OTHER WORKS BY SHAUN O. MCCOY

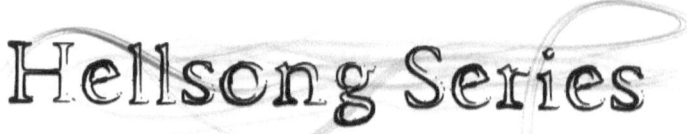

Hellsong Series

BOOK III

MARCH TILL DEATH

SHAUN O. MCCOY

SISYPHEAN PUBLISHING

PRAISE FOR SHAUN O. McCOY AND THE HELLSONG SERIES

"March till Death is McCoy at his best. A heart-pounding adrenaline rush with characters deeper than the Hell they are damned to."
—*Matt Michaelis, Author of Kids Summon the Damndest Things*

"McCoy caps off his series with a work of pure brilliance. In this volume Hellsong goes from being a captivating read to a life changing one."
—*Monet Jones, Author of the Captive Youth Trilogy*

"McCoy's unrivaled setting meets its match in a tightly woven plot and some truly extraordinary character arcs. In a genre rife with tropes and forgettable stories, March till Death stands out as being both unique and powerful."
—*Thomas the Younger, Author of These Windows*

"McCoy is a talented and bright young writer. Knight of Gehenna is a new kind of novel—a page turner in the truest sense—wrought from equal parts brawn and brain."
—*B. Butler, Author of Murder in Cairo*

"McCoy is a brilliant writer; insightful, intelligent, articulate, imaginative, and funny."
—*McKendree Long, Author of No Good Like it is*

"In Knight of Gehenna, McCoy masterfully creates characters, scenarios and the Hell where they live. He writes with a passion, layering emotion on fantasy and science fiction, drawing in readers from beyond his genre."
—*Ginny Padgett, President of SCWW*

"Shaun is the real McCoy."
—*Laura Valtorte, Filmmaker, Author of Family Meal*

"With the visionary aptitude of such writers as C.S. Lewis and J.R.R. Tolkein, McCoy further illustrates his unique underworld that has produced the spiritual vagabond Arturus in this sequel

to Even Hell Has Knights. Arturus' quest for purpose in Hell is not unlike man's quest for purpose on Earth."
—*Len Lawson, Author of City of David*

"McCoy has a queer ability to highlight the most delightfully horrific details imaginable. I grimace, suck air through my teeth and squeeze shut my eyes. Then I open just one so I can keep on reading."
—*Fred Fields, Author*

"In Even Hell Has Knights, McCoy depicts dark landscapes filled with fiery fury. His characters are soulful, at times wonderfully craven, surprising us with their humanity and evoking our laughter in unexpected ways."
—*Chris Mathews, Author of GARGOYLES*

"McCoy writes with a passion for action. He introduces us to graphic characters and takes us on a hair-raising journey through crumbling underground landscapes where battles rage to protect a magical child. This is a borderlands for where the quest for survival has never been so grueling."
—*Bonnie Stanard, Author of Master of Westfall Plantation*

This is a work of fiction. The damnation portrayed in this novel is fictitious, and similarities between it and any actual damnation are strictly coincidental.

MARCH TILL DEATH

Copyright 2014 © by Shaun McCoy

All rights reserved.

Editor-in-Chief: Matt Michaelis
Associate Editors: Leigh Thomas, Justin Williams, Jody Mobley
Consulting Editors: James Mobley, Gabrielle Olexa

Title art: Thomas the Younger
Title Layout: Kirill Simin

A Sisyphean Publishing Book

http://hellsongseries.com
http://sipublisher.com

ISBN-13: 978-0692223734
ISBN-10: 0692223738

First Edition May 2014

Printed in the United States of America

0 9 8 7 6 5 4 3 2

For Rusty Hess

ACKNOWLEDGEMENTS

While I was writing this book, a fan of the series and friend of the family, Anders Kaufmann Sr., passed. For some ridiculous reason, I felt terribly guilty for having left him at a cliffhanger in book two—and I feel guilty still—although I'm sure that the worries held for fiction seem fickle indeed to a person dealing with the rigors of life and death.

I no longer believe in places like Heaven or Hell, but if there is such a place where people live on in some meaningful way after death—and if in such a place people still do things like read—I would beg some angel pass him a copy.

MARCH TILL DEATH

From Neostoicism: Philosophia

When I was alive, I had always believed death would bring me answers. I think we all thought that. Then maybe you can understand that my greatest disappointment was not then that I was damned, but that death only brought more questions.
    —Endymion

The greatest gifts the gods ever gave us were our enemies, for we must better ourselves to defeat them.
    —Ares

Part VII:
Sinners of the City
of Blood and Stone

From Gehennic Law: The Sadist and the Jew

Herod the Great, Ruler of Judea, enjoyed nothing more than torturing the children of Yahweh. One day, as his charge lay dying, Herod noticed that the man was smiling.

"Why do you smile?" Herod asked. "I have ripped out your guts, and you are about to perish. Soon I will do the same to your entire family. How could you be happy?"

"Because I am a sinless man," the Jew answered. "I and my Rabbi performed my sacrifices and propitiations in accordance with the scriptures. After you slay me, I will be resurrected at the end of time to be by the side of my God."

Herod was enraged and became determined to find some way to stop the resurrection of his victims. Seeking advice on how to do this, he called for the wise Rabbi Hillel to dine with him. During a public dinner, he interviewed Hillel, and the Rabbi gave him this advice: "Place your Jew in a room, leaving with him only pork. He must either choose to eat the meat—a sin—or he must starve to death of his own will—a sin. Then he shall not be reborn at the end of days."

Herod thanked the Rabbi and took his wise council. He would place a Jewish man in a cell with only pork to eat and wait for him to die. By keeping him away from any Rabbi who could help him with a sacrifice, Herod ensured the man's damnation since the Jew must either choose to commit suicide or eat the unclean animal.

Many Jews he tortured in this way. To a man, they refused to eat the pork and died. Herod was happy since his torture would not now reward its subjects to a second life.

But one day a child of Yahweh was put in the cell who did eat the pork.

"Why?" Herod asked. "Why would you eat the pig knowing

that you are to be damned?"

"The inevitable is inevitable," the Jew replied, licking his fingers between lusty bites, "but it hasn't happened yet."

1

Alice must think I'm dead.

Magma had once poured down these spiraled corridors, filling the complex of chambers below with a knee deep layer of molten rock before solidifying into the stone rivers and lakes upon which Arturus now stepped. The stone itself was grey and pitted with an unfathomable number of tiny holes. Aaron had likened them to crab dens in a beach's sand. Above the now solidified floor were black and purple hellstone bricks, each one about six inches in length, rising up to form the low hanging domes and narrow arches which surrounded him.

And in a way, Alice would be right.

They had gone so deep into the Carrion that they had almost come out the other side. Even now the shores of Sheol, where this afterlife was separated from the next, was only a half hour's walk from him—but he was dead in other ways too. The Arturus who eagerly joined the Harpsborough hunters with dreams of a heroic rescue had most certainly perished.

He couldn't quite pinpoint when he'd lost himself. Maybe it was when Maab picked him in her ritual. Maybe it was when Patrick died. Maybe it was when he killed Pyle. Maybe it was when he'd stood idly by when they'd abandoned Kyle to his death. Maybe it was when he'd slit the throats of those helpless dyitzu.

I'm a killer now. Killers don't need fond memories of pretty girls. Killers don't need hope. Killers need victims.

Those victims were nearby. Somewhere in this hellacious

wilderness of frozen lava and spiraled corridors were Tamara's captors. It was possible that the men of the City of Blood and Stone had broken her already. If that were the case, the City's soldiers could even now be marching on Calimay's sanctuary. That meant Calista, the girl who was supposedly carrying his unborn child, would be killed. That meant they would never meet the person who was to guide them down the river Lethe. That meant that Arturus would never get home.

I have to find Tamara.

Galen had split them into two groups. The wounded Avery and Dakota were left with Johnny to watch over them in the aqueduct. The healthy members, which included himself, Kelly, Aaron and Galen, had split up in these halls with hopes of intercepting Tamara's captors as they made their way back to the City of Blood and Stone.

But if I find her . . .

Galen had made it clear that rescuing Tamara was only one possible way to keep her from talking. The other should have been unthinkable—but it wasn't. If Arturus saw her, if he had the shot, he was going to take it.

I'd spare her their torture. Would that be merciful?

Maybe.

"Kelly," the priestess announced her presence as she entered the room. "Galen spotted them. Tamara's not with them. He thinks they may have already left her at the prison or . . ."

Her black robe was wearing thin. There was a hole at one of the elbows, and the cloth was nearly see-through at the other. Even so, she cut a striking figure. Her black hair was pulled back into a ponytail behind her pale face, and her sharp features and dark blue eyes were entrancing.

"Or what?" Arturus asked.

"There's a chance Tamara was important enough to take her straight into the heart of the City of Blood and Stone. Then again, we could just have the wrong group."

We'd better not.

There was a pocket around the city where the dyitzu and the hounds weren't so thick, and it was here that Galen set up their perimeter. But traveling this close to the City of Blood and Stone also meant that they were constantly ducking the city's combined devil and human patrols. Arturus could not count the number of human slaves he'd watched pass by in single file lines. That sight, at least, had broken through his wall of apathy.

I'm still a little human.

Kelly must have noticed his distress. She came close to him, too close. "Come on," she breathed, her lips only inches from his. "We've got a plan to execute."

Arturus nodded.

Chains clinked as Kelly pulled a set of shackles out from under her robe. "Help me get these on."

The irons had been warmed by her body. They were heavy in his hands. Kelly turned around, holding her arms behind her. The shackles were hinged along their sides and could be tightened by a pair of adjustable screws. The locking mechanisms clicked as he closed them, one after the other, around her slender wrists.

"Do you like me better chained?" she whispered.

Arturus started. "What?"

"Do you like me better chained? I mean, after what I did to Avery, I thought you might enjoy it more if you felt like you were in control when we—"

"I was fine with Calimay's daughters." Arturus had hoped the statement would put her off a little, but Kelly seemed unaffected.

"Yes," she answered, the corner of her lip curling up slightly, hinting at a smile while she looked back over her shoulder at him, "but you didn't have any choice in that. I want us to be different. Untie my hair, would you? I don't think a prisoner would look so well groomed."

Her hair had been bound with a black strip of silk. Arturus noticed his hands were shaking as he untied the knot in the smooth fabric.

I'm nervous—probably because we're about to meet those soldiers.

But he wasn't nervous about that, and he knew it.

The shackle on her right wrist slid off. Kelly wasn't nervous. Her hands were as steady as rocks.

Kelly laughed as he bent down and picked up the fallen restraint.

The adjustable screws wouldn't tighten while the shackle was closed.

"Damn," Arturus said.

"Key's in my pants," Kelly informed him as she turned around.

Arturus reached in through her robe and felt around for a pocket. She moved closer as he did so. Arturus felt his heart quicken.

"Galen and Aaron," Arturus' father announced as he and Harpsborough's Lead Hunter entered the room. Each was wearing a black uniform with a dark red, upside down cross sewn into the right shoulder. In theory, wearing the uniform of the City of Blood and Stone was supposed to help Galen gather information about Tamara.

Galen paused for a moment, regarding Arturus and Kelly. "Am I interrupting something?"

They would come in at this exact moment.

Arturus felt a flush on his cheeks. "I'm just getting the key for the shackles."

"Wrong pocket, love," Kelly said.

For some reason, her use of "love" as a term of endearment only embarrassed him further. He rifled through her pockets awkwardly until he found the key.

Aaron had a bemused smile on his face.

"Hurry," Galen said, "there's not much time."

Marcus felt uneasy guarding the entrance to Harpsborough. He'd felt uneasy when he'd woken up this morning. He'd felt uneasy the entire fitful night he'd spent in his hovel.

It wasn't the battle he'd had with the corpsemen. Nor was it the gaping hole in the Carrion barrier that even now was open to whatever horrors Hell had to throw at him. Or rather, it wasn't just these things. It was also the strange type of corpse which Martin had fought. It was the way the bullets had dropped off it like lead beads of sweat. It was the thing's black eyes.

It was the fact that the thing had once been Kyle.

If ever Marcus needed confirmation that Aaron was dead and that Julian would never return, then the Kyle-thing was it. Worse, it had been no normal corpse. Something had to have created it.

"You alright there, Marcus?" Tucker's voice startled him slightly.

Marcus had been so focused on his fear he'd almost forgotten the other hunter was there.

Tucker laughed. "Little jumpy there, man."

Marcus shook his head, trying to clear it. He put his 700 Remington down, leaning it against the rock wall before running his nervous fingers through his hair. After a moment, he took a deep, shaky breath.

"I'm all fucked up, too, man," Tucker said. "That raid on the corpses, I can't get it out of my head. What could convince so many people to become lepers? Something wasn't right in that place."

"No shit, Tucker." Marcus said, picking his rifle back up.

"And it don't feel right, that Carrion barrier being breached. We should be out there building it back up right now. And I mean right fucking now. I don't care what Mike says. Was he there? Did he see that black-eyed thing laugh at our bullets?"

Marcus shook his head. "It ain't safe, and you know it."

"I'll tell you what ain't safe. What ain't safe is leaving that barrier open."

"What if another column of corpses came while we were trying to build it back up? What if something came in from the Carrion? Scouting is the right way."

Tucker shook his head, turned away from the exit and looked Marcus in the eyes. "Every second that barrier is down is another moment when one of those Kyle-things can come through and get us. Fighting Kyle was tough enough, what if the next one is Aaron? There's a reason Michael Baker is scared shitless of the Carrion. There's a reason none of the Citizens talk about that place without flipping out."

"Don't neglect your post," Marcus said, but his heart wasn't in it.

Tucker stared him down for a long moment before turning back to face the wilds.

"Maybe you're right," Marcus admitted.

Then he heard footsteps. Marcus raised his gun to his shoulder. Its stock felt cold against his skin even through his hoodie.

"Don't shoot, please," a feminine voice called from the wilds.

Marcus sighed and lowered his weapon. He shared a look of relief with Tucker, who had drawn his pistol.

Molly rounded the corner. Marcus almost picked his rifle back up.

Tucker's head jerked back when he saw her. "I thought you were dead."

Fear took Marcus suddenly, and he looked carefully at her eyes. In this lighting, and with her on the other side of the room, he couldn't tell if her eyes were green or blue, but they definitely weren't black. He breathed out another relieved sigh.

Molly walked forward like she was about to enter Harpsborough, but Tucker stopped her, holding his rifle up sideways as a barrier. "Miss, I don't know if you're allowed in. What you did to Graham was pretty bad."

"Take me to Klein," Molly ordered. "Tell him I wish to confess."

Arturus lay in a tiny alcove that was barely large enough for him to wedge himself into. Aside from its claustrophobia-inducing confines, his hiding place was well chosen. Both Galen and Aaron had said they couldn't see him from the room beyond. Arturus was nearly at the level of the twenty foot tall ceiling, and the height gave him a good vantage point to shoot down into the room. The light grey color of the solidified stone floor would also help him by making the darkly dressed soldiers of the City of Blood and Stone stand out. If things went badly during the firefight, though, there would be no easy way out.

He was going to have to worm his way forward and drop headfirst towards the floor, something he wasn't looking forward to even if everything went well and their enemies were defeated, so he shuddered to think about attempting a retreat in the middle of a shootout.

His shotgun lay against his right side, caught between himself and the stone, while he held his pistol at the ready. Since Galen, Kelly and Aaron would be mixed in with the enemy, a shotgun would be too dangerous to use—not that he would have been able to aim the bulky weapon in such close quarters.

Arturus took in a few deep breaths to steady himself. With

each breath, he could feel his chest pressing into the cool rock.

He heard voices. At first they were too quiet for him to make out, but they grew louder as they grew closer.

Be ready, Turi.

"Yes," said an unfamiliar voice. "We'd caught one, too, though she was nowhere as pretty as yours. One of the purple robed bitches. I'm telling you, if you need to take them, it's not that hard. You just have to belt their pelvis down. They can't get ya if they can't move their hips."

Arturus felt angry. Kelly'd been hurt enough.

"Don't know that I'll take my chances on that," Galen said.

"Jarvis here likes to cut 'em too," the voice went on, getting louder as it got closer, "one deep line along their left side—"

"Right side," another voice corrected.

"Whatever, I'm sure it doesn't matter *which* side, but it should keep your pecker safe. Don't know why you're such a pussy about it, Jarvis. Why bother cutting 'em, just break theirs before they break yours, right?"

Arturus felt blood rushing into his head.

I may actually be looking forward to shooting these people.

The unfamiliar voices continued talking, but for some reason, they had stopped coming closer. Hopefully they were still coming into this room. If not, Arturus wasn't sure how he was going to coordinate his attack with Galen and Aaron.

What could they be doing?

Arturus couldn't fathom why raping a woman would satisfy a man. It seemed somehow to be missing the point. If you weren't getting love from it, why not just work everything out on your own? But then, he couldn't fathom why a man would work with demons either.

Just hang on, Kelly. We'll kill them quickly.

"But to answer your question," a voice was saying, "those harpies are nasty. There are about six or seven dens to the east. They don't listen to Crassus or even One Horn. They killed a couple of our men last week, that's why we steer clear of 'em. Makes getting back a hell of a deal. Can't wait until we dig out Tu-El. He'll fuck them up for not doing what One Horn told 'em."

"You already dumped your priestess?" Galen asked.

There was some laughter, and Arturus gauged the echoes,

guessing that there should be at least ten of the enemy.

This is going to be tough.

"Dumped whole loads in her," another voice said. "But yeah, dropped her at Cul' Nahedran. She wasn't in very good shape, though. Them priestesses ain't used to not being in control . . . and she sure as hell wasn't ready for Jarvis."

There was some more laughter. "She damn near bled to death."

I'm sorry, Tamara. Even you don't deserve this.

"Didn't talk though," said another. "Stubborn little bitch."

"Why aren't you all still with One Horn?" Aaron's voice asked.

They still weren't getting any closer.

Come on!

"We got in a firefight out there, man. They gave us the slip. One Horn said they actually went into an aqueduct, one that the ancients built. He said it would take him a couple of days to get in, but that he and his dyitzu would hunt them down after."

Suddenly gunshots were ringing out. They sounded like Galen's MP5 and another weapon of some sort. Maybe a pistol. Arturus switched his safety off and pointed his weapon towards the entrance.

There was the shout of a man in pain, another gunshot, and then silence.

"Holy shit, Galen," that was Aaron's voice. "Why in the fuck?"

"Gather their weapons and ammo. Be quick. Kelly, unlock yourself."

"Yes, Galen." Kelly seemed distracted.

"Galen," Arturus' father announced moments before poking his head through the entrance to Arturus' room. "Get down from there. We're moving out, now."

"What happened to the plan?" Arturus asked, squirming forward so that his torso was hanging free in the air.

He lowered his shotgun down to Galen.

Galen grabbed the weapon. "No time. They said it would take the Minotaur two days to get into the aqueduct."

Arturus dropped to the ground, trying to cushion his fall with his arms. It worked, sort of. He rolled over to his side as he fell, but he still felt like he had bruised his hip. He stood up and accepted his shotgun back. "And?"

"Turi, we've been here for two days."

So if the Minotaur was two days behind us, then . . .

"Oh shit," Arturus said.

2

"You have any idea what this is about?" Graham asked Martin as the pair mounted the stairs leading up to the Fore's parlor.

Martin noticed that Graham's dark hair was a tangled mess and that his stubble was only a couple days short of a beard.

I'm not really a sight to behold at the moment, either.

Katie had hardly wanted to look at him after the bruising he'd received from the Kyle-thing. He touched the swelling under his right eye.

"What'd you say?" Martin asked.

"You know why we're here?"

"The Carrion breach, I'm guessing."

"Don't see what there is to discuss," Graham said. "Fill it. What's the big deal?"

The big deal is that we just watched a fuck ton of undead walk through that hole. The big deal is that there might be more of those Kyle-things out there. The big deal is that I had to fight that damn monstrosity while you were out there nursing your balls.

"Guess we're about to find out," Martin said as they reached the third floor landing.

They entered the parlor room. Its lavishness always disturbed Martin for some reason. The couches and seats, covered in earthen hued blankets, would not have looked out of place in an old world mansion—except for the fact that they were made of stone. Guns hung on the wall, many of which might still serve the hunters of Harpsborough well. Michael's push-fed Winchester Model 70, for instance, could do a lot more good in the hands of a hunter than it would gathering dust on the Fore's wall.

Michael and Mancini sat across from each other, Michael in his favorite chair and Mancini on the couch. A chess board was set up on the woodstone coffee table that was between them, the pieces in their starting positions.

The light orbs were particularly bright today. Martin almost wanted to put a few more blankets on to dim them, but this wasn't his home. Besides, Davel Mancini, Harpsborough's brewer, was notorious for liking the darkness, and Martin could stand to see the guy looking a bit uncomfortable.

Mancini had dark circles under his squinting eyes. Martin thought it was fitting that a deceitful snake like Mancini would be bothered by the light.

And he probably wouldn't have those headaches if he wasn't plotting his little brains out all the damn time.

"Have a seat," Michael said, his voice grim.

Martin would have felt uncomfortable sitting next to Mancini, so he hung back until Graham took the middle of the couch.

"Some bloodwater?" Mancini asked.

"Please," Graham answered.

Martin nodded, sitting down next to Graham.

Mancini clapped his hands. The young boy, John, entered the Parlor room at the summons, coming in through the curtains that led to the balcony.

"Bloodwater," Michael told him.

"Yes, First Citizen," John answered. He even gave a little bow.

Martin watched the young boy walk across the room to where the wine sat on an end table. The glass decanter clinked against crystal glasses as John poured the four of them bloodwater. The liquid was so bright it almost looked like old world Kool-Aid. They always had the good stuff here in the Fore.

Martin felt his mouth watering.

John passed out the glasses. Mancini and Michael absently swirled their bloodwater as they received their drinks. Graham was copying them. Martin took a swig. The sting was pleasant in the back of his throat, and he felt the bloodwater's comforting burn as it made its way down to his stomach.

Martin leaned forward, glass held tightly in his right hand. Soft blankets shifted beneath him as he did so. "You called us here?"

Michael frowned. "I did. I have to ask you to do something, something I don't want to ask you to do."

Graham rubbed at one of his eyes. "I thought this was about the Carrion barrier."

Mancini leaned back into the couch, swirling his bloodwater as he crossed his legs. "It is."

"It's too dangerous to leave open," Michael said, setting his glass down next to the chess board. "And, it's also too dangerous to close."

"We can close it, sir," Graham said. "You saw how fast we bricked up Julian's."

The memory still hurt Martin. That was the day he'd known they'd lost Aaron. Aaron had been a good leader, Aaron had taken care of him, Aaron had opposed the Fore's hoarding even though he'd benefited from it, and Aaron had been a damn good fighter.

He wouldn't have shut the fuck down in the riverbed when fighting the corpsemen like I did, that's for sure.

Mancini shook his head. "Julian's opening was only a few feet wide. We're talking about an entire barrier here. It could take days to seal that thing."

As usual, the bastard was right.

"Did Copperfield refuse to help?" Martin asked.

"No," Michael answered. "I thought he'd be afraid, too, but he's volunteered to go and help mix the mortar on site. With Rick and Galen gone, he's one of the only people left who knows how to do that."

"Who else?" Graham asked.

"Chelsea."

Martin and Graham shared a look.

I'd take her ass over Copperfield any day of the week.

"So it'll be a little longer," Graham said. "Give us the hunters. We can survive a day or two without hunting. It's not like we pull in that much meat these days anyway."

We bring in plenty. You *didn't bring in jack shit.*

"We're worried about risking so many of you," Mancini said, though his voice sounded remarkably unconcerned.

"He's right," Michael leaned forward and rubbed the back of his head. "If another column of corpses comes through, we could lose you. And Martin, you know Hidalgo reported that there were hundreds of harpies heading into the Carrion at the end of those columns. That's why we want Graham to scout around the area on our side, make sure no more are coming."

Martin felt Graham shift on the couch beside him. "Not a problem, sir. I'll take my collectors."

Michael leveled his gaze on Martin. "But there's another direction trouble could come from."

You've got to be kidding me.

Martin swallowed. "The Carrion . . ."

"That's right. We want you to take a small crew and scout the Carrion."

Martin felt his testicles drawing up to his body. He stood quickly.

"A small group, Martin. Just to make sure we can repair the breach safely."

"Aaron went in there. Aaron. And he's dead. I'm nowhere near as good a hunter as he was."

Mancini nodded. "You're not."

Thanks for agreeing with me, asswipe.

Michael gave Mancini a sideways glance and then stood up, grabbing Martin's shoulder. Martin was surprised by how strong the grip was.

"You don't have to be as good as Aaron. You're just going a little ways. Not far in at all. Aaron had to find Julian and a cache of devilwheat. You just have to make sure there isn't an army hiding within earshot of the breach. If those corpses decide to turn around, if those harpies come back, well that's a force that all of Harpsborough couldn't face. That's why you have to do this. That's why you have to wall them in."

"I say we just build the wall," Graham said. "We can skip the scouting."

Michael turned his back on them and walked to the balcony's door curtain. He stopped before it. "Too much noise. If there is a dyitzu pack, or some hounds, or an army of harpies and corpses, they'll be drawn to you. We can't have you start until we're sure it's clear."

Martin could see a sliver of the world beyond through the crack in the curtain over Michael's shoulder. Harpsborough was out there. Katie was out there.

God, I could use her support about now.

"Alright," Martin said. "I'll get some guys together."

"Let Huxley lead the normal hunting," Mancini suggested. "He's capable."

But Huxley's one of the best we have!

"I need Hux with me," Martin said.

"We're still in a famine," Mancini shot back.

Michael turned away from the curtain, holding up a hand. "Choose who you need. Take the best men you can find. But do it quickly. We have no idea what dark things are crawling in from the Carrion with that barrier down."

"Aye, sir," Martin said, glaring at Mancini.

"That's First Citizen," Mancini corrected. "If you're going to be a Lead Hunter, you need to make sure you follow protocol."

I want to punch that man right in the nose.

"Protocol won't do me a lick of good in the Carrion," Martin told him.

Michael looked lost in thought, his eyes staring towards the wall. "It won't, Martin. It won't."

Aaron, why'd you die on me?

Father Klein looked back over his shoulder to see who had entered his church. Two hunters stood in the open doorway, flanking a woman—it was Molly.

"Bless you, child," he breathed. "You're alive."

She walked into his church. The hunters stood awkwardly behind her.

"You can go," Father Klein told them.

They looked hesitant, probably remembering what this girl had done to Graham. Was it possible that she had come in to the church to reap her revenge? Unlikely. You had to corner Molly to get her violent. Her anger, when it overflowed, was usually self destructive.

Besides, if she tries to get me like she got Graham, she's going to be in for a shock.

"It's okay," Molly assured the hunters. "I've come home. It happens sometimes, people lose their way. But then they learn. They humble themselves. They come home."

Bless you, child. Can this be true? Can Molly really have turned her soul around?

Father Klein nodded and the hunters closed the church's double doors behind the girl.

Molly began the long walk down the central aisle of the church, the shadows of the crucifix-filled windows rolling over her body. She had lost a lot of weight, Klein realized. Had he been anyone else, he'd have found her tempting.

Father Klein moved to the center aisle to meet her. Molly stopped before him and knelt.

"Father," she whispered. "I'm so sorry, Father. When last we spoke I said terrible things. Things that didn't belong in your church. Things which didn't belong in me. And I wish they hadn't been inside me so that they wouldn't have had a chance to come out."

Can she be telling the truth? What could she have left to lie about?

"Father, I wish I could say that I stopped doing wrong the second after I attacked Graham. But I'm through with lying. When I crawled out of the river, I kept doing wretched things. I traveled. And when I got so far from myself that even I knew I was going wrong, I remembered what you had said to me. You said that I could come and confess. That I could tell you the truth about what had happened in those conversations between myself and Cris. I've come to tell you that now. And I think it's better, because even if I had told you what I thought was the truth before, it wouldn't have really been the truth—because I didn't really know what had happened—until now."

Father Klein knelt beside her. "Molly. It is never too late for us to forgive one another. Jesus teaches us that."

"Will you listen?" Molly asked, clasping her hands together in front of her chest. "Will you be my confessor?"

"To the best of my ability, child. I am little without God, but we can do as we should have done in the old world."

"Good," Molly took a deep breath. "I've realized you're right about that as well. I was trying to fight Satan with my own wit, but I'm only human. Of course I failed. The only way to fight him is the way God told us. But you know that. You tried to tell me that before, I just couldn't listen."

Father Klein nodded. "It is not an easy lesson to learn, for any of us. Our pride, it tells us that we can make the right decisions, but that's the sin the Devil knows best. Yes, tell me about Cris, about that conversation."

Tears began to flow down her cheeks. Not the tears Molly usually gave, which were cloaked in self pity and self interest, but actual tears. True tears. Tears of genuine sorrow.

"I loved him, Father," she said between sniffles. "I loved him. You had all been so mean to me. I wanted to think that somehow it was you all who were wrong. That way it wouldn't have been *my* problem. I must have known I was a terrible person, because I felt like . . . like if a single thing I had done had actually been my fault, then it would have been enough to make me worthless. I guess I forgot that we were all damned and sent to Hell. I guess I forgot that we were all terrible people, and by forgetting that, I forgot my personal responsibility. I forgot who I was. I wanted to go on f . . . having sex with men. I wanted to think it was okay. Most of all I wanted to think that the sex I'd had already wasn't done in sin. Cris told me consensual sex was no vice. He told me that *you* were the ones who were evil. He told me I was worthwhile. He told me exactly what I wanted to hear."

"He appealed to your pride. You should not hate yourself for falling into that trap. The Infidel Friend, they're vile creatures. They know how to widen the cracks in a man's faith."

Molly gripped the hem of his robe. "But when I was out there, out there in the wilds, I was confronted by Satan. Not literally, but He's out there, Father. I could *feel* him. I could feel his breath coming down the back of my neck. No human can withstand him. I was trying to use my own mind to fight Hell, but my own mind is worthless. The Devil got in there. I went astray, so far astray. But there was always this light leading me back. I started to wonder how could it be that all of you, *all* of you were in the wrong. I just couldn't believe that all of Harpsborough, all of my brothers and sisters here, that an entire society, was in the wrong. It *had* to be me. But I buried that thought deep.

"Time passed. Satan was winning. I was sure of myself. I

was sure my arms were long enough to box with the Devil . . . but I was a fool. Only God could fight Satan, and only he could give us the path to do so ourselves. I don't want to be a demon, Father. I don't. You all are my family, and I was mad at you. Children do that sometimes, don't they, Father? They think they hate their parents."

"They do."

Molly's blue eyes were red with sadness. "And the children, sometimes they don't realize that they love their family. But I love you all. I do. I realized that out there. I remembered your teachings. I found my way back. It's so funny. It was the sex that did it. I just wanted to believe it was okay. But it's not okay to have sex like I was having. I had to think of what God would have said about it. I don't know what God would say about everything I've done, I'd need to discuss that with you, but in my heart I knew He disapproved. I knew it. So I had to admit I was wrong."

Father Klein stood up. "I hear you."

She reached out and grabbed his wrist. "Don't let them put me through the Golden Door. Don't let them take me to trial."

"It would fill me with joy to put in a good word for you, it really would," Father Klein said. "But I know you, Molly. You're a smart girl. You're capable of deceiving me."

"Father!" she choked, and her face suddenly turned red with anger. "You don't trust me now? After I poured my heart out to you?" She stood up and shoved her finger into his chest. "Do you think I'm stupid?"

Father Klein took a cautious step back.

"Do you think I'm stupid?" she repeated.

Molly was many things, but she was not stupid. "No, I—"

"And you know that I've been out there. That I've been in Hell facing these realities that I'm talking about. Do you think any intelligent person could experience those things and not realize that you're right? Do you think that any person could have these ideas, and seriously consider them, and then think they should turn the other way?"

Molly had a strength in her he had not seen before. It was a strength that reminded him strangely of Cris, but it expressed itself in a completely different way. What a Christian Cris would have made! What an excellent tool for God. It was a shame he'd chosen the Devil's path. But Molly, Molly was a different story. She had that strength, certainly, that will to be her own person, and that's why her willingness to toss aside that personality, to humble herself before the will of the Lord, was even more powerful.

"I believe you," he told her. And he meant it. He felt the truth in his heart. Molly had come back from the darkness. "Welcome home, child," he said, tears in his eyes. "Welcome home."

"Tsup Reg," Martin greeted the bird depiction painted onto the front of his girlfriend's door blanket.

"Is that you Martin?" Katie's sweet voice came to him from beyond the bird.

"Sure is, ma'am."

"Come on in, we're decent!"

Martin slid the door blanket aside, dropped to his knees and crawled under the low archway into Katie's hovel. Erica was there, too. Martin was glad to see her. At one point, when the famine was at its worst and before the Fore had agreed to the feast days, he'd feared she was dead.

"I was just headed out," Erica said, smiling. She crawled by Martin, leaving them alone. Martin watched the door blanket as it waved back and forth for a moment. It stopped.

Katie looked beautiful in the soft light. There were still dark circles under her eyes, but they didn't look so bad now.

"Hey, princess," Martin said.

"Hey, Lead Hunter," she giggled after the title had left her lips.

The giggle made Martin feel very warm. "That's *acting* Lead Hunter, technically."

"It's all the same to me. But I miss when you were just Martin."

Martin had to admit to himself that the fight with the Kyle-thing, hell, the whole incident with the corpsemen, had shaken him deeply. He couldn't disagree with Katie. A part of him wished he was just Martin as well.

I need to have a long talk with ole Bense, he'll help me sort this all out.

"What's wrong?" she asked.

Girl can see right through me.

"I got a bad assignment," he said.

Katie frowned and wrinkles appeared on her forehead. She suddenly looked more tired. For a second she looked almost as bad as she had right before the feast, but then her frown lessened a little. "You can't like, delegate it?" She tried a smile.

"No, no I can't. Came straight from Michael." He settled down on the blanket she used as a bed and put his head on her pack-turned-pillow. "And I don't know that I would if I could."

He raised his weak hand and looked at it. He could hardly tell that it had regrown, now. Hell did indeed heal all wounds. He made a fist with it. Light came in from a gap between the tarp they used to cover the hovel's roof, illuminating the middle two knuckles of his fist.

All wounds.

"They're treating you wrong, Martin," she said. "I hate to see you treated wrong."

"It's fine, Katie. They'd have given Aaron the job if he was here."

She leaned over and put her hands on his raised fist, guiding it down to his belly. "But Aaron was a Citizen. He got rewarded for all the work that he did. He got to sit up there in the Fore and eat all that dyitzu and hound meat. He got to drink Mancini's wine every night. He got to suckle on sweetened hound's milk and sleep in an actual bed in an actual room."

"I'm not the Lead Hunter. I'm the acting Lead Hunter. I'll get those privileges if the Fore decides I'm capable. Then they can vote me in. Besides, being Lead Hunter is different now. They've got Graham doing some of the stuff Aaron used to do."

"What more could they possibly have you do to earn it?" she asked, squeezing his fist.

Martin pulled his hand free. "I don't know. I just need to do more, is all."

"You already went out and fed all those people who were dying in the halls, and out of your own food. Then you fought the Kyle-thing, which no one else could kill. You led the attack on the corpse eater lepers. You deserve it already. They're not going to give it to you, honey."

Martin half sat up, pushing his torso up with his elbows. "That's not true."

Katie looked like she was going to cry. "It is true. I know it's true. They're not accepting any new Citizens. They've made you and Graham take on all this shit, and they aren't paying you for it. It's because they want to keep it all to themselves."

Martin sat all the way up. "Maybe, but it doesn't matter. I wouldn't gluttonize anyway. It's a good thing they don't let me in the Fore, because I'd empty the whole damn store room and give it to the hungry people. The only thing I really wish I could do is . . ."

"Is what?"

Martin sat all the way up, leaned forward and kissed Katie. "I used to watch Alice and Aaron eat up there on the Fore's balconies. I wish I could treat you like that. I want to be able to give you those things."

She turned away from his next kiss. "You deserve that, Martin. They're just keeping it from you. You need to go in there and tell Michael that you won't let him mistreat you."

"God damn it, Katie. They need me."

Katie crossed her arms over her chest. "They need Aaron."

Martin hung his head.

I need Aaron.

"Maybe they do," Martin said.

A long, long, long talk with ole Bense.

Katie looked back at him, tears in her eyes. "They put you through all this, put me through all this. I can't. I . . . I . . . I can't just sit here while you go out and do the most dangerous things the Fore can find. I know you say that the Kyle-thing won't happen again, and I know there won't be wars every day, but it kills me inside. Every time someone speaks about danger in the wilds, every time I hear a rumor about something terrible coming, I get sick inside because I know that you are the one they're going to make fight it. I can't eat, Martin. Promise me, promise me that you won't do anything dangerous for a long time. At least a month."

"They need me."

Her eyes narrowed and her nostrils flared. "Promise me."

"I can't."

"God damn it, Martin! I love you, but you have to do some things for me. I can't take it." A tear rolled down her face. "I can't. I literally can't eat. And I need to. When I get a chance at some food I have to take it, because I might not get another full meal until next Feast Day. But when I do, I just throw it back up."

Martin swallowed. "I'll get you more food, Katie."

That means that I'll lead an expedition into the Carrion on an empty stomach, but if that's what I have to do.

"Just promise me!" she was almost shouting.

"The thing they have me doing, Katie, I'm . . ." Martin stopped.

Katie was furious now, and she wasn't going to take the news well. He didn't want to tell her.

"What?" she snapped. "Tell me."

"I'm going into the Carrion, Katie."

Her eyes widened. "Why?" She started shouting. "God damn it Martin, tell me why!"

"We've got to fill the hole, and they're worried that—"

She grabbed him by the shoulders, shaking her head furiously. "They can't make you do this. You can't go in there." She stopped.

Martin met her gaze. "Katie, I'm going."

She picked up her pack and threw it into the wall beside her. A rock tumbled down from the side of her hovel, letting more light in from outside, but she didn't seem to care.

"Katie, I—"

"Don't talk to me."

"Katie. I have to go. You don't understand. I just—"

"I said don't talk to me!" Her face was red. "Get out!"

Martin shook his head. "Princess, it's got to be done. You have—"

"I said get out! I don't want to talk to you right now! Get out!"

She started shoving him.

"Okay, b—"

"Don't talk! Go!"

Martin left the tent.

He was greeted by the curious, annoyed, and occasionally sympathetic stares of roughly half of Harpsborough's villagers. Up on the balcony he saw Copperfield and Herod the gunsmith—both of them staring right at him.

He felt empty inside. Now was the moment when he had to

be at his best. He had to gather his men and go into the God damned Carrion. He had to be as alert as he had ever been. He had to be ready to fight harpies and an army of the undead, and it was entirely possible that he'd run into another Kyle-thing. Maybe several of them.

Now how the Hell am I supposed to do all this when all I want to do is go find a corner and die?

 — 3 —

For some reason, not being able to see made time impossible to judge.

Johnny sat in the darkness, close enough to Dakota that he could feel the wounded soldier's body heat and the gentle tickle of his slow, even breath. Johnny was afraid to leave Dakota's side. Galen had nearly killed the man, and in those brief moments when he was conscious, Dakota had trouble seeing straight or remembering things that had happened even a few moments ago.

It had been too dangerous to keep the wounded soldier in the service corridor near the Erebus, where his somnolent nightmares might end his own life—so they'd carried him gently back to the aqueduct proper.

In the beginning, Dakota had awakened every few hours, and each time thought himself blind. Galen said that he'd probably survive if they kept him from moving too much. Of course, he'd said that *after* they'd dragged him out of the service corridor. There could still be bleeding in the brain, but Hell was different, Galen had explained to him. In the old world, the brain damage could have been permanent. Here, whatever Dakota lost would be restored.

Which is a fucking shame. Sooner or later he's going to remember that it was Galen who did this to him, and he's not going to be very happy.

Avery was also nearby. At first he had tried to join Galen

and the others while they frantically searched for Tamara, but the man's pain had ended up being too much. Now Avery was just resting. Johnny wasn't wounded, but someone had to watch Dakota, and Avery was as likely to kill the man as help him. That, and during those times when the injured man did wake up, Johnny found he was able to calm the man faster than the others. For some reason Dakota trusted him.

Which is fucking amazing considering that he hated my guts just two days ago.

It had stung Johnny when the man had called him a chink. It hurt him deeply still—but somehow being next to Dakota when the Carrion man was near death had softened his feelings. The trust Dakota showed him was endearing, too. It was hard to hate someone, Johnny found, who needed him so badly.

But when he's healthy again, will we still be friends?

Johnny didn't know.

If he calls me a chink again, I'll just let Avery be his nurse.

"Did you hear that?" Avery's whispering voice came in from the dark, featureless space to Johnny's right, interrupting his thoughts.

"Galen coming back?" Johnny asked.

"No, something else."

Johnny stood up into the blackness and listened.

Nothing. "I don't hear a thing, man."

"I swear I'm not imagining this. I heard something."

It wasn't hard to imagine noises, or to turn benign ones into horrors, when one could not see. Johnny had freaked himself out a couple times today already.

"Maybe," Johnny said softly. "Maybe you heard something from outside of the aqueduct."

"Maybe." Avery did not sound convinced.

Johnny stood in silence for a moment longer. "You're getting fucking paranoid, Avery."

He sat back down next to where he knew Dakota must be. Then he heard it. The sound of a distant hoof clopping against stone echoed down the aqueduct. Johnny shot back up.

"I hear it," he whispered.

Avery said nothing, but Johnny could hear his breathing.

"It's got to be above us," Johnny said.

The sound continued, slow, rhythmic, as steady and as even as a metronome.

"I think it's inside," Avery's voice cracked as he spoke.

Johnny fished around his pack and drew out his torch. After a little more searching, he produced the firerock Galen had left him. Johnny slammed the rock against the stone wall, lighting up the area with a shower of sparks. For a brief moment he caught sight of Dakota's peaceful, sleeping visage, but the torch didn't catch, so the soldier's face faded away. Johnny tried again, and again.

Then one spark caught and the torch flared into life.

Johnny looked down the aqueduct in the direction where the sound had come from. He saw nothing, and at first he couldn't hear the hoofsteps over the fire of the torch, but then one came through clearly.

"It's got to be above us," Avery said.

Johnny stepped over Dakota's unconscious body. "It could also be on the other side."

He took a few running steps down the aqueduct and tossed the lit torch as far as he could down the tunnel. The quick movement of the torch through the air caused its flame to die down to embers. Sparks flew as it clattered across the stone. For a moment, all was black again except for the barest hints of red where the torch smoldered. Then the fire lit back up.

The flickering light illuminated two hooved, hairy legs. The legs ran up into a broad human torso. The torso had the head of a bull, and one of its horns had been broken off. Behind it, in the shadows of the flickering torchlight, were the red, slinking forms of dyitzu. A hoofstep echoed again down the chamber, along with the hushed sounds of dyitzu breath and the noise of their claws scratching across the stone.

Johnny shook Dakota. "Wake up! Wake up!"

Dakota groaned.

"Time to go!" Avery shouted as he turned and ran.

"Dakota, so help me God, brother, you have got to move!" Johnny screamed.

Dakota sat up putting a hand to his head.

"If you don't move right now, we're going to die." Johnny reached down and dragged him to his feet. "Move!"

Dakota ran.

Martin's boots felt heavier than usual as he approached Hidalgo's home.

The hermit lived in a cave he'd blocked off with a wall of stacked woodstone planks. It had a single window with a row of iron bars that guarded a pair of closed woodstone shutters. Skulls of varying types, both human and devil, formed a line near where the woodstone wall met hellstone.

Martin did not feel comfortable asking Hidalgo to help him again, but he was too afraid to enter the Carrion without the man. With Aaron, Galen, and Rick gone, Hidalgo might be the single best hunter left in the area. The only problem was that Hidalgo was not a member of Harpsborough, so Martin could not simply order him to go. Even worse, Martin already owed the hermit a favor for his help in fighting the corpsemen and the Kyle-thing.

Martin stepped reluctantly onto a mat made of a coiled sinfruit vine and knocked on the door. "Hidalgo?"

"I be," Hidalgo's raspy voice answered.

"Hidalgo, I've come to thank you for your help against the corpsemen."

The door opened. Hidalgo stood in the doorway, his dreadlocks loose about his shoulders, his long arms open wide. "I be thanking you for your thanks. But Martin, you thanking me for something I be glad to do."

"And I've come to ask for your help again."

Hidalgo's mouth broke into a wide smile. "You be needing me, Martin? They not make you famous leader?"

Martin sighed. "I need you. They're sending me into the Carrion."

Hidalgo's grin disappeared. "Harpsborough, they can't be sending you there. They be sending Galen into the Carrion, and he never come back. You be new, Martin. You be very new. You know I coming from there with Klein and Charlie and Severn and Michael."

"That hole is open, Hidalgo. I've never been to the Carrion, but I know there are things in there we can't fight. And we can't close that hole until we make sure the noise won't draw one of those things to us."

Hidalgo looked angry. "I be telling Hidalgo that he never be going back there. I be saying this many years. Never. Never. Never."

"I'm scared, Hidalgo," Martin admitted. "I'm fucking terrified. I'll be leading a team of people who've never seen the Carrion. They've never had to face it. They don't know what's in there. I don't either. My girlfriend is so scared shitless that I might die, she won't even talk to me."

The beads in Hidalgo's dreadlocks rattled as he nodded his head. "But Martin, you be coming to me to ask me to be doing you favor. You a fool, Martin. You a fool. I live closer to the hole than Harpsborough. Martin, you be filling that hole, you be doing me a favor. I help you."

Thank the ever loving Christ.

Martin let out a long breath. "Thank you. Thank you so much, Hidalgo. We won't go in far. We're just going to scout."

Martin felt his stomach grumble. He'd forgone eating and given his food to Katie. It was the least he could do for putting her through all this.

"You be right, Martin man. We not be going in far. We not being able to, even if try."

"We won't try," Martin assured him. "I'll be back with my team."

Martin turned around to leave, but one of Hidalgo's long arms reached out and grabbed him. Martin turned around and was surprised to see how close Hidalgo's face was to his. He was staring into large, white, bloodshot eyes.

"Your girlfriend," Hidalgo said. "You be going to her, and telling her goodbye. You be making things so she is okay when you dead. Understand?"

Martin froze, his mouth hanging open.

"Understand?" Hidalgo demanded.

"Yes," Martin said. "I understand."

Johnny ran headlong into the pitch black tunnel. His shin collided with a jutting rock. He reeled through the darkness, his shoulder skimming against the wall to his right—but there was no time to stop and catch his balance.

He tripped again, falling headlong over Dakota's grunting form. Johnny broke his fall with his forearms and then sprang back to his feet. He reached out, catching hold of some part of

Dakota's clothing. With a heave, Johnny pulled the man to his feet.

Avery's voice called back at them from further up the tunnel. "Run run run!"

Suddenly the tunnel was lit by a dim, ruddy glow. Johnny saw the aqueduct's metal pipe just inches to the right of his face. Skull shaped stones glared at him.

The light was from dyitzu fire. Johnny ducked as the fireball rushed over his head.

"Dakota!" Johnny screamed. "Move it!"

The fireball nicked the pipe and splattered across the corridor in front of him. Dakota tried to stop, but Johnny pulled him through the fire. The intensity of the firelight had half blinded Johnny, and its smoke filled his lungs.

He and Dakota coughed as they sprinted forward.

Avery had climbed up the tunnel's exit ladder and was busily turning the wheel which would unlock the exit hatch.

"Wrong way, Avery!" Johnny shouted. "You're turning it the wrong way!"

"Shit!"

Avery frantically spun the wheel in the other direction. He shouted in frustration, ramming his shoulder up into the hatch to see if it was open. He fell back down a rung and redoubled his efforts.

Johnny fired his shotgun back down the corridor. Dakota leaned against a wall and vomited.

Jesus, he's in bad shape.

Avery rammed his shoulder up into the hatch again, and this time it burst open. "Got it!" He shot up out of the tunnel.

Johnny fired another shell with one hand, the kick knocking his shotgun out of his grasp. The weapon went spinning across the floor as Johnny shoved Dakota to the ladder. Avery pulled him up.

Johnny looked to the charging Minotaur and the army of dyitzu which followed him.

I'm going to make it!

Johnny ducked a pair of dyitzu fireballs and started climbing. Another fireball hit him in the side. It knocked the breath out of him and he nearly lost his grip. Avery reached down and grabbed his forearm. Johnny's shirt was on fire.

The beat of the cloven hooves increased in intensity. Fear of the Minotaur and Avery's strength powered Johnny upward.

The chamber they found themselves in was covered in mist. It was dark, but they were illuminated by flashes of blue light coming from down one corridor.

Avery slammed the hatch shut. Johnny threw himself down, rolling across the stone floor to try and smother the flames. The roll only lessened the fire a little, but Dakota and Avery were already running for an exit, so he chased after them, beating at the remaining tongues of flame which licked up at his face while he ran.

Avery was leading them away from the flashes of light, away from the Erebus.

Dakota's strides were uneven and lurching, as if he'd lost either his balance or his vision.

"Galen!" the warrior's voice announced from beyond the corridor ahead of them.

Thank God.

"It's us!" Johnny shouted.

Galen, Aaron, Turi and Kelly were in the next room.

"Minotaur!" Avery warned as the two groups came together.

Galen had already turned around. "Follow me!"

Together they ran, following Galen through the maze of Carrion corridors.

 — 4 —

"Other way!" Galen shouted as he burst back into the chamber.

He was followed by half a dozen dyitzu fireballs.

Arturus pivoted on one foot, leveling his pistol behind him at the exit. He ran after his father, gunning down the first dyitzu that came into their room. A second entered, and Arturus took aim, but Dakota's lurching form blocked his line of fire.

"He's herding us!" Aaron shouted as he and Arturus ran into the next chamber.

The pockmarked grey surface of the solidified magma lake blurred under Arturus' feet. The stone ripples threatened to trip him as he ran, and he found himself looking down as often as he looked over his shoulder towards his pursuers.

"He's driving us towards the city," Galen said.

"Any chance we can survive that?" Aaron shouted back.

"No."

Arturus saw another pair of dyitzu across a one hundred foot chamber. He didn't even bother trying to shoot them. One got off a fireball, but it sailed behind Johnny. Then Galen led them rushing into another room.

"Johnny's not looking good," Kelly reported.

Kelly was right, Johnny seemed almost as bad off as Dakota. What remained of his shirt was smoking. Some of the cloth had been burnt into his skin. He looked like he was close to shock.

Their next room had no exits along the ground. The molten stone had poured into this room from a chute that was perhaps fifteen feet above them. A solidified stone waterfall descended from it providing a way to climb up into it.

"Up up up!" Galen shouted.

Aaron and Turi tried first. The stone felt odd under his fingertips, and he was afraid that his grip might slip, but the climb was easy, nonetheless. Arturus turned around and helped Aaron crest the solidified stone waterfall.

Johnny and Dakota came next, with Avery trying to push Dakota up from below.

Galen took off his pack and threw it upwards. Arturus caught it, confused as to why his father would have done such a thing—then the Minotaur entered the chamber.

Its red eyes were wide with anger. Sweat made the thing's grey skin glisten. Its veined muscles rippled as it walked towards them.

"Climb!" Galen ordered.

The Minotaur snorted as Arturus' father advanced on the beast.

Arturus and Aaron reached down, grabbing Johnny's arms and then yanking him up between them. They reached down again for Dakota, but he was having trouble. Avery had stopped pushing him and was trying to climb around. Kelly was just beneath them on the wall.

Galen threw an overhand right which caught the eight foot tall Minotaur on its snout. The smack of the blow reverberated across the room. Arturus doubted that, had the beast been human, it would have survived the blow. As it was, the Minotaur took a step back. Galen followed his punch in, pushing the massive bullman back into the wall and throwing knees at the thing's hairy legs. The Minotaur stomped down with its hooves. Galen moved his feet away from the crushing hooves, but doing so disturbed his balance, and the beast was able to push him away.

Kelly had climbed higher than Dakota and was trying to pull him up by his collar. Finally Aaron was able to grab him, though Dakota's wrist was just out of Arturus' reach.

"Climb!" Kelly screamed.

Finally Arturus got a hand on him. He and Aaron pulled Dakota up.

Galen danced back from the Minotaur. It lowered its one-horned head and tried to gore him. Galen stepped off at an angle while launching a shovel uppercut into its face. The beast leaned back, snorting from the pain, but then it continued forward. Galen caught one of its arms and dropped for a suicide throw. The beast kept its balance however, and Galen ended up on his knees, his back to the creature which was bent over him. It tried to bite him, but Galen, with the Minotaur's arm still caught over his shoulder, lunged forward. The Minotaur dropped its hips, making sure that it did not topple over Arturus' father.

The sound of dyitzu hisses came in from the room beyond.

Arturus and Aaron were helping Avery up into the chute. He reached out again for Kelly.

The Minotaur, having resisted both throw attempts, tried to strike the back of Galen's head. Galen sat out, moving his body from hands and knees into a crab position. In so doing, he was suddenly out from under the Minotaur. He sprang to his feet. Galen did not turn to face the Minotaur as it lumbered upright but instead charged the stone waterfall. He leapt into the air, found his footing on the wall and leapt again. Arturus and Aaron didn't even have a chance to grab his wrists before he was between them in the chute.

"Move!" Galen yelled.

Constance, and a crew of over fifty volunteer workers and hunters were busy transporting mortar and stone to a room Martin had guessed to be a safe distance from the breached Carrion barrier. Even without all of their materials, they were ready to begin repairs to the barrier at any moment. When Martin gave his go ahead, they'd begin work and send a man back to Harpsborough to bring in Copperfield. Graham's people were even now scouring the wilds on their side, and though they had shot down four dyitzu, their initial reports were that there was nothing out there the Harpsborough hunters couldn't handle. Everyone was waiting on Martin.

Martin had gathered the three people who were, in his opinion, the best warriors he knew. There was Tucker, who had proved useful in the fight against the corpsemen. There was Huxley, who Graham had chosen as a right hand man for good reason. And there was Hidalgo, who Martin was glad to see wasn't wearing any beads or unclean clothes.

Of the three, Hidalgo's the only one I trust with my life.

"Four damn dyitzu," Tucker was saying. "Maybe we shouldn't even close up the barrier, you know? We could use that kind of food. That's more than we found during the entire time Graham was Lead Hunter."

Huxley nodded. "He's got a point, sir. I wouldn't mind heading back to town and talking more about Molly."

Martin shook his head. "First, Hux, that's the wrong girl to get caught up on, I don't care what Klein says about her. She's smarter than he is, and I don't trust a woman who's smarter than her priest. Secondly, I'm scared shitless of the Carrion. Shitless. I would jump at the first excuse not to go in there. Try bringing it up to Mike, or to Klein, or even to Hidalgo here. They've been through that place, and ain't none of them right about it."

Hidalgo nodded gravely. "It be in my head. I never be right again."

"That Kyle-thing, it came from in there. And there must be other things, things people don't even want to talk about, which we cannot allow coming across."

"Banshees," Hidalgo said. "There be banshees, they be screaming so loud that your ears bleed. Found many a dead man, they not be wounded, but they having pools of blood coming from their ears. There be packs of dyitzu, they be fifty strong or more. There be Minotaurs and there be hounds, they be large as elephants. There be harpies, smell so bad your eyes be watering. And there be worse things. There be a woman named Maab, and the men she commands. They be taking things from Hidalgo's soul, and Hidalgo never be getting them back. Not after all these years."

Huxley shrugged, but Tucker seemed appropriately fearful.

"Besides," Martin said, "those are our orders from the Fore. This ain't the time to question them. Now get your head on straight, Hux. You're new, so you don't know nuthin' but winning. Mark my words, Son, we don't always win. Aaron went into the Carrion. He's twice the hunter I am, and the Carrion beat him. Beat the best hunters we had. So stay sharp, and we'll get out of there as soon as we know it's safe."

Huxley straightened. "You'll get my best, sir."

Martin put a hand on the man's shoulder.

I just hope your best is enough.

"Follow me," Martin said.

His growling stomach tied itself into knots as he brought his team through the winding passages of the wilds towards the corpse eater village. He brought them down to the dried river bed and into the dead hungerleaf forest. Then he brought them into the halls which led to the village itself.

It looked no different than when last he'd left it, except that the bodies had been crushed into the loose cobblestone floor— probably by the stamping feet of a thousand corpses. Martin looked to his men. Hidalgo did not look well, and his hands were shaking. Tucker was nervous, jumpy. Only Huxley looked calm.

He's just too damn stupid to know any better.

Across the cobble plain, and on the far side of the Hellenistic marble temple, was the fallen Carrion barrier. Martin led them in that direction, stepping over the smatterings of dried blood and splintered bone; the remains of the casualties of their war. As they neared the temple, they found bodies which had not been trampled down into the stone. There was the body of a corpse eater, and there was the Kyle-thing's body, grinning up at him, seemingly untouched, with cobblestones scattered around it.

Martin was still bruised from that fight. Bruised on his palms from falling to the ground. Bruised on his head from where it had hit him.

There had better not be any more of those back there. I don't think I could even bear to face an Aaron-thing.

It struck him suddenly that the only reason he'd been able to beat the Kyle-thing was because of the cobblestones. In the Carrion, there might not be such convenient ammo lying around. He unslung his pack, picked up a stone, and tucked it away. As he was putting his pack back on, a hand on his shoulder made him jump.

It was Hidalgo's hand.

I can't be helping morale, jumping around like I'm new to

Hell.

"I be speaking with you. Alone."

"Sure, sure."

Hidalgo led him to the edge of the chamber and crouched down. Martin did so as well.

There was a cubed purple stone beside them, perhaps three feet tall, lying in front of the open corridor which had once been blocked with a wall of stone and gravel. Martin wondered if it was his imagination, or if he could really feel the cold emanating from that place.

Hidalgo drew out some dried dyitzu jerky from his pack, but kept it low so that Martin's body would hide it from the others.

"You be eating this," Hidalgo said.

"I'm fine," Martin answered.

Hidalgo's dreadlocks swung around his head as it shook. "No. You not be fine. Your stomach, it making loud noise. It roaring, and dyitzu, they hearing this. Martin, you be eating."

Martin nodded, accepting the gift. He took his first bite . . . then his second . . . and then he devoured it. Dyitzu meat had never tasted so good to him.

He was still hungry. Worse than that, he was still starving, but the meal had taken some of the edge off.

"Thank you, friend," Martin told the hermit.

Hidalgo smiled. "My friend, Martin man, you be ready to do this? You never seen this place before. It be . . . it be . . . it be *wrong*. It be wrong in a way that hurts you . . ." Hidalgo put his fist over his chest. " . . . here."

Martin noticed that his own hands were shaking. "I'm not ready. Not at all. Not even Aaron was ready."

He stood up and, together with Hidalgo, he rejoined Tucker and Huxley.

"This way," Martin said.

He walked towards the Carrion. The cold wasn't his imagination, he realized, and it was darker in the corridor beyond as well. The barrier had been reduced to two piles of stones on either side of the dim corridor. There was some loose gravel and a few random cobblestones that the undead troop must have tracked in here. The detritus crunched under his feet. He felt goosebumps rise up on his arm, either from the cold or from his own fear—or both.

I'll be careful, Katie.

Behind him he heard Huxley chamber a round into his 700 Remington. Martin drew his pistol and flipped off the safety.

The Carrion lay before him.

Galen froze.

Arturus watched his father intently, looking for a clue as to why he had stopped. Arturus turned back and saw the rest of his friends come silently to a halt. They were watching Galen too.

His father began creeping backwards, taking care to stay quiet. The room beyond was better lit than the corridor they were in, causing Galen's long shadow to fall at Arturus' feet. The shadow got closer as Galen inched backwards, covering Arturus' boots.

Kelly was at Arturus' side, and he felt her tense.

A dyitzu's shadow crept into view, overlapping with Galen's—the image in profile, its angular head crossing from Arturus' right to his left. It moved just a little beyond Galen's shadow and then stopped.

Did it hear us? Smell us?

Then another shadow appeared. And another. And then the black elongated shape of a person—or a corpse. He tried to judge its identity from its limping gate, but the walk seemed a little too smooth for a corpse, and a little to jerky to be human.

They can't be with One Horn, then. He only had dyitzu with him.

More devils, and then more humanesque shadows, made their way across the passage.

Galen's measured retreat continued.

The shadows kept coming—then a larger one, with a bull's head and one horn.

Damn.

Kelly's eyes widened and she clutched Arturus' arm. She pulled at him, and like his father, Arturus also began inching backwards. The one horned shadow moved on and more dyitzu followed.

Finally, those inching steps brought them back out of that room.

"This way?" Aaron whispered pointing to another corridor.

Galen shook his head. "That leads back to the city. We have to go this way."

A light mist hung in that corridor.

Arturus shook his head violently. "We can't!" he whispered harshly. "That leads to the Erebus."

Galen nodded.

Aaron threw his arms out wide. "But the Furies? You said nothing can withstand them."

Galen turned to face Aaron. "Nothing. Not me. Not you. No devil nor angel can withstand a Fury. Not even that Minotaur."

Galen walked into the mist. Arturus could do nothing but follow him.

"Quickly," Galen shouted, "there's no way to know how much time we'll have."

The mist in the air conformed to Arturus' will. He could shift it, move it to one side, or make it thicker elsewhere. The stone had become natural, and there was no evidence that any of it had been cut or worked over, even by Hell's architect. Flashes of blue light would illuminate the caves at random intervals. Arturus watched his feet cut through the supernatural mist.

The mist that obeys my mind.

He remembered Galen's warning about being this close to Sheol. He remembered how thoughts here could subtly affect reality, how hellsong might bend to his will—and how a moment's fantasy might be enough to kill.

The passageway opened up to the Erebus, the river of darkness.

This was the second time Arturus had seen it, but he was no less in awe for having experienced it before.

The river itself was a dimness that filled the chasm between the two Hells Arturus had heard called Gehenna and Sheol. Through the darkness swam cords, thick as trees, made out of a blue light so intense it hurt to look at them. Those cords swept across the chasm, breaking, forking in two before binding together again, weaving themselves into a tremendous tapestry that hung down from the infinite heights above to dangle into the infinite depths below. Their light cut through the dim water-like vapors that were the Erebus, creating pockets of visibility around themselves through which Arturus could see the stone shelf of Sheol—the Hell beyond his own. The place that, unless the stories were mistaken, he was destined to go to if he should die here. A place where every Carrion born he'd ever killed might be waiting for him. A place where Saint Wretch lived.

There was a howl, distant, but louder than anything else he'd heard in Hell.

"It's like a train," Aaron said.

Kelly nodded.

Galen moved out onto the ledge that had formed where the tunnel ended, looking around. "There!" he shouted, pointing upwards. "Look! If we climb there, the Minotaur will not be able to catch us."

Arturus looked to Johnny. The man had been burnt badly and was nearing a state of shock. Dakota swayed where he stood. His eyes were still unfocused, and he didn't seem to have a good understanding of what was going on. Avery seemed unnaturally pale, but at least he was alert.

We might lose any one of them in this climb. Any one, or all three.

The howl stopped, but only for a moment, and when it came back it was louder. Arturus saw them, two Furies, coming up the Erebus. They were distant, two tiny lights on the edge of his vision.

Or all of us.

Arturus looked up the rock face to the opening where his father had pointed. It was about fifty yards up. The gradient of the slope was steep, but it wasn't completely vertical, and there were many handholds. It would have been an easy climb had they not been saddled with wounded and forced to reckon with the threats of the Furies and the Minotaur.

Arturus leapt up to the stone and started climbing.

"Don't worry," Galen said. "The rocks are steady and easy to hold on to."

At first Arturus could hear the others behind him while they climbed, but as the Furies got closer, he could no longer hear their grunts, nor the sound of displaced pebbles skittering down the side of the cliff.

He looked back to the Furies. They were closer now, but not by much.

We might make it.

He looked down when he'd made it halfway. Galen had climbed off to one side, perhaps so that he could come across and help anyone in need. Johnny was keeping up, and the danger of the climb seemed to have given him focus. Avery was lagging behind, though. Arturus waited for him to get a little closer. Avery's pants were stained with fresh blood.

His stitches must have opened again.

Dakota was the worst off and the farthest down. Kelly was just above him, trying to coax him upwards.

The gradient of the climb for the second half was more forgiving, and Arturus was glad for it. As he gauged the distance of the oncoming Furies, he felt that they would need to make better time.

"He's here!" Kelly shouted.

Below, on the ledge they had left behind just five minutes before, the Minotaur stood, looking up at them. There were dyitzu there too, flanking him. Arturus could tell, instinctively, that they were afraid, though he could not remember having ever seen them fearful before.

The calls of the Furies mixed together, becoming loud enough to hurt Arturus' ears. For a moment one was silent.

"Take cover!" Galen was shouting. "There are dyitzu below!"

Arturus climbed so that a large jut was below him. With that, and the change in the slope of the cliff, the dyitzu wouldn't be able to get a clean throw at him. Aaron was coming up next, and Arturus waved him on.

"Keep this rock behind . . ." Arturus shouted, but the noise of the Furies was so intense that he couldn't hear his own voice.

He waited until one was quiet. "Keep this rock behind us! They can't see us."

Aaron nodded. Then he climbed by.

Dyitzu fire spun upwards into the chasm above. The fireballs passed freely through the dark portions of the Erebus, lighting up the stones and the blue cords around them with their red firelight. When they touched the blue cords, they exploded, raining down droplets of liquid fire. Arturus had never seen a sight more terrifyingly beautiful.

Galen was firing one handed back down the cliff with his MP5. Avery and Johnny, one bloody and the other burned, came up around the jut next. Arturus climbed to one side so he could look down.

He searched for Kelly, but he couldn't see her.

"Where's Kelly?" he screamed at Avery and Johnny.

"What?"

"Where's Kelly?"

Waves of dyitzu fire swept past the jut Arturus was using for cover.

That was close. As they climb higher, they'll have better shots at us.

"She's with . . ." the rest of Avery's sentence was blocked out by the twin calls of the Furies.

"What?"

"Dakota. The bitch is with Dakota."

The Furies were getting ever closer. They seemed to be made out of the same kind of effervescent substance that he might have imagined angels were made out of—except these things were no angels.

Arturus climbed to one side so that he could see Kelly. He saw a dyitzu far below, climbing up the rock. It formed a fireball. Arturus drew his pistol, but the thing had already hurled its fire at him. Arturus climbed over to his left, firing downwards. One bullet caught it in its face. The dyitzu fell backwards, bouncing off a stone and tumbling into the Erebus, spinning through the dark gaps between the blue cords until it touched one—the dyitzu's corpse erupted into a shower of blood.

Oh hell.

Arturus holstered his pistol, climbed a little farther, and looked down. There Kelly was, side by side with Dakota, shouting at him. They had found a fissure that was keeping them safe from the dyitzu fire. In a moment where one Fury's call ceased, he heard more of Galen's gunshots.

Arturus looked up to their destination. Aaron was already there, standing on the ledge.

I could be with him in a second.

Aaron bent down and helped Avery up. Johnny was nearly there too.

Arturus looked back to the Furies.

They were larger than he expected. The light that made them was shaped like warrior women, each one perhaps twenty feet tall—it was hard to tell at this distance—but their light spread out behind them on all sides in wing-like streams.

Maybe a thousand more yards?

Kelly and Dakota were rushing up through a part of their climb that left them vulnerable to dyitzu fire. The fireballs tore through the air around them. One impacted with the rock next to Kelly and sent its burning droplets across her. She didn't slow down at all, but climbed on.

Galen was coming towards Arturus.

Arturus climbed farther up, stopping again to look. Dakota had slipped and was falling back down towards the fissure. He was going to die.

Kelly went back for him.

"No!" Arturus screamed down to her. "Kelly, let him die. There's no time."

But the sound of the Furies was too intense and there was no way that she could have heard him.

A few of the dyitzu crawled onto a stone ledge. From there they threw their fire more rapidly and with better accuracy. Arturus redrew his pistol and fired. He dropped one, but the others moved so that the jut which had saved him earlier was blocking his line of fire.

Kelly had been forced back into the fissure to avoid them.

Galen was beside him now. "Go!"

Arturus had no trouble hearing his father's voice over the Furies' call. "I can't!" Arturus shouted back. "Kelly!"

"She dies!"

"I love her!" Arturus paused for a moment after he shouted it.

Did I mean that?

Galen's face went pale. "Climb, Son."

"She can't—"

"I said *climb!*"

Arturus moved up the wall and grabbed Aaron's reaching hand. Harpsborough's Lead Hunter pulled him up onto the ledge. Arturus looked back and saw Galen. His father had climbed down towards Kelly and Dakota. Galen could go no farther without exposing himself to the hail of dyitzu fire.

He'll die. He'll die trying to save a girl I don't even know if I love.

The light of the Furies was illuminating the rocks around them now. Their faces were tortured, or horrifically angered, or both. One's mouth was closed, but it opened, and she issued forth her call with a vehemence that Arturus had never before heard.

Galen's booming voice carried over the Furies. "Kelly listen, and listen closely. If you're going to live, you're going to have to do exactly what I say. Understand?"

There was a pause, and Arturus could only hope that she had been able to reply.

"Stay down," Galen continued. "The Furies will reach the dyitzu first. When I shout 'go,' you have to climb, and you have to climb as fast as you can. You can't stop to help each other. If you do, you will both die. You both have to make it. Understand?"

There was another pause.

"And does Dakota understand?" Galen asked.

Another pause.

"That'll have to do."

The noise of the Furies shook the stones beneath Arturus. He could feel their calls vibrating up through his boots to hum in the hollow of his chest. He could even feel their sound in his teeth. The twin woman warriors were only moments away, their flowing trails of light spread out behind them. They had eight arms each and in the hand of every arm was a blade. They disappeared beneath the jut.

"*Now!*" Galen boomed.

Arturus watched his father scale the cliff at a pace he would not have thought possible.

The dyitzu blood splattered freely out from behind the stone jut, showering down into the abyss. Kelly and Dakota came into view, and no fire harassed them. Arturus looked back to the dyitzu. They were spreading out along the cliff, climbing in all directions, struggling to save themselves from the relentless Furies. One dyitzu threw a fireball in some pitiful defense, but the fire passed right through the Fury's light. The Fury howled so loudly that the dyitzu clutched its hands over its ears. It fell, but before it could drop more than even a few feet, two slashing blades of light tore it into pieces.

Kelly was coming up faster than Dakota. Arturus dropped to his belly, reaching out with his hand. Galen lay down beside him.

"When we get her, run with her back into the corridor," Galen shouted. "I'll get Dakota, if I can."

Kelly was close, twenty feet away. Fifteen.

One of the Furies came over the jut. Four of her arms were stretched towards them, brandishing swords. The other four, the lower arms, had sheathed their blades and were pushing up off of the rocks as she soared upwards.

Arturus stretched his arm out as far as he could.

Ten feet. Five. He clutched at her wrist. Galen grabbed her, too, pulling her up so fiercely that Arturus wasn't sure if he'd helped at all. Her momentum practically carried him back down the corridor. Arturus scrambled to his feet and ran with her away from the Erebus.

Galen came after, dragging Dakota as he ran. But then he dropped the man. At first Arturus thought his father was abandoning Dakota, but then his mind processed what he'd seen.

Galen had only dropped the top half of Dakota.

 — 6 —

The cool air of the Carrion sent shivers up Martin's spine. It was a dark place, so dark that many of the rooms were entirely lost in shadow. He and his men dared not speak. Out of all of them, only Hidalgo was succeeding at being perfectly quiet. The rest, including Martin himself, had spent most of their time hunting in the wilds around Harpsborough. They'd had no fear, then, no reason to learn to stay *this* quiet.

We were so arrogant. So prideful.

Martin was doing his best. He kept his footfalls as soft as he could. He tightened his pack around his back in order to lessen its movement. He was careful not to let his clothing brush against any walls.

The archways that led from one room to another were always built with huge violet keystones. He tried to memorize the path they'd taken, but the darkness and his own ever present fear made him unsure about their direction.

"What's that?" Huxley whispered.

Martin hadn't heard or seen anything. He raised his hand in a fist in the same way that Aaron had sometimes. His men stopped moving, freezing in place. Now that he was still, Martin could hear his own breathing. The cold was causing him to wheeze ever so slightly, and that single small whistle seemed to drown out every other noise.

There didn't *seem* to be anything out there.

Martin turned to Huxley, whose eyes were narrowed in

concentration. "What did you hear?"

Huxley held up his rifle and shrugged. "I don't know," his soft voice reported. "Something. I swear it was something. Like scratches."

"Dyitzu?" Hidalgo asked.

Huxley shook his head. "No. Something different."

Harpies?

Martin held them still for a few minutes longer, but when he heard nothing, he motioned his men onwards.

The next room was lit by two dim rocks in the ceiling, but a chest high outcropping of natural stone left most of the room in shadow. Hidalgo was in front, and he stopped, pointing to the ground.

Martin hadn't seen them at first, but there were a pair of stone mounds on the floor. He bent down to inspect them. They had been made of loose gravel, but the stones had started to heal together. They looked like they might be hollow. Martin began to stand up, but as he did so, he thought he saw something deeper in the mound. He dropped back down.

"Flashlight," he ordered.

Huxley walked up next to him, unslung his pack and pulled a flashlight out of one pocket. He offered it to Martin. The rest of Martin's men knelt beside him, which made him feel nervous.

"Watch the exits, Tucker," Martin ordered.

The flashlight's handle was a long, black metal tube. It would have made a fabulous club. Martin's thumb found a switch which had raised rubber bumps on it. Martin flipped on the flashlight.

He peered into the center of the mound. Inside it was a dead body dressed all in grey.

"Shit," Tucker said.

Martin looked up at him. "I said watch the exits." He turned off the flashlight and handed it back to Huxley. "Move it."

They'd explored enough, Martin figured, to justify turning around. If they headed back, they should run into another barrier. Then they could follow the walls until they found where they'd entered.

Then we'll be halfway done.

He could feel his men's relief when he turned them around, but it didn't last long.

"There it is again!" Huxley's said harshly.

"You're dreaming things," Tucker accused.

Martin held up his fist again, though his men had already stopped.

Hidalgo's throat issued a low rattle. "He right. There be something."

"That way," Huxley said.

Please let it be nothing.

They followed the young hunter as he led them beneath a violet keystone topped arch. Now Martin could hear the noise as well. It was like a scratching, but different somehow from the sound of dyitzu claws scraping across stone. Martin didn't know if he'd heard such a sound before.

It got louder as Huxley led them into another room. This chamber's floor was almost completely covered by the stone burial mounds. Huxley stepped around one and found an aisle where he could walk between them. Martin did the same. The scratching grew in volume, louder and louder, until it was intense enough to drown out his footsteps.

Huxley stopped at the end of the chamber and looked back. He seemed confused. Martin looked behind him to see Hidalgo and Tucker picking their way through the mounds. The scratching stopped for a second . . . and then started again with renewed vigor. Martin realized where it was coming from.

He looked to the burial mound to his right. "Light," he ordered in a hoarse whisper. "Huxley, quickly. The light."

The young hunter hurried back, unslinging his pack again. He reached in and produced the flashlight. Martin flipped it on, pointing it at the mound. He could barely see through the stacked stones, but there inside, something was moving.

"He's still alive," Tucker said.

"Tucker," Martin ordered, "Watch the exits again."

Martin tried to pull at the stones. A few came loose, breaking off from the gravel they'd healed into, but most wouldn't budge. "Does anyone have a crowbar?"

"I've got a pick, sir," Huxley's voice cracked when he spoke.

Martin looked towards him. Before they'd entered the Carrion, Huxley had seemed to be the calmest of all of them. He was not calm now. His hands were shaking.

"That'll do." Martin leaned closer to the mound. "Don't

worry, we'll get you out."

Martin accepted the pick, took a deep breath, and then tapped it into the gravel. The sound of the metal banging on stone reverberated through the chamber. He gave it another two strikes, and then a large section of the mound gave way. Martin pulled out a few handfuls of broken stones and dumped them behind himself.

A human hand emerged from the mound and grabbed Martin's wrist. Its veins were black rivers running through its pale skin. The tip of its fingers had been worn away, perhaps by the constant scratching, so that white bone protruded out of the flesh at the end of each undead digit. Martin let out an involuntary shout, but that was eclipsed by Huxley's high pitched scream.

Martin struggled to get his wrist out of its grip, but the thing's cold fingers would not loosen. Hidalgo brandished his hellstone tomahawk and brought it down on the offending limb. Black blood spurted up into the air, spreading across them all. Hidalgo brought the tomahawk down again and again, and finally Martin was able to pull his wrist free.

The bare boned tips of the thing's fingers had ripped through the fabric of his hoodie, leaving four long lines of blood across his forearm.

He looked to Huxley, who had dropped his rifle and placed both of his hands over his mouth.

For a few heartbeats Martin waited, expecting all manner of devils to come answering Huxley's scream.

Except for the clawing of the half severed corpse arm that thrashed about at Martin's feet, all was quiet.

Martin picked up Huxley's rifle and handed it to him. "Get your shit together, Hux."

Huxley nodded as he accepted the rifle. "Yes, sir."

Martin led them through the next arch.

Copperfield usually set himself up on the second story balcony to do his business, and one of the things he'd enjoyed the most about it, in the old days at least, was eating during his meetings. Doing business without food, well, it was a good way to get indigestion.

Cindy, his main assistant, was just getting up to leave. She was the one who coordinated the five men who mined the woodstone. She was the one who traded his torches and his lumber to the villagers. She was the one who delivered the firewood to Mancini's still and to Kylie's Kiln. But she was also the one he'd shown how to mix saw dust, sinfruit juice and a pinch of ground firerock in order to make his torches, and it was for that reason that he was thinking about having her killed.

Copperfield watched Cindy walk away from him. He'd miss her figure, sure, but since she'd never bed him, what did it matter? Most women would sleep with him for a meal, but meals were how he paid Cindy for her work, so she was rarely wanting.

If I paid her less, she might come around.

But she wouldn't. She'd resent him if he cut her pay, and he couldn't have that since, technically, she could go into business all by herself.

Then I'd really have to kill her, and before she showed anybody else the secret.

His stomach growled angrily, and he felt a little sick. Not for the first time, he resented the law that forbid any eating on the balconies. Copperfield had never approved of the law, but now that they were feeding the villagers on Feast Day, he felt that the law was especially outdated. He had plans to try and strike it down at the Fore's next meeting, but for the moment that statute still held.

He appreciated the island of bodies that surrounded him and protected him from Hell, but now that Hell was getting significantly less dangerous, he wondered how much he really needed them. The hunters would have to stay. After all, someone had to fend off the corpse eaters and repair the Carrion barriers, but the villagers themselves were getting to be too much of a liability. They were draining the Fore's resources in addition to upsetting his stomach.

We should at least halve them.

Copperfield's belly rumbled again.

I'd better get back inside and get some food.

John's sandals slapped against the stone balcony. "Someone to see you, Citizen."

Copperfield sat up straight in his woodstone chair. "A

Citizen or a villager?"

"Villager," John answered.

Copperfield slumped back. "Send them up."

John's sandals slapped their way back into the Fore and then down the stairs. While Copperfield listened for their return, he heard a conversation coming down from above him. He couldn't quite make out the words, but he could tell that the voices belonged to Michael and Mancini.

Maybe I can get John to give me some bloodwater. There's no law about not drinking on the damn balcony, is there?

He looked across the village of Harpsborough with irritation. The slapping of the sandals returned.

John had brought Molly.

Well, this is going to be interesting.

"Really?" Copperfield asked. "The hell could you have to say to me?"

Molly sat down across from him. "It's true, I said some bad things about you when I was Mike's. I'm not proud of it. I know it took a long time for people to realize that those lies were lies. It was shitty. Damn shitty."

"You don't say?" Copperfield was surprised how much bitterness was in his voice.

"I'm doing what I should have done before," Molly said. She seemed different somehow, from the Molly he'd known, and her expression was strangely unreadable. "I was doing bad shit, Copperfield. Really bad shit. I was trying to find a way behind the Golden Door and—"

"I know what the fuck you were trying to do, Molly. I think you should face charges for it. I plan to bring it up."

Molly nodded and frowned. "Jesus Christ, you know, I hope you do. And you know what else? I tried to convince Mike to charge me. Klein wouldn't let him. But if you push it, it might go through the Fore. I know I don't have shit for influence with the Citizens anymore, but if you can do anything to make sure I go to trial, let me know. I'll help you."

You can suck my cock, you little slut. You can suck the cock you told everyone was small and crooked.

It was a little crooked, and it wasn't huge, but it certainly wasn't small. Copperfield had measured it in the old world to make sure. Because of the small bit of truth to her lie, it had taken nearly a year before people had stopped calling him "Little Capn' Hook."

Molly's blue eyes were intent on him.

Copperfield felt the acid in his stomach creeping up into his throat. "Look, you made your own bed—"

"They had revoked my right to be in the wilds right before I left. I thought it was a death sentence. I thought there was no way I could live in Harpsborough, do you know why?"

Copperfield glared at her.

"Do you know why?"

He shook his head.

"Because I'd burned every bridge that I'd ever built. I'd made enemies of all my friends. And before I escaped, in my little fucked up mind, I would have rather starved to death than come back and apologize or make amends. I'm not that chick, Copperfield. I'm not her anymore. I was out there, alone. Hell got to me Copperfield. It got to me. I started to think about the things I'd done. And I started to think about the ways I could make it up to people. The ways I could undo all the pain I'd caused." She leaned forward. Her shirt wasn't exactly revealing, but it was loose enough to give Copperfield a sudden glance of her infamous breasts. "That includes you."

He shook his head. "You haven't changed, Molly. You just want something from me."

Molly stood up and walked to the balcony. "I have changed. But you're right. I do want something from you, and I want it bad."

"And that is?"

"I want to work for you, Copperfield," she put her hands on the railing and leaned forward over the edge of the balcony.

"I've already got a manager. You're no match for Cindy."

"I meant in the mine. I want to mine woodstone for you."

Copperfield sat back. Before the famine, he'd had ten people working the mines for him. Now that things were getting a little better, he could probably stand to have six, particularly since Mancini had hinted that he'd need to buy more woodstone soon.

"I could, if I were to hire you, pay you what I pay the men, but only if you pull out as much woodstone. It's outside of Harpsborough, though. You think they'll let you go?"

Molly nodded. "I think so. Most days your people get

escorted by hunters on their way out to hunt, right? That should give Mike enough confidence. Besides, I don't know if that restriction still applies to me."

Copperfield pursed his lips.

I hate to trust this woman, but, if she's working for me . . .

"Okay. I'll try you out. We'll be fixing a broken Carrion barrier in just a few hours, assuming Martin survives. No promises. If you work well with me, you're in. If not, you're out."

She smiled. "Thank you!" She walked over from the railing and bent down to hug him. He felt her breasts pushing into his shoulder. "Thank you so much. You won't regret it. I'll start, uhm, undoing my previous lies too. Unless you think that would be too indiscreet?"

Copperfield shook his head. "No no! Just don't . . . you know."

"Oh, I won't let anyone think that," Molly said. "Am I free to go?"

Copperfield nodded. "Just keep an eye out. Come with me when I leave the Fore."

He had to admit that Molly was more exciting to watch leave than Cindy.

They had finished scouting, to Martin's satisfaction, the upriver side of the Carrion. Now they were close to finishing the downriver portion.

Just another half hour, maybe fifteen minutes, and I'm free.

Then he could go back to Copperfield and feel justified in asking him to start building the wall. He could go back to Michael and report. He could go back to Katie and make things right with her. He would kiss her and hold her and tell her how terrible the Carrion was—and she would kiss him and hold him and tell him how much she loved him.

The hellstone here was either black or purple. It was difficult to tell which. A vein of lighter hellstone swam through the wall to his right, illuminating the giant room they were in. The room was perhaps a hundred yards wide and half that in height. The purple vein, however, seemed oddly dim in many places. Martin walked up to the wall and held his hand against the lighter purple rock. The edges of his fingers glowed violet as he touched the stone. Even this close to the light source, he could not make out any details in the wall.

"Light," Martin whispered.

Huxley was there in a moment, passing Martin the flashlight with his shaking hands. Martin flipped it on. Hidalgo sucked air in through his teeth.

The entire wall was scarred with fire. Martin ran his finger over the stone, finding an oily residue.

"Dyitzu fire," Martin said.

The floor and ceiling showed signs of burn marks as well. There must have been thousands and thousands of fireballs thrown in this room.

"How many dyitzu would it take to do this?" Tucker asked.

"Maybe few," Hidalgo said, "throwing fire for long time. Maybe many, throwing for shorter time."

Martin turned off the flashlight and handed it back to Huxley. Their revelation hadn't made him any less nervous.

"But where they'd go?" Martin asked.

Hidalgo let out a low, throaty growl. "The dyitzu shun the undead, but they not be killing them. When the corpse army come through, they must scare dyitzu. We finish scouting fast, build wall fast, before they be returning.

"Agreed."

The Carrion didn't get any easier to navigate as they traveled deeper. Winding staircases appeared which dead ended into stone walls as often as they led to other floors.

The next room was so completely dark Martin almost called for a flashlight outright, but he thought he heard something, so he held up his fist instead. It sounded like breathing—or wind. Probably wind.

Martin held out the palm of his hand to his people, hoping that would keep them back, and then entered into the pitch black room alone.

No sense in everybody dying.

He felt claustrophobic.

The walls must be only inches away.

The floor of this room was more natural, and it was sloped upwards. As quietly as he could, Martin picked his way across the uneven stone. He kept one hand raised before him, expecting to run into the ceiling at any moment, but he did not. He climbed higher and higher.

He stopped for a moment, and in the silence, thought he heard voices.

They *were* voices, but they echoed oddly. It almost seemed like they were coming from under him.

At least they're human.

He climbed even higher.

I think.

There was light. He found himself at the top of a precipice, looking down into a cavern below. It was shaped like half of a caldera, its circular base bisected by a natural-looking cave wall. At its center, a stage had been built, and men filled the surrounding area as if it were an amphitheatre. The whole of it was lit by a single white light orb suspended in the air near the back wall, perhaps a hundred feet lower than Martin, yet one hundred feet or so higher than the stage.

Oh my God.

Martin eased himself to the stone floor and looked straight down the cliff. Just below him, perhaps only ten feet or so away, sat the top row of the crowd. They were still—dreadfully still. He could smell their wet swampy rot from where he sat. Some were corpses, but not all those in the crowd were. Though it was hard to tell which was which since the light was so dim this far out from the stage, he could tell that some of these people were lepers. In fact, almost all of those that filled the front rows seemed to be lepers. Martin could identify them, not because he could make out any details about the persons, but because they were filled with a nervous energy that the dead lacked.

It was not wind I heard. It was their breathing.

The men in the front rows were dressed almost exclusively in dark clothes, though a few who sat amongst them wore grey robes. On the stage, raised up on knee high stone sepulchers and well lit by the brilliant white light, were the bodies of four black robed women. A black robed man stepped up from behind them.

The breathing that had sounded like wind stopped. Then someone shouted.

"Nephysis!"

The shouter had been in the crowd, one of the members in the front row.

"Nephysis!" shouted another.

The corpse eaters began to chant that strange word, their fists pumping in the air.

I've heard that word before. The corpse eater I interviewed—what was his name?—said Nephysis was God.

It must be Nephysis then, who stood on the stage, and that man raised his hand. The chanting stopped, and all was silent. Then, his arm still held high, he walked along the back of the stage behind the women, stopping in between the center two. He raised his other hand as well.

"You asked for freedom, and I have given it. You asked for rapture and I have given it. You asked for ecstasy and I have given it! Yet it is still Friday . . . but Sunday's coming."

The last part confused Martin. Who cared what day it was?

The lepers cheered.

Nephysis took a step towards the crowd. His robe swirled about him as he motioned to his people. "I have delivered unto you these four women. Are you not thankful?"

The crowd answered in a roar. "Yes!"

"You should be, Gods be damned. They tortured you. They broke you. They stole parts of your body with rust rock so that they would not regrow. They raped you. They did things to you which no human could withstand. You thought them invincible, but here they are . . . Maab's priestesses. Their Minotaur-blood potions offered them no protection. Their spells and incantations failed them. Their God, Ahuramazda, abandoned them." There was a long pause. "And here they lie. Are you not happy?"

The crowd roared again. "Yes!"

"You shouldn't be." Nephysis sudden reversal of expectation quieted them all. "It's Friday, but Sunday's coming."

Martin felt his heart thudding in his chest. He tore his gaze from the spectacle and looked back behind him to see if any of his men had come up this way, but their shadows remained in that distant purple light which outlined the arch at the base of the hill. They had not come. They would not come, somehow he knew that. They had heard Nephysis' voice and were afraid.

"Did you hear me?" Nephysis called out to his people. "I said it's *Friday*, but *Sunday's* coming. Is it fair that these women who lied to you, who did so much wrong to you, got to escape the wrath of your revenge?"

"No!" answered the lepers.

"Is it fair that these people who robbed you of body parts escaped dismemberment?"

"No!"

"Is it fair that these people who tortured you escaped torture?"

"No!" The air was crackling with the lepers' passion.

Nephysis voice lowered. "Is it fair that those who raped you not be raped themselves?"

"No!"

"Amen," Nephysis said. There was a pause after he said the word, an intake of breath, as if the crowd feared that the utterance of those two syllables would bring about some terrible calamity. "Amen, my brothers and sisters. It's Friday, but Sunday's coming."

Silence, fear, anticipation, ecstasy. Martin could feel the energy of the crowd.

"But would it mean a damn thing if you were to remove the body parts of these unfeeling corpses? Would that do anything to sate your lust for your rightful and righteous retribution?"

"No!"

Martin felt himself shaking his head with them. Whomever these women were, desecrating their bodies would do nothing to their souls.

"Would beating and torturing these dead priestesses of Maab cause them any pain?"

"No!"

Nephysis' voice lowered again. "Would raping these still, cold bodies give you any pleasure?"

"No!"

"It's Friday, but Sunday's coming. Can I get an Amen from you, my children?"

They were too terrified to say the word. Martin understood why. This did not seem like the time to be invoking God.

Nephysis walked up to the front of the stage and paced to the left. "But I promise you, there is a way we can go on hurting these women. There is. Can I get an amen for that?"

"Amen," a man in the front row said.

"You'd pray for that wouldn't you?" Nephysis said, stopping in front of the leper who'd spoken.

Even from this distance, Martin could see the leper shrink back in his seat.

"I'd pray for that. Remember there was a time, not so very long ago, when I served Maab, too. I'd pray that these women could have lived long enough for you to murder them, dismember them, torture and rape them a thousand times over."

"Amen," a few spoke this time.

"I'd pray that you were the ones who had a chance to do that."

"Amen!" the crowd spoke as one.

"It's Friday," Nephysis boomed, "but Sunday's coming. Know you that there was a time when the Jews hated one of their own so badly that they were willing to see him crucified. They beat him and tortured him and stabbed him, but they were fools, because they beat him too badly. Crucifixion on its own is a slow death, but these people had cheated themselves of their revenge, so eager were they for blood. That Lord on his cross looked up to the uncaring stars and said 'oh God, why have you forsaken me!'" Nephysis paced back across the stage and stopped near the middle. He leaned in towards the crowd and spoke to them conspiratorially. "That was on a Friday."

Oh, shit.

The crowd began to cheer. They raised their hands and stood, hooting and hollering. Only the corpses remained in their chairs, but Nephysis raised his hands and even they stood.

Nephysis paced back amongst the four bodies of the dead women. "And God looked down upon that tortured man and thought that perhaps he deserved more. Perhaps that crucified Lord deserved to be tortured for all eternity, so He used His might and sated the violent lust of those Jews. He brought that bastard back to life so we could kill him all over again—oh, if only it were that way now! If only there were some god that would look upon your anger and bring these women back to life. Oh! Oh! Oh! The horrible things we'd do to them."

Nephysis drew a dagger and slit the sash which tied closed the robe of the first woman. "If only there was some way that these bodies could be reattached to their souls so that you might wreak your revenge. If only there was some God who would take pity on your wrongs and let you get your fair retribution." He spread wide the priestess' robe revealing that the woman's torso had been split in two and that her intestines had been removed. "Well if you're looking for a God like that, I'm your huckleberry. I tell you, brothers, amen."

"Amen," the lepers responded.

"I tell you, *amen*, brothers."

"Amen!" the lepers shouted.

He walked along the sepulchers, opening the robe of each woman, showing that they had been similarly prepared. Then Nephysis pulled out a red colored pouch. "It's Friday, but Sunday's coming. And did you know that on that third day they came to the tomb and found that Jesus had been raised from the dead? Did you know that? Did *you* know *that*?"

"Amen!"

"I say to you that it's Friday, but Sunday's coming. Say it with me now!"

"It's Friday," the crowd chanted, "but Sunday's coming."

Nephysis opened his bag and reached in. "Say it with me now, children."

He withdrew his hand from the bag and threw red dust up into the air. It hung there in a long arc, ten feet or so above his head, motionless.

"It's Friday, but Sunday's coming." The dust sprinkled down upon the dead bodies as the crowd shouted out its mantra. "It's Friday, but Sunday's coming!"

"Witness then," Nephysis' voice filled the huge chamber, "the miracle of the resurrection. It may look like you're down. It may look like your soul has taken its last beating, but by my magic, I tell you, that ain't right. You may be dead, but I hold for you the promise of everlasting life. My brothers and sisters. My children. People who have slaved under the dominion of Maab for so long that you've lost yourselves, Friday can't last forever. Now know this, Sunday's coming. Can I get an amen from you now?"

"Amen!" they shouted, and Martin even found himself mumbling the word along with them.

"Amen," Nephysis shot back at them.

"Amen!"

Nephysis put away his pouch and drew another. He threw its contents into the air. "Amen!"

"Amen!"

White dust drifted down upon the bodies. Nephysis' hands shot back up into the air and shouted to his people again. *"Sunday's coming!"*

The dust settled, and for a moment, all was still. Then one of the dead women's feet twitched. Nephysis' raised his hands again.

"Amen!"

And again.

"Amen!"

And again.

"AMEN!"

"So be it."

The first woman stood. For a moment, nothing happened, but then a corpse eater charged the stage. He was followed by many others, and suddenly Martin could not see the women any longer. Finally, one appeared, as if cresting the wave of lepers. Her clothes had been stripped off. She was screaming in terror even as the last pieces of her guts fell away from her body. They were raping her. They were raping a corpse, or a Kyle-thing, or a resurrected body, Martin did know what, and he didn't care. He turned and ran back down the dark slope.

"Run!" he ordered his men.

"What's going on?" Huxley's shaky voice asked as Martin ran by.

"I said *run!*"

Screams of terror ripped Michael's attention away from the chess board. He leapt to his feet and charged to the balcony, tearing aside the curtain that blocked his vision. Only once before had he heard screams like this. Once when Charlie had been the leader of Harpsborough—when a pack of dyitzu and hounds had broken in while their hunters were out. The reason, or one of the reasons, why Michael had gunned him down in cold blood was that it had been Charlie's decision to leave the village undefended—and somehow Michael had made the same mistake. Martin and the best hunters were out scouting the Carrion, leaving the village all but undefended.

"Please!" a villager was shouting, "please!"

His first thought was for the Fore. As soon as he took stock of the enemy, he had to get a gun and guard the doorway. The villagers could come in and hide here, or, assuming Klein could find someone to help defend it, they could shelter in the church. He charged along the balcony and looked out over Harpsborough's motley hovels towards the entrance. He came to a stop.

What the hell?

The villagers had formed up in a half moon around the entrance. They were leaning back, terrified, though one woman stood apart from the others. She was shouting.

"Please! I beg you! Don't hurt my Marcus. Please don't hurt him."

The two hunters responsible for guarding Harpsborough were on their knees, their hands behind their heads. Standing behind them were two people covered in body armor. They were wearing what looked like the helmets riot police wore in the old world. Even at this distance, Michael could tell what kind of rifles were leveled at the back of his hunters' heads.

They were M-16s.

Infidels.

There were four of them. Two, who were pointing guns at the back of his people's heads, and two more; a taller one with broad shoulders, and a small, diminutive one. The small one took off her helmet. It turned out she was facing the balcony, as if she knew to look for him.

"My name is El Cid, Michael." The little woman's voice echoed across Harpsborough.

She knows my name. The infidels know my name.

She strutted forward, her rifle swinging at her side. She stopped before the pleading villager. "And don't worry, Miss, I've come to talk."

Galen led them up into an enclosed series of chambers, some of which were no larger than coffins. The lighting here was as dim as in the rest of the Carrion, and the cool thick stone around them served to enhance Arturus' feeling of oppression.

"Where the hell are we?" Avery's voice was shaky.

Arturus looked back at him. Galen had given the hunter a cloth to make sure that he wasn't leaving a trail of blood. The cloth made an odd bulge in the man's pants.

Thank goodness I'm not injured like that.

Johnny was wheezing badly. His burns looked serious.

Aaron, though, seemed as strong as ever. He was almost untouched. With Galen around, it was easy to forget how capable a fighter Harpsborough's Lead Hunter was. Aaron's jaw was set, his eyes peering fearlessly into the darkness.

Kelly seemed also to be gaining in strength.

Her ribs must be nearly healed.

"Rest here," Galen ordered.

"Will we be safe?" Aaron asked.

Galen shrugged. "I don't know. This place was once a part of the City of Blood and Stone, centuries ago. Slaves lived in here, once, but it has since been abandoned. It is as safe a place as I can find on short notice."

"I don't think One Horn was killed when the Furies came," Arturus said. "He'll be looking for us."

Aaron looked at him and nodded. "I think you're right."

"Be that as it may," Galen's deep voice intoned, "Tamara *must* be either rescued or killed. Johnny and Avery *must* rest and heal. The devil men said that Tamara was in Cul' Nahedran. I will attempt to save her. If I fail, then I will make sure she doesn't give away Calimay's position."

Avery sat down gingerly, leaning against a stone wall that separated two coffin sized cubbyholes. "Who gives a damn about Calimay? Let them find her. We just want to get home."

"Do not forget that we need her guide to navigate the Lethe," Galen said. "Don't forget that Calista has Turi's child growing in her belly. And don't forget that Harpsborough needs someone on their side in the Carrion, lest they be conquered by the armies of Maab or the City."

Kelly looked at him suddenly. "You care for her, don't you? Calimay, I mean."

Galen gave her a wan smile. "There are slaves there too, remember."

Kelly nodded.

"Now I'll seal you in when I leave," Galen continued. "If I'm not back in two days—measure them as best you can—then leave this place and search for food and water."

Aaron sat down next to Avery. "If you don't return, what chance will we have to make it home?"

Galen looked at him gravely. "None. Come with me, Turi. I'd speak to you for a moment before I go."

Arturus followed his father through a small maze of corridors and rooms. Galen turned around at one point and then knelt. Arturus also dropped to his knees.

Galen reached out with both of his hands and put them on Arturus' shoulders. "Son, it is possible that the Minotaur will find you here. You will hear him coming when he breaks down the door and slaughters your friends. Take Kelly and run down this corridor. At its far end is another sealed off stone passage. You will be able to lever it open. It will lead you through the ruins of the old city and into the City of Blood and Stone itself.

You will be a slave there, but you will be alive. It is possible that I will come and find you, but it is not likely. As a slave, Arturus, I have found it is best not to have hope. It hurts too much. You won't be able to help yourself, I know, but try. If there is a resistance, join it. Convince its leader to help you escape. Find Rick."

Arturus nodded. "Do you think it's likely? That I'll have to run, I mean."

Galen looked over his shoulder into the dark corridor. "I don't know, Son."

"It's still okay for me to have hope now, though, isn't it?"

Galen's head turned back towards him. Arturus noticed that his father's beard was a bit unkempt. "Find Kelly. Make sure she's near you so that you two can escape together. Tell her how you feel. You might not have another chance."

Galen stood and walked back to where the others were resting. Arturus couldn't get his father's response to Aaron's last question out of his mind.

"If you don't return, what chance will we have to make it home?"

"None."

Michael ripped his Winchester down from its display and tossed it onto the table. Chess pieces scattered, bouncing and rolling across the floor. He whipped open a cabinet and pulled out his body armor. He slipped it on over his shoulders and fastened its buckles.

Kylie ran up to him. She was close to tears. "Michael, don't go down there."

Michael shoved his hand into the cabinet and brought out a fistful of bullets.

"Michael!" she shrieked. "Don't go!"

She clutched at the bullets in Michael's hand, sending them scattering across the floor.

Michael shoved her away. She was propelled backwards into the wall, banging against the mirror. She fell to the ground amidst the bullets and looked up at him, tears in her eyes.

"Who then?" Michael demanded, pointing to his own chest. "Who would you send other than me?"

She no longer looked like she was about to cry. Her lips

pursed as if she was thinking. "No one." Her eyes narrowed as if in thought. "No one, Michael. You're the one I trust to handle this."

Michael grabbed another handful of bullets. Kylie made no move to get up. Michael left her there, charging down the stairs. He stopped in the waiting room on the first floor to jam a couple of shells into his rifle—then he chambered one round.

Mancini came up behind him. He was not alone, the rest of the Citizens were gathering in the hallway or were huddling up in the stairs. They wouldn't dare go out and show their faces, Michael knew that much already.

And why should they? That's the promise of the Fore. Once you're in, you've seen the last of danger.

Only, for some reason, that had never applied to him.

"Anyone going with me?" Michael asked.

No one volunteered. Mancini looked away, and then at the floor, and then away again. The bastard manipulator was never around when you really needed him.

Then Chelsea stepped forward. She was dressed in a nightgown. Obviously she'd been sleeping when the commotion had occurred. "I'll come with you," she said.

Thank you. I forget sometimes why we brought you into the Fore. Thank you.

"You want a gun?" Michael asked her.

She shrugged. "What good would it do me against *her*?"

Probably none at all. But this motherfucker in my hands just might pierce an infidel's armor.

With Chelsea at his side, Michael exited the Fore. The villagers were all there, most of them gathered about the entrance. They were staring at him. Some of the ones nearest him were noticeably shaking. Worry was in their eyes. Fear.

If I had been a better leader, my presence would have taken their fear away.

"Move aside," Michael ordered.

Slowly, almost begrudgingly, the terrified villagers opened a path. Michael looked through the parting sea of humanity to the diminutive Infidel Friend that he had to face. Michael looked over to Chelsea for support.

She smiled at him. "If we die right here, I want you to know that, for what it's worth, I think you've been a better leader than

Charlie."

"Thank you. I just wish that they'd come when we'd had more hunters around."

She shook her head. "It's too convenient to be a coincidence. They must have someone on the inside. Someone spying on us."

Michael snorted. "Well that's going to make me feel more comfortable while walking through this crowd."

It was a long walk. Michael stopped well short of El Cid, who stood a few feet in front of his two kneeling hunters. Her black hair was pulled back and bound up behind her head. A loose strand of it fell across her angular face and rested against the pale skin at her neck.

I've never seen eyes so green.

"Are you Michael Baker?" El Cid asked as he stopped.

"I am."

"Good. Now you're not cold blooded killers, so I know you won't let your men die. And we're not cold blooded killers, either, so we're not going to kill them. I say we stop pretending." El Cid turned her back on him and spoke to the other infidels. "Let them go."

His hunters were dragged to their feet and shoved into the crowd. The crowd accepted them with protective arms.

"More comfortable?" El Cid asked.

Not at all.

"I've always been comfortable," Michael lied. "I could have you shot down right now. I have snipers up on the Fore."

El Cid gave a laugh that sounded like a little girl's. "They'd better not miss. Besides, you know what happened to Hellespont."

Fear erupted throughout Michael's body, spreading out from his belly and settling in the small of his back. Father Klein had spoken of that city. The infidels had come and slain them, to a man. To hear Klein tell it, there had only been three infidels.

"As you said, I'm not a cold blooded killer." Mike sneered. "But since you mention Hellespont, we know you are."

El Cid stepped closer to him. Michael felt a visceral reaction to her nearness and stepped back. He could not believe he was so terrified of someone so tiny.

She's an Infidel Friend. You should be scared of her. She's got a ton of heartless bastards ready to kill on her command.

"War and murder are different things," El Cid said. "One of ours was murdered in Hellespont. The village's destruction was an act of war. Surely you know the difference. My scouts say that you had a war just a while ago against a pack of lepers. You killed them because they murdered some of yours, did you not?"

How does she know these things?

"Why have you come?" Michael demanded.

"First, I'd like to commend your mercy. My understanding is that instead of killing one of our people for a crime they didn't commit, you exiled him."

Oh, somehow I knew that was going to come back and bite me in the ass.

There was some movement to Michael's right and Father Klein burst in from the crowd.

I knew I had a few friends worth a damn.

"I assure you, woman," the Father said, "he was most certainly guilty of his crimes."

El Cid gave Klein a patronizing smile. "Let me guess, was it blasphemy?"

Klein nodded. "It was."

"My apologies, Father," El Cid said, her smile sharpening, "but being a God damned idiot will not spare you from infidel justice."

Father Klein rose up and shouted. "Speak your words, infidel, but this is a Godly town. You will not speak His name in vain!"

She looked at him slyly. "Still can't read Hebrew?"

"I can."

"Then you should know that taking the Lord's name in vain refers to Yahweh's true name, which tradition dictates is a sin to speak. Surely you can see my trepidation in trusting you when the thing you worship is known as 'He Who Shall Not Be Named.'"

Father Klein took a step closer, leaving the half circle of villagers behind him. "You have the devil in your hearts. I know what the scriptures mean because I have God in mine."

"If God is in the heart of the body you think the devil gave you, you are in some serious shit."

"You twist my words."

El Cid raised one eyebrow.

Father Klein would not relent. "This body is God's body, not the Devil's."

"Let me offer you peace, then, man who would be of God. I know Maab took your genitals. I know she used a method that made them not grow back. The condition is not irreversible. I can make you whole. Will you accept?"

Father Klein sneered. "I'm a better man for their loss. I'd not be swayed again by temptation."

The crowd groaned suddenly. They had not known. Michael's jaw dropped. He had not expected Klein to admit his infirmity.

Such a brave man.

"Well I suppose that's for the best," El Cid said, "I preffer my cowards dickless."

Father Klein's jaw clenched. "You come offering peace, you say? You come offering to enable my own temptation. You come trying to give back to me what the devil can use to warp my will. You come offering only damnation. Do not think your motivations are anything other than transparent to these people."

There was a murmur of fiery agreement from the crowd.

Good, let them see their leaders resist the infidels. Let them feel empowered by our strength.

"Why have you come?" Michael demanded.

El Cid turned her brilliant green eyes back towards him. "The 'mercy' you showed my man was . . . admirable for people of your backward understanding. I commend you for it. Know that in the future you are to release the Infidel Friend you nurse back to health. If you are unable to do this, then simply do not attempt to aid them."

"And if I don't agree?" Michael asked.

"Then my helmet goes back on."

"Very well," Michael said. "We will not exile your people through the Golden Door, but we will exile them from Harpsborough. That includes you."

"No!" Klein shouted. "We cannot do this, Michael. Every Infidel Friend we leave alive allows them to spread their code.

Spread their ideas. They infect souls, Mike."

Michael put a hand over his eyes for a moment. "I know what you mean, Klein. I agree with you, I really do. But we're all damned. I'm not going to turn my back on my morals Father, but I'm not going to put Harpsborough at war for something that doesn't change anything."

Klein grabbed Michael firmly by the shoulder. "They change *everything,* Mike, this is our people's last chance."

"I'm sorry, Father. I can't let what happened to Hellespont happen here."

"If you cave on this, they'll know they can make you do anything."

Michael looked to El Cid. She reminded him of Cris. She reminded him a lot of Cris.

"I've made the concession," he told El Cid. "I'm sticking to it."

El Cid nodded. "Agreed. That should fix any future transgressions, but you still need to make amends for your first one. Our man, Cris, was sent through the Golden Door. These doors were used by the ancients to block off safe passageways for their runners to bring messages between towns. Now that the ancients have fallen, many of these doors lead nowhere . . . or worse, to places held by Archdevils."

"He deserves that fate," Klein said.

"For washing up on your riverbank?" El Cid asked.

"For being one of you. For being a member of a group that would massacre a helpless village. For being a ruthless killer no less evil than Maab."

El Cid's fake pleasant demeanor dropped away. "You speak of events in ways they did not happen because of what Maab did to you. That's where your anger lies, fool. I've offered in reality to repair the damage she's left you, and you've turned it down because of a fiction you maintain in your own mind to protect you from that same damage. That fiction is killing you, Klein. It's poisoning you and this entire village with it."

It was Klein's turn to smile. Michael could not understand what fortitude the man must have to turn down such an offer because it was the right thing to do.

"You are poison," Klein said.

"Let me help you," El Cid offered. "No payment required. No

strings. Let me do what good I can."

For a moment Father Klein looked down.

Are you right, Klein? Are you being tempted by the Devil right now? Has Satan wormed his way so deeply into these infidel hearts that he's able to use them to get to you?

Father Klein's eyes narrowed. "I'm a better man this way," he said around clenched teeth.

Michael nodded, pride swelling in his heart. They needed to make a stand, to show these infidels that Harpsborough wasn't going to be pushed around, no matter what had happened to Hellespont.

El Cid shrugged and Michael felt her attention as it rested back on him.

"You were saying?" Michael asked politely.

"We need the ability to save our man. Or if he's dead already, the chance to prevent his body from becoming a corpse."

Michael Baker nodded his head. "That you may do. I'll have one of my men show you the Golden Door. We'll even show you the walls around it so you can try and find a way in."

El Cid pursed her lips. "I meant that you would open the door."

"Don't give in to her," Klein said. "We don't know what terrors lie beyond that door, but if they have a key, they might well leave it open. I know these infidels. They would kill us if we threaten their people, but they won't kill us to save themselves a long walk—even if it is through the Carrion."

"He's right," El Cid said. "I'll not slaughter your people because you won't open a door, but a man's life is on the line here. You never even have to give us the key, just open the door for us. And Cris' work was important. Many more depend on him. Even you. Have you not been in famine lately?"

Michael raised his chin. "I will not be fooled into thinking that you infidels can control the comings and goings of devils. I will not let you through that door."

"I thought throwing infidels through the Golden Door was kind of your thing?" her faux-pleasant demeanor returned.

"Surrender your weapons and throw yourself at the mercy of the Citizen Court, and I'll see what I can do," Michael quipped right back.

Mancini would be proud of that one.

El Cid shrugged. "Very well. You have made the concession we seek."

"We'd ask a concession of you as well," Michael said, his words stopping her as she turned around.

"Oh?"

"Come to our church. Listen to Klein. Try walking in the way of God. You all could do so much good if you were only fighting for the right things."

El Cid gave a rueful smile. "We fight for humanity, all of it, and that includes you. The fact that you oppose us should give you a hint as to where your self-destructive impulses lie," she turned to her soldiers. "Move out."

El Cid watched her men exit Harpsborough. She paused in the entryway, and turned back, looking over her shoulder at Michael. "We'll be in the hungerleaf copse that your people have stripped. We'll be there for the next couple of days to keep as many of the trees from dying as we can. If you change your mind, bring the key to us, and we'll see that it's returned."

"There's no chance of that," Michael answered.

"I'll tell Cris you said so."

 — 8 —

Arturus had chosen a larger room with two stone bedlike blocks. He made sure it was close to the passage Galen had ordered him to retreat through—just in case.

Kelly leaned against one side of the small doorway. "This where you're going to bunk up?"

Arturus sighed and nodded.

"A chance for rest, Turi. You should be happy."

Arturus nodded again, even more glumly. "The Minotaur will find us, I know it."

"Why do you think that?" she asked.

Arturus was looking towards the back of the room, but he heard her as she came closer to him. "Because that's how things have been going. Every time we think we're going to get a chance to go home we end up going deeper in. It just figures that we'll run right into the City of Blood and Stone."

She walked past him and sat on one of the stone bunks. "Well, if we run, we don't have to go *that* way."

"We do, actually," Arturus said. "Galen showed me a secret escape. He ordered me to take you with me down a corridor which will lead into the City, if the devils come."

"Why did he want you to take me?" Kelly asked.

"Because I told him . . ." He looked at her.

Because I told him that I love you.

Kelly was supernaturally beautiful in the dim light. Her tattered robe fell around her slender shoulders, open in the front. Her black hair made her inviting ivory colored skin stand out. Her cruel cheekbones and sharp features drew him to her.

He sat down beside her on the cold stone bunk. "I told him we'd been kissing," Arturus lied.

She scooted back across the bed until she was leaning against the chamber's wall. "Well I'll tell you something, Turi, One Horn will not come. He can't pick up our trail at the source because of the Furies. Galen brought us along the halls of the City of Blood and Stone. The Minotaur won't think to come here, and even if he did, our trail will be crisscrossed with hundreds of other groups of men and devils. Your father made a terrible gamble, but it paid off. So this is what's going to happen. Your father is going to rescue Tamara. Your father is going to return. Your father is going to lead us back to your home . . . so you can be reunited with whatever little girlfriend you've got back there . . ."

Arturus shook his head. "I don't have anyone waiting for me back home. Except for Rick, of course. Not a girl, I mean."

Her cruel lips formed a soft smile. "Do you think I could live where you live, Turi? Would the people accept me there? Or would they be like Avery?"

I have no idea.

"They'd accept you," he said. "I'd make them."

She slid her legs under herself so she that was kneeling next to him on the bed. "Say it again, Turi. Say it like we're going to make it."

"They'll accept you. I'll make them."

She reached out her hands. Arturus took them in his own.

She drew him close so she could whisper down into his ear. "It's not fair." Her nearness was causing Arturus' heart to beat faster. "It's not fair that you had to be given to Calimay's daughters as part of a deal. You and I, we were supposed to do that."

Arturus swallowed. "I don't care for them."

"I know," her whisper continued. "It's not the same when two people don't care about each other. Don't love each other. I know that better than anyone else, believe me. Turi, I'm being torn up inside. I feel so angry at them. How dare they take you? You're *mine.*"

Arturus' blood was pumping. He didn't know what was

happening to him. He felt his body responding to Kelly in the same way it had to Maab. Was there some magic about this woman? He drew back and looked into her eyes, her dangerous eyes.

He was new to this. His emotions were an uncontrollable flood. First he'd loved Alice, then Maab, and now her. Kelly's blue eyes looked like black pools in the dim light. This woman was seducing him. This woman knew what she was doing. This woman was certainly *not* in love. She was using him, manipulating him, bending him to her will so that . . .

"I need you, Turi," her words interrupted his thoughts. "And I need to tell you why. I was someone different in the old world. I didn't enslave men and torture them. Watching your father work, well, I think maybe our way isn't the only way. Maybe men don't have to be slaves. Maybe their mindsets don't bring about ruin. Everyone needs a second chance, Turi. I didn't lead the life I wanted to before I died.

"I wanted to get married, but . . . well . . . that doesn't matter now. What matters is that you are *pure*, Turi. You are innocent. You really care for people. You really love people. You could really love me. And I want that. I want you to love me because then I can love you back. Then I can admit to you the way you make me feel. Please make them accept me in your home, Turi. Let us find something here, in Hell, that . . . I've said too much."

Maybe I've misjudged her.

Galen always said that people could be redeemed. There was nothing Galen loved more than humanity.

But Galen had also warned him about women. Rick didn't agree with that, though. Of course Kelly would want something different than what Maab's people had offered her. She wanted to be loved, didn't everybody? She must now know that the slaves who'd given her attention before didn't love her, couldn't love her, because she held them in thrall. This would be different for her. This would be a chance for her to really feel loved. And even if there was some part of her hedging her bets, using him, wouldn't it fade?

"I've scared you off," she was saying.

"No," Arturus told her. "No you haven't."

He bent back his head and kissed her. Kissing was a new

thing for him, exciting. All five of the women he'd kissed had done it differently. Maab kissed him like he was a delicate thing that could have been easily crushed. Calimay's women had all been different, too. Teasing, or confronting, or, as in the case of Calista, submitting.

Kelly was different though. Her small tongue moved slowly in his mouth, tasting him, drinking him in. His ears rang, so hard was his blood pumping through his body. Her hands cupped his face, then descended down his neck, then found their way across his chest, and abdomen, and hips, and farther down until a small part of him screamed that she might do to him what she'd done to Avery. But she kept kissing him, and kept touching him, and that screaming voice was drowned out in the flood of emotion and the beating of his heart and the ringing of his ears.

Martin was out of breath by the time he'd crested the stairs, but he charged into the parlor room anyway.

Michael and Mancini looked up from their wine glasses.

"Jesus," the First Citizen said, "what's wrong?"

"Where's Copperfield?" Martin shouted.

Mancini stood up and set his glass on the table. "Martin, take a few deep breaths, and explain to Michael what's going on. Things have been happening here, too. Big things, important things."

Martin nodded and bent over, his hands on his knees. He felt the rolls of his remaining belly fat rubbing against each other. Sweat poured off of his brow. "Where's Copperfield? I was in the Carrion. No time. We have to build the wall now."

Calmly, Michael set his own glass aside and stood. "Martin, the Carrion is a terrible place. If you saw an army of dyitzu in there, or a harpy or even a Minotaur, it's not safe to build a wall. I know it seems terrible, but if we wait, even if the devils come on to our side, they'll break up in the wilds of Hell. We'll be able to build the wall in a few days. We have to be smart about this."

Martin looked all around the room for something he could use to beat a lick of sense into Michael.

You have no idea what I've seen.

"What did you find?" Mancini asked. "Report, soldier."

Even though Mancini was about as far from being a commanding officer as Martin could imagine, for some reason the Brewer's tone and order gave him a moment of clarity.

"There was a ritual," Martin said. "There was a man there, who said he was fighting Maab's priestesses. They had some of them, dead, tied down on stone blocks. His name was Nephysis, he . . ."

At the mention of Nephysis, Michael's face went pale. He stumbled back, bumping into the table and sending his crystal glass careening off the edge. It bounced across the dyitzu skin carpet, spilling its contents in long streaks up the side of the table leg and across the floor.

Mancini looked confused. "Who's Nephysis?" he asked.

Michael seemed not to have heard him. He was trying to sit down, his hands waving around behind him in search for the chair's armrests. Finally he touched one and eased himself down.

"What's going on?" Mancini demanded.

For a second, Michael put his head in his hands and looked at the ground. Then he sat straight up and took in a quick breath.

"No wonder they're here." His head tilted back, eyes wide as if he'd just been struck with a sudden epiphany. "Where's Copperfield?"

Arturus awoke, shivering, his naked skin pressed against the cold stone. Kelly was next to him. She had put her robe back on at some point. Her body was warm, so he wrapped himself around her. She was holding her left arm up, as if examining it.

She lifted her head for a moment so that he could slide his own arm behind her. Then she snuggled into the crook of his shoulder.

"I'm proud of you," she said.

"For what?"

"You didn't break."

Oh, hell. I've got to get out of the Carrion.

But as terrifying as the thought was, there was something dreadfully erotic about the situation—about how she had to be so careful to keep him safe. It reminded him of Maab. Except that Kelly seemed as submissive as Calista. Arturus found the combination intoxicating.

"I have one dark hair on my arm," she said, holding it over to him, "do you see it?"

"No."

She pointed at a spot just below her ivory wrist. "All the other hairs are light, but that one is dark. I never noticed it before. I wonder if it was that way in the old world."

Arturus couldn't see the hair, and he didn't feel very motivated to find it. Instead he pulled her closer. She turned on her side, draping one arm over his chest.

She's so warm.

"Was there any girl back home that you liked?" Kelly asked.

Arturus thought first of Alice, and then he thought of Ellen. "Yes. But she . . . well. I didn't know anything then. I never kissed anyone, or know what it meant.

Kelly fiddled with his hair. "Was she pretty?"

Arturus smiled. He remembered Alice's blonde hair, tied behind her head, bouncing as she climbed the Bordonelles. "Yes, she was pretty."

"As pretty as me?" Kelly asked.

She seemed pre-occupied, her finger tracing strange shapes across his chest.

Hell, even I know better than to say yes to that.

"No," Arturus said, as if he'd just thought of it. "No, I suppose she isn't."

He tried to imagine Alice, to hold a picture of her face in his mind so he could find out who he really thought was prettier, but he couldn't think of Alice right now. All he could see was Kelly, her black hair cascading down one half-bared shoulder.

God, she is beautiful.

She was about to say more but the black pools that were her eyes looked at the ceiling. Then she jerked up into a seated position. Arturus heard the sound of stone grinding on stone. He leapt to his feet and grabbed his pistol. There would be no time to get his clothes.

Then he heard his father's voice.

"We don't have much time."

"You've got her!" That sounded like Johnny.

"Yes, and they know she's gone," Galen said.

"There are patrols after me already," Tamara's voice warned.

"She's right, get ready to move out."

Arturus pulled a shirt over his head and went for his pants. He'd just gotten them on when Galen poked his head in through the door.

"Time to go, Son. You ready?"

Arturus grinned. "Yes, sir!"

Arturus had never seen caverns like these. They didn't look like they'd been touched by Hell's Architect, but they also seemed too well polished to be natural. Perhaps they had been smoothed by running water. The tunnels themselves were a chaotic mess of paths cut into the dark grey stone. No one path went more than twenty feet before crisscrossing with another. Small chambers appeared where the corridors dead ended, shaped in perfect spheres, their stone so smooth that they cast back misshapen reflections. Arturus guessed that this place was like some sort of city, and that the tunnels were highways leading from chamber to chamber.

"What is this place?" he asked.

"Once it was a colony of vyn worms," Tamara answered, "but now they're all dead."

She was dressed in brown shorts and a white top they'd made by cutting a neck hole into a blanket. Without her robe, she didn't seem very impressive. Her determination was there, certainly, but it no longer matched her physique.

Galen was nodding in agreement. "It does look like a vyn colony. I must admit, I did not know of this place."

"It leads us under the Deadlands," Tamara said. "Not even the infidels know of it. A Shadow Mother showed it to me when I was still Maab's. No one will find us here. Not the Minotaur. Not the Infidel Friend. No one."

Avery looked like he'd just eaten something rotten. "Any chance of running into Maab's people down here?"

Arturus stopped to examine his warped reflection in the smooth curved wall of the tunnel. Johnny limped by him. The hunter hadn't talked much—nor had he made any jokes—but he was keeping up just fine, and he no longer appeared to be in shock. The night of rest must have done him some good.

"I doubt it," Tamara was saying. "I never quite got around to reporting this place to her. After we killed that Shadow Mother's people, Maab granted the Deadlands above us to Nephysis. I doubt he ever bothered to come down here. I doubt he's even found this place."

Galen stopped, examining one of the smooth grey walls. "It doesn't look like any human has been here in some time. You say this will lead us back to the mines?"

Tamara nodded. "This goes all the way under."

"What's a vyn?" Aaron asked.

"A worm that can tunnel through rock," Tamara answered. "We think they come over from Sheol."

Galen shook his head. "That is not true."

Tamara shrugged her shoulders. "True or not, they did us a favor by carving this place out."

"Any chance we'll run into one of them?"

Galen shook his head. "I doubt it."

Avery frowned, looking unconvinced. "What about One Horn? You think we ditched him?"

Galen shrugged. "He picked up my trail when I was going into Cul' Nahedran. Had some wights with him, which was odd—I'm not sure when or how he got those to follow him. Tamara and I ran through a harpy nest to shake him. When we left, his dyitzu were fighting the harpies, and he was fighting a twelve winger. Normally I'd say a twelve winged harpy male would stand a good chance of defeating a Minotaur, especially when surrounded by its wives, but in this case, I doubt it. One Horn is one of the more intelligent members of his species."

"I thought they were all supposed to be smart?" Aaron asked.

"Most are," Galen's voice was gruff. "Others are more—bestial."

"I heard something." Kelly said.

Arturus turned around to look at her. Everyone had stopped to listen, except Tamara, who crossed her arms impatiently.

"I told you, this place is abandoned," Tamara said.

Kelly cocked her head to one side. "I think it was coming from behind us."

Galen drew his MP5. "She's right, we're not alone." He pointed forward down the tunnel.

A pack of dyitzu spilled out into the corridor ahead, maybe a hundred feet away. Arturus couldn't begin to guess how many there were. A familiar snort echoed in from farther back down that passageway.

He's found us.

The corridor was narrow, and they were standing right by a bend, so it was easy for them to move aside to stay out of the dyitzu's line of fire.

"Take us back," Galen said to Tamara, firing his MP5 around the corner. "Can you find a way around?"

Tamara sneered at Kelly. "I think so."

She turned and ran back down the tunnel. Arturus looked to Avery and Johnny. Johnny's face showed no emotion, but Avery was horrified.

Poor bastard. But he deserves this. He tried to rape my girlfriend.

Arturus ran after her, but Tamara stopped before she'd made it twenty feet.

"Blood of Mithras!" Tamara shouted. "They're behind us too!"

Arturus took two steps up the side of one of the circular tunnels so he could see over Avery's shoulder. Tamara was right, the dyitzu were behind them as well. Tamara began running for a tunnel that led upwards.

"No!" Galen boomed. "The Deadlands are up. We go down."

He led them into a different tunnel whose walls were even smoother than the rest.

Avery followed, his gait uneven because of his wound. "What if it dead ends?"

Galen didn't answer.

Shit.

The dyitzu filled the halls behind them, and their fire

started soaring in. Galen led them back and forth through different passages, keeping them out of the line of fire, and taking them steadily downwards. They came around a tight turn, and Arturus saw light coming from the passageway ahead.

"There!" Aaron said.

But Galen had stopped. Arturus looked back around the bend. Behind them, the pale, smooth faces of the dead had joined the ranks of dyitzu.

Avery leveled his shotgun and fired. Somehow, he missed.

Or did he? Some wights are like Icanitzu.

"Can't go back," Arturus warned his father.

With a curse in a language that Arturus didn't understand, Galen led them onwards. The floor to the cavern fell away, becoming a sloped cliff. The cliff was not made of rock, but of loosely packed earth. It looked like there was a forest of dead trees rising out of some mist far below. Arturus ran up to the precipice. Corpses were moving around down there amidst the trees.

Galen turned to Tamara. "You said we were *below* the Deadlands."

Tamara's eyes were opened wide with terror. "I thought . . ."

"They're coming," Aaron warned.

"Climb down," Galen ordered.

"Into the Deadlands?" Kelly shouted back. "Can't we climb up?"

But there was nowhere up to go. The tunnel's ceiling was level with the giant chamber it had dumped them into—a chamber that was so large that Arturus couldn't see the end of it through the fog.

Galen was the first to start climbing. His movements sent streams of loose earth and stone cascading down the sloped cliff. Arturus and Kelly followed him as quickly as they could. Dyitzu fire screeched over their heads, shooting out into the Deadlands.

We should have known better than to listen to Tamara.

Martin's arms shook with the strain of carrying the gravel bags back and forth towards the wall—but he dared not stop. As exhausted as he was when he'd arrived, he'd not bothered to rest before he set about working. Copperfield hadn't even arrived yet, even so, Martin did not care. The gravel could be moved closer. The mixing barrels for the mortar could be readied. It was true that only Copperfield knew how to actually make it, but there was no reason not to get everything set up for him.

Hidalgo, Tucker and Huxley worked with similar abandon. The other hunters and villagers around them could not match their intensity. They hadn't seen what Martin had seen, nor heard Nephysis' speech like Hidalgo, Tucker and Huxley.

The workers knew to be terrified, surely. They even fed off the nervous energy Martin and his men exuded, but without having experienced the Carrion themselves, they could not *really* know how badly that wall needed to be built—nor how quickly.

Sometime after he had lost himself in his work, Copperfield arrived. At first Martin saw that the Citizen was reluctant to match the furious pace of the villager workers, but Copperfield had brought Molly along, and she managed to motivate him. Martin had no idea what it was she had whispered into the man's ear, but it got him mixing fiercely. Martin had always hated Molly a little, but today he gave her a small bit of respect. If nothing else, she and Copperfield made a good team.

The construction plan was simple. They were going to build one wall closer to the Carrion and another wall closer to their side of Hell. Then they were going to fill the intervening space with gravel. It was the quickest way to build a solid barrier that they knew of. Martin had not been there when the people of Harpsborough had fled from the depths of the Carrion. Martin had not been there when Michael and Rick and Galen and the founders of their village combed through the wilds and repaired all the barriers. Martin had never before understood why the mere mention of the Carrion set First Citizen Michael Baker into fits.

Now he knew.

He lay down his bag of gravel and returned, jogging back along the line of his own workers, Huxley in tow. Together they picked up another pair of bags and jogged back.

I might work myself to death.

But better that than face Nephysis' army. Better that than face whatever else roamed the Carrion. Better that than face another Kyle-thing.

Martin deposited his next bag. He doubted he could make the jog back. He shared a glance with Huxley, and it didn't look like the hunter could either. Somehow they found the strength to do another run, and another, and another.

Martin felt a hand on his arm.

He stopped, panting, his vision shaking. He turned to look at who had stopped him.

Molly's blue eyes pierced his soul.

This girl has changed.

"What?" he asked her.

"There is a time when working too hard slows your progress," Molly said.

"The hell there is," Martin shot back.

Molly didn't blink, she held his gaze even as she held his arm.

Well, technically she was right. He could theoretically work himself until he fainted, and that would make everyone else stop and take care of him. It might hurt their morale, too. But Molly didn't understand. He wasn't the kind of guy who had the willpower to work himself until he fainted. That was the kind of thing that Michael and Aaron could do.

I'm just not that strong willed.

He held up his hand to wave her off. It shook badly.

Oh. Oh, shit.

Martin felt his heart beating in his chest. Sweat poured off his body. Had he ever worked so hard? Had he ever been so motivated?

Am I afraid for myself, or for them? For Harpsborough?

But it wasn't a *they* he was protecting, it was a *she*.

I'm afraid for Katie.

"Okay," he told the steely eyed Molly. "Okay. I'll rest." He turned to his men. "I'm going to take five. Keep up the good work."

"You earned it, boss," Marcus said.

Martin grinned at the hunter and followed Molly back to where she and Copperfield were mixing the mortar. He collapsed into a corner, his chest still heaving. Molly handed him a canteen before she returned to her work with Copperfield.

Martin dumped the first half of it over his face. Then he

drank the rest. Finally, when he'd swallowed the last drop, he felt sated. The cool stone was a blessing on his back. He wiped the sweat off of his brow. He noticed his hair was drenched.

God damn. I feel good!

The revelation was a surprise to him. He thought he should be terrified. He thought he should feel the horror in his stomach. But he didn't. The hard work of his men, the hard work he'd been doing with them, it raised his spirits. It put air under the wings of his soul. It made him feel like he belonged.

He breathed, slowly and deeply, and then, his eyes closing, he leaned his head back. He had never felt so peaceful. Molly and Copperfield were talking to each other.

"No," Molly was saying. "I really am impressed. I never really knew you. I would have never guessed that you'd have come out here and risk your own life to mix the mortar."

But of course Copperfield would. The only thing more important to Copperfield than his life was his food. If he taught people how to make the mortar, they'd be able to mix it without him. If they did that, he wouldn't get paid.

Surely Molly knows that about him.

"It just has to be done," Copperfield replied, as if he was doing something that was somehow more admirable than the rest of them.

"But you served your time!" Molly's voice seemed surprised. "You're a Citizen. You're not supposed to ever have to risk your life. It's unfair for you to have to go back out into danger."

Unfair my ass. Unfair is that he gets to make us do it for him.

"This is the best way," Copperfield's voice seemed deeper than usual. "It would be wrong for me not to make this sacrifice."

Sacrifice! Really? I mean, come on.

Martin fought to keep his mirth on the inside. He looked to the line of his men, villagers and hunters and even a few of Constance's people, doing the heavy lifting, getting right up there next to the Carrion. Sacrifice?

Martin looked back to Copperfield. The Citizen was bending down to pick up another bag of some ground substance or another. In doing so he ran into Molly's butt. He stood up embarrassed. From this angle, Martin could see the inviting smile that Molly gave the man.

She's seducing him?

No wonder she was filling his ass with smoke. Molly may be a changed woman, but she still knew how to get what she wanted.

The more things change . . .

Handfuls of loose earth broke off beneath Arturus' grasp as he climbed quickly for cover. He could see the one horned Minotaur standing head and shoulders above the six foot dyitzu that flanked him. There was another thing on the ledge, too—a tall, humanoid thing with yellow, rotten skin.

Fire sizzled over Arturus' head. He found Johnny already sheltering under cover he climbed behind.

Galen's MP5 went off a few times. Then a dyitzu went toppling by down the cliff.

How does he even aim while climbing?

Arturus jammed his feet into the earth, found a rocky handhold with his left hand, and drew his pistol with his right.

"You're going to fight back?" Johnny asked, incredulously.

"You want to just die?" Arturus shouted.

The look on the hunter's face was despondent. He was still wearing the shirt that had caught on fire. The cloth had been burnt away on one side, exposing the horrific burns and boils below on Johnny's skin.

He's in a lot of pain. Death might seem sweet to him.

Arturus climbed a little to the left, looking out over the raised piece of cliff which was his cover. He took careful aim with his pistol and fired. The bullet missed, but he'd gotten their attention. The dyitzu fire started pouring his way. As quickly as he could, Arturus climbed back behind his cover. Dyitzu fire bombarded the earth above, sending clumps of mixed dyitzu fire and dirt raining down through the air behind himself and Johnny.

The earthen cliff Arturus clung to was not very tightly packed, and the vibrations of the fireball impacts shook some of it loose.

Arturus looked frantically about him.

Kelly was sheltering under a boulder to his left, and he knew Galen was somewhere to his right, but he wasn't sure where anyone else was.

"We can't go down!" Kelly was shouting.

"No choice." Galen yelled back.

"Just look down!" Kelly answered.

Arturus made the mistake of doing what she said. He had never been afraid of heights, but a fall from here would surely kill him. The cliff they were on wasn't really a cliff, he realized, but a low point in the ceiling. It didn't actually make it all the way to the forest below. The forest wasn't that thick, and the area beneath them was more like a giant plain. Now that he was lower, he could see that the hills were covered with a dark green grass and the occasional white flower.

On those fields were the corpses. The chamber might well contain thousands of them, even hundreds of thousands. Though they weren't that thick below, the noise of the battle was drawing more of them.

"Oh shit!" Aaron screamed from somewhere above. "They're coming. The dyitzu are climbing down."

"Everyone get as low as you can," Arturus heard his father's voice over another barrage of dyitzu fire. "We're going to drop to the plains and make a run for it. The dead seem pretty thick out there, but I've been in the Deadlands before. They should thin out."

Arturus mapped out a path downwards and then began to take it. He looked up. Johnny was still behind the cover, pressing himself desperately to the wall.

"Come on!" Arturus shouted.

Johnny looked lost.

"Please!" Arturus pressed. "I need you."

Johnny let go with one hand and began to climb down, but the earth gave way beneath his feet and he stopped, clinging to the cliff.

"Galen will get us through this!" Arturus shouted. "He always does. It's going to be okay."

Johnny nodded, seeming to snap back into alertness. He climbed after Arturus. Kelly was coming too.

It's going to be a long drop when we make it.

A dyitzu was tumbling down the cliff. Arturus hadn't heard anyone shoot it. Maybe it had just fallen. He tried to get another look at One Horn, but his view of the passageway was blocked.

"To your right!" Johnny shouted.

Arturus understood why Johnny wanted to go that way since it did appear to be closer to the ground. It would, however, leave them open to dyitzu fire.

"We can't," Arturus said. "We'll be in the open."

"We ain't going to survive that fall!"

Arturus tried to judge the distance. It was difficult from their perspective. Tamara was down that way already.

Arturus shook his head. "We won't survive the fire, either!"

"It ain't so bad," Johnny said. "Slide!"

He's right.

Arturus looked up at Johnny. The hunter's eyes were wide with terror, but he looked determined.

"I'll see you down there," Johnny said.

Johnny spun around, putting his back to the cliff, and then he let go. He slid by Arturus amidst an avalanche of dirt and pebbles.

Hell.

Arturus turned around as well and followed. Dirt came up in clouds around him. From the billowing dust below, he heard Johnny's high pitched scream of exhilarated terror.

Damn you, Johnny.

 — 10 —

Copperfield awakened.

His heavy body ached from the pleasure he'd received. Molly had been a holy horror in the sack. The woman had brought him to the edge of climax so many times he'd thought his balls were going to explode. She'd driven him to the end of his physical endurance, demanding that he fuck her against the wall. Then, finally, she let him cum.

He was sure he hadn't orgasmed so hard since his fourteen year old self had found his father's porno VHSs.

That's one hell of a woman.

To tell the truth, it was about time he'd gotten her in bed. The others in the Fore wouldn't touch her, but Copperfield didn't give a damn about her reputation. Michael might be pissed at him for doing it, but fuck, right now, Copperfield didn't give a damn about Michael either. It was only a matter of time before Mancini and Graham replaced him and Martin as the ruling First Citizen and Lead Hunter.

Besides, Molly was a changed woman. Changed how? He couldn't say. It was just that she wasn't the same Molly which had gotten her ass exiled out of the Fore for being a horrible bitch.

Oh shit, she was banned from the Fore even before she left. I probably broke that.

Copperfield turned to look at her, but he found that he was

alone in his bed.

She's in a hell of a lot better shape than I am. She probably didn't need to sleep as long.

But it felt like their sex had happened only an hour or so ago. Maybe she had left in disgust. Some of the other women who slept with him did that because they were only fucking him for food. Still, he'd swear that Molly was genuinely interested. There had been no hints at her displeasure like there had been with the other villagers. Copperfield couldn't shake the feeling that Molly truly cared about him. Besides, he'd offered her a good job already. If she didn't actually want him, or at least didn't want to pretend to want him, fucking him now would make it look like she was the same old Molly. She would have erased whatever goodwill she'd earned by being a prodigal son of sorts.

She does want to be with me. She must have just gone out. Maybe to piss.

If there was one thing Copperfield knew, it was that people were self interested. Now it was still possible that Molly might be playing the long con on him. To tell the truth, he wouldn't mind that at all. Sure her love would be dishonest, and it would end eventually, but wasn't that the way of all love? When you got down and really thought about it, there wasn't much difference between a long con and a marriage. But no, it had to be either love or duper's delight which had set that warm smile on her sleeping face. He just couldn't imagine a motivation she might have to fuck him and leave him.

I mean, she'd have to not want to stay in the village. And there's nothing outside the village she could want . . . except.

Copperfield shot up in his bed. He threw off his covers and ran across the plush houndskin carpet to his shelf. The box was missing.

No . . .

"Staunten!" Copperfield shouted, snatching a pair of pants from the floor. "Staunten!"

He pulled his pants up under his belly, not even bothering to put on a shirt, and burst through his door curtain. "Staunten!"

Citizens woke, coming out of their rooms, but Copperfield ignored them. He burst past Herod the Gunsmith and a curious

Chelsea before charging down the stairs to find Staunten's room.

"Staunten!"

The man was one of the few people to have a door. Copperfield banged on it with both fists. "Staunten, so help me God, you had better get your ass up right now."

"I'm sleeping, Copperfield." His voice was muffled by the door.

"God damn it. It's that bitch, Molly, she stole the spare key."

"What?" the voice was frantic.

Copperfield heard items crashing in the man's room. Staunten opened the door, his dark hair a disheveled mess, his shirt buttoned wrong, and his pants skewed awkwardly to one side.

"What did she steal?" Staunten asked.

"I don't know," Copperfield said.

Staunten charged past him. "Thinking with your damn dick, Copperfield."

A line of Citizens had showed up in the hallway behind them, but Copperfield paid them no heed.

Copperfield waddled by them. He wasn't used to exertion, and earlier this day he'd helped mix mortar, traveled back and forth from Harpsborough to the Carrion barrier, and gotten his brains fucked out by a thief. His legs were understandably shaky.

Staunten pulled the key necklace over his head when he reached the giant woodstone storeroom door. He pulled it open as fast as he could and charged in. He looked about him, checking the stacks of devilwheat sacks and picking up dyitzu hocks. He moved over to his old world paper lists and started checking his inventory. Slowly, his frantic expression was replaced by one of confusion.

"I don't know," Staunten said as he counted the black barrels which contained the preserved birthing milk. "If she stole something, it was small."

Copperfield knew where to look, however. He walked past Staunten and the riches which Harpsborough's Citizen's kept safe from Hell. He came to a stop before a drawer. He moved a bucket of shotgun shells out of the way so he could open it.

This was where they kept the key to the Golden Door.

Staunten gasped when Copperfield opened it.

"It's gone," Copperfield said. "The key is gone."

He turned around and saw Michael and Mancini standing at the storeroom's entrance.

"The key to the Golden Door," Copperfield explained to them. "Molly stole it. I'm sorry, I should have—"

Michael held up one hand. "Is Martin still repairing the Carrion Barrier?"

"I think so."

Michael nodded. "Get him. Get him now. Send him to the Golden Door."

There was a terrible pop when Johnny landed. Arturus came down just a moment later, the ground hitting him hard enough to knock the breath out of him.

Please Johnny. Please be okay.

The corpses were all around them. Arturus tried to breathe, but the air wouldn't come into his lungs. He struggled to his feet, but he couldn't straighten his torso. He'd lost his breath like this once in boxing practice. Galen had ordered him not to fall down, so Arturus had just stood, hunched over, doing his best to keep boxing. As always, the lessons which had seemed the cruelest were the ones that saved his life. Unable to straighten himself, Arturus drew his pistol and fired at the closest corpse. Some of these undead moved smoothly, almost like men walking. They were wearing styles of rotten clothing Arturus could not recognize.

"Johnny," he wheezed, but he wasn't sure if his voice was loud enough. He tried for more air and spoke again. "Johnny!" This time it was loud enough. "Can you stand?"

"I think I'm fine," the hunter answered.

Johnny struggled to his feet as Arturus took aim at an approaching corpse and shot it down. The hunter limped over to Arturus.

"I'm wrong. I'm fucked up," Johnny reported.

"Tamara fell over there," Arturus managed to say.

They moved towards her, and Arturus was finally able to stand straight. Tamara had landed on top of a hill. She was struggling to her feet.

"She's alive," Johnny said. "That tough bitch."

She was moving awkwardly, not like a human recovering from a fall, but like a newborn corpse standing for the first time.

"No she didn't," Arturus said. He dropped her corpse with another pistol shot. "Corpsedust. It's everywhere in here."

Arturus looked around. The Deadlands seemed different from ground level. Rolling hills, full of grass and asphodel flowers, surrounded him. Sparse groupings of trees, dirkenwood if he remembered his lessons right, raised their gnarled trunks and empty branches up into the mists surrounding them. On one side, the trees thickened into a forest. Towards the other, they thinned into a field of white asphodel flowers. The ceiling of the chamber hovered over their heads, coming down in places so that it almost touched the earth. In a few spots, the ceiling had collapsed onto the ground. Corpses were spread out around them as far as he could see through the haze. A stone structure, perhaps only containing a single room and a small watch tower, was on the edge of his vision. It had to be at least half a mile away, but there was nothing else nearby which could give them shelter.

Arturus heard more gunshots.

Kelly was trotting towards him, her pistol blazing as she passed the scattered corpses. Aaron was coming too, with Galen behind him. Galen had Avery slung over one shoulder.

Tamara was the only one we lost in the fall.

A dyitzu was getting up from where it fell, but the undead were all over it.

That's odd, these corpses kill devils?

"Turi!" Galen shouted. "The building. Do you see the building?"

"Yes, sir."

"Then run."

Arturus jogged down the slope of the hill. He wanted to run faster, but Johnny wasn't moving well, and he knew that his father was burdened with Avery. The trees thickened as they moved. Corpses came at them, appearing suddenly from in between tree trunks or from behind the hills. Arturus shot only those that were the closest to him and did his best to outrun the rest. He cast a glance over his shoulder. He saw the rest of his group spread out behind him. They were running too, often having to shoot down the undead which Arturus had spared. High above them, on that low hanging portion of the ceiling, Arturus saw the corridor which had led them into the Deadlands. Standing in it was One Horn. Below the Minotaur, the yellow skinned rotting monstrosity of a human figure was climbing down.

Arturus turned his attention forward.

Jesus, the corpses aren't thinning out. They're getting thicker.

He found himself using more bullets as he ran. Johnny had drawn his own pistol and was firing as well.

"We're not going to make it!" Arturus shouted. "We have to move faster."

He caught a glimpse of Johnny's ankle. Arturus was surprised that the hunter was still running. The swelling had practically torn open the man's boot.

"Then run faster!" Johnny pointed his gun forward and pulled the trigger, but he was out of ammo.

Arturus looked ahead of himself long enough to kill the corpse Johnny had been aiming at—then he looked back again. The rest of his group had caught up. Galen and Aaron were running side by side, and Kelly was just behind them.

"Can you run faster?" Arturus asked Johnny.

"I worry about me, not you!" Johnny shouted. "You run."

Another corpse was in front of him. Arturus pointed his gun and pulled the trigger. Nothing. And he had no more magazines. Arturus, mid stride, kicked it in the chest and then passed it by.

"I'm out!" he reported.

"Coming!" Galen shouted. "Avery, I'm going to have to put you down in a minute. You'll have to run."

"Take my gun!" Avery said. "I've got ammo left."

There were a few more pistol shots, and some of the dead closest to Arturus dropped.

The building was getting closer. He could see that it was little more than a gatehouse built into the side of a hill. The tower was a spindly stone thing, maybe only five feet wide. If there was anything more to the structure, it was hidden underground.

Maybe it hides a passage that leads to where Tamara had

wanted to take us.

Only that wouldn't do them any good now since Tamara couldn't guide them.

"I thought you said they'd thin out!" Aaron shouted.

"It's different than before," Galen answered. "There have never been so many dead here."

"Nephysis," Kelly shouted, "he's been busy."

But why did the corpses attack the dyitzu? Can Nephysis really control them?

Another corpse drew near enough to grab him. Arturus expected his father to shoot it down, but instead he heard a click.

Oh shit.

Arturus kicked it backwards.

The building still looked awfully far away, and if anything, the corpses were thicker around it.

"We're all out!" Galen shouted. "Everyone run! As fast as you can."

Arturus heard Avery give out a shout of pain. A grim faced Johnny sprinted by him. Arturus sped up, passing back by Johnny, dodging in and out of the groups of undead. He tried to lead the corpses away from Johnny, but he wasn't sure if he was helping. Galen rushed ahead, a blur of motion. Arturus knew his father was fast, but to see the man's speed now was breathtaking. Galen barreled through the undead, knocking them off their feet as he passed with his head and shoulder lowered.

Johnny was lagging behind. Kelly passed him, her long black hair streaming back behind her. A corpse reached out. She dodged it, but stumbled.

Jesus!

She regained her balance and continued running.

The building was just ahead. Galen had stopped at its iron gated door.

"Locked!" Galen shouted. "Defend me!"

"We've got no weapons," Aaron shouted back.

"I need time."

"Defend you with what?" Aaron asked.

"Your hands if you have to!" Galen yelled.

Arturus knew what needed to be done. "Form up around

me," he ordered.

It was the first order he could remember giving to the group. They obeyed.

The gate was in a slight alcove. Arturus took up a stance where he hoped their human wall would allow his father time to work the lock. Aaron stood at his left and Johnny took up his right. Avery joined the left wing and Kelly came in on the far right.

Then the undead were upon them.

 — 11 —

Martin had never felt so gloriously tired in his life. The Carrion-side wall had been completed, and the near-side wall was about halfway finished.

And I feel safe. Time for another break, I think.

He'd never paid much attention to the Carrion barriers before. He'd known what the purple cubic marker stones meant, but even so, the barriers had meant little more to him than any other wall. Now he had the horrible premonition that he was going to start seeing them as thin and breakable eggshells on which his life depended.

Ignorance is indeed bliss. But then, so is sleep.

His sore muscles relaxed as he leaned up against a wall and slid down it. He closed his eyes.

"You going to sleep there, sir?" Huxley asked.

Martin opened one eye. "You're damn straight I am."

"Are you sure that's safe?"

"Didn't you know?" Martin asked, closing his open eye. "I'm the God damned acting Lead Hunter. I say what is safe and what is not, and I'm telling you, Hux, that this spot is safe. And I'm going to rest my ass here until ya'll springy fuckers are finished."

A few of the men working on the let out a round of tired laughter.

"Then again," Martin said. "It might be a good time to call it a day."

"Should we sleep here or head back to Harpsborough?" Huxley asked.

Here, because I'll be fucked before I move my ass.

Stone had never felt so comfortable.

"Here," Martin said. "Gather up the boys. Tell 'em four hours sleep, then we finish the barrier and head back."

"Aye, sir," Huxley said, his own voice weary.

Martin opened his one eye again. "And you're not eligible for watch, Hux. You've been working too hard."

"I think I'm the most—"

"Who's in fucking charge here?" Martin asked.

"You are."

"Then I say you fucking sleep. Make Graham do it. He's good for watches."

Graham cleared his throat. "You know I'm right here."

Huxley laughed. "Yes, sir."

Martin heard shouting.

Christ. Well at least it's not coming from the Carrion.

He opened both of his eyes. Constance was sprinting across the cobbled room.

"Martin!" he was shouting.

As beleaguered as he could ever remember being, Martin pulled his aching body to its feet. "This had better be God damned important."

Constance stopped, panting. "Molly. She's got the key. The Golden Door key. We think she's headed there right now."

Holy shit.

"Hunters," he ordered, "form up. Follow me."

Arturus bludgeoned one corpse with his pistol, but the weapon made for a poor club.

Hell.

He threw the pistol aside and let his inhibitions go. Galen's training spewed forth from him as he let his fists fly. The corpses were too slow to defend against his assault, so his punches sent them back a few steps. Even so, their mass was building. Johnny was beating one in the face with Avery's shotgun. Aaron was holding two back.

"Father!" Arturus shouted.

Arturus grabbed the corpse in front of him by putting both

of his forearms on the thing's shoulders and his hands on the back of the thing's neck. He kept his elbows in tight.

The corpse tried to come forward, but Arturus forced it to bend down at the waist by pulling down on its neck. Then he shifted his hips back and started throwing knees towards the thing's head. His first couple of blows knocked the corpse back into an upright stance. Arturus pulled it down again and gave it a couple more. He heard a crunch as his knee crushed bone, breaking the rotten skull.

He kicked the thing away. Another corpse was clawing at him with rotting broken nails. It cut him across his face, and Arturus tasted his own blood as it poured into the corner of his mouth.

He had to step back because his friends were losing ground. Arturus caught the hand of the attacking corpse in front of him. It was a monstrous thing, surely, but it had human anatomy. Arturus tried a wristlock on it. On a person, the hold would have been almost impossible to execute, and if he'd managed to get it, his opponent would have dropped to his knees as his joint was locked and his tendons were pulled taut. The corpse, however, was too slow to avoid it, and its joint and tendons snapped. Arturus let go and took another step back. The corpse's arm hung loosely at its side. Arturus hit it with a couple of punches and then kicked it away.

Another corpse stepped forward. It was dressed as some sort of ancient soldier. The helmet on top of its head sported a ruddy Mohawk of bristles. It had a large square shield which covered its body on one arm, and it brandished a short sword with its other.

A gladius.

Galen had taught him how to fight a man armed in this way, but he had only gone over it once, and Arturus couldn't remember much of the lesson. It struck out at him, its technique surprisingly crisp. Arturus hated to think how long a corpse would have to be dead to move so smoothly—or to be wearing such outdated equipment—but something in its motion awakened Arturus' instincts. The strike was linear, heading straight for his body. Arturus pivoted to one side on his right foot, letting the strike go by. With his left hand he caught the corpse's sword arm at its wrist and then threw his right shoulder into the large square shield—knocking the corpse backwards even while he kept the creature's sword arm close. Then he turned his back on his foe, wrapping his right arm around the corpse's sword arm. He kept a firm grip with his left hand and then grabbed his own wrist, his limbs intertwining with the corpse's as he completed the hold. He spun back around, pivoting as hard as he could. All his body weight and momentum was applied to the corpse's arm. The hold was supposed to be a shoulder lock, but the arm broke at the elbow. Arturus moved his hold further down the arm, grabbing the wrist at the end of the limp appendage. He broke that too, spinning back around—and then took the sword out of its undead hand.

He looked to the undead mass.

Now you all fall.

Arturus struck out with the gladius again and again, his father's training guiding his blade. The corpses before him fell, one after the other, helpless before his sword. He started slicing at the ones in front of Aaron and Johnny. Suddenly Arturus and his friends weren't being pushed back anymore. They were gaining ground. Arturus' heart beat as he continued the slaughter. Hope and adrenalin filled his veins.

Then he looked up.

The corpses were coming towards them like a tide. He had thought there might be hundreds of thousands in the Deadlands, but he had obviously underestimated their number. No amount of killing would save them. He would simply drop from exhaustion before the dead stopped coming.

"Father!" Arturus shouted.

"Almost," Galen answered.

He could hear the sound of metal on metal. Arturus had no idea what his father was using to try and pry the lock open. However, he did notice when his father stopped prying and switched to bashing.

Arturus turned his attention back to the tide.

Come on then.

Arturus renewed his efforts. He struck straight forward to make sure he didn't hurt his friends beside him. He stabbed the corpses in the face, in the chest, in the gut, all with quick snaking strikes.

"In," Galen finally ordered. "Everyone in."

The gate had been opened. Arturus ran through it. Johnny hopped in behind Avery. Aaron and Kelly followed.

Galen slammed the gate into the mass of corpses. "Use your weight!"

Arturus reached out, pushing forward. Aaron was beside him. The corpses' hands were on Arturus, reaching in through the gate. Their mouths tried to bite at his fingers. Frantically, Arturus slid his hand up and down the bars to keep them safe while he stabbed at the corpses with his sword.

Aaron gave out a painful shout and pulled back, one of his fingers bloodied.

Galen tied his MP5's shoulder strap around the center of the gate. Any fool could undo the knot, or cut it, but the corpses were less than fools. They simply pushed forward.

"Their weight will be too much." Galen warned. "Farther back. We have to leave their sight so they stop pressing."

Arturus ran down a tight stone corridor. The gate's tunnel had been dug into the hill. It turned to the right and emptied out into a room. The room was full of sarcophagi and what looked to Arturus like iron maidens. Hooks, most covered with dried, black blood, lined the walls and hung from the ceiling. Rusted tools, cutting implements mostly, lay about.

From the thick layers of dust, Arturus guessed that whatever this place had been, it had stopped being it long ago.

There were two doorways leading out of that room. Galen ran through one, and they followed him. The room it led to had no exits. Galen ran back and tried the other. Also a dead end.

No way to get back to the vyn tunnels.

Galen ran to one of the contraptions on the wall. They looked like shackles. With a heave, Galen ripped a pair down.

"Wait here," he ordered. "I'm going to secure the door."

Martin and Graham slowed to a jog, rifles raised as they entered the chamber with the Golden Door. They stopped in the middle of the room. The Harpsborough hunters entered in their wake, spreading out all around them. Half blinded from sweat, Martin ran a hand over his forehead and eyes to clear his vision. He had never expected to see this.

A crew of Infidel Friend were standing there, decked out in

their armor, M-16 assault rifles pointed at his men. Molly was there, her face a mask of confidence. Martin had never seen that look on her before. But Ellen was there too, that nice little girl that lived with Rick and spent time with Turi. And Rick himself, and Massan. Shit, even Alice.

Holy hell. What have I gotten myself into?

It wasn't just that he knew that the Infidel Friend could probably slaughter his men, it was that he didn't even know if he could bring himself to shoot at Alice, Rick, Massan or Ellen.

What the hell are they doing with Infidel Friend?

"No one moves!" Martin shouted.

"You," Graham's voice was filled with hate.

He had spotted Molly.

"Hold your fire!" Martin's voice cracked as he shouted. "No one moves, and no one shoots."

He took stock of his men. They looked nervous. Worse than nervous—they were scared shitless. One of them could accidently fire at any moment.

I can't let that happen.

The Infidel Friend seemed completely unfazed. Martin didn't have to worry about his enemies starting this—unless they actually wanted blood.

Please, we don't want a fight.

"Stay calm," Martin tried to keep his voice from cracking this time, but it cracked anyway. "We're going to talk this out. No one shoots. You hear me, Graham? No one shoots."

Graham's eyes were fixed on Molly.

Guy's losing it.

"That's our key," Martin said, pointing to the golden item in the diminutive infidel's hand.

The smaller of the two female infidels nodded, her green eyes focusing on Martin. "It is."

She held the key up before her, then placed it in the keyhole . . . and turned it. Martin heard the Golden Doors unlock. The woman made no move to open them though.

She removed the key and tossed it to him. Graham jerked, but the man managed to stop himself from firing. Martin caught the key and pocketed it. When he looked back at the infidels he noticed that their demeanor had not changed—it was just that two of them were now pointing their assault rifles straight at

Graham.

God damn we're outmatched. But we outnumber them four to one, maybe. We should win. Right?

The infidels were covered in body armor, and they were notoriously quick shots. His men were protected by little more than hoodies. They'd have to get head shots to win, probably. Worse than that, his men were armed with 700 bolt action Remington rifles. The infidels were carrying semi-automatics.

Push better not come to shove.

"No one moves," Martin ordered. "Ellen, Rick, Massan— Alice. I want you to come over here."

They didn't obey him. They drew closer together around Rick.

"We're going to lock that door," Graham said. "And then we're going to take our people into custody. If you don't comply—"

"Quiet, Graham!" Martin shouted.

Graham kept his rifle trained on Molly. His nostrils flared with his anger.

"She's an outlaw," Graham said. "She needs to be tried. And these people," he motioned towards Rick and his huddle of former Harpsborough people. "They should be tried too, to determine if they're guilty."

"Stand down, Graham." Martin shouted.

"You're breaking the law of the Fore!" Graham insisted. "These are infidels. They're evil, and our people are with them. This *must* be stopped."

The small female infidel was watching them with a cruel detachment.

Well they sure as hell ain't afraid of us now. Nice united front there, Graham.

"I'm the acting Lead Hunter," Martin told him, "so my word is the Fore's law. Now stand the fuck down."

"You stand down," Graham shouted, and suddenly the rifle was pointed at Martin. "It's clear what's to be done. Hux, take his weapon."

The infidel woman cocked her head to one side.

Huxley drew his pistol and pointed it at Graham. "Martin's going to run this show."

Thank you, Hux. Jesus fucking Christ, thank you.

Graham slowly lowered his rifle.

There was the sound of stone grating on stone, and then Martin thought he could hear metal gears, or a winch, or something of that sort.

"I said no one moves!" Martin screamed.

But no one was moving. Everyone had frozen still. Even the infidels seemed confused.

It's the grate. There is a grate behind the Golden Door. It's being raised. But how?

Martin looked at the chain which the Harpsborough people used to open the grate. It was still, and no one was standing near it.

The noise stopped.

The Golden Doors burst open.

Martin heard Ellen's gasp.

Cris stood there, in as arrogant a posture as Martin thought a man could hold, dressed in full body armor like the other infidels. Like his compatriots, he had an M-16, though it was slung across his back. Whatever wounds he'd had before appeared to have healed. Cris crossed his arms over his chest and leaned up against the doorway.

Martin felt dumbstruck. "You."

A grin spread across Cris' face as he looked over Martin and the Harpsborough hunters. "Ya'll fuckers miss me?"

"Don't go down that hallway," Arturus warned Kelly. "The corpses will see you and try to break in." He knelt down by Johnny and inspected the man's foot. "There are some tables in here. Some of their wood isn't rotten. We'll be able to make a splint."

Johnny nodded, his breath labored. The man was obviously in some pain.

"I can't believe you ran on that," Aaron said.

"It didn't hurt at the time," Johnny replied through clenched teeth.

"Adrenalin." Avery's voice was also strained. "Brought me through it too."

Johnny's swelling was coming up over the top of the boot.

Arturus shook his head. "I'm going to have to cut the boot off. I'll show you how to sew it up like Galen did to mine when you can get it back on."

Johnny nodded.

Arturus pulled out the laces first. Normally he would have cut them, except he doubted there were any spares. Arturus went for the razor blade in his pocket. He inserted it into the instep and started sawing, careful not to cut his friend.

Galen came back into the main room while he worked. Galen was inspecting the wall. Pushing and pulling against bricks. Tapping on them. He had already spent some time on the floor and journeyed up into the tower.

Arturus kept sawing and the boot came loose. Johnny let out a sigh and then leaned his head back against the stone wall.

"Who built this place?" Aaron asked.

"I bet it was Nephysis' laboratory," Kelly said. "An old one. It doesn't look like he's been here for a long time."

"That wood is fresh," Avery said. "It must be new. Things must rot in here pretty damn fast."

Kelly gave him a wry smile. "It's been treated. Only the treated wood is fine. The rest has rotted, look at that table over there. No one's been here in years, I'd bet."

"She's right, Avery," Galen said from where he was checking the wall. "Be careful going up into the tower. The hill allows the corpses to get on the roof, and if you go up there, you'll see there are places they can break in."

"How are the dead looking?" Aaron asked.

"Numerous," Galen answered, "more than I would have imagined possible. There's no room to even try to make a break for it. They're shoulder to shoulder.

"Maybe Calimay will come find us?" Johnny tried.

Kelly snorted. "No one comes to the Deadlands, not devils, and not humans. No one."

Galen stopped and sat down with the rest of them, his face as calm as ever. At first Arturus was confused, but then he realized that Galen had completed his circuit. There was simply nothing left to check.

Johnny looked to Aaron, but the Lead Hunter wouldn't meet his gaze. Then Johnny turned to Galen. "Alright, what do we do?"

Galen did not answer.

"Well? We can escape, right? Is there a way down into the tunnels?"

Galen shook his head.

Johnny frowned. "Then we'll make a run for it. You can splint up my leg and we'll run."

"No," Galen said. "Even alone and with a full complement of weapons and ammunition, I wouldn't have a chance of making it. The Deadlands is over thirty miles wide. There are wights up there, too. I saw them. They're intelligent. And they can run."

Johnny seemed confused. "So what then? What do we do?"

Galen didn't answer.

Johnny's face grew red. He struggled up, standing on his good leg. "What do we do?" he shouted.

Galen looked at Johnny. Arturus watched his father's face. Slowly, like a mountain eroding away, Galen's stoic veneer crumbled. His face was stricken with sadness. An old sadness. Arturus felt it must be older than himself. Maybe as old as Hell.

"What do we do?" Johnny demanded.

"Calm down, Johnny!" Aaron ordered.

Johnny wouldn't listen. "What?"

Galen looked for a moment towards Arturus. Arturus rarely saw naked emotion on the man's face. There was love on it now.

"What do we do?" Johnny hopped forward and put a hand against the stone over where Galen sat. "Tell us what to do God damn it!"

Galen looked up at him. "We die."

From Neostoicism: Philosophia

Did I play my part well? Then applaud as I exit.
—Augustus Caesar

Let he who is without sin cast the first stone.
—5th Century Christian Monk

Part VIII
Fields of Asphodel

From Gehennic Law: The Emperor and the Bridge

When Xerxes' army came to the Dardanelles, they stopped and waited for their engineers to fashion a bridge out of boats and flaxen ropes. The engineers worked tirelessly through the day, and by evening, they had bridged the narrow sea.

Now on that night there was a storm, and the ropes were broken and the boats were washed away. When Xerxes saw this in the morning, he was furious.

"What happened?" Xerxes asked. "Was the bridge built too weak?"

"Nay," answered the engineers. "The bridge was built correctly. It is the waters that are at fault."

Xerxes was angered. "Could you not have lowered anchors on either side of each boat to better keep them in place?"

"We could," they answered, "but the bridge was strong enough. It was the fault of the water."

"And could you not have used winches to keep the tension between ships?"

"We could," they answered, "but the bridge was strong enough. It was the fault of the water."

"And could you not have built the bridge in the lee of that shoal so that the storm would not so trouble our construction?"

"We could," they answered, "but the bridge was strong enough. It was the fault of the water."

"And could you not have doubled the ropes and built the bridge two boats thick?"

"We could," they answered. "But the bridge was strong enough. It was the fault of the water."

"I see you are right!" Mighty Xerxes said, and he strode grandly before his troops. "What is at fault here are these waters. Take up your whips! Light fires and heat the brands so that we

might mark the Dardanelles with shame! Today we shall spend thrashing the waters and marking them for their treachery.

And so it came to pass that all that day the engineers whipped and branded and jeered the waters. Xerxes came to them as the sun was setting.

"Look now at the waters!" Mighty Xerxes commanded. "Do they look pacified?"

The engineers looked at the waters, but they did not look pacified. They were a turbulent mass of anger.

"No," said the engineers.

"Do they look like they have learned their lesson?"

The engineers examined the waters, but they did not look any different.

"No," said the engineers.

Xerxes held up his hands in dismay. "But the branding! Tell me at least that you can see the brands you have made on the sea so that others might know of its treacherous nature?"

The engineers looked at the waters, but they could see no markings left from the hot iron.

Xerxes turned to his armies. "You see, punishment is wasted on those who cannot learn."

And then Mighty Xerxes put his engineers to death.

The sky was a chaotic mess of dark thunderheads. Lightning swam through them in long forked chains, flickering like Tiamat's tongue.

Carlisle looked along the ladder which shot upwards through the tumultuous lightning filled skies. Then he looked down at the rock where Benson lay, the man's soul chained there by steel shackles. Those shackles had been forged by Mephistopheles' will, so they were well nigh unbreakable. They shined like polished silver in the storm's flickering light.

Benson struggled against them pitifully.

Soon.

"It was in a storm like this that Jephthah sacrificed his daughter," Mephistopheles' warm voice washed over Carlisle.

"Who was Jephthah?" Carlisle asked.

The shadow that was Mephistopheles turned to him. "He was a servant of your God, Carlisle."

Carlisle nodded. "A good man, then."

"As holy as you."

Carlisle turned to the struggling Benson. "You will die slowly," he said.

Mephistopheles' shadowy form circled the knoll on which the ritual stone table sat. Then the devil returned to Carlisle. "It is time. Climb the ladder. As this man dies in Sheol, you will get closer and closer to his body in Gehenna. I will make sure that his march to death is a smooth one. Even as the last shred of Benson leaves this plane, you will enter into his Gehennic body. You will be barely able to move, and your form will be beset by malnutrition and atrophy. It will take great will on your part to defeat the stilling and move. Accept the help of your fellows, but leave as soon as you can. As your body heals, it will grow to look more and more like you. After a week or so, you will be yourself again. Then you can complete your quest. Then you can find the Child of Heaven."

Carlisle sneered. "Good. Thank you Benson. Any words you wish for me to give to Harpsborough?"

Benson had stopped thrashing. "Go on, Carlisle. But you will never make it. I will stop you."

"He shall not," Mephistopheles said. "I shall see to him." Then the devil passed a stone dagger to Carlisle.

Carlisle held it up over his head. The air was roiling with

energy. The thunderheads billowed, rushing in waves across the sky. The wind picked up and pressed his clothes into his body. He felt his hair whipping about his head.

This was the turning point. This was the moment in his death where he stopped growing farther and farther away from his Heavenly Father. This time he was going in the right direction. He was blessed, so blessed that even the demons were forced to help him. He would climb up into that maelstrom of clouds and wind and find himself one step closer to the angel's get.

He would be one step closer to Heaven.

Down plunged the dagger into Benson's stomach, cutting deep through the flesh of the man's abdomen. Benson let out a long wail. The wail dissipated, torn away from the tortured man's lips by the power of the wind.

CLIMB, CARLISLE! Mephistopheles' words rang in his head.

Carlisle climbed. The rungs in the ladder were easy to grip. He felt light, as if the wind itself was lifting him upwards.

I have purpose. I mean something. I'm important. God makes this so. Without him I am nothing.

He could practically hear the song of the angels in the wind.

He started taking the rungs two at a time, then three at a time. He had never been filled with such energy. It was as if the Holy Spirit was streaming down from Heaven, cutting through the Earth, slicing through Gehenna before finally infusing him with its glory.

He looked down below him even as he climbed and saw that he'd left the stone table miles below—but he had more distance to travel.

How long had it been since he'd felt this way? How many sacrifices had he been forced to make in the attempt of holding his convictions? What lows had he been forced to sink to in the service of his God?

The music was growing louder now. It echoed in the spaces between the clouds, singing to him loudly between thunderclaps . . . only he had heard it before. It reminded him of something—of someone. A woman. A devil.

"Can you hear me Carlisle?" A low, sultry and feminine voice asked.

The voice was not loud, but it seemed so because it was so

close to him.

Carlisle stopped climbing. "Who is this?"

"You don't remember me, do you, my sweet? You don't remember when I tried to save you? You don't remember when I tried to heal you? When I tried to save you from your faith?"

"Lilith? Impossible." Carlisle looked all about him in the turbulent wind tossed sea of clouds, but he could see no sign of Benson. "Mephistopheles defeated you."

"Look down, my sweet. Benson found a friend."

"Liar! He has no friends." Carlisle said. "I killed the only person who ever loved him."

Her laughter was a gust of wind, shaking him so he was forced to cling to the ladder lest he fall. "Are you sure about that? Are you sure there isn't someone else out there who loves him simply because he's human?"

Carlisle continued climbing, but his limbs felt heavy. Each new rung was an effort.

What's happening? Someone who loves him just for being human? The fool. She thinks God is on Benson's side.

"God's not here, Lilith," Carlisle shouted over the wind.

"It's not God who helps him, Carlisle. What's that pouring out of your side?"

Carlisle felt the blood running from his wound. It was drenching his pants and dripping off the bottom of his booted feet. The blood was soaking the ladder.

My wound. It bleeds like never before.

Lilith spoke again. "Didn't that devil friend of yours show you how to see across long distances? How to have the eyes of an eagle?"

Carlisle changed his eyes and looked down, but he could not see far enough. He applied his will carefully to his vision until he could see the light even farther down. It gave him the sensation of plummeting even though he knew that he was still on the ladder. He saw Benson, sitting up, his chains clinging to his wrists. The black wings of Mephistopheles covered the man, but they seemed almost transparent.

Benson was shouting something.

Carlisle reformed his ears, focusing on those distant words.

"Infidel!" Benson was screaming. "I need you. You were right. The Christians here do the Devil's work. I was wrong.

Don't let them use me! I won't be their puppet. Save me. *Save me!"*

The Infidel approached, walking through Mephistopheles as if the devil were mere illusion. The wind picked up all around him. Benson's sacrificial robe flapped back and forth in the gale. The grass wavered and the trees shook, but the Infidel was not touched.

He heard Lilith's sensual breath in his ear. "And that's not even my lover, Carlisle. That's just the *idea* of my lover. He can win here because in Hell, your God is only an idea. There is no difference between the two of them. Don't you understand? This Hell, it is based on perception. In Gehenna, there is no God to answer your prayers. But in Sheol—if the amassed weight of men's perceptions can make the shade of a man, didn't you ever stop to think that they could make a God?"

Carlisle was stunned.

My God, he could be here?

"But after Gehenna, Carlisle, the God men bring with them to Hell—well, let's just say he's more of the vengeful kind. More of a Luke 19:27 God than a 1 John 4:8."

Then that's why I feel the Holy Spirit! There is a God here, I must succeed.

She had said it was a vengeful God, but that would only help him, right? He needed God to strike down his enemies. He hadn't done anything to anger God. He hadn't done anything to bring about His wrath. He had been a good person. Anyone could see that. Anyone.

The chains fell away from Benson's wrists. The Infidel handed Benson the sacrificial dagger.

"A lie!" Carlisle screeched. "The chains were unbreakable!"

Lilith sighed. "I told you he had a friend."

The Infidel reached out one hand at put it on Benson's shoulder. "Are you sure you wish to do this?"

"No!" Carlisle yelled. "Mephistopheles! Stop him."

"He can't hear you," Lilith's sultry voice caressed his soul. "Devils dare not come close to the Infidel shades."

Mephistopheles, please, fight them!

"I do," Benson was saying. "Do you think I am doing good?"

"I do not know," the Infidel replied. "I'm not, in truth, here. You must ask yourself if this is the right thing to do."

"Don't listen to him!" Carlisle shouted down to Benson, his voice a whisper on the edge of the storm. "He's evil! What I'm doing is right. I'm in the right, Benson. You just can't see it because I'm trying to destroy you."

But Benson did not seem to be able to hear him.

"It is," Benson said. "Carlisle is not a good man. Whatever the devils have turned him into is vile. If I am to die, then let my death mean something."

The Infidel nodded. "As you will it."

Benson took the dagger and shoved it into his chest.

"Climb!" the distant voice of Mephistopheles ordered. "If he dies faster, you must climb faster."

Carlisle grabbed the next rung, pulling himself upwards. He climbed with abandon, but he felt his legs burning. Sweat poured off his body and mixed with the blood pouring out of him. The wind buffeted him, slamming him into the ladder, and he felt the weight of his wound, all those thousands of tons of dirty blood, pulling him down like a chain.

With all the will he could muster he tried to make himself stronger. Then Benson died, and the ladder was broken.

Carlisle was falling—falling at a speed he had not thought possible. He wasn't falling through space, but through emotions. They crashed by him, slipping in through the perforations of his self and polluting his existence with their substance. Agony, as he had never felt before. Despair, as if God had abandoned him. Ire, as if some stranger had come to kill his mother. Indignation, as if some entity had stolen from him his dignity. Horror, as if he had awakened to find that he had raped his sister. Indifference, as if the world was peopled by automata. Mania, as if every girl in the world was in love with him. Vanity, as if he were the apple of God's eye. Jealousy, as if he'd sacrificed his son to a people who'd left him for his enemies. Pride, as if he was the leader of all mankind. Lust, as if forty nubile virgins lay spread out before him. Hatred, as if he had been made to finally know himself. Each emotion was more intense than the last. Then the final one dissipated and he fell still farther. He saw the masses of Hells laid out beneath him.

I'm dying. I'm dying again.

He broke out of the land that he knew as Sheol. His soul wheeled about, trying to find purchase on any of the universes that he was now plummeting past. They were terrible, each more horrific than the last. He had to stop himself, he had to land now. There was no way he could exist in these vile places. He couldn't let them get any worse.

But there was a weight beneath him, dragging him downwards, forcing him through each new land of horror.

Help me!

He tried to scream, but without a place for his soul to inhabit, he had nothing to scream with. No mouth to open. No voice to issue. No air to exhale.

He had to grab onto something but found himself lacking a physicality to grab with. Somehow he had become unstuck from the Hells during his fall. For him to stop falling, some part of him, some part of his soul, would have to be able to latch onto one of these damnations.

He spread himself as thin as he could, hoping against hope that he would touch down on the shore of some distant Hell.

And then he did.

— 12 —

"That's it," Johnny said. "Everything's been rationed, even all the food from Galen's pack."

Arturus looked at the two strips of hound jerky and the handful of devilwheat which lay in a small pile in front of him. In his canteen he had a few swallows of water.

And there's nothing here to hunt.

Kelly came climbing down from the tower. "Galen's right," she said, casting a glance at Arturus' father. "They're thick out there. Shoulder to shoulder, like he said. We wouldn't make it five feet. It's like they can smell us or something."

Arturus looked to Galen. The man sat cross-legged against one stone wall, leaning forward, his left elbow resting on one knee while his left hand supported his chin. He seemed to be deep in thought.

"Maybe we could make a rope," Johnny suggested. "Tie it off on the tower and climb down to where they're thinnest."

She shook her head. "Go up and look yourself."

Johnny pointed to his swollen leg. No one had bothered to splint it.

Kelly sat facing Johnny, putting a hand on his knee. "I couldn't see the end of them."

Johnny started crying.

"Oh Christ," Avery said, "could you cut that shit out?"

Galen spoke, "All we've left to do is die, Avery. Our last task is to do that well. If Johnny needs to mourn before that happens, that is his business."

Avery threw his canteen across the room.

Aaron stood up. "Cut that shit out. That's an order."

Avery leapt up to his feet, wincing with pain. He threw his devilwheat across the room. The grains scattered in the air and drifted down onto the stone floor. "Yeah? I'm done taking orders from you. You're shit, Aaron. You've let Galen take us all this way and look where we are. Look where we are! Whatever weird ass funeral you guys want to have for yourselves . . ." Avery's voice cracked.

He must have wanted to say more, but for some reason Avery stopped talking.

"I know," Aaron said.

Avery bowed his head, putting up one hand to cover his eyes.

"I know," Aaron repeated. "I wanted to make it home, too."

Aaron bent down and picked up Avery's canteen.

Johnny slid himself along the floor and started picking up the scattered devilwheat. "Let me help you get this back together."

Avery managed a smile.

While they worked, Arturus walked over to his father. Galen was deep in thought. If he noticed Arturus' approach, he showed no sign of it. Galen was disturbed, of that much Arturus was certain. Perhaps it was their coming deaths that bothered Galen, but Arturus suspected there was something more. He doubted that death alone would be enough to cause worry to pierce is father's stoic veneer.

It's me. He thinks he's failed me.

Arturus knelt beside him. "Father, it's okay. You don't have to be sad. I'm not what everyone wanted me to be. I know that now. If I was, then the Furies would not have come to kill me. You're only losing a son. You're not losing all the hopes of all the damned."

Galen looked up. His eyes were a torrent of thought, not just emotion. He was making a decision, or weighing some alternatives. Or something.

"Oh," Arturus said. "There's more to do?"

Galen nodded. "Dying well is no easy task, Son. You see how Avery is acting? Soon those feelings will be on your shoulders. In a few hours, or few days, it will sink in. If you can do this last thing, if you can die as the man you are, that is a truly great accomplishment."

Arturus frowned. "But no one will know how we died. No one will care. What does it matter?"

"Because in those last moments before death, you will have to face yourself. As a person dies, their world shrinks in around them, getting smaller and smaller. Imagine two universes. First, the one where you behaved as you thought you should. The one where you consoled your friends and did not hurt them. The one where you made your last goodbyes and told Kelly you loved her. Then imagine a second universe. In that one, imagine that you yelled at Kelly and made her cry. Imagine that you threw your food around as Avery just did. Imagine that you told me you hated me. Now in that last moment, when your world has shrunk to a size so small as to only include yourself, and you find that you have only your own misery for company, in which universe would you rather find yourself?"

Arturus imagined these things. But he wasn't worried about when his world would be at its smallest. He knew, just moments before his soul left his body, that there would be a time when his world shrank down to where he would just be aware of his father and himself. There were two possibilities for that time too. There was the Arturus who had died poorly, who would have to suffer his father's disapproval. There was also the Arturus who had died well, who could bask in the knowledge that his father was proud of him. More than that, he knew his father's pride would be justified because this last battle would be no easy thing to win.

But those moments would be short.

"Such a small thing to fight for," Arturus mumbled.

Galen nodded. "Perhaps. Maybe it would be more accurate to say that it is all we have left to fight for. A doomed man and a man with a bright future, when they die, they both only lose the present. Do you understand?"

Arturus shook his head.

"For you, and for me, if we only had five minutes left—if our hourglass was nearly empty, those five minutes would be all of our lives. How is it any different when you are fighting for a future that might span millennia? Five minutes or a thousand years, for you, it's all you have."

Arturus nodded. "And then we do it all again."

Galen smiled. "Think not of the next life, Son. Nothing you can do in the here and now will affect it. Finish this one first. Drink it in. Let it fill your thoughts. Let it be all that you are."

It doesn't matter if I go on, or if I don't, or if there will always be a Turi or not.

"Do you think Rick will know it, when we've died? Do you think he'll somehow feel it?"

"He knows already, Son. He's known for a long time."

Ellen had forgotten how beautiful Cris was. When she had seen him before, naked in the river room, he hadn't been able to stand straight. Even then, she had been struck by his figure. And now, though the physique which had sent fingers of lust all across her body was hidden, she could feel his presence filling the room.

Graham had taken a few steps back.

Martin's jaw hung open. "You," he breathed.

Cris leaned against the wall of the doorway, a smile spreading across his face. "Ya'll fuckers miss me?"

Molly ran to him. She encircled her arms around the infidel and clung to his side. Then she sneered at the hunters.

"Sorry," El Cid said to Martin, "but for your own sakes, we have to find out what's going on in the Carrion. You may think us your enemy, but at least know that we also fight the devils. Why stop your enemies from killing each other?"

Martin nodded. Strangely, Ellen felt that she had somehow missed the man, although what he was doing ordering Graham around escaped her.

"Alright," Martin shouted. "Hunters, no shooting. If the Infidel Friend want to go play in the Carrion, we're going to let them."

Everything was quiet.

Slowly and carefully, the infidels began moving. Q and El Cid went first, their M-16s held steady as their small, even steps brought them past Cris and Molly. Ellen began to follow them, but Rick grabbed her, hands on her shoulders, and held her back.

"Let me go!" she shouted, struggling against his grip.

"You can't," Rick said.

"It's my decision!" Ellen screamed. "Mine! I want to find him. I want to go help him. I don't care if I die."

Rick spun her around. He bent down and leveled his intense gaze at her. "But you will die. You won't do Turi a damn bit of good if you go in there. And the infidels, well, they're not looking for my son. They're looking for Lucreas Crassus and Saint Wretch and all manner of terrible things. And they're infidels, Ellen. That means they might find those wicked people. You and I, we don't have what it takes to journey there and fight those things."

Jessica, Eagan and Q passed through the doorway. El Cid handed her gun to Cris and walked back out. She brushed Rick aside and took Ellen's hands.

"Rick isn't quite right," El Cid said. "He is good enough to come with us. He would help us in the Carrion. But you aren't that good, yet. The Carrion isn't like this part of Hell. Everyone has to know exactly what to do at all times. In there, all of our lives depend on our fellow soldiers. I realize you are willing to sacrifice your own life, and I laud that. But please ask yourself if you're willing to sacrifice the lives of my soldiers, too."

Ellen felt tears in her eyes.

I'm a fucking idiot. El Cid will never respect me if I cry.

But the tears were impossible to hold back. They filled her vision and then dribbled down her cheeks. She felt Rick's warm arms surround her. She let herself get lost in that warmth. When she looked up she saw that El Cid had joined the others.

How come Molly gets to go with them?

The Harpsborough hunters kept their weapons trained on the infidels as the gate lowered.

"Hey, Cris," Martin said.

Cris stepped up to the grate, his eyes focused on the hunter.

Martin lowered his weapon. "Fuck 'em up in there."

Cris smiled.

Rick walked up to the doors and closed them.

"So," Graham said as he advanced on Massan, "you were going to get a ring for Kara, huh?"

Arturus woke to find himself sitting, his knees pulled up to his chest, his back pressed against the stone wall. Kelly was resting her head on his shoulder. Someone was talking. Arturus focused on their words.

"And you're okay in there?" Johnny was asking.

"It doesn't bother me," Avery answered.

"But the corpses are right on the other side. You can see them through that crack. How could you have slept in there? I mean, you can hear them clawing at the walls for God's sake."

"They can't get at me."

Arturus left his eyes closed, but he imagined that Avery was crossing his arms. The thought of the hunter's idiosyncratic pose brought a small smile to his face.

Everything was quiet. The walls creaked, and the air from the vestigial breathing of the hundreds of thousands of corpses outside combined to make a noise sort of like wind. The gate which Galen had fastened shut with shackles creaked gingerly, probably from the weight of the dead outside. Kelly's breath was warm on his shoulder. Each exhalation left a bit of condensation on his neck.

This is not the way I would have chosen, but it is a way. It is better than many others.

He remembered Pyle. He remembered the man being flayed alive by the silverleg spiders. He remembered the man asking for mercy. Arturus hadn't given him that.

Maybe I should have respected him more.

He found that, more than anything else, he wanted Rick to be happy. He hoped that Rick had found someone. Someone that would fill the hole Galen and Turi had left.

"So, when the first one of us dies," Johnny said, interrupting Arturus' thoughts, "should we eat them?"

Oh, hell.

Arturus opened his eyes and looked around. His father was still sitting cross-legged, his chin resting on his hand. Slowly, perhaps because of what Johnny said, Galen's eyes focused on the hunters.

"That's bullshit, man." Avery crossed his arms. "That is absolute bullshit. Cannibalism ain't right."

"I want to hear you say that in three weeks when we're starving to death," Aaron said.

"I ain't joking, man." Avery was wide eyed. "That ain't right."

"Would you rather your friends starve?" Johnny asked.

"Hell, you're going to starve to death anyway," Avery shot back. "I'd rather do it without committing any great evil."

Kelly was stirring on Arturus' shoulder, but she hadn't awakened fully yet.

"It can't be evil," Arturus said. "It doesn't hurt anyone."

"A thing doesn't have to hurt someone to be wrong," Avery answered.

"Quiet," Galen said. "Turi is right. Unless someone is hurt by an action, it cannot be a wrong one."

Avery sneered. "I know that ain't right. Thinking angry things is wrong. It's committing murder in your heart. It's an affront to God."

How could he . . . after what he's done?

"Then God's the one who's hurt," Galen said.

Arturus stood, waking Kelly.

"After what you've done," Arturus said, "you'd argue about an affront to God? After what you did to Kelly?"

Avery spat. "What about what she did to me, Turi? You give a damn—"

"Quiet." Galen's soft voice silenced them.

Avery looked up at the ceiling angrily. Arturus wished Kelly was still sleeping. It seemed like sleep was going to be the last time that any of them got any peace.

Arturus sat back down and Kelly rested her head on his lap.

Not for me. I'll have nightmares.

He could feel the nightmares coming. They were there, just waiting for him on the other side of consciousness.

Calista had given him a lock of hair to remember her by. It had made Kelly angry. How silly that all seemed now.

Avery was whispering something.

"What?" Johnny whispered back.

"I said you can eat me."

"Jesus, Avery. You just said you didn't want me to."

"If I'm fucking dead, and you want to live longer—if you're hungry, I want you to."

"It's cool man."

"I'm fucking serious, Johnny. You eat me. I don't want you to suffer. When I'm done with me, you can have me."

 — 13 —

Ellen was certain that they couldn't tell the truth and hope to be spared by the Harpsborough hunters. They were going to have to lie, and Ellen could only hope it was going to be a good one.

"We deceived you," Rick said.

Oh, no, Rick. Your stupid honor. We should have all gone through with the infidels.

"No shit," Graham spat. "Hux, give me my damn gun back."

Huxley turned to Martin. Martin had a lot on his mind, of that Ellen was certain. He'd lost a good amount of weight since she'd first met him by the Fore. He seemed sadder, somehow. Maybe it was the fact that he was sober. Or it could just have been that he was in charge now, and that his responsibilities were weighing on him.

Martin nodded, and Huxley gave Graham his rifle. Ellen felt more than a little relieved when the hunter slung it behind his back.

Graham returned his attention to them. "Now I think we're all going to take a little walk to—"

"Molly was in the boat when you stopped us," Rick interrupted. "We took her to Tucumcari so she could meet with an Infidel Friend and beg them to help Cris. We did this because she thinks she loves the man."

Graham's mouth formed a sneer. "You aided an exile. You lied to me. To *me*? You—"

"Then we traveled with the Infidel Friend on our way back," Rick continued over Graham's hateful words. "We deliberately lay silent as they discussed how they would negotiate for the key. Then, when negotiating did not work for them, we did not warn you that they were coming to steal it. At every step that we could have stopped them, we chose not to."

"I should shoot you—"

"But we've killed no one. We've stolen nothing. We haven't hurt a soul. We haven't endangered Harpsborough or her people."

"The hell you haven't!" Graham spat. "You led those infidels here. They could have attacked the village. You had no way to know if they would or wouldn't. You didn't see the showdown in Harpsborough when they came. We could have been the next Hellespont. You sick fucks. Get in line. Men, we're taking them to the Fore."

"Funny, that," Martin said loudly. "I think that going forward, before you give orders, you are going to ask me, first."

Graham's eyes were wide with incredulity. "You deny they broke the laws of Harpsborough?"

"I ain't denying shit . . . 'cept you."

Graham's sneer faded into an angry grimace. His brow furrowed. His hands were visibly trembling. Ellen had always remembered him being unpleasant, but there was something worse in Graham now.

What in Hell could have made him so angry?

He certainly wasn't angry at Rick or her or Massan.

Molly. Molly humiliated him, and now she's gone, and he blames us for it.

"I'm the collector. The Head Enforcer," Graham's voice was slow, and he seemed like he was just barely able to contain his anger. "I speak for the Fore."

Martin leaned back against the wall and crossed his arms. "Great. What taxes do Massan and Rick owe? What stash have they not claimed?"

Graham's eyes were stuck on Martin, but he didn't say anything.

"Because the way I see it, when Rick left, the Harpsborough people went through and stripped the Hungerleaf Grove down so badly that those trees nearly died. Hell, for all I know, they did die. So if you want to speak for the Fore, maybe you could give an apology. Maybe you could let Rick know how we're going to make it up to him?"

"They're criminals," Graham insisted.

"We'll let the Fore decide that," Martin said. "In the meantime, I can't spare the manpower. We've got to fill in that barrier. Hunters, collectors, Graham, you're all with me."

Graham's hand went to his rifle, but then fell to his side. "You can't seriously just let them go."

"Oh I can," Martin said. "I can because I know Rick is a good man. Because I know that he's not going to run." Martin walked up to Graham, and as he did so, his voice got louder. "Because I know that if we saw things from his perspective, that we might understand why he did what he did. And I know he'll gladly tell the Fore about everything he's done. I know that we've robbed him and that Constance's people tried to mug him." Martin was shouting now. "But you wanna know why? You wanna *really* know why I'm giving this order? Because there's a *God damned* breach in the Carrion barrier, Graham! A God damned breach. Because on the other side of that hole is the biggest fucking army I've ever seen. *I* had to fight that Kyle-thing. I don't know if I could beat another one." Martin's face was red with fury. He was only inches away from Graham's cringing visage. "Because Rick is the most experienced builder we have. He's the one that fucking showed us how to repair the Carrion barriers to begin with. And I need his God damned help. Is that clear, *soldier?*"

Graham was silent.

"I asked you a fucking question, soldier. Is . . . that . . . *clear*?"

"Yes."

"Do I look like your fucking friend?"

Graham was confused. He looked around to the other hunters for support, but found none.

"I asked you a question, soldier. Do I look like your fucking *friend*?"

Graham held his hands out wide, obviously unsure of what Martin was trying to ask him. "I don't . . . I don't—"

"Do I look like your fucking peer? Do I look like some villager?"

"No," Graham managed.

"Damn straight I don't. But you know what I do look like? I look like your God damned commanding officer, Graham, so I had better hear a 'sir' come out of you. So let me try one more time. Is what I said perfectly fucking clear?"

"Yes, sir."

Martin looked slightly pleased with himself. He turned to Rick. "Would you mind terribly helping us repair the Carrion barrier?"

Rick had a slight smile on his face as well. Ellen had seen that look before. It was a look of approval.

"I'd be delighted," Rick said, and then he motioned towards the exit. "After you, Lead Hunter."

One of the rooms in the complex had a one inch thick gap in between two of the walls. The corpses would look through the crack, and a few had managed to wiggle their fingers into it. Because of this, it was the only room that offered any privacy. Arturus doubted that the privacy was worth it, though.

Kelly led Arturus in.

He could hear the undead brushing against the crack-ridden walls.

She sat down on the stone floor, the dust stirring around her and clinging to her robe. She looked up at him, and Arturus sat beside her.

She took his hand in hers. "I wanted to say goodbye," she told him. "I wanted to tell you all the things I was going to tell you, but never got the chance because our future was cut short. I love you, Turi. Maybe I don't know you well enough. Maybe I'm in love with the idea of you that I have in my head. Maybe, but I don't care. I love you. We were going to make it back to your village. They'd be skeptical of me at first. They'd think I was some kind of witch. But you'd go on being you, and I'd earn their trust. First, they'd just think I was useful because I could give them insights into their enemy. Then, after a while, they'd learn to truly accept me. It would be at about that time when I would have told you that I wanted to have a child with you. And you would have made a wonderful father. Galen would make a terrific grandfather. Imagine, please Turi, imagine, the pain I went through at childbirth. Imagine your joy as you see our first child. Imagine the fights we have over naming him. Imagine his first steps. His first words. His first everything. Imagine how ferociously we would fight the devils knowing that we have to protect our son. And imagine him growing up and living on his own. And then we turn and look at each other. We who have been through all those experiences. Then, those two people, they could say they loved each other. They could really say it. You and I, we don't know. We feel it, but maybe the feeling wouldn't have been enough. Don't be you, Turi. Be that man who raised a child with me. Be that man who really loves me."

Arturus looked up from the dream she'd laid before him. The Kelly in front of him now was a dangerous woman. A woman who could take advantage of him. Who could break his heart. Who could have used him to gain the trust of his village before betraying them. But this other Kelly, the one that had been faithfully by his side for a lifetime. The one that had borne his child and who had helped him raise it. That was a Kelly he could love.

Then let this Kelly be that one.

Of course he loved this woman. She wasn't dangerous. There was no way she could betray him, now. She could only be as faithful to him as any woman could be.

Arturus squeezed her hand. "It is as you say. We have done those things. Let us die that way, together."

She leaned forward and kissed him, more passionately than she had before, more desperately—more honestly.

"I don't want to be a corpse," she whispered. "If I die before you, will you burn me?"

"I shall."

"And if you die before me, I'll burn us both."

Arturus nodded. "I wish we were on Earth, so that a miracle could happen, and we would be saved."

"We're alone, here, my love. There are no gods to save us. No one to even know why we died."

He remembered what Galen had said about dying. About how Galen said his world would shrink in until he was alone with himself. How would Arturus then feel, knowing that all his efforts had been in vain? Was there any one thing he had done in his life that he could really say made the experience of living worthwhile? Was there anything he had accomplished, or experienced, that made damnation a price worth paying?

No. But no one asked me if I wanted to be born, so I just did the best I could.

Kelly threw herself into his arms, knocking him back a little from where he sat so that his back touched the uneven wall. He held her, seeing the corpses through the crack over her shoulder. One's blood blackened eye was pressed up to the gap. Another had shoved its finger so far in that the skin had been rubbed off it. Black, half coagulated blood dripped down from the flayed digit.

Mother, whoever you were, I hope you would have been proud of me.

It occurred to him then that there was no reason left for Galen to keep any secrets.

It's time. I will at least get to know the truth before I die.

He held Kelly a little longer because she was crying. She was probably thinking about her life. About what it had amounted to. Maybe she had come up with the same answers he had. But eventually her crying stopped, and her breathing evened out, and her body went limp in his arms. He laid her gently against the stones—and stood.

He walked back into the main room to find out where his mother was. To find out how his father had fallen in love with an angel. To finally find out why it was he'd been given the birth he'd never asked for.

 — 14 —

Arturus saw that Galen must have found time to tend to his beard while he and Kelly had been in the other room; it was as well trimmed as ever.

It's death. He's preparing for death.

Turi walked up next to his father and sat down beside to him.

"Tell me a story," Arturus said.

Galen smiled. "It has been a long time since I've told you a story, Son."

"They were never just stories," Arturus said. "They were lessons. They were your way of sharing with me what you'd learned. I want that very much right now, to know what you know."

"Was there a story you wanted to hear in particular?"

"The one about my mother."

Galen looked up to the ladder which led to the tower. The sound of metal scraping on stone filled the air for a moment. Outside there must be a corpse, perhaps wearing armor or with some other metal accoutrement, who was being pressed into the stone. Then the noise stopped.

Galen took a deep breath and closed his eyes. When he opened them, they were no longer focused. He wasn't staring at anything in *this* room, Arturus knew. He must have been looking at events which had happened long ago.

"Things were different," Galen said. "The Carrion was a vile place, but not so horrific as today. The armies of Blood and Stone were still sleeping in their city. Maab was not yet the supreme leader of the Mithric tribes. She was second to another woman, just as terrible but not quite as smart. Her name was Igraine, and she lived in the compound from which Maab now rules.

"Charlie, who you may remember from when you were a young boy, and Severn, Michael and Klein, they were all her slaves. Maab's slaves in particular, but under Igraine. They wanted freedom. They wanted to be able to worship their God. It was Maab who instituted the practice of castration. Before it hadn't mattered so much what the slaves believed. Igraine had thought there was no way to really change peoples' minds. Maab proved her wrong. Maab found a way to bend people to her will. Then Igraine spread the practice. You can imagine the pain and suffering that was inflicted.

"But there was hope. The crux of the power of the Mithric tribes was a man named Lucreas Crassus. He was the one who taught La'Ferve how to fight. He was the one who taught Gilgamesh how to control the hounds. Who taught Nephysis how to raise the dead—though on that score Nephysis may have surpassed his tutor. This man was intensely interested in the Infidel Friend, and he knew they were looking for something. They were looking for a fallen angel. Not a Grigori, mind you, but an actual fallen angel, straight from Heaven.

"Oh, the infidels had always been searching for one, ever since anyone could remember—but this time it was different. This time they knew they'd seen one. They used some form of alchemy on the feathers she'd molted and found her to be legitimate.

"It was this that gave Charlie a purpose to live. Not that he liked the Infidel Friend, mind you, but he loved God. And the idea that there might be an angel here, well that filled him with hope because if he could speak to her, he figured he could find out what it was that God wanted him to do. He might learn who God actually was, and how he could earn his way into Heaven."

Arturus felt a pang of nostalgia so strong that it almost made him double over. This story, to be sure, was nothing like the stories Galen had told him when he was a child, but the feeling was the same. He felt . . . safe, and he hadn't felt that way in a long time.

"Now, I told you that the Infidel Friend used alchemy on her feathers to verify that she was from Heaven," Galen was saying, "but I didn't need alchemy to know. I *knew*. I found her with the initial stilling, who knows how far she'd fallen and for how long, lying vulnerable in a room. Usually devils ignore those with the stilling, but there was a Minotaur that had detected her. Perhaps it simply had acquired a taste for stilled souls, or perhaps it could somehow tell that she was from Heaven, and the idea angered it, but whatever the case may be, it tried to kill your mother.

"I fought it as best I could, with all my knowledge and all my skill I held it off. It would lead me out into the wilds and try to circle back to get her. It would call its dyitzu to its side and send them at me. When finally I managed to get her moving and was able to drag her through the halls of Hell, it sent hounds to track me. We ran and we ran and we ran, but it would not relent.

"She sang to me, sometimes, when we occasioned to feel safe in a chamber for a night. She sang to me the Song of Heaven. I learned things that would terrify Charlie. I learned that she had never met God. That she had never met anyone who had. I learned that she didn't even know if He had existed. I also learned her name, which was Evariel.

"Now angels may be holy to those people in Harpsborough, but believe me, they are very terrible things. It's not that they are evil in the way the Father Klein understands evil, it's that they don't view human life like we do. It's not sacred to them. Evariel was evil in the way that I view evil. But as I fought to protect her, she began to see me as more than just a damned soul. She saw me as more than human. I was her friend. Rick was with me, then, of course. She saw him as a friend, too.

"I would tell her stories, just like I am telling you now, during that long chase. She learned about humans for the first time. About our wishes. Our loves. Our pains. And one day, she cried. It is a terrible thing to see an angel cry, Son. It is good that you'll never have to experience it. There is something so pure about them, so . . . perhaps holy is the right word. I grabbed her up in my arms and I begged for her to tell me why she cried. She said that now she knew why she had fallen—why she'd been exiled from Heaven.

"'Why?' I asked her. She told me they must have known that she had developed the ability to love a human. She believed, even though she had not yet committed the crime, the fact that she *could* have was why she was cast down. On that night, Turi, we loved each other. In the morning she was horrified. She could not believe that she had done what she did. She felt as if I had dirtied her. She told me I had taken advantage of her in her weakness.

"Then she ran."

Galen paused for a moment. The undead rustled softly against the stone walls. The gentle snoring of Johnny, who was asleep in one of the other rooms, came and went. Came and went. Came and went.

"I chased her," Galen's face, which had remained expressionless for nearly all of Arturus' life, was forlorn.

I never knew him. I never saw his mettle tested. Whatever the horrors the Carrion has brought me, it has at least let me know my father.

"I chased her," Galen said, "not to break her wishes, for I accepted that she no longer wished to see me, but to protect her from the Minotaur which tracked her. Sadly, the Minotaur found her before I did. I came upon them as they fought. Your mother was formidable, and it might be that she could have defeated a normal Minotaur, I don't know, but this one was different. This one was somehow more terrible than the rest. I came to her aid and was able to distract the beast. When finally I was able to escape its clutches, I set about searching for her, but she was gone.

"Unbeknownst to me, she had found one of the forgotten passages into Igraine's compound. A guard hadn't discovered her, but Charlie had. Now Maab had already made the Christian's recant, but some of them weren't willing to let go, even though they had pretended to. Charlie picked up one of her feathers and used it to show his people that there was hope. Your mother, she had been wounded badly, and she couldn't remember much at all. Charlie was convinced that when your mother regained her memory, she would be able to tell them about God. It was this hope that allowed him to unify the Christians and win them to his banner under Maab's very nose.

"But they were betrayed. One member amongst their ranks went to Igraine and told her the truth. Igraine bade the man take his time and worm his way into Charlie's inner circle.

"The Minotaur which I had so long fought also found out that Evariel was in Igraine's compound. He arranged for himself to be captured and brought in. They kept him chained in a room where they would sacrifice unruly prisoners.

"Then, Igraine's spy finally entered Charlie's inner circle, and they let him meet the angel. Then he told Igraine how to find your mother. Your mother was captured and put in a cage where all the slaves could see her. It was clear now that she was with child. Then, before long, you were born.

"That was when the Infidel came to me."

Arturus had let the voice of his father lull him into a state very near sleep, but at the mention of the Infidel he snapped into sudden alertness.

"The Infidel?"

"He spoke to me. He too was looking for Evariel. I told him she had been taken, but he'd known already. He was the one who told me that she'd had you. I was overjoyed because I'd feared she was actually dead. I was overjoyed because I learned that you existed. But I was in misery, too. Your mother and I had parted on terrible terms. You and your mother were being kept in one of the most impregnable fortresses ever devised in Hell. Your mother had found a way in, but try as I might, I could not. Then I came up with a plan, and the Infidel agreed to it. I would rescue you, and he would pretend to steal you. He would lead the forces of Igraine astray.

"But why?" Arturus asked. "Why would the Infidel help you?"

"A couple of reasons. Back then he wasn't interested in you, Son, he was interested in your mother. Also, he owed me a favor."

Arturus wanted to ask why the Infidel would owe his father a favor, but Galen had started to talk again, and he was loath to interrupt him.

"So I went in that place. Like the Minotaur before me, I allowed myself to be captured. They took me to be sacrificed to it, but instead of me dying, I slew it. Then I found your mother. She was still in her prison. I took you out of her arms. She wept, and I left. The Infidel kept his part of the bargain. He led a merry chase. In the aftermath, Maab came to power. She sent men after you, but they all chased the Infidel. Then Charlie's people revolted and Maab stopped caring about you. Charlie and his men broke out and made their way across the Carrion, Maab's soldiers in pursuit. By then Rick was helping to raise you. We agreed that we wanted you out of the Carrion, so he took you for a while and I led Charlie's people out. Then we all settled down."

"But what happened to my mother?"

"The Infidel had helped me, so I agreed to help him. I left you with Rick at Harpsborough and traveled back into the Carrion to find your mother. Maab had moved her to one of her other compounds, and it took some time to find her. When we did, Son, it was . . . horrific. It's not that they hurt her, Turi. They turned her. When we found her she wanted you dead. The Infidel did his tests on one of her feathers. She had fallen too far. Her body was no longer of Heaven, she'd turned into a Grigori. I couldn't, I couldn't make myself kill her, and it didn't matter one way or another to the Infidel. So she's still there, in that compound. And she wants you dead, Turi."

Arturus took a deep breath.

Galen's eyes returned to the present. "I promised Rick that we would tell you about the angel that we knew. The one that befriended us and learned to love humanity. He didn't want to tell you about the devil she'd become. I have broken that promise, but I think he'd approve."

"Maab did that to her," Arturus said. "Maab turned her into a monster."

"Perhaps. Perhaps it was I who drove her away from humanity. Perhaps it was the fall from Heaven. Perhaps, but no matter. Now she's just another one of Maab's captured play things."

Galen stopped talking.

"There's more, isn't there?" Arturus asked. "More secrets?"

"Yes," Galen said, "but I think you know what concerns you. The rest, well, I can tell you if you wish. Those secrets aren't about you though, so I don't think it will change the way you die."

Suddenly the idea of dying horrified Arturus.

I can't die. I have to find my mother and make her love me. I have to show her Kelly. She should have a grandchild. It's not supposed to end this way.

Arturus suddenly remembered Father Klein's church. He remembered praying to God there, even though he knew God could not listen. It seemed somehow terribly wrong that there wasn't some God for him to plead his case too. This wasn't fair. It had to be changed. Anyone could see that.

There are no miracles in Hell.

That's what people said, but Galen would sometimes give a different quote.

In Hell, a man makes his own miracles.

Arturus sat up straight. Then he leaned forward, coming to his knees, and he grabbed his father by the shoulders. "Save me, Father."

Galen's face was expressionless. "I don't know how."

"I don't care what we have to do. I don't care if you have to make a deal with One Horn. Save me. Find a way."

"I shall think again, Son."

— 15 —

"My God, Martin," Michael said, "you look like shit."

Martin was too tired to be insulted. His eyes were stinging and his eyelids seemed determined to close themselves. Whenever they managed to, he felt himself drifting off—even though he was standing.

He felt lightheaded.

Martin did his best to focus on Michael.

Michael seemed to be waiting for a response.

"Long day," Martin said. "Think it's been a couple. I'm ready to sleep."

"I understand your men are doing that right now?"

Martin gave up trying to focus on Michael. Instead, he just faced the blur. "Yeah. Four hours. Carrion-side wall is up already. Just need to finish."

"Graham came and leveled some pretty big accusations at you."

I bet that fucker did.

Martin felt even more tired. "Sure. He disobeyed me in leaving the breach. But hell, who cares about the chain of command these days?"

"I do," Michael's distant voice said.

This is important. Wake up.

Martin clawed his way back into consciousness. Michael was expecting a response.

"I'm sorry," Martin said. "Could you repeat that?"

"I said I do. I care about the chain of command. That means that no matter what we decide, Graham's going to be punished for not listening to you. Also, no matter what the Fore rules about Rick, whatever decisions you made will not be held against you. You were under a lot of pressure. You had just been to the Carrion. You were sleep deprived. Your number one priority was to seal the breach, and I agree with that."

"That's good to know, sir."

The blur that was Michael stood up and walked closer to him. Now that he was closer, Martin was able to see his facial features. Harpsborough's First Citizen seemed remarkably unconcerned considering all that had happened.

Michael stopped a pace away from him. "What I want to know, though, is why you made the order you did."

Martin felt a rush of emotion coming.

Don't do it, Martin. Don't you say what you actually think. You know better than that.

But the words came out anyway.

"Because we're in the wrong. Because you slimy bastards sit up here in the Fore and pretend that somehow you earned it. Because you use your control over my men to starve my friends, hunters, and girlfriend. Because Cris didn't ask to be brought into this God damned town, and we did him wrong by sending him through the Golden Door. Rick was making it up to the Infidel Friend. You owe him a bit of gratitude. Cris was alive, surely you heard that. He was decked out and armed and ready to go. Whenever he was done doing whatever he was going to do, that motherfucker was going to come back anyway. I'd have been fine. I helped him, but the rest of you? I don't know. He might have killed you all. So we owe Rick one. Or maybe Cris wouldn't have done that. Maybe I just wanted Cris to come and level this place because I am sick of watching you all sit up here in the Fore with food and bloodwater while you act like it ain't Hell out there. But it's Hell. We've lost people. We've lost the best of us. The best of us went out there after Julian and the Carrion just ate them. Then it spat out their shells and made me fight one. And up here you sit. You act like because you ran around Hell a couple of years ago, you get some special privilege. And maybe you deserve something. Maybe you even deserve to be protected by my men. But you *don't* deserve to rob us of what we've earned. You *don't* get to design a system where we can't earn a place among you. You *don't* get to cause people to suffer and starve until they have died, not just so that you can eat, but so that you can eat as much of whatever it is that you want. We can't afford luxury, but rather than admit that, you make us die so you can have it anyway. Fuck you. Fuck you for agreeing to this. Fuck you for letting the Fore bully you into this."

Michael returned to his seat and sat down. "That's just the way things are."

"Funny. To me it looks like you're the leader. It looks like you are the *reason* things are the way things are. I mean, I don't know why Satan even bothers making dyitzu when he's got men like you."

The blur that was Michael shifted. "You're lucky, Martin, that I know what it feels like to be in your shoes. You're lucky that I sympathize with you. I know you're tired, too, and that you aren't thinking clearly. But Martin, I've got to talk to the Fore tonight, and I've got to give them a good reason as to why we shouldn't throw Rick and his friends through that Golden Door right after El Cid and Cris."

Martin steadied himself, then he walked over to the couch and sat, not on the end in Mancini's usual place, but on the middle cushion. The soft blankets and pillows welcomed his body and begged him to sleep, but Martin had found that he'd become a very stubborn man.

He leaned forward over the coffee table to try and keep himself awake. "Why do you want to help Rick?"

Michael pinched the bridge of his nose with his thumb and forefinger. "Because of Galen."

"He's dead now, though."

"We owe Galen so much. He was a guide during our exodus. If I were to exile Rick, well, it would be like spitting on his grave. And Rick's lost a son. I can't fault him for making stupid decisions. I wish . . . I wish you had arrived just a little bit late, and we never knew that they had been conspiring with infidels."

Martin's foggy brain tried to come up with something. Some way to spin Rick's actions into a light which would please the Fore. "He did wrong. He did wrong by the way the Fore sees things."

Michael nodded. "I was afraid you'd say that. Mancini wants him exiled. I'll have to fight that tonight. I'll come up with something. Don't worry."

Martin leaned back into the couch. He let his tired mind try to work at the problem. Rick. Rick was a nice guy. That was all there was to it. It was as plain as day. Easy to see.

"It's just going to be a hard sell, since Mancini will be fighting me," Michael's voice said inside his head. It was weird, how the First Citizen's voice got inside his head.

That . . . wherever he was—was he sitting down?—it sure was comfortable. Wasn't there something he had to do? He was sure there was something, somewhere, a task he had to complete. Whatever it was, Katie would have to accept that he was going to do it later. He would explain how comfortable it was. That would be enough. She would understand. Michael's voice was buzzing some more. It was a comforting sound. Comfortable. Very comfortable.

There was a voice, someone whispering. Arturus focused on it.

"We've been talking," Aaron was saying.

"About what?" Avery asked.

"About how we want to die."

"And?"

"Galen told me that we won't even have to worry about eating each other. There's corpsedust all over this place. If one of us dies, then we'll rise. The rest of us will probably be too tired to fight it off."

"Holy fuck," Avery said.

Arturus opened his eyes. When he'd fallen asleep, Kelly had been resting on his shoulder. She'd gone somewhere, however. He saw her across the room, sitting, staring at the ladder that led to the tower.

"I know," Aaron said.

"Okay." Avery sat up. "I'm listening."

"We're thinking about splinting up Johnny's leg and going out there. We've got some things we can use as weapons. You saw Turi go mad ass on those fuckers with his sword. If we're going to die, then that's the way I want to do it."

Arturus considered this.

That's not a bad idea. It's not as hard as dying bravely while sitting still. Let's just go into the fields and fight our hearts out.

Avery's eyes were wide. He started to breathe harder, but then he looked down. "You've got my vote, but what about Johnny? Johnny might not want to."

Johnny laughed. "You guys don't whisper too well. I'm in. If that's what you want to do, I'm in."

Galen stood. Everyone fell silent. Even the corpses outside seemed to still their breath just for him. "No," he said.

"You don't want to die fighting?" Avery asked, incredulous.

"We might still do that," Galen said, "but I've got an idea."

Johnny was suddenly grinning like an idiot. Kelly rushed over to Arturus and grabbed his hands. Tears were in her eyes.

"You know a way we can live?" Aaron said.

Galen took a deep breath and nodded. "There is a way we might make it. I don't know if I'd call it living, exactly. It's a long shot, but this one's worth trying."

"Well spill it, man!" Avery said, getting up.

"Corpses don't attack lepers."

Oh my God.

Avery's face fell. He sat back down.

Kelly's exuberance died away. Her hands went limp in Arturus'.

"I can hack a few of their limbs off at the gate and bring them back. We're going to have to get right on the line between life and death," Galen said. "With so many corpses packed so tightly, they'll attack anything that's even slightly living. For this to work, we'll have to be right on the edge. We'll be hallucinating badly. If your will's not strong, if you're not committed, you'll probably cross over to being a full on corpse."

Aaron put one hand over his eyes. "You want us to eat corpseflesh?"

Galen nodded. "I do. You don't have to, but if you want to live, it's the only option I have to give you."

Arturus watched his friends' faces as they tried to process the information. Maybe this wasn't worth it. Maybe they'd be better off just fighting the corpses in some sort of heroic last battle. At least that way they'd die cleanly.

Aaron looked up. He'd made a decision. "Well, someone had better start putting that splint on Johnny," he said.

16

They could not break him. They could try. They could work him all day. They could tie him to the slab and have men rape him until he was torn—and then they could pulp his nuts like they were fruit. They could do whatever the hell they wanted.

Julian didn't care.

He had a secret, and that secret made him strong.

It was the only thing he could think of when he lay down at night. It ran through his mind while he was working. It gave him strength when they hurt him. It comforted him when he was miserable. It kept him going when any other man would have quit.

And he no longer considered it to be a dangerous secret. He was beyond the need for physical wellbeing. For the first time, Julian knew what it was like to be willing to die for a cause. But he was willing to do more than that. He was willing to be castrated. To be mutilated. To be tortured until his body ran out of ways to receive pain.

Still, he had to be careful not to be too bold.

Not all of his disciples had come as far as he. All of them wanted to reach transcendence, but few had come to that state where they truly felt that their secret was more important than their bodies. He couldn't let them get caught. For that reason, he kept his peace. For that reason, he didn't stop in the mines and shout out to the uncaring Hell his love.

So he stayed quiet. So he bided his time. So he made his

conversions in inches. One person, then another. And then another. Slowly but surely, their numbers grew. Julian was certain that Selena would find out eventually. But let her. Let her find out when most of her slaves had already left her foul religion. Then, oh yes, then there could be a reckoning. They could rise up. Yes they could.

All of the prisons seemed pitch black when you entered them, but a few had enough light so that Julian could see shadows moving amongst the chambers after his eyes adjusted. He saw one of those shadows moving now. It stopped where Brother Jim, one of Julian's most fervent followers, sat.

The shadow's whisper was too soft for him to hear the man's words, but Julian was able to make out his own name.

Brother Jim motioned in his direction. The shadow approached.

As it got closer, Julian was able to tell that shadow was George, one of his most recent converts.

"I've got news for you," George whispered.

"Good?"

"I think so," George sat down beside him. "It is an opportunity, at least. It carries some risk, but it might help us. I don't know if you'll like it."

Julian was worried. "Do you intend to take this opportunity, whether I decide to or not?"

"I do, but just hear what they have to say. I won't do anything to risk us. I won't agree to any Christian's involvement without your consent."

"Who?" Julian asked. "Hear what who has to say?"

"The infidels. There's one named Cris. He found a way into our compound, one not even the Priestesses know about. He spoke to me before. They may be able to help us, Julian."

Infidels.

"Those people are evil, George."

George nodded. "Maybe. But the enemy of my enemy—"

"Is not always my friend," Julian said. "We don't make choices between the devil we know and the devil we don't. We don't side with any devil. We must have a purity of purpose. We cannot compromise our values."

George put a hand on his shoulder. "Let me be honest with you. I don't believe in your God or your Christ. I support you, with all my life and all my heart and all my soul, because I believe your way is better than Selena's. I believe it as strongly as you hold your faith. I am willing to die to keep our organization strong."

I should have known. He'll compromise us.

George could never make it to the point where he could resist torture. He could never reach transcendence. No man could on his own. Human beings just weren't that strong. Without faith, a person just couldn't withstand those things.

"I'm glad you admitted that to me," Julian said.

"And let me tell you something else, Julian. I know you want to have a pure path, but that has never been possible. You can only have purity of goals. Trying to have a pure method will only doom you to evil. What do you think you do all day? What do you think shoveling all that stone around accomplishes? You are already serving Selena, and by doing that, you are supporting Maab. You have already dirtied your purpose. Now, I beg you, Julian, listen to these infidels. Hear what they have to say. If they can somehow convince you that what they offer is a better course than supporting Selena, then let's take it! If they can't convince you of that, even if they say they will and you don't believe them, then we'll come back. Nothing will change."

Julian thought about this. "Very well. I will meet with them, but I promise no more than that."

"Good!" George said. "Get picked by Truscan tomorrow. His workers will be assigned to the prison where we can meet Cris."

"What if he doesn't pick me?" Julian asked.

"He will," George said.

This rebellion, it seems, is larger than just my group.

Watching them brick up another Carrion barrier had been traumatic for Ellen. This time she hadn't expected Arturus to come shouting for help before they'd added the last stone, and somehow that made the whole experience worse. It was clear to her now that El Cid and her infidels would never find Turi. Her hope had become the empty thing Rick had promised it would—a thing more painful than she could bear.

I told him it was okay. I told him we would only hope for a little while. Then we would give it up. Only we never did.

The Carrion was simply too large. The infidels were too few.

Or I never did, until now.

She had put her grief off for too long, she knew. As Rick, Massan and Alice helped build the barrier, Ellen began to mourn. It might not have been so painful if she'd simply accepted the truth in the beginning. Then she would have only lost a childhood crush. But she had kept him in her heart. She had kept him there against all reason, against all the arguments that Rick had given her. And her denial had grown there, spreading its roots through her. Her optimism had festered in that heart—until now. Confronted finally with the cold reality of Hell, Ellen felt her denial break. It was as if her soul was pouring out through the cracks.

She sat down while the others filled in the breach, staring into nothingness.

Maybe I'll never move again. What reason could I possibly have to keep going?

She wasn't sure how long she sat like that.

Rick's face intruded, breaking the hypnotic spell she'd cast on herself. "You alright, Ellen?"

"Fine," she mumbled.

"Let's get you moving," Rick said. "We've got to keep the stilling off of you. And besides, it's time for us to leave, anyway."

"Home?"

"Not yet. I'm sorry, but not yet. We have to go to Harpsborough. The Fore is going to have a meeting in the church. We're to be put on trial."

They'll sentence us. Just like Cris. They'll throw us through the Golden Door. Wait! That means we'll be forced to go after Turi!

For a second that hope flared up inside her, but it would not hold. Without these Infidel Friend, they would die. With the Infidel Friend, Ellen knew that she would cause them to die.

I'm not good enough. I didn't learn fast enough.

Not like Molly. Molly had spent every minute she could training with the infidels.

Martin's hunters surrounded them. Martin looked a little better than the last time she'd seen him. He still looked tired, but he didn't look like he was about to topple over.

He must have gotten at least a few hours of sleep.

"Come on," Martin said, "let's get this over with."

Massan and Alice shared a look.

They passed through the wilds of Hell quickly. Ellen noticed that Martin's men were on edge. She didn't know if it was because of how long the breach had been open, or if perhaps they were unhappy escorting prisoners which they thought weren't guilty.

How could I deserve this? I just got here. How could they think I'd know what was right and what was wrong?

But maybe her recent arrival is what had let her see what good and evil were here. After all, the Infidel Friend were nothing like she had expected. They seemed to be many things, but they weren't evil. If anything, they wanted to fight for the wellbeing of all people. How could that be wrong?

There was a large crowd in Harpsborough. Rumor must have gotten around and drawn the people back in from the wilds. Some looked angry. Others were sad.

I'm sorry. I know you think I betrayed you, but I didn't.

Martin led the way, the crowd parting before him. The hunters did their best to keep the villagers back, but one woman was struggling, and she managed to force her way through.

"Kara!" Massan shouted.

The woman threw herself into his arms. Massan looked overwhelmed.

Martin waved his men back, and their procession stopped.

"Tell me it's going to be okay!" she said. "Tell me you did nothing wrong."

Massan stepped back so he could look at her, his hands gripping her shoulders. "I'm sorry, Kara. I think I'm in serious trouble. I don't know, I don't know if I'll survive this."

Kara looked down at her feet. "They may kill you?"

"They might. Or exile. Or something worse."

"Worse?"

"It's true. We conspired with Infidel Friend, I . . ."

Kara looked back up at him. Ellen was struck by how genuine the woman's love seemed.

"Then tell me this," Kara said, "tell me that you did this while following your heart."

Massan wrapped his arms around Kara and held her tightly. "I did. That I promise you."

She held him for a long time, then she let go and stepped back. "I love you."

"I love you, too, Kara."

The hunters looked towards Martin. Martin grimaced and then nodded. Their procession continued. In front of them were the open doors of the Fore, and beyond that, the men who would call themselves her judges.

They can't hurt me. I have nothing left.

She looked at Rick. The man was suffering.

Except him.

"Hope you're a good climber," George said to Julian.

"I'm alright."

George led him through the prison. It had been some time since they'd finished their day's labor, so most of the other prisoners were sleeping. Strangely, they'd had no trouble with Kruks even though Edmond, by far the worst Kruk Julian knew of, was in their same cell. Kruks never seemed bother George, for some reason.

Oh, hell. If he gets baptized by Maab, he'll deliver us all to Selena.

Two men stood up as they approached one of the shitholes.

"It's okay," George said.

They moved aside.

The shitholes were basically outhouses. Plumbing wasn't the best, but when they got too full, Selena's people were able to divert a nearby river through them to clean them out. For a moment Julian feared that they were going to crawl down through all that waste, but then he remembered that the holes were too small for people to fit through. He looked around to see where the secret exit might be.

Is this a trap?

But surely Selena wouldn't have bothered with an elaborate ruse. She'd simply torture him. And even if George wanted to beat him up or hurt him on behalf of some Kruk gang, he could have done so without such a complicated lie.

George knelt by the shithole and pulled up the stone plate. Now there was room for a person to fit.

"Trust me," George said, "you'll want to leave your robe."

Damn.

But Julian was beyond the flesh. If he'd withstood the torture of conversion, he could withstand this. He crawled down after George. Beyond the flesh or not, he puked his guts out.

When he had finished vomiting, George led him through the shithole's equivalent of a septic tank. There was a grate where the river would flow through to wash out the refuse, but it had been sawed through. Julian did not envy whoever had done that.

"This way," George said.

There was no light at all after they entered the empty waterway. There weren't many twists and turns, but even so, Julian wasn't sure if he could make it back without George's help. Then George stopped, opening some kind of hatch above him. Julian and he crawled through it and then up into a room.

Julian was thankful that he could see again. George held up a finger to his lips.

We're still in the Carrion.

George closed the hatch behind him, which looked like normal rock from this side. Then he motioned for Julian to follow him. There was a river nearby. Julian could hear it, and as they walked, it came into view. George dropped, slave clothes and all, into the river. Julian did likewise.

George swam to the far side.

Julian followed. He felt the cold Carrion water as it rushed around his body and soaked his clothes. It washed the refuse away.

George left the river. He removed his grey slave clothes, shameless of his nude body, and then began to wring them out. Julian did likewise, but felt horribly uncomfortable. He would have left his underwear on had Selena provided him with any.

"Come on," George said. "It's not safe to be out in the open like this."

George led him down a few more passages. Julian felt his heart beating. It had been a while since he'd roamed the wilds, and even when he lived in Harpsborough, the Carrion had always terrified him.

And this time I don't even have a weapon.

It was a different kind of fear than he faced in Selena's complex. Dying there would mean martyrdom. Dying out here would be meaningless.

I'm God's. I have to remember that.

George led him to a chute that ran up and out of the room. He climbed it and Julian continued to follow. After a time, the chute leveled off. It reminded him of climbing through the Carrion barrier. The memory unsettled him. He had come into a position of strength through his faith, but remembering all his friends—it made him feel weak.

And Turi. What happened to him?

The chute opened up into a small room. There were no bricks here. The entire chamber had been carved out of a single piece of stone.

George moved to one corner and sat down. "Good time for a nap. We'll be back in our prison cell before our shift starts, but you'll be better rested if you catch some sleep now.

That, Julian knew, would be impossible.

17

Ellen had never been inside the church before. She was amazed that people could have built such a thing. Its ceiling soared up above her. Open arches near the top let light in from the Harpsborough chamber. Crosses lined those openings, casting their long shadows down across the pews. It seemed like a place where a Harpsborough villager might come to forget about Hell for a while. It would have made her feel safe, too, except that the church was full of Citizens.

Ellen was surprised how many there were. Their voices coalesced into a single hum as they shared what details about the case they had heard. In a moment, she knew, they were going to start asking questions, and Rick was going to tell the truth again.

He might as well, there was no use lying now.

For the moment, they were being left alone. Two hunters stood at the door of the church, guarding their weapons. Ellen had been surprised how hard it was for her to give them up.

"Rick, you could have consulted us before you started spouting out truth." Massan's voice was venomous.

"I'm truly sorry," Rick said. "Do you hold it against me?"

Ellen watched intently as Massan considered this.

"No," the trader said finally. "No, I guess I don't. You know, everyone knows everyone in Harpsborough. Sooner or later the truth was going to come out. I guess the worst they can do is send us through the Golden Door, yeah?"

The hum of the Citizens ebbed for a moment before returning, perhaps louder than before.

"You think we're going to be okay?" Massan asked.

"I don't know," Rick said.

I have got to talk to him about lying at some point.

A table had been set up in front of the pulpit. A line of Citizens were walking towards it. Ellen recognized a few of them. The red haired woman, she remembered, was Chelsea. And father Klein was there. Mancini ascended the stairs next. Then came a large man whose name she thought she knew.

Copperton? Something like that, anyway.

Michael entered from a side room. His face was serious, stern. He looked like he was a man ready to do battle.

But against us? We're at his mercy already.

He sat down at the center of the table. The voices of the Citizens died away. One coughed, and the sound echoed throughout the church. Michael raised a granite orb as if he was going to slam it down into the table, but as the room had already quieted, he simply set it down.

Michael looked at them. "Now, you have all been accused of aiding infidels. Additionally, you were said to have helped Molly, who was confined to Harpsborough by order of the Fore and who escaped by assaulting one of our hunters. Furthermore, it is said that you had foreknowledge of the theft from the Fore. Lastly, it is said that you endangered Harpsborough through a combination of all the above listed actions. How do you plead?"

"I plead guilty, and I ask for your mercy," Rick said.

Alice stepped forward. "I am guilty. I ask for your mercy."

Massan stepped forward. "I am guilty. I ask for your mercy."

"I am guilty of those things, except the last one," Ellen said. "I would never endanger you guys. I care for you very much."

Mancini snorted. "You think bringing Infidel Friend to Harpsborough was somehow not endangering it?"

"There was no way she could know, Mancini," Rick said. "She was only in Hell for a month, and staying with me for that time. I did not give her enough information for her to be able to make that determination."

Mancini shrugged. "Well, they've pled guilty. I guess it's not necessary that we go through any testimony."

The Citizens murmured their agreement, but Chelsea cut

them short. "So you say, but these are people we know well. Who here hasn't done business with Massan? Who here hasn't been surprised by his honesty? And Rick, for God's sake. This is Rick we're talking about. The man just came back from helping fill the breach."

Mancini rolled his eyes. "He'd already been caught and confessed. Good behavior is no surprise from a prisoner who knows he's about to be sentenced."

Michael cleared his throat. "Mancini, I think Rick would have helped anyway. You weren't here then, but when we first came out of the Carrion, almost all of the barriers were in disrepair, and Rick helped us build them. There was a time when a settling knocked a couple down, and Rick was right there. Rick helped us fill Julian's breach in too. Not to mention the time when he helped hunt the Icanitzu. If you're looking for good behavior, this man's got it in spades."

"As always," Mancini said, "I must tell you I wasn't here in the beginning, so I can't begin to understand how you feel about these things. All I can do is tell you what I see from my new perspective. Weigh it as you will, but Rick hasn't done anything for us lately that we couldn't have done ourselves."

Chelsea shrugged. "Nor has anyone. We're a community. The point is that Rick volunteered. We had to pay the people of Harpsborough to help fill in Julian's barrier, and they wouldn't even do that until they knew we'd bricked up the far side. Rick didn't get a single ration. He didn't ask for one. You know why? Because Rick's always got our best interests at heart."

Father Klein sighed. "A fool can have the best intentions, but if he intends to remain a fool after he's committed his wrongdoing, he must be stopped. Rick, I ask you, do you think the infidels are evil?"

Ellen looked at Rick.

Now would be a great time to learn how to lie.

"Like all men," Rick said, "they are a mixture of both good and evil. The only difference is that they don't hold God in their heart."

For a second Ellen was shocked, not because Rick had lied, but because he hadn't. He had answered in a way that Father Klein would certainly misinterpret. Klein would think that Rick meant the infidels were evil because the alternative meaning was unthinkable. The alternative was that Rick didn't think a godless heart was a bad one.

We're all in Hell. Here, all hearts are godless.

"It doesn't matter what they say," Mancini announced. "What matters is that there is no way that we can be sure they aren't lying to us. There's no way that we can be sure they won't do something like this again."

I have something to say.

Ellen raised her hand.

It looked like Father Klein and Mancini were about to say something, but they both stopped and looked at her curiously, as if stunned by her gesture.

"Go ahead," Michael said softly. "You can speak."

"If you're looking to know that we'll never do anything like that again, I can tell you why."

Father Klein nodded. "It would fill my heart with joy."

"I didn't know enough when we started the journey to know that we were doing wrong. But these other people did, and they are good people. You must be at least a little confused as to why such good people would do such things?"

She looked around. She had every Citizen's complete attention. Even Mancini seemed intent on what she had to say.

"But if you think about it, all of us, even Molly before she left, all had something in common." She paused. No one spoke, so she continued. "We all have lost someone we love. Or in Massan's case, feared it. Alice watched Aaron go into the Carrion and never come back. Rick and I, we watched Galen and Turi leave. Molly had seen Cris exiled through the Golden Door. When Molly came to us it was just after we'd found the corpse eater. Do you remember?" They were nodding. "Massan knew, we all knew, that there was something terrible out in the wilds. Molly had spoken to Cris, and she told us—and we believed her—that the source of that evil was in the Carrion."

Chelsea nodded. "And in fact, it was."

"It was," Ellen said. "Normally danger would have never made Rick do what he did. He would have worked with you all to defeat it. It's just that the infidels represented more than just a reprieve from danger. They were our hope. We cried together, he and I, about the decision to get them. It was my fault because he didn't want to have hope that Turi would come back, and I did." Ellen fought to keep her voice steady. "I told him it was okay. I said that we'd hope for just a little while. That we'd let it go before . . ." She had to stop. She just couldn't say any more.

The Citizens were silent.

"It doesn't change the fact that they are guilty," Mancini said. "they confessed."

"Maybe not," Chelsea's voice was sweet and compassionate, "but there is more to this trial than just a guilty or not guilty verdict. Once we declare them guilty, Michael has to decide a punishment. I think what they had to say was very important because our judge has to decide what leniency to give them."

Ellen decided that she liked Chelsea.

"Very well," Michael said, "raise your hand for a guilty vote."

As one, the Citizens raised their hands.

Michael looked at them. Ellen realized now why he'd been preparing to fight a battle earlier. It wasn't a battle against her and Rick. It was a battle against Mancini and Klein and Copperton and whomever else was bloodthirsty and intolerant amongst the ranks of his followers. And knowing those people, it must have seemed like a terrible battle to fight indeed.

I hope I helped you.

"Very well, guilty you are," Michael said. "I have decided the sentences. Rick and Ellen, what you did was foolish, but it was done out of love. We all had someone we care about disappear in the Carrion. For that reason, I'll grant you as much leniency as I can. We ceded to you the Hungerleaf Grove for services rendered long ago. It will now be returned to the Fore. Alice, I know how much Aaron meant to you. I know that you would have done anything to bring him back. Your actions are, therefore, understandable. I sentence you to six months indentured servitude to the Fore."

Alice's head bowed under the weight of the proclamation. Her blonde hair fell over her face, covering her blue eyes.

"Massan. You are a good man, and I know you want to keep Kara safe, but what you did endangered her and the rest of us. I give you a choice. You can either be exiled through the Golden Door or you can lose your hand."

Alice's head snapped back up.

"No!" Ellen cried.

Everyone was looking at her.

"How could you do such a thing?" she asked.

How could these people, these *fucking* Fore idiots who didn't even have to risk their own lives, call for something so evil?

"No!" she shouted. "That's barbaric!"

Father Klein nodded sadly. "In the Good Book, there were terrible punishments for certain crimes. Rebellious children were to be stoned. Cities that harbored apostates were to be put to the torch. In the old world, that sort of justice seemed cruel to us because we led blessed lives. In the old times, when God's people were nomads roaming in the desert, if someone did something wrong, it could cause the whole tribe to be killed. That's why conformity was so important. That's why those laws seemed so harsh. Here, in Hell, we can now see God's wisdom in giving such laws. Here we are, in a place where a single person can bring about the destruction of our entire village. It is still possible, if the Infidel Friend come back, that your actions have doomed us. That's why our punishments seem so barbaric to you."

"Seem!" Ellen was seething with rage.

El Cid would never allow something like this.

Massan put a hand on her shoulder. "Be easy, Ellen. It is okay."

He looked as calm as she had ever seen him. He wasn't even sweating.

Massan stepped towards the table. "You are very generous, First Citizen, to allow me to choose my punishment. You know I cannot choose exile, because I love Kara too much. I must stay with her. I offer you my hand."

Ellen wanted to shout at them. She wanted to throttle them.

These people are evil. They stopped thinking, hoping that would defeat Satan, but all that did was let the Devil in.

But it was more than that. These people were rotten. Maybe they had been born rotten. Or maybe someone had planted a dark seed deep inside their hearts—a seed that grew up to poison their souls. Ellen looked at Chelsea. There was look of disgust on the Citizen's face, and instinctively Ellen knew that the woman agreed with her.

"It was worse in Hellespont," Rick whispered. "That's why El

Cid had to do what she did. They had become so much worse."

If Turi was here, if he hadn't died, he would have redeemed these people. He would have grown up and talked sense into them. I know he would have.

Maybe that was the important thing Rick had spoken of, the thing that Turi had to do.

And if I am to replace Turi in Rick's heart, does that mean I have to redeem these people?

 — 18 —

"Cris!" George said, his voice loud enough to wake Julian.

The Infidel Friend George had called Cris crawled out of the chute. He stood in an odd manner. First he held his torso up with a posted arm and then he swung one leg under himself. The infidel named Cris crossed the room and shook George's hand.

"I'm glad you're alive," Cris said.

More Infidel Friend were coming. There was a tiny girl with dark hair and brilliant green eyes. There was a blond man who looked like a statue come to life. There was a tall, lithe black man with a shaved head. There was a couple, a man and a woman, who shared a kiss as soon as they entered the room. All of them stood in the same way Cris had.

Then Molly came through. Unlike the others, she scrambled clumsily to her feet.

Julian felt his jaw grow slack. At first he couldn't believe he was seeing her, but then after he closed his eyes and looked again, his heart began leaping in his chest.

She had changed. She was svelte, as thin as he could ever remember her being. Her face seemed more grim now, more serious.

But doesn't mine?

"Molly!" Julian cried.

He stood, rushing towards her.

A surprised grin spread across her face. "I thought you were dead!" She caught him up in a fierce hug. "Oh, God, Julian. We thought you were dead. We were sure you were dead!"

Julian's blood ran cold. This conversation couldn't continue. If it did, he would have to tell her what happened to him. He would have to explain about how they'd raped him. About how they broke him. How he had given up God. These were things he wasn't ready to talk about. Worse than that, with her here, he no longer felt strong. He felt like the little boy who'd dared the Carrion in secret each and every day to access his cache of devilwheat. The boy who'd been forced to get that devilwheat so he could afford to buy the love and acceptance of the Harpsborough people. That Julian couldn't withstand Selena. That Julian couldn't survive the Carrion.

He noticed her face had changed too.

What is she doing here with these Infidel Friend?

She must also be feeling shame. Only, where Julian's experiences had made him more holy, Molly's had obviously done the opposite.

"What about Aaron?" Molly asked. "Or Patrick or Kyle? Or Duncan? Have you seen them?"

Julian shook his head. "I saw Turi and Galen. Turi said that Aaron and some others were waiting for me, but . . . well, he was able to get away. Maab sent some soldiers after them, though. I don't think that . . ."

Molly nodded. "I was just hoping, you know, for Alice's sake.

Alice.

"And who's Julian?" The tiny Infidel Friend motioned towards him.

"Julian's a community leader opposed to Selena," George said. "I brought him because he's got a group of Christian converts. He's anti-slavery. I'm planning to help him if there is a rebellion."

Cris cocked his head to one side. "You from Harpsborough?"

Julian had never seen the man before.

"Yes," Julian said.

Cris snorted. "Figures. George, let's get down to business. How much time do you have?"

Molly stepped back to stand by Cris' side.

She loves him. She's fallen for an Infidel Friend.

George shrugged. "At least a couple hours, but we should be quick, just to make sure. Hard to measure time, you know."

The tiny one nodded. "Very true."

Molly, the infidels and George were standing in a circle. Julian joined them.

"She's in charge, George," Cris said, pointing to the tiny one. "You can report to El Cid here."

"My soldier contacts have been getting promoted," George said. "I'm a little afraid of them exposing me now, but I think I should be safe. If they rat me out, then Selena is going to catch on to the fact that they were part of my organization for years, and that won't be good for them. The positive part is, though, that I'm getting a lot more news than I used to. There was a full on battle with army of Blood and Stone. Rumor is that Lucreas has returned, and that he came to speak to Maab. Maab refused to obey him, so that's what started the war."

"Makes sense," Cris told El Cid. "Maab is the nastiest woman you'd ever meet, but even she'd not deal with devils."

El Cid nodded. "Go on, George."

"Anyway, the City people started coming in and took over some of her food caches. A lot of Maab's deep tribes were cut off. Some haven't reported in almost a year. Others have managed to sneak some messengers through. Maab has no idea how many of them are left. Food got tight for a little bit, but Maab struck back. First she buckled down on local raiders. Anyone who was tapping a cache was killed. Then she attacked. La'Ferve, Gilgamesh, and Nephysis ambushed a Blood and Stone army and were able to defeat it."

El Cid smiled, crossing her arms under her tiny breasts. "Good contact, Cris."

George smiled. "There's more, too. Right now Maab suspects Nephysis has turned against her, or that he's at least playing both sides. Her scouts have found corpses that look like they were raised by Nephysis in the deep. Supposedly, they are being used to build bridges and dig. Maab thinks they're trying to dig out an Archdevil named Tu-El.

"I think Maab's putting a group together to try and sabotage their digging efforts—"

El Cid held up a hand. "You said he had undead building a

bridge?"

"Yes, or practicing building one. I'm not sure if I believe my sources. Apparently they were building the bridges randomly, ones that didn't have any purpose. I don't know, again, my reports are all second and third hand."

The blond one spoke. "Do Furies attack corpses, Father?"

Cris nodded his head. "My understanding is that they do only when the corpses are under a devil's control. Nephysis, though, must have found a way around it. I saw them prepping construction by the Erebus."

El Cid took in a deep breath. "That's why you were so worried."

"That means they're trying to rescue Saint Wretch?" the female of the couple asked.

Cris nodded. "Go on, George. Anything else?"

"Yes," George said. "There's something called an angel's get running around. They're trying to catch it."

El Cid's lips pursed for a second. "So the worst case scenario is that we face an army led by Lucreas Crassus and a recovered Tu-El—who's nice and pissed off after being buried for a millennia and a half—along with Saint Wretch himself and his pet Archdevil."

"That's going to be one hell of a call they'll put out," the male of the couple said.

"You sure we can't fight alongside Maab's armies?" El Cid asked Cris.

Julian was terrified by the suggestion.

If Maab and the infidels were to work together . . .

Cris shook his head. "Sorry. She's evil."

El Cid looked surprised. "More evil than Saint Wretch?"

"I've infiltrated both her complex and the City of Blood and Stone. I'm not joking when I tell you I preferred the City. That bitch is rotten to the core. If we're going to use a local army, it's got to be one raised from rebellions."

El Cid frowned. "When Ares came through here he reported that the culture was intractable."

"Possibly," Cris said. "But things are different now. We've got Malkravyan set up with Calimay. We've got Julian here. It could be possible. Free the slaves, set up little governments, get them ready to fight."

Julian felt a shiver run down his back when El Cid turned her gaze towards him.

"How many men do you have?" El Cid asked.

"I don't know," Julian said. "I wouldn't tell you if I did."

George sucked air in through is teeth. "They're set up in cells. It's smart, so that if one group falls, the rest won't go down."

"Effective at keeping your movement alive," Cris said. "But you're going to have a hell of a time figuring out when you're capable of striking."

"I'll tell you this," Julian said. "I've heard you speaking, and you're talking about using us. If I do gain control of Selena's complex, I have no intention of turning it over to you."

Molly frowned and shook her head.

El Cid approached him. Instinctively, he took a step back.

"You won't be serving us," El Cid said. "What we'd ask is that you'd work with us. That you'd fight beside us against the City of Blood and Stone. Trust me, at that point, they'd be attacking you anyway."

Julian looked away.

The female of the couple snorted. "Ares was right. Intractable. We're going to have to send out our own call. Bring an infidel army. I mean, if it really is Saint Wretch coming, we all knew it was going to come down to that at some point."

El Cid looked back towards the chute. "If it's Saint Wretch coming, an army might not do any good." She turned to George again. "You sure you don't have enough men to stage a revolt?"

"I'm afraid not. My contacts are good for information, but I think they want to play both sides here. In the end, their loyalty is with their priestesses. Julian is the guy who has people willing to fight for him."

"Very well," El Cid said. "We appreciate your time. We're going deeper in, George. It looks like when we come back this way, we're going to try extraction."

George nodded. "I long to be free. Come back soon, huh?"

"I know you hate us, Julian," Cris said to him, "but we can take you, too. Drop you back at Harpsborough."

Home.

Julian felt as if the air had been knocked out of him. He could be free. He could taste the honey again. He could spend time laughing with the Citizens.

They never cared about me. They cared about the devilwheat, and I won't be able to get that now.

And it was the wrong choice, besides. The Infidel Friend were evil. He couldn't abandon all his brothers back in Selena's compound.

"No," Julian said.

Cris shrugged. "Let us know if you change your mind."

"Julian!" Molly said.

Julian turned his head away.

"These are good people, Julian! They don't hoard food like the Fore. You don't have to pay them to make them accept you. They're good for Hell."

"Go," Julian said.

"Julian, you don't understand."

"I said go!" he shouted.

Molly walked towards him, so he held out a hand to stop her.

"Julian I—"

"I won't speak to an Infidel Friend!" Julian insisted.

"No." Molly's voice cracked. "No, that's not what I mean. I've just been in Harpsborough. Do you want to know about anyone? I can tell you how they're doing. Mancini's still making that new brew. They made Martin Lead Hunter. Would you believe that? Lead Hunter. He's done pretty good, too, from what I hear. John's still in the Fore . . ."

Tears were building up in his eyes. He pushed Molly away, but she kept talking.

"Massan might be in some trouble, but he's going to do a union ceremony with Kara. I saw Chelsea, she was your favorite Citizen right? She was—"

"Shut up!" Julian shouted.

He couldn't take this. The memories of his friends, of his life, they were tearing down the walls of Faith he had built up around his soul. Couldn't she tell she was hurting him? Or did she just not care because she was an infidel now?

"She was standing on the balcony," Molly continued. "She was sad, Julian. She was so sad. She was looking out here, to the Carrion. It think she hasn't been right since Aaron left—"

"I said shut up!" Julian screeched.

His tears were running freely down his cheeks. He covered his face with his hands.

"Go!" He yelled. "Just go. I have nothing to say to you. I have *nothing* to say to you."

He dropped to his haunches and looked up at her.

She seemed like she was about to cry. Julian had never seen Molly hurt like this. Before, her tears had always been shed to cause someone else pain.

The one called Cris put his hand on her shoulder. Molly stepped back.

One by one, the Infidel Friend crawled back out. Julian made sure not to look at the hole until he was sure that Molly had gone through it.

He turned to George, but the man wouldn't meet his gaze.

19

Arturus watched as Johnny doubled over and vomited bile and chunks of partially digested corpseflesh. The scent was unbearable and the vapors made his eyes sting.

Johnny rolled over to his side, crying. "I can't. I can't."

Galen was standing over him. "We don't have any water left to keep you hydrated, Johnny."

Johnny looked back up at him. His eyes were terribly bloodshot. "I'm trying!" he shouted. "Please, God. I'm *trying!*"

"If you do not do this," Galen said, his voice calm and even, "you will die."

Johnny's mouth hung open as he tried to catch his breath. He gave a few dry heaves. Some bile dribbled down his chin. "More. Give me more, I will try again."

"I will not risk another trip to the gate."

"You want me to die?" he asked, pointing towards the splint they'd made for him. "You can't leave me like this!"

"No Johnny, that's not what I'm saying."

Johnny's brow furrowed in confusion. His eyes searched all around before meeting Arturus' gaze.

Arturus looked towards the puddle of vomit and corpseflesh.

Johnny's face froze. For a long moment he lay there, motionless. Then he turned back to Galen. "I can't."

Galen nodded. "It is possible you are telling the truth. Your body may not allow you to do this. It cannot know that this is the only way, the only possibility you have to live."

"No," Johnny said.

He was beaten. His downcast eyes looked lost. This was the same expression Arturus remembered seeing on Johnny's face during their climb down into the Deadlands.

But then something clicked inside the hunter, and his nostrils flared with anger. "I won't quit." Johnny faced the vomit. "I won't quit." He stared at it. He cried.

Arturus turned to his own portion. Several hours ago, he had mixed what corpsedust they'd extracted with his water and drank it—but it was not enough. The corpses would still know he was alive. He had to take in more. Already he felt the poison in his body—and in his mind. There were whispers, voices which belonged to no one. Sentences that went nowhere. The walls moved, back and forth, sometimes melting into the floor.

Aaron cried out in frustration.

Avery was holding his nose as he chewed.

Kelly's face was as pale as Arturus had ever seen it.

"You will be nearly dead," Galen's monotone voice informed them. "You will feel the death in your soul. You will succumb to the illusion that you are being separated from your body. You must not give in to this. You must not pass on to the other side. You may hallucinate that you are already dead. In your feverish delusion you might already think you are a corpse. You cannot do this because that path may lead you to a place you can never come back from. Your will alone will keep your body moving. Your will alone will keep you alive."

Arturus picked up the severed arm that lay before him and bit into the bicep. The dead flesh was unlike any meat he'd had in his life. It tasted—rotten. The skin was dry, almost flaky. Its bitterness filled the back of his mouth. Then it crept up into his nose and inched down his throat.

"We will be surrounded by dead on all sides," Galen continued, "and we will be walking, hand in hand, across the fields of asphodel. We will see things that aren't real. We will sense danger where there is none. Whatever weapon you wield, know that you are very likely to use that against a friend because what you think you see is not what you see. Because what appears before you is not what is before you. Yet, you must remain vigilant. You cannot simply ignore every threat.

There are wights out there. Undead which have the left over intelligence of the bodies they have taken. Undead which you cannot hurt with your old world weapons, be they knives or bullets. You can only strike at them with fists, or rock, or whatever Hell stuff surrounds you. Sometimes they even have the remnants of that body's personality. While the corpses will not be able to tell that we are living, the wights can. They may ignore us. They may attack us. Some can even direct the dead around them. Should one strike at you, you may not know it is a wight. You can tell what they are because they have black eyes, like a dyitzu, but now that I have told you this, you may see black eyes on your friends. On random corpses. Or it could be that your mind exaggerates the danger. You may see an attacking phantasm that you know *must not be real,* however, that phantasm can simply be the mask that you've placed on a real danger. There will be no way to know with any certainty that the choices you are making are the right ones. There will be no way to eliminate doubt. There may be no time for skepticism, and you may not be able to afford the foolishness of faith."

Arturus swallowed down the bitter undead flesh. His stomach heaved, trying to reject what he was giving it.

No. I know better than you, my body. Let me show you what happens if we're wrong.

He let the dark thoughts come in. He let his fears touch his body as surely as the hands of the corpses would. They put their fingers in his mouth. One was biting at his ankle, ripping through his flesh. He felt the muscle of his calf give way. A tooth caught on his Achilles tendon. He tried to shake his leg loose but they were all around him. Clawing him. Covering him. One's hand reached down into his belly and caused it to erupt with a fiery pain.

See! Look at what I show you. I have to eat this.

He picked up the arm. It was moving. Fighting him, clawing at him.

Let it fight.

Arturus took another bite, and another.

"We have miles to cross, and only a general direction to head in. Our senses will be disturbed. Yet, we must move quickly and efficiently. If we stay here too long, we might succumb to death or begin to come back to life. In either case, we will be dead. If you get lost, if you let go of the hand in front or behind you, there will be no time to come back for you. Know this, that hand is the only thing that keeps you alive. You must cling to it as you would to your very life. Nothing, and I mean *nothing* can separate you. It simply cannot be."

Arturus' lips felt dry. The blood in his body was sluggish. Coagulated. His skin was already a grey color. Lesions had appeared on his arm, though he could not say if they were real or dreamed. Spots of dead flesh covered him.

"If we have been out there too long, we may have to kill a corpse and eat from it to keep our balance. You cannot all attack at once. Only one of us will make the kill, and the rest will consume the meat off of that corpse. If you attack one, and damage it sufficiently, it will respond with violence. In our weakened state, such an attack might prove more than we can overcome. It will not take much in the way of damage to push us over the line from barely living to barely dead. There is no return after you have gone too far. There is no coming back."

Arturus' tooth hit bone. The rotten substance crunched under his bite. He chewed it, grinding up the bone between his molars, and swallowed it. To his right, Johnny was struggling to eat some more.

Kelly looked at him. Her eyes were staring right through him. Her pink lips were now grey. Her pale ivory skin marked with the scars of rot. It had spread across her quickly, or at least that's what he imagined. How long had it been since they'd started? Hours? Days? Who knew? He'd thought it had not been long, but certainly he was no judge of time.

"I'm sorry," Arturus told his mother.

"I know you are," the angel responded.

"I didn't mean to be something you hate."

"You are an abomination. Your father and I should never have consummated the feelings we had that night. You are a thing that should not be. But this, this that you are doing now, I approve of it. The closer you come to death, the closer you come to my acceptance. The closer you come to my love."

"I—"

"Hush now, young Turi. Your father is speaking. Listen to him. He wants what is best for you."

" . . . to clear the fields, then we will be in the mines. Assuming that I have control of my faculties I will lead us to as safe a place as I can find. I will, if I am capable of doing so, get you some food and water. If I am not able to do so, one of you must. It is possible that, by will alone, you can begin the healing process. However, it is not likely after such a harrowing journey that any of us will have the fortitude to do so. For your body to help you with this fight, you must feed that portion of you which is alive. That means food and water. I can tell you that if you don't get these things soon after we arrive, it is unlikely that any of us will live. Now I have instructed you to eat all your food. If you have hoarded some for whatever reason, know that after crossing the fields of the dead it is unlikely that your food will have made it untainted. Eating rotten food will only push you farther towards death. What guns you have with you may fail. Your clubs may break. Your boots may rot off your feet. Your clothes will rot off your back. Your body will rot from the inside. But you must keep going. You must not let go of that hand. And if you are dismembered, you must hang on by any means that you have left at your disposal."

Arturus saw that Johnny was bent over on his hands and knees. He was lapping up his own vomit with his tongue.

"Do you see that, mother?" Arturus asked the angel.

"Humans are just animals, Turi. There is nothing sad to see there."

"But it's Johnny. He's my friend."

"Abominations don't have friends, Son."

"I think you're wrong. I think he is my friend. I think that he is in a lot of pain. You're an angel. Can't you bless him? Can't you use your holiness to give him some sort of reprieve from Hell?"

"I can," said the angel, "but I choose not to."

"You are very close, Turi," Galen's voice came down to him from where he stood, high on a mountain top over the ceiling. Clouds of mist broke over his shoulders like a wave of water cresting him. "Just a little bit more. Take two more bites and stop. Wait. I will give you further instructions."

Now that Arturus was nearly dead he could hear the corpses better outside. He could feel their wants. He could sense their memories. Many of those memories had been taken away, as if they'd been drinking from the river of forgetfulness. Yes. As if they had drunken from the river Lethe. But some memories remained. Some few. More like impressions of memories. Just the echoes of the great despair they felt.

"I loved a woman," said one.

And it had loved a woman. Arturus wasn't sure where she'd come from or where she'd gone or if the man had been able to marry her or not, but he had certainly loved her. There was an image, a Minotaur above her. Staring down. The man screaming for her to run. But she couldn't, she wasn't fast enough.

"I know you're in there," said another voice. "I will not be fooled. If you come out pretending to be dead, I will follow along with you, and just when you think you are safe, I will strike at you."

"Not me," said another voice. "I need not follow you. You'll die on your way. I'll not spend the effort. You'll join me on your own."

Those must be the wights. The intelligent ones. I hope Galen heard them.

Johnny had been moving the vomit with his tongue. He had pushed it so far across the floor that it had started to climb the wall. Johnny crawled along the wall after it, lapping it up. Avery was there too, defying gravity.

"You can't catch us," Arturus told the wights outside, "we can climb walls."

He felt then the ability to fly, only when he soared upwards his body wouldn't go with him. He decided that he would float through the wall and see the wights.

Don't go far. You know Galen told you not to fly too high. The sun might melt your wings.

Arturus left his body behind and passed through the wall. There they were, the wights. They were inhuman looking. Bulbous faces and rotten appendages came out from all portions of their bent and elongated torsos. Huge black eyes, faceted like a diamond, stared down at him.

"I'm going to eat you," said one.

"I'm going to kill you, and when you are just a wandering corpse, I'm going to take you across the Carrion—no one will bother us while dead—and then I will take you past the barrier and leave you for Rick to find."

Arturus shook his head. "You will not. I will not let you."

"That is enough," Galen said, taking away the corpse's dismembered arm.

"If you are not sure if a thing is real," Galen said, "ask your friend to confirm it for you. Don't tell him what to confirm, because he may then see it as reality—not because it is real—but because you put that thought in his mind. Know also that you can hallucinate his response to your question. It may lead you astray into believing what is false, or disbelieving what is true."

Galen might not even be speaking right now. He could have said that a day ago. An hour ago. He might say that in the future, and I'm just remembering it now, before he says it.

"We are ready," Galen said. "Stand."

On shaky legs, Arturus stood.

"Now take my hand," Galen said.

Aaron grabbed it. Then Avery grabbed Aaron's. Then Kelly grabbed Avery's. Then Arturus grabbed Kelly's. Then Johnny grabbed his.

Outside, the undead called to him, a chorus of wailing voices.

"Follow me," Galen said.

The gate that separated them from the undead was a shaky, brittle thing. The shackles that held it shut might have been strong, but each of the two rusty doors looked as if they might easily break off of their hinges.

Galen took them to those doors.

The corpses on the other side paid him no heed. He unlocked the shackles and tossed them aside.

Arturus remembered what Kelly had said to him once.

Do you like me better chained?

Galen led them into the sea of undead. He could not go quickly because there was barely any room to move. The dead were packed close together, their vestigial breaths filling the air with their sorrow. Arturus could see the dead's memories drifting out of their heads as they forgot them. They could try to hold on to the memories, but eventually they would all fade. One was trying to keep his memories in. Its hands were on his head, but the memories slipped right through his fingers.

"I'm sorry," Arturus told him.

The corpse pointed to Arturus' head, and Arturus saw that he was losing memories too. They were floating away. He saw the one where he'd learned of his mother.

Oh. I liked that memory.

And then another, from when he'd made a mistake and shot a man.

I won't miss that.

But though it would free him from guilt, forgetting that moment would be a horrible thing. Then he might kill someone else again in the future because he couldn't remember the lesson that he'd learned with that man. Then his experience would have been for naught. He would have shot someone and had it mean nothing.

No, I can't forget you.

But the memory floated away.

Every step was a battle. The undead were pressing against him from all sides. Their fingernails, long and yellow and rotten, scraped against his skin. Their lifeless visages passed by him, only inches away, each one more rotten than the last. Pale paper thin skin stretched taut across their faces. Rotted through cheeks revealed the hollows of mouths. Chest wounds showed the grey innards of kidneys and intestines and lungs.

Kelly's hand seemed to be slipping away. He grabbed it tighter. Then it slipped again. He grabbed her around the wrist. She looked back at him. The left side of her face was all rotten, the right, pale beyond possibility—but her eyes were pools of blue fire.

I will not let go. I will love you.

"Even if we die," she said, "don't let go. Let us wander these fields of asphodels for all eternity, hand in hand."

I will not let go. Not even in death.

"I'm following you," said the wight.

No you're not.

"Yes I am."

Ha! I fooled you. If you were a wight, you wouldn't be able to read my thoughts.

"You are very wise."

Wiser than you.

"Don't worry. I will continue to follow you. Sooner or later I will convince you that you are not real. When you are not real, then I will be as real as you, and then I can attack you like I promised."

I will never be a dream.

"So you say. But all men dream. Wouldn't your mother like you better as a figment of her imagination? That's where you can go, if you become a dream. You can go to her and she can dream you, and then maybe she can love you."

Galen loves me. Rick loves me. I don't need a mother's love.

"All people need a mother's love, Turi. Even a dream."

And it seemed very sad that his mother didn't love him. He wanted to cry, but corpse's eyes couldn't cry. That seemed the saddest of all—that the dead couldn't cry. It seemed like they were the ones who needed to the most.

He kept a tight grip on her wrist while Johnny kept clung to his other hand, and together they waded through the undead masses. The tide began to thin. There was space around him, now. Galen was leading them up a hill. Or was it Death? Was Death the leader of their column? Was it he who they followed? How could a man know when death comes to everyone?

The asphodel flowers were brilliant candles of white light at his feet. Red lines of blood ran through the centers of their petals. They were so beautiful. They waved in the wind that was the breath of all the corpses as Arturus and those whose hands he held climbed higher, and higher.

And then, there they were, at the precipice of this hill, looking all around them at the sprawling Deadlands. The fields looked endless. Here and there, more packs of corpses wandered. Some so thick that the dead were forced together, shoulder to shoulder, and there would be no room to move between them. Other packs were looser so that one might wind their way in and out of the crowd. Trees, living dirkenwood trees, shot out from the hills at random places, spreading their dark green leaf laden branches low over the flower pocked grass of the fields.

The ceiling of the cavern dipped low in places, nearly touching the ground, and then soared back up in others. It was as if he was looking at a formation of upside down mountains. Maybe there was another Turi on those slopes, walking upside down.

He saw mist pouring in from one direction. The mists rolled along the hills, spreading out between the trees and covering the asphodels. It rolled over corpses and settled in the flower strewn valleys.

It was in that direction, towards the mist, which Galen led them.

20

Someone has to stop this.

Ellen stood close to Rick at the edge of the crowd of Harpsborough villagers. The balconies of the Fore above were filled with brightly dressed Citizens. No one was horrified. No one was outraged. It just seemed that people wanted to watch this happen.

"They can't let this go on," Ellen said.

"Were you the queen of a city, Ellen," Rick said in a hushed voice, "I would live in it."

"But these people are modern people! They lived in America. How could they do a thing like this?"

Father Klein's words haunted her. Not their meaning, but that he believed them. She had heard people argue like that in the old world. They would defend the uglier parts of the book most people had long since attributed to metaphor. She hadn't thought it was dangerous then. She hadn't understood why anyone would even bother arguing with them—but now she understood.

This is what happens when people like that get power.

"It'll be okay, eventually," Rick said. "It'll heal."

Like that's any excuse.

Martin led Massan up to a woodstone table. "Just be calm, keep your hand as still as possible."

"I'd much rather you do it," Massan replied.

"I wish I could, too," Martin answered. "I've experienced

this, myself. I just can't. Man, I could try, but I can't be a part of this."

Massan nodded.

Ellen turned to Rick. "Please stop this."

"It is beyond my control."

Massan dropped down to his knees and placed his hand on the table. A leather strap was used to hold his hand in place. Men stood nearby with cloths ready, Ellen assumed, to stop the bleeding.

Massan had a calm look on his dark face.

How can he not be afraid?

Graham walked up to the table. He had a cleaver in his right hand. His face displayed a frozen grimace.

At least this hurts him. At least this is a painful thing for him to do.

Massan looked into the crowd. His gaze settled on one place and stayed there. Ellen watched his breast swell. It was as if he was drawing strength from someone.

Kara.

Ellen turned, and indeed, it was Kara that Massan was looking towards. The woman was close to Ellen, not more than twenty feet away. Her hair was a disheveled mess, her eyes were red and puffy, her hands were held over her heart. Kara gave a smile, a smile that conveyed her support.

Massan's head was as still as a statue. He did not move as Graham walked up and stood over him. Massan did not move as Graham raised the cleaver. He did not move when Kara shouted.

"Stop this!" Kara's voice was desperate.

She was crying openly.

A ghost of a smile appeared on Graham's lips, but it quickly disappeared.

You sick bastard. You're enjoying this.

"Go on," Michael called from where he stood on the balcony. "No need to draw it out."

The cleaver descended as Graham brought it down with a shout. It slammed into Massan's wrist and blood went flying from the blow. When he raised the blood splattered cleaver, Ellen gasped.

The cleaver had not severed the hand.

The men who held the bandages jumped forward, but stopped, unsure of what to do. Massan's blood poured out of his wound, but he did not shout in pain. His face held that same calm expression. Kara was the only thing he was looking at.

"Quickly Graham!" Martin shouted.

Graham raised the cleaver and struck again. And when that wasn't enough, again.

Finally the hand came off, and the hunters rushed forward to stop the bleeding. Massan had yet to cry out. Ellen rushed to his side, Rick right behind her. Kara was screaming.

"Are you okay?" Ellen asked Massan.

"No, Ellen. I am not. But I am home. I am with Kara. That is all that matters."

And there was Graham, looming above them. The man was grinning.

I hate you. I hate you, and some day you and all the people like you are going to suffer.

"Quit whistling, Johnny," Avery's voice was harsh.

Arturus looked back at the hunter. The man made noise as he moved, certainly, but that was coming from the odd splint that Galen had placed on his leg. The wood came down farther than Johnny's foot, so that the weight of his body was actually on his knee. The pain should have been unbearable, nonetheless, but perhaps it was hard to feel that kind of pain this close to death. There was, Arturus knew, another more pressing agony closer at hand. It was the feeling of rotting from the inside out. It was the slow push of coagulated blood that dribbled like sludge through Arturus' veins. It was the unreal universes that his mind created and tried to map onto the real one.

"Jesus, Johnny, quiet," Avery's voice was louder this time.

"He's not making noise," Aaron said.

"What? Are you deaf?"

"Focus, Avery," Galen said. "Is it like hellsong? Will the notes follow where you will them to?"

"Yes."

"Then it is not Johnny."

"Well whoever it is had better shut up."

Avery quieted as the dead began to thicken again. The mist

was heavier here. It obscured the ground just a few feet away. Branches pierced it in places, attached to trees that Arturus could not see. The dead came out of the haze, as well. Walking, stumbling, crawling.

Kelly's wrist was so small. He feared that he might break it. He felt his fingers squishing into her skin. It must be hurting her. Arturus looked up to her, but she did not appear to be in distress.

Maybe she cannot feel it.

His fingers touched each other. He looked down and watched in horror as her hand fell to the ground.

Or maybe it's not real.

He was still holding on. Her hand was still there.

"Is that wind?" Aaron asked.

Of course it's not wind. You're losing your mind.

But it *was* wind. It was a cool breeze which brushed across his face. It set the mists swirling about through the trees. He heard the branches creaking and their leaves rustling. Over the next hill he saw the asphodel flowers waving back and forth.

They continued walking.

Ahead was another tree, larger than the rest. The dead became more tightly packed together as they drew closer to it. Nooses dangled down between the leaves. Some were empty, others had broken off so all that was left were frayed ropes attached to the branches. Still others suspended the bodies of the dead. Arturus could tell from their dark uniforms and robes that they were priestesses and soldiers from Maab's army. Their heads were swollen. Their bodies still kicked. Their hands clutched at the air.

Who would do this? Why? Is it even real?

There was no way for him to know.

They had to fight to pass through the dead again. Cold bodies bumped up against his. The sleeve of his black shirt was coming off. Then the corpses started moving as one—like a herd—dragging Arturus and his line along with them. To keep following Galen, he had to push against the crowd. None of the dead were strong individually, but as a mass, their power was formidable.

Or maybe I'm just weak.

It was hard to stay together. He had the hallucination

where Kelly's hand dropped off again, but he dared not let go. Suddenly he was hit from the side by a corpse wearing some sort of metal armor. He lost hold of Johnny's hand, but only for a second. He gripped it harder. Johnny was slowing, but Arturus couldn't let him stay behind. He tugged and he tugged. Finally the press of corpses started to thin.

"Everyone okay?" Galen asked.

No one answered.

The copse of trees in front of them swayed back and forth in the wind. These ones had no leaves.

Arturus looked back. The face behind him was unfamiliar. Long white wisps of hair hung back from a thick jawed dead man. It's eyes were milky white. It did not look like it was going to attack him, but it was very close.

Wait, I'm holding its hand!

He was holding the hand of a stranger.

It was a random corpse he was dragging along with him.

Johnny! I must have lost him.

He looked back into the field of the dead, and there the hunter was, struggling forward with his limping gait.

"Wait!" Arturus said.

The noise brought the attention of the dead all around them. They looked. They pondered. Then they came closer, standing next to the wispy haired man.

Arturus remained perfectly quiet and did his best to breathe shallowly. He waited, and after a few moments the corpses began to wander again.

Arturus felt something grab his hand. He almost shouted.

It was Johnny.

Arturus met his father's eyes.

They began marching again.

The wind died down. Soon after, the mists began to lift. The fields and hills passed by under his feet. Arturus could not say how long it had been since they'd started walking. He just knew that, as far as he could see in any direction, there were more of the asphodel fields. More of the hills and the trees and the dead.

Another crowd was ahead. It was a looser group than the last, and Galen was able to thread their line through its members. Only this one was much larger. They walked and they walked and they walked, and they were still in the midst of the pack. Arturus looked back, and was happy to see that Johnny was still behind him.

We're going to make it.

Ahead of them, standing alone amidst a sea of moving corpses, one of the dead was still. It seemed peculiarly rotten, its skin a jaundiced yellow hue. Perhaps it was so old that it could no longer move. Its head was bowed, as if it might be in prayer, or contemplating some great mystery. It looked familiar somehow.

The other dead parted around it, moving like a river around a rock.

The thing raised its hand, and all of the dead stopped.

Galen stopped too, and so they all halted. Arturus was aware that he and his friends were facing in a different direction than the dead. The wind blew a little, a soft breeze. The branches creaked and the leaves rustled and the last of the mist curled in the air.

It, or something near it, gave a short series of whistles. The tone was not random, but seemed to be part of a melody. The melody seemed familiar somehow. Arturus didn't think it was something that Rick or Galen had ever sung, though. This was something different.

This must be a dream.

No one moved.

The whistle came again.

Arturus looked at all the dead around him. They were as still as statues.

Then the raised hand of the corpse ahead lowered slightly. The other hand, the left hand, came up to cover its heart. It began snapping, slowly and rhythmically.

Then it sang, *"Ezekiel cried, 'Dem dry bones!' Ezekiel cried, 'Dem dry bones!'"*

The corpses all around them raised their hands and began snapping along with the rhythm. The one closest to him had no right hand, but its stub joint waved in the air as if there was a phantom appendage keeping time with the rest.

"Ezekiel cried, 'Dem dry bones!'"

"The fuck is happening?" Avery's half dead eyes looked wild.

Kelly looked back at Arturus. "Galen's gone, hun. I'm sorry.

Your father, he's gone."

But Galen was right there, ahead of them.

What was she talking about? She must be hallucinating.

But then he saw that his father's right hand was snapping to the rhythm of the dead around them. The noise grew in volume as the corpses, all over the nearby field and perhaps all over the entirety of the Deadlands, began to join in. For as far as Arturus could see in any direction, the dead stood still, snapping.

"Oh, hear the word of the Lord."

The yellow corpse ahead of them raised its head from its prayer and opened its eyes—its black obsidian eyes. Now Arturus knew why it looked familiar. This was the wight One Horn had sent into the Deadlands after them.

"The foot bone connected to the leg bone."

Its right foot began to tap against the ground. The motion began to spread amongst the corpses across the fields. The thumping grew louder and louder until it drowned out the breathing of the dead and the creaking of the branches and the rustling of the leaves. The asphodels trembled from the vibrations.

"The leg bone connected to the knee bone." Its voice was growing louder and deeper as if it was drawing strength from the masses around it. The tone was resonant. It shook Arturus' heart along with the vibrations of the stomping feet.

And then the dead changed their movements again. Before, their stomping had been a small, quick motion. Now it became exaggerated. The feet of the dead were rising higher into the air before dropping back to the ground. One of the corpses, unable to stand, lay on the grass, its half leg rising and falling in unison with the rest.

"The knee bone connected to the thigh bone."

And the stomping grew even higher now, each corpse raising their knee up almost to their abdomen before sending their foot crashing down. Galen remained in step with the rest.

"The thigh bone connected to the back bone," the wight sang, its dead voice echoing off the distant hills in the cavern.

It began moving its body from side to side, as if it were mimicking some sort of stiff dance. The pounding of its foot continued, and its swaying motion spread throughout the fields of the dead.

"The back bone connected to the neck bone."

The corpses stopped snapping as one and started slamming their hands together in the same rhythm as the stomp. The dry skin of the undead crashed together, the pop echoing along with the last musical refrain of the thing's voice.

"The neck bone connected to the head bone."

The corpses continued rocking side to side as they clapped and stomped. The one without a right hand acted the same as all the others, perfect in its limbless mimicry. Galen's face was as empty and as blank as all the rest. Somehow Arturus hadn't thought it would come to this. He couldn't imagine that it would have been Galen that succumbed. Then he turned to look at Johnny.

The man was shifting, ever so slightly, from side to side. His hands were twitching as if he wanted to clap.

"No, Johnny. Don't."

"Oh, heeeeeeeeeeear . . ." it sang, its voice louder than Arturus thought was possible, it's tone sending shivers through his body as the stamping rhythm echoed in the hollow of his chest, "the woooooooooooooooooooooooooooooord . . . of the Looooooooooooooooooooooooooooord!"

Its black eyes were opened wide as it started dancing, hopping back and forth from one foot to the other. *"THEM BONES THEM BONES GONNA WALK AROUND!"*

And the dead surrounding them turned and struck. Avery screamed in pain as Aaron fought back with his fists. Arturus drew his sword and started hacking about him. He tried to pull Kelly back, but she tore her wrist free from his grasp, brandishing her shotgun as a club.

Johnny was right behind him. The hunter stumbled into him.

"Damn it, Johnny," Arturus cried, "you're still alive."

"THEM BONES THEM BONES GONNA WALK AROUND!"

Arturus' sword caught on the collar bone of one corpse. Another ran into him, its arms circling around him. Arturus struggled to pull his sword free. There was a loud crack and the one grabbing him fell beneath the walnut stock of Kelly's shotgun. Arturus put his foot against the chest of the corpse before him, jerking his sword free. The collar bone came out with it, but it broke away during Arturus' next stab.

"THEM BONES THEM BONES GONNA WALK AROUND!"

The wight was approaching them, its arms held wide.

Galen was wrestling with Aaron, his body moving in jerks.

It's over.

Aaron pushed Galen's form away with a tremendous heave and then turned to face the wight. Suddenly Galen recovered, spinning on his heel. Galen's forearm snaked across the dead thing's face, turning its head to the side. Galen stepped back, the momentum pulling the wight against him. The hold his father was using on it kept its neck locked to one side, held still against his chest.

Arturus knew that when the human head was turned as far as it could, it could not bend forward. But Galen made it do that anyway, pulling the wight back faster than its legs could allow and then dropping his weight downward. The thing folded under him, sending a giant pop up across the caverns of the Deadlands as its neck broke. Its head now facing the wrong direction, its body crumpled, the wight reached up, trying to grab Galen. Galen ignored it, rolling it to one side, shrugging off the undead that harried him from behind. Arturus rushed to his father's aid, slashing and stabbing to keep Galen safe, unable to take his eyes away. Galen shoved his thumb down into one obsidian eye. Then he pulled the eyeball out.

"Try it, Turi," Arturus' mother said, "use your sword on the wight."

But Galen said old world weapons can't harm it.

"Did you not see the mark of the Infidel on the pommel, young man? Your father taught you better than that. The Roman weapons, they are almost always hellforged."

Arturus touched his father on the shoulder. Galen pulled back, making room. He heard Kelly grunt as she fought to keep a corpse off of him. Arturus stabbed downward. The sword cut through the wight's throat.

I thought you didn't love me? Why would you tell me this?

"Because I'm you, Turi."

The dead kept attacking after the wight stopped moving, but now their assault was uncoordinated. They attacked corpse and human alike, overtaken by some murderous fugue. Johnny had finally regained some of his senses and was trying to stay behind Kelly and Avery. Aaron was using the handle of his pistol to club the corpse that was missing its right hand.

Galen never left me, he was just tricking our enemy!

"Run!" Galen shouted. "Fight and run!"

 — 21 —

Arturus looked back to make sure Johnny was okay. The hunter's splint had come off, so he was moving as fast as he could, limping on his ruined foot.

Arturus found that he could not run in this condition. His body didn't have the coordination for it. He walked desperately forward, slashing any corpse he could reach. Galen had produced a pick from his pack and was brandishing it about. Aaron and Kelly moved in step a few paces back, flanking Johnny and attacking any corpse that came close.

Undead came at Arturus from all sides. Their disfigured, pale faces blurred together into a nightmare of black blood and sunken eyes. Some were missing jaws, others ears, others parts of their skull. There was something about their visages that began to bother him. The tiny pieces of fear they caused started building up in the back of his mind. It was as if the terror was touching him on some preternatural level which he'd never been aware of before.

As often as they attacked him, those corpses attacked each other. They grappled with one another, trampling grass and asphodels.

And then it stopped. It was as if there was some invisible line beyond which the corpses were no longer afflicted with madness.

I'm safe.

Arturus cleaned his blade on the grass and sheathed it. His

shirt was gone. It had rotted off of his back. His pants hung in tatters around his legs. His belt seemed okay, but his boots were marked with dry rot. They probably would not last much longer. He realized he couldn't feel his feet—the death inside him had robbed him of that ability.

Galen had been scratched at some point in the fight. The wound had torn off the dry skin around his cheek. Grey, dead muscle showed from beneath the broad cut. There was also a spot of pink, the evidence that he was still alive.

"Hand in hand," Galen said.

"I can't," Avery said, "can't go on."

Johnny was strangely silent.

He must be too tired to even complain.

"Look there." Galen pointed ahead. "Do you see that wall?"

Avery shook his head.

"Well it's there, Avery. Just ahead. The exits are raised so that the dead can't get out, but I'll help you up. Then we'll be free. We'll be able to descend into the mines of the Carrion. Remember when we were showing Tamara where the rustrock was?"

"Yes."

"It's right there. Then we'll rest. Remember how close it was to Calimay's?"

"Yes."

"That's why we have to keep going."

Avery stumbled and fell to his knees. His pants had rotted away completely, and Arturus saw the horrid black stitches that had been sewn into his manhood. Corpseblood was seeping out of the wound.

Kelly bent down to Avery's ear. "I'm going on, Avery. I'm going to keep on walking. You hate me. If you ever want the chance to get revenge on me for what I did to you, you have got to keep going."

He struggled to stand. Kelly got her shoulder under his armpit and pushed up. Avery came staggering to his feet. They moved together, passing Galen.

Arturus, Aaron, Galen and Johnny followed the struggling pair. The wall beyond got closer slowly, almost imperceptibly so.

Arturus felt like centuries were passing by. Then he noticed that the dead were beginning to pay more attention to them.

They were starting to look their way for longer periods of time. Some even took to following them for a while before losing interest.

"Father," Arturus warned, "we're starting to draw attention."

"That's a good sign," Galen answered. "It means we're coming back to life."

The loose gravel crunched under Ellen's feet.

Home.

She passed Arturus' room—her room, and the hall that led to where Rick stayed. Shortly thereafter, she walked by where Galen had once lived. She entered the battery room. She stepped over the lip that kept out the gravel, crossed the stone floor, and sat down at the door-turned-table. She ran her finger along the woodstone at its edge. Her finger dipped into one of the depressions that had once housed a door hinge.

Ellen put her arms on the table and rested her cheek on her folded hands. She heard Rick approaching across the gravel behind her. He entered the room too. He sat down on one of the seats that had once been a barrel and leaned back against the stone wall. She could hear the gentle squeaking of the waterwheel. Somehow that noise made the place seem more quiet.

"How long will it take Massan to heal?" Ellen asked, her voice cutting through the still air.

"Depends. His will seems very strong now. Those who have the will to live usually heal faster. Perhaps as few as two weeks, or as many as a month. It's hard to tell in Hell. You have to learn your own moods to know how long it will take."

She nodded. There was a piece of gravel on the table. She wasn't sure how it had gotten there. Maybe Alice or Molly, or even Massan, had placed it there. She picked up the rock and used it to trace designs on the woodstone. The wood was lighter under where she moved the rock. For a long while, the sound of the waterwheel and her rock on the woodstone was all there was.

"I didn't like what I saw today," Ellen said.

"I know. You'd be a bad person if you did."

"I mean I really didn't like it." She looked up at Rick.

"We must not do anything rash."

Ellen nodded. "But I'd like to. I'd like to make them suffer. Maybe we could get all the Citizens to agree to trade places with the villagers for a week."

Rick chuckled. "I wish."

Ellen drew a small spiral. It looked sort of like a snail's shell. "We don't have to live here, do we?"

Rick shifted, causing his barrel to scrape across the floor. "It would be hard to replace all that we have. The battery, the waterwheel. Those things weren't easy to build. Without Galen, I don't know how long it would take me to figure everything out. He was the one who made these things."

"But we could replace them, couldn't we?" Ellen asked. "If we worked hard enough and for long enough."

Rick nodded.

"El Cid told me there were Infidel cities. She said they were much better off than Harpsborough. That they were near the populated center of Hell."

"Normally, she'd be right. But there are so few devils here, now, there would probably be more if we headed toward those cities."

"But we *could* go."

Rick closed his eyes and tilted his head back.

Ellen waited for his answer, but he didn't give one. "When you're ready . . . I mean, I know you've spent a lot of time here. I know it's hard for you to let go. But someday you have to. We can go to one of those Infidel Friend cities. You belong with them, Rick. You heard what El Cid said, you're good enough to go into the Carrion. The way you fought that harpy. You're as good as they are, Rick. I don't think anyone else in Harpsborough is."

Rick didn't move.

"Just think about it. Sleep on it. You don't have to answer right away. But tell me this, do the Infidel Friend cities chop off people's hands?"

Rick opened his eyes. "No, Ellen. No, they do not."

"Do they have a rich bunch of fuckers who hide their worthless bodies away from Hell while they make other people withstand the torture that they should be receiving?"

"There is some of that, but it's not nearly as bad."

"Do they have people like Galen?"

Tears began to form in Rick's eyes, but he breathed in deeply and looked up to fight them. Then he blinked a few times, recovering his composure. "No. Nobody has people like Galen. Ever, anywhere."

Ellen stood up and walked around the table. She bent down and kissed Rick as if he was her lover.

His lips were still for a moment, but then he began to respond.

"I'm too young for you," Ellen whispered. "I'm in love with your dead son. In the old world, me kissing you would be so fucked up. Or we would have at least thought it was. But I do love you, Rick. I want you to be happy. I want what's best for you. Of all the people in all of Harpsborough, you're the only one who I figure got cheated when he was sent to Hell. You're too good for this place. Let's find what happiness we can. Let's take it. No one would begrudge us that. Would Galen disapprove?"

Rick shook his head.

"Then this must be the right thing." She kissed him again.

Ellen stood straight and walked back to the doorway. "Think about it," Ellen said. "You don't have to tell me the answer in the morning. Or tomorrow, or the day after that. But someday, let me know if we can find a place where we belong. Where there are people who I wouldn't mind fighting Hell with."

The gravel crunched beneath her again as she walked to the room that had once been Turi's. She entered it and lay down on the blankets he had once used as a bed. She looked up to the stone ceiling that he must have watched on those nights when he couldn't fall asleep.

Ye swore.

He felt dead.

Am I? Did I go too far?

He felt sick inside. In his belly, in his arms and legs. The muscles behind his right eye were an epicenter of pain, shooting wretched waves of agony through his head and down the back of his neck.

"Where am I?" Arturus asked around his dry tongue.

"You passed out," Kelly's voice was weak. "Galen carried you. We're in the silver mines. We're out of the Deadlands."

Arturus' hands were shaking. His stomach felt like it was burning.

"Galen's gone for more food," Kelly said. "Eat this. He told me to make you eat it when you woke. And there's water. But drink and eat slowly. Very slowly. Trust me."

Arturus didn't know if he was famished, or if he never wanted to eat again. He put some of the raw dyitzu meat in his mouth. He could barely taste it on his tongue. He chewed a little, but his mouth erupted in pain. He swallowed, and the meat was fire running down his throat. His stomach churned.

"What's happening to me?"

"Water," Kelly demanded, "just a little."

Arturus drank a sip. It was worse than the dyitzu meat. He felt it sinking into the nerves in his teeth. The pain was more than he could bear. He swallowed it just to get it out of his mouth, but the pain didn't stop. He felt his stomach grumbling.

"What's happening?"

"I don't know," Kelly's small voice belied her tears. "I wish I knew. It hurts so bad. So bad. Maybe it's the dead parts of us. Maybe it's withdrawal. I don't know."

Arturus crawled over to her. The effort it required was mindboggling. He lay down next to her and pulled her close to him. They lay together. They suffered together. They ate and drank measured bites and sips together. They threw up all over each other. But it didn't matter. The vomit and the bile and the tears and the snot, none of it meant anything to Arturus. It was nothing compared to the pain of the death inside him.

Aaron woke up for a while and ate. Then Avery did.

Then Galen returned. He brought more water and another dyitzu body.

"How long?" Arturus asked through clenched teeth. "How long will it hurt?"

In the dim light of the mining cavern, Arturus could see the bright pink of his father's cheek muscle beneath the wound that he'd received.

"I don't know," his father's calm voice said. "It is different for everyone. But as always, my son, the more you want to live, the faster you heal."

Arturus looked to Kelly.

I want to live.

"Has Johnny woken up yet?" Galen asked.

Kelly shook her head. "He's still breathing though."

"Give him another few hours," Galen said. "If he's not up by the time I get back, I'll wake him."

None of Galen's clothing had rotted. Kelly had mentioned that things could be treated to withstand the rot when they were in Nephysis' old lab, and Arturus remembered his father telling him as much when he was younger.

Galen didn't seem to be in any pain, either, though Arturus knew he must be feeling the same things he was. Only Arturus didn't see how it was possible to work or think through this kind of agony.

"Father, how can you still move?"

"You, Turi."

"What?"

"I can move because of you, Son."

"What do you mean? Because I'm an angel's get I give you power?"

"No." Galen shook his head. "I love you very much, Son. Very, very much. And that means that I have a reason to live. Because of you I want to live more passionately than I ever have before. That means I heal quickly."

"I love you, too, Father."

"Now rest, and heal. I have work to do."

"And miles to go before you sleep."

Galen nodded. "Yes, like the poem Rick loves. Miles to go before we sleep."

22

Kelly started to give off warmth. That was around the time Arturus realized that he was freezing. Or maybe he was burning up. He couldn't tell. All he knew was that he was both shivering and sweating. He was hungrier than he had ever been, thirstier than he thought possible, but eating and drinking were tortures beyond his imagination. His hands shook so badly that he could barely open the canteen. His vision was blurred by the pain. Kelly was crying into his shoulder.

Avery lay on his back, his eyes were wide open. He was staring at the ceiling, his jaw clenched. He was breathing heavily enough to send flecks of spittle into the air.

Johnny sat up slowly.

Oh thank God.

"Johnny." Arturus said. "Food. You have to eat"

Johnny struggled to his feet.

"No." Arturus muddled through the pain in his mind to form the words he wanted to say. "Stay down. Your ankle."

But Johnny didn't seem to know where he was. Perhaps he had been fighting for so long, trying to run for so long, he didn't know he was safe.

Arturus gathered his will and forced himself to his feet. The nerves in his body protested so loudly that, for a moment, he couldn't see. But this was Johnny, the only hunter Arturus was sure he loved. He had to help. He picked up a canteen.

Johnny was limping away.

"Wait!" Arturus choked over the word.

Arturus followed after Johnny, each step sending blinding waves of agony through his body. Arturus caught up with the hunter and turned him around.

"Here," Arturus said, offering him the canteen with shaky hands.

Johnny looked at him. Or seemed to. Or maybe looked right through him. He was so pale. His mouth opened and closed. There wasn't a single bit of pink in his tongue or gums or in his mouth.

Maybe it's just too dark.

"Johnny, listen to me."

It's too dark. If it were brighter, I could see the living parts of him. He's not moving like a corpse. He's moving like a person with a fucked up ankle.

Johnny stumbled back. Then the hunter started limping towards him.

It's just the way that he's injured that makes him walk that way. Johnny's fine. He's alive. He's going to make it. Galen would have warned us if he was going to die.

Johnny raised his hands.

He made it through all this. Through the spiders and the Minotaur, the climb and the walk through the dead. He wouldn't come this far only to die now.

The hunter swung, and Arturus ducked under the attack.

"Johnny, wake up!"

He's just in so much pain. He's not dead. He's not dead.

Arturus pushed the humter back, adrenalin giving him some temporary relief from his pain.

"Johnny!"

The hunter fell down stiffly. With arms and legs barely bending, Johnny climbed back to his feet.

"You're not dead!" Arturus shouted. "You're not."

But Johnny was.

Arturus saw his sword lying there next to Kelly. He looked back at Johnny, or rather, at what had once been Johnny.

I'm going to miss you.

Arturus bent down and picked up the sword.

The corpse walked closer towards him.

Arturus shoved the gladius into his friend's chest. Then he

pulled it out. The black blood of a corpse spilled out of Johnny's body as it fell to the floor.

Arturus dropped the sword. It clattered against the stones.

He lay down beside Kelly and cried.

From Neostoicism: Philosophia

Whether you kill an old man or a young man, you take from him just the same—you take from him the present.
—*Marcus Aurelius*

Pause, for a moment, and imagine your own death. Try hard, dig deep. Make yourself face your own mortality. I'll wait. Does it disturb you? When you have done this, imagine what ills, what evils scare you more than death. Those things, the ones worse than death, those are the things worth fighting.
—*Ares*

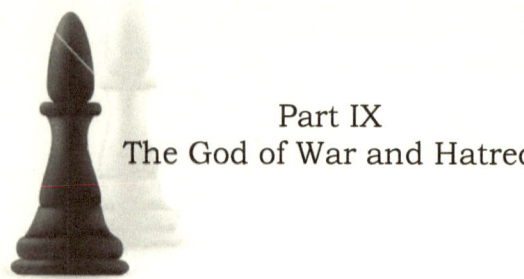

Part IX
The God of War and Hatred

From Gehennic Law: The Court Swallow

There was once a young bird who, when fluttering through the skies, sought a place where she could build her nest and lay her eggs. It was such trouble, building a nest, and it was very difficult to find a warm, dry place to put it. So she flew over the human city of Athens and descended upon the roof of their court building. The roof seemed steady, and it was waterproof, so she thought that it must be a place of perfect shelter.

"Whosoever has built this place will not mind if I rest here for a while," she thought.

She flew into the building and found that the Athenians had placed straw along the roof as insulation. Happy then, she landed and, with minimal effort, made her nest there. So it came to pass that this was the place where she laid her eggs—then she waited for them to hatch.

While she was waiting, she listened to many law cases and enjoyed seeing justice dispensed. She began to feel that this court building was the most important of all the buildings in Athens, and that it was, in a way, a pillar which supported their society.

Then one morning she flew out to find some food, leaving her eggs safe in their warm and sheltered space.

But there was a rat who had also found shelter in the court building. It was dry and safe for him as well, and the men who came there often left crumbs for him to feast on.

Seeing that the swallow had left, the rat climbed up a pillar and ate the swallow's eggs.

Then it so happened that the swallow returned and saw that her eggs had been eaten.

She bemoaned her fate and shouted up to the uncaring gods, "Oh what unfairness has been visited upon me, that such injustice strikes my family in this house of law."

.

He had a body, clad in a grey robe. He hadn't during the fall from Benson's ladder.

I'm not bleeding.

It had finally stopped. He wasn't sure how long he'd bled—but at the moment, he was unable to remember a time before he'd borne the wound. Certainly he'd been bleeding through the entirety of his last life. But there was an earlier time, a time before he'd been stabbed, he knew there was—only the memory seemed distant. Far, far distant.

He was lying on a black plain. It was featureless, smooth and endless, expanding out from him in all directions towards some invisible horizon. There was light which he could see by, but it seemed wrong somehow. It reflected oddly off the blackness around him.

Am I the source?

Perhaps he was, but he wasn't glowing. Carlisle struggled, climbing up to his hands and knees.

Where am I? What Hell is this? Should I even call it Hell?

His early memories—maybe they could tell him what was going on, but they were so distant. He remembered Benson and Mephistopheles and Simeon. Those faces were fresh, crisp in his mind. But there were other faces, faces from long ago. The Infidel, for one. Maab, for another. But there were other memories even farther back than that. Memories of a cornfield—of Anna McNamara. He tried to remember how she had looked on the day he had sodomized her, but the memory was too far distant. It was as if he was looking at her through fogged glass.

She was bearing my child. She died, and the child died with her.

The light started to bug him. There was something wrong with it, but he couldn't figure out what. He waved his hand in front of his eyes. He saw the light whirl a little.

That's what's wrong!

He had seen light move before, in a way, but it had always been an illusion. It had been fog, or glass, or something else that had actually been moving. This was different. He actually saw the light *itself* move. It was almost imperceptible, because it was so fast, but he could see its minute oscillations as it sped through the air. If he ignored that, then he could see normally.

Whatever substance was beneath him, it was not rock. He bent down and pushed against it with his fingers. At first the blackness gave a little, but the harder he pushed, the more firm it became. He could make a depression about an inch deep, but nothing more than that.

He didn't know where to go, so he picked a random direction.

After a few steps, he stopped. This was not a featureless plain at all. In places there was a ceiling, or a wall, or some combination of the two. They were formed out of odd geometric shapes which met each other at clean lines. Between those lines he could occasionally catch glimpses of some world that lay beyond this one.

It was full of brilliant colors—reds and blues and purples and greens, each intermixing with the others. He saw living beings in that fluid. They were in agony, their bodies being rent in one direction or another. The agony did not seem natural, and Carlisle could feel the pain of their torture as if their discomfort were heat from a flame.

As he walked, however, he began to doubt that the colorful Hell he thought he saw was real—or if it was real, that it was real in a sense that Carlisle wasn't familiar with. Each time he got a chance to see under or over one of the cracks, the sea of colors wasn't there.

He saw a person, dressed in a grey robe, lying down on the black plain. Carlisle wandered towards him. There were others near the man, perhaps a dozen, all dressed the same way. It was the way Carlisle himself was dressed.

The man saw him and raised a finger to his lips. He motioned for Carlisle to come closer. Carlisle had no other course of action but to accept the man's invitation.

"Don't move," the stranger whispered. "Lie down and keep quiet. Do you know where you are?"

Carlisle shook his head.

"You are very lucky my friend. You have fallen into the space between two Hells. We are not supposed to be here. Kaider, over there, has enough power from Aezcherbaelyn to keep us alive."

"How long must I stay quiet?" Carlisle asked. "How long must I lay here?"

"Forever."

Carlisle balked at the idea. "Surely we must . . ."

The man shook his head. "I'm not sure what Hells you have been through, young man, but believe me, an eternity of silence is an embarrassment of good fortune. And take care, if you call attention to yourself, you will destroy us as well. You will expose us to the demons in there." The fellow pointed towards one of the cracks. "That is where I fell from, young man. Trust me, silence without torture, it might as well be Heaven."

How has it come to this?

Carlisle lay down on the black floor. There was a woman across from him. She looked at him with pleading eyes.

Stay silent, those eyes said. *Stay still.*

So that's what Carlisle did. And he waited, though he knew not for what.

23

Upon awakening for the second time, Arturus regretted being alive. He hadn't imagined that such pain was possible. Galen had told him that he was in an unnatural state—that in the old world it wouldn't have even been possible to stay alive like this, and that the pain was the only way his body knew how to process its current condition.

He had been hurt, he had been hopeless, he had been almost down, but he had never experienced anything like this before. The closest he'd ever come was when, in his childhood, he'd fallen during one of Galen's climbing lessons and crushed his teeth on a rock. The exposed nerves had given him a sensation beyond excruciating agony. It was like that, now, except all over his body. He hadn't imagined such misery was possible.

He was ashamed of this, but in the throes of his pain, Arturus wished for death—only he was too hurt to do anything more than think about it.

Maybe it wouldn't be so bad if I just drifted off?

Then it passed. Oh, the pain remained, but he no longer wished to die. It was okay, Galen had taught him, to have moments of weakness. As long as you survived them, they let you know where your weak points were.

If that's my weakness, unimaginable pain, I guess I'm doing alright.

He had always believed, in those days when he'd lived

outside of Harpsborough, that he had an unbreakable spirit. The Carrion had destroyed that petty illusion, again and again.

It wouldn't be possible to withstand such agony and stay strong.

He thought this, but he knew immediately it was not true. Somehow Galen had.

All these people care that I'm the son of an angel, but they missed the point. Her blood might have diluted his.

The thought was amusing. It hurt to laugh, but not so badly now that the worst had passed. He was recovering more quickly than Aaron or Avery or Kelly. They were just now entering the horrific phase he was leaving.

Maybe I should be proud of how fast I'm healing. My will is strong.

Galen entered. He met Arturus' eyes and nodded towards the others. "How are they doing?"

"The pain is coming to them. They're all tough. They'll stay quiet."

Galen nodded, considering this. "I believe you are right about that. It should only be a few hours until the worst passes and the withdrawal kicks in."

"I remember it being longer."

"So will they," Galen said. "We'll move shortly."

"Oh? Are we in danger?"

Galen shook his head. "No, we are lucky. Some of Calimay's people are in the mines nearby us. They are gathering the rust rock."

Finally, we've had some good luck.

Arturus wanted to tell this to his friends, but the person he wanted to share his joy with most was Johnny.

Why did Johnny die and the rapist live?

"I'll tell them," Arturus said.

"Good, I shall sleep. Wake me when their pain passes."

"How long has it been, Father, since you've slept?"

Galen shrugged. "I do not know, Son."

"Your clothes didn't rot."

"They've been treated."

"You withstood La'Ferve's bullets."

"Body armor."

"You recover too quickly."

"My will."

Arturus stood. "Are you the angel?"

Galen cocked his head, regarding him for a moment. Then he smiled. "No," he laughed. "I am human, Son. And so are you. And someday, when you are grown, men will look at you and ask you why you heal so quickly, and why you are so well equipped and so well armored. They will ask you why you don't need as much sleep as them. And do you know what you will tell them?"

"No."

"You will tell them goodnight."

Galen set his pack against the uneven mine wall. He lay down, closed his eyes, and fell almost immediately to sleep.

Arturus heard a whimper behind him. He looked back. It was Avery. Tears were pouring out of his eyes.

Arturus sat down next to him.

Avery grabbed him with a shaky hand. His eyes were wild. Foam was collecting around the corners of his mouth. "He—lp me . . . please . . ."

Arturus gripped Avery's hand back firmly and met the hunter's desperate gaze. "I have been there," Arturus told him, "and I know there is nothing I can say to make you feel better. All I can tell you, Avery, is that this will pass. Do you hear me? This too shall pass."

"That's—from the Bible."

"Is it?" Arturus didn't know. "I remember it from a story."

Avery's half dead body shook. "Tell . . . me."

"I'm not good with—"

"*Tell me!*"

Arturus nodded. "Galen told it to me long ago. There was once a Sultan, and he was afflicted with powerful emotions. They were feelings so strong that they drove him to distraction. There was a mania that made him think he was invincible, and a depression that made him think he was so worthless he couldn't even be bothered to kill himself. He went to his Magi and asked for them to make a ring, filled with magical power, which would make him sad when he was happy, and happy when he was sad. As a reward, the Sultan promised that he would marry the Magi's daughter who cured his malady.

"Now the least of the Magi was a man Ferdowsi, and

Ferdowsi went home to his daughter and told her of the Sultan's reward. Now the daughter wanted to marry the Sultan very much, and she told her father that he must make this ring. The father lamented, saying 'it is beyond my power.' His daughter replied that philosophy was more powerful than magic. She asked that he make a simple gold ring and give it to her, and that she would make the enchantment herself.

"Now Ferdowsi knew better than to laugh at his daughter, for she was very wise, so he forged the ring and gave it to her. She spent the night with it and returned it to him in a locked box.

"On the next day . . . Avery? Avery!"

Avery's body was shaking uncontrollably. He pissed and shit himself. The foam at the corners of his mouth spread, running down his cheeks.

Arturus leaned in close and held him.

Avery shook his head, suddenly furious. He pushed Arturus back with weak arms and looked over to Kelly.

"Are you okay?" Arturus asked.

"*I'm fine!*" He managed to say through clenched teeth, his gaze still on Kelly. "So long as your . . . your fucking girlfriend lives, I'm living, too. I hate her. I fucking hate her, Turi. I'm going to do such terrible things to her. I am."

Arturus grabbed the hunter's hand more tightly. "Yes. Live for that, Avery."

Avery's eyes lost their focus. "What happened?"

"What do you mean?"

"To Fedor, what's . . . his name? His daughter. What happened?"

"Avery . . ."

"*Tell me!*"

Arturus nodded.

Avery's breaths were coming in a series of little jerks. His eyes were squeezed tight against the unbearable agony that Arturus himself had gone through only hours before.

"So all the powerful Magi gathered and presented the Sultan with their rings. Each one was more magnificent than the rest, and Ferdowsi could see that they were imbued with powerful enchantments of a nature that he could never hope to match. But each one failed. Finally the Sultan came to

Ferdowsi's. The Sultan had come to him last because he knew Ferdowsi was the weakest of the Magi, and he knew that the man's ring would most likely be a failure. He unlocked the box and he took out the ring.

"There was no magic on it at all. It just had an inscription. It said 'this too shall pass.' So the Sultan put it on and married Ferdowsi's daughter."

Avery was still shaking. "Is it true?"

"I don't think so. I think most old stories are lies. I think the truth is in the lesson."

"No, I mean . . . is philosophy—stronger . . . than magic?"

"Of course," Arturus said, "philosophy is real."

Avery turned over on his side. Aaron was whimpering too, now.

Thank God this hasn't happened to Kelly yet. I don't know if I could withstand her suffering.

He looked over to her. She had her back turned to him, but she wasn't in agony yet. He walked over to her and knelt beside her.

He was wrong, she was in pain. Tears streamed down from her eyes. She looked at him. She was angry, as angry as he'd ever seen anyone be.

"My love," he breathed.

"The Devil will pay," she spat.

"I'm sorry."

"You went through this?" she asked.

"I did."

She nodded, the muscles standing out on the edges of her clenched jaw. "Yes, the Devil will pay. No one gets to hurt you like that, Turi. No one. I'll break his soul for you."

Arturus was taken aback by her passion. By her protectiveness. By how similar she seemed in that moment to his father.

"This too shall pass," Avery was whispering. "This too shall pass." He chanted it again and again, his arms crossed over his belly while he lay in a fetal position, rocking back and forth.

Aaron screamed for a second before clamping his hands over his mouth.

Arturus looked at Johnny's body.

At least you didn't have to go through this, friend.

24

Galen led them through the mines.

Woodstone planks, the Devil knew how old they were, supported the walls and the ceiling of the hellstone tunnel. In places, the beams of the roof bowed under the weight of the stone above them. Piles of rubble lay along some of the branching corridors, letting Arturus know exactly what would happen if one of those woodstone planks over his head were to give way.

Avery had one arm over Arturus' shoulder and the other over Aaron's. Kelly took up the rear. Arturus kept his sword in his left hand, trying to keep it pointed away from Avery. He could feel his bone handled razor in the right pocket of his pants.

His pants had almost rotted away and his boots had fallen apart completely—so now he walked barefoot.

Aaron's clothes had fared no better, and Avery was naked except for the thin remains of his shirt. For some reason Arturus could not fathom, Kelly's robe was still in one piece, and of course, his father's treated clothes and armor showed no signs at all of their march through the Deadlands.

Galen stopped for a moment.

Aaron shook his head. "In the name of the Lord, don't be lost."

"Hell," Avery said, "be lost. Just don't say you heard something."

"It's okay," Galen said, "just echoes."

"You sure?" Kelly asked.

Galen turned back, grimacing. "You want an answer?"

She shook her head.

The next time I'm surrounded by corpses, I'll just die. Easier that way.

Galen led them down a long, dusty ladder to a lower level.

The woodstone supports seemed weaker here, and every so often, a collapse forced them to double back.

If a settling comes . . .

Arturus thought he heard voices. He froze.

"It's okay," Galen said without turning around. "Those are Calimay's people."

The voices grew louder as they approached.

"Galen," Arturus' father reported. "I'm coming with four men."

"Understood," a voice called back. "We won't shoot."

One of Calimay's purple robed priestesses was sitting in a bubble of soft blue light that was emanating from a skystone vein. Around her were a couple of soldiers dressed in black and grey. There were sounds, though distant, of picks chipping at the stone.

They must have slaves down there.

Calimay's priestess stood. "Oh Mithras, you all look bad."

Arturus tried to grin at her, it didn't work. He and Aaron lowered Avery to the ground.

"I told you, we had to eat corpsedust to survive the Deadlands," Galen said.

She nodded. "But I'd no idea that . . . that it was this bad."

"You smell, too," one of the soldiers said. "We'll have to bathe you before we try to trek home. Yesterday our scouts detected a Minotaur on the loose. He had stone wights in his thrall."

"He didn't have one horn missing, did he?" Aaron asked.

The soldier nodded. "Crafty bastard. Calimay has traps set up throughout the wilds. We had to lead him into one to shake him."

Galen looked to Arturus for a second. "He followed us all the way to the City of Blood and Stone and back. He's the one that chased us into the Deadlands."

"I don't like the bullmen," the soldier went on, "they're all crafty. They're all holy horrors. But this one, this one is different. This one is worse."

Kelly opened her canteen before draining it. "That's the truth."

"He may have been the one that issued the call," Galen said.

"No call, friend," the soldier disagreed. "Not from the City of Blood and Stone, at any rate. Devils would have gotten lighter around us, not thicker."

"That depends," Galen answered.

"On what?"

"On how big the call was."

The priestess snorted. "You can scare the shit out of yourselves in the morning. In the meantime, get some rest. There is a river down that path. I suggest you all bathe before you sleep."

Hell seemed different to Martin this morning. He had fallen asleep next to Katie. She was gone when he awoke.

Who knows how long I slept?

He hadn't noticed the difference at first. He only noticed it when he pushed aside the door curtain and said bye to Reginald.

The buildings were all the same, of course. The Fore balconies didn't have any Citizens on them, but that was pretty normal these days. The right amount of villagers were around. They weren't doing anything special, but something was different.

Or maybe it's me who's different.

He had said things to Michael that he could not unsay. Michael might pretend not to hold that against him, but the First Citizen would now know where his heart lay.

He knows how much I hate the Fore.

Martin wandered towards the building that housed the people he hated. He stopped for a moment and looked at where they'd severed Massan's hand. The table was gone, but some of the blood remained. That blood had dried to form the edges of an empty square where it had dripped down the table leg. In other places it had dried in long shooting lines. He knelt down over the smooth stone floor and looked at the texture. There was grit all over the floor, grains of sand tracked in from the wilds along with the dust of clothes and skin. The blood had drawn the grit into little lumps so that it looked like curdled black milk.

Martin shook his head.

He took it well, though. Hell, he took it a shit ton better than I did.

Some of the villagers nodded at him as they passed by. People looked at him differently now. He was a leader. He was the guy that fed the people. He was the guy who conquered the corpsemen.

I wish I felt different.

He stood up from where the blood had been spilled and continued around the Fore. He let out a hopeless sigh before plopping down on the stone next to ole Bense.

I wonder if he's even noticed that I haven't talked to him in a while?

"The hell, man," Martin told Benson, "what do you mean you don't know? You've been avoiding me. I ain't talked to you in ages."

There was some shouting coming from the other side of the Fore. At first Martin was alarmed, but then he realized it was just a lover's spat.

"Don't say it's all my fault!" Martin said to Ole Bense. "Don't give me that shit. Just because I'm acting Lead Hunter doesn't mean I let it go to my head. And I sure as hell haven't forgotten 'bout you man. Sure. Sure I've been spending time with Hidalgo, but that's fighting stuff, you know. If you're going to get jealous about it, you might as well just get up and come fight with me. I thought not. So it's settled then, it's your fault."

The fight of the lovers ended with the girl leaving. Martin saw her run across the village, dodging between hovels. She made it to the chamber's exit and ran out into the wilds.

"Sarah!" the boy shouted after her.

Martin watched him run by those same hovels.

"Shit man, I know what that guy feels like," Martin told Benson. "But I need to talk to you. I need to talk to you bad. I've been through some serious shit. I know you've heard about the Kyle-thing. I'm scared, Bense. I'm real scared. And the worst part is, you know, that I can't tell nobody about it. I have to be all strong and shit now. I can't tell nobody but you."

Benson's still, lifeless eyes stared out across the village.

"Oh, you're worried about the couple?" Martin asked. "Don't worry, they'll be fine. Katie and I are like that, too. Sometimes. But we manage, you know. We manage. Look, I've got to tell you what I've been thinking. That Kyle-thing, it got in my head. It's fucked me up, deep down. I think the whole battle did, really. I was scared, Bense. I was scared like a leader can't let themselves be, you know. But Chelsea, she brought me out of it. She brought me . . ."

Martin stopped mid sentence and stared at Benson more closely. "She brought me . . ." He wanted to say more but he couldn't. Benson's eyes were the same as ever, just as shrunken. Just as lifeless. His cheeks were just as hollow. He was a man with the stilling, after all.

No. Please not this.

The staring eyes were dry. The man's emaciated chest was still.

"Bense?"

Martin leaned forward, putting a hand in front of the still man's mouth. He felt nothing. He pushed a little on Benson's chest. No response.

Martin felt as if he'd had the wind knocked out of him. He let his head fall back against the stone wall of the Fore.

Ole Bense had died.

Molly found Cris more intimidating, more intriguing, than any man she'd ever met. It had been easy, as they crept through the Carrion, for her to avoid speaking to him. Now, however, while they sat and waited for the coming of their contact—supposedly safe in this stone room—she was drawn to him. She wasn't looking at him, but she could feel where he was.

I should talk to him.

The idea scared her in a way that crawling through the Carrion did not.

What would I say?

She had every right to talk to him of course. He wouldn't think less of her. Hell, he owed her at least that much for crossing half of Hell to deliver his message. Even more so because now she was going to become an infidel herself. He should at least be okay with talking to her, even if he didn't want to sleep with her.

But there was danger, too. He and El Cid had something. An understanding, perhaps; a past, definitely—and maybe something more. Realistically, Molly wasn't sure how anyone, let alone herself, was going to be able to compete with a force like El Cid. The girl moved mountains. She fought bare handed against harpies and won. The infidels, even Cris, leapt to do her bidding. And she had that human shadow, that blond haired six-foot-plus Adonis of death they called Aiden, following at her heel.

Aiden is Cris' son, but is El Cid his mother?

Molly stood up, ducking her head to avoid hitting the low ceiling, and walked down the narrow chamber, passing the infidels. She sat down next to Cris.

Cris glanced up at her from the M-16 he was cleaning before looking over towards where Aiden stood watch at the room's exit.

Molly realized her hands were shaking, so she put them behind her in the small of her back and let her weight push them into the stone. "How long do we wait?"

Cris shrugged and then went back to his work. He was brushing out the trigger mechanism. "Malkravyan will be along. There was probably trouble, if he's this late, but I would trust him to come out on top of it."

"That Minotaur we saw? The one with one horn?"

Cris shrugged again. "Could be."

"Aiden seems very close to El Cid."

Cris held the trigger mechanism up, though there was very little light, and examined it. "She helped raise him," He held the trigger closer to his eyes and peered at it. "since he was a young man."

"She's not his mother?"

Cris shook his head and started to reassemble his weapon. "No. Aiden's mother fucked him up. Nearly turned him into a wight. You have no idea how hard I had to fight to save him. El Cid made that possible."

"Your son is very beautiful," she said, and then immediately regretted it.

He shrugged for a third time. "I breed well."

She laughed softly. "Do you think if we had a child, he would look as good?"

Cris grinned slyly. "A gentle touch, you show, when you like a guy."

Her heart froze in her chest.

He's an infidel. They speak openly and honestly about things that we would only hint at. I said nothing out of line, and nor did he.

"You and El Cid, do you love each other?"

"Off and on," he answered.

"Is there room, in your heart, for another?"

Cris folded up the cloth kit which held the tools he'd used to clean his rifle. He tucked it into his pack.

He did not, however, answer.

"I crossed Hell for you," she said. "I went and found an Infidel Friend, just like you asked. I brought them back while you healed. I abandoned everyone I knew for you. My entire village, my best friend. I need to know if it was a good choice."

She looked intently at Cris, but it was Aiden's whisper which came to her ears.

"He's coming."

Now? He had to come now?

"They would be," Cris said.

Molly wasn't sure what he was talking about. "What?"

"Our hypothetical child, I think they'd be as beautiful."

 — 25 —

Julian's soul was like the pick, and Selena, she was like the rock. She thought she was hard, she thought her faith was strong, she thought that she was in control—but that was just because she'd never met true faith. True faith was like steel.

He thought of this as he slammed his pick against the stone. In the beginning, his hands had formed blisters. Those blisters had bled, making the handle hard to grip. The pain had driven him mad. But now his hands were as rough as cured dyitzu skin.

In the beginning, he had hit the rock as hard as he could with every blow. It had taken so much out of him. He didn't understand how the others could work for so long, but now he knew the secret. Now he knew that he didn't have to swing hard, just fast, and that the weight of the pick would do all the work—and just like his faith would make mincemeat of Selena's belief in Ahuramazda, so too did the rock crumble into rubble beneath his rapid blows.

Brother Jeremy was coming. He was the only Christian that Julian knew of on this detail, though he thought there might have been others. There was an empty wicker basket in his hand. He stumbled and fell. Nearby, one of Selena's darkly dressed soldiers stood watch. Julian hurried to Jeremy and helped him to his feet.

He must be near exhaustion.

"Are you okay, brother?" Julian asked him.

But when he saw Jeremy's face he knew the man was not tired at all.

Jeremy gripped Julian's wrist so hard it hurt. "George has been taken to a Little Lady," he whispered. "They suspect him of fostering a rebellion."

Julian felt cold. A shiver ran along his body from his feet to his shoulders. He wanted to ask Jeremy more, but that soldier was looking right at them. Julian watched his fellow Christian walk away. Jeremy was still feigning tiredness, but when he glanced back, Julian saw only worry in the man's eyes.

Julian did his best to return to his work as if nothing was wrong, but his pick seemed heavier, slower. His heart was a stone in his chest, refusing to beat hard or fast enough. His fingers were tingling and his arms felt weak.

Jeremy had been terrified, but he hadn't looked hopeless. That was because he didn't know about George. Jeremy thought George was a man of faith, but Julian knew he was a pretender. No matter how strong George's convictions, they would be nothing compared to the torture of a Little Lady. Julian had been through that horror himself. No, George only thought he was strong, but he had no spirit. No real strength. The body was *weak*. Even to Julian, who had given himself over completely to the Lord, the calling of home and honey had nearly caused him to give up on his friends and flee. Without that armor of Faith, George would crumble. He would give them all up.

Poor George. I wish you had listened. I wish you had found God.

Julian felt the steel of his soul inside him. He felt the invincibility it offered.

Come what may, I am yours, Lord. Let them do their worst. I am dedicated to you. My soul is in your keeping. They can destroy my body, but my heart will be yours, forever and ever, amen.

As he worked on through the rest of the day, he felt a deep sorrow in his heart—not for himself, but for George. It seemed terrible that the man could have been so close to true happiness, and yet eschew it. If he had just opened his heart's eyes, not his mind's, he would be invincible. George was a good man, he truly was. He wanted what was right for people—but he was only a man. Human beings couldn't face things like that. They didn't have the will.

The flesh is weak.

Now they would all pay for George's lack of faith.

And then the shift was over. The soldiers came, as they did every day, and took them away. By this point George would have broken. At any moment, Selena's men would come for him.

The flesh is weak.

He had been assigned to one of the lower rooms. These were the darkest and usually where the Kruks preferred to hunt. Julian didn't have the energy to resist when one of the cruelest Kruks, Edmond, and his gang came to him. Julian let them strip him bare and turn him over. There were only three of them, so he knew it wouldn't take too long.

They pushed him into a corner and bent him over at the waist. He let them pound him rhythmically into the wall, but he made no sound.

The flesh is weak, but I am the pick, and you, Selena, are the rock.

 — 26 —

Kelly had waited for Aaron and Arturus to finish bathing before she came to the river. She wanted privacy.

Only Avery hadn't washed so far, but it hadn't looked like he was going to wake up any time soon.

Her robe was so threadbare she figured it would be see-through in bright light. Her clothes beneath the robe were in tatters. She doubted that she would even bother to put them back on after she took them off. Her shoes had worn so thin in the soles that she could feel the texture of the rock through them, and at one point, under the ball of her left foot, she could feel the cool stone of the floor directly.

She shrugged off her robe and what was left of her shirt fell in tatters to the ground with it. Her pants were a few strips of rotten cloth attached to her waistband. With a negligent gesture, she tore them off, feeling then the cold air of the Carrion on her skin. Goosebumps rose on the parts of her flesh which were alive.

The rush of the water was calming.

For a moment she closed her eyes.

I'm ready. I can do this. I just have to be strong.

Even so, she hesitated. She opened her eyes and stared up at the ceiling.

Just be strong.

She looked down at her rotten body.

Flakes of skin were peeling off her arms. Dark splotches of

necrotic tissue covered her over, looking worse than any rash she'd ever seen. Blackened pus was leaking out of her body in places. Around those dead patches, the skin was wrinkled—not like she'd spent too much time in the water—but as if she had the skin of a woman succumbing to old age. She could not even make out her belly button through the decayed mess of her abdomen. There was an open pocket there, an abscess maybe an inch deep, where her body had rotted out completely.

I can't let Turi see me like this.

The water was swift enough to distort her reflection, a fact for which she was grateful. She tried dipping her toe into the water, but she couldn't feel it at all, so she lowered her leg deeper.

Suddenly she could feel the cold water on her naked nerves, and the agony knocked the wind out of her. She yanked her foot out, collapsing to the ground and fighting to hold in a scream.

So much pain.

She closed her eyes again.

Be strong.

She tried a second time, this time letting her body descend slowly into the water. For all she could tell, she was descending into a pool of fire. Tears ran freely down her cheeks as the pain covered her over. She let her head descend beneath the surface, and for a moment, she was alone with her agony. There was nothing else in Hell but herself and the wretched, insidious and all consuming sting of the cold water on her half dead flesh.

This is what it is to be alive.

She felt the sludge that was the mix of human and corpse blood thin in her body from the sudden power of her beating heart.

This is my fire. When the fire is done burning, only I will remain.

She felt the dead skin washing away from her limbs. She stayed beneath the water until the pain had dulled. Then she surfaced. With her back still to the bank, she pulled herself out of the water. Parts of her skin looked restored, and she could see places on her arm where her typical ivory coloring had returned. In other places, however, the dead flesh had become swollen, bloating like a dead body might. She saw, as she inspected her arm, a single dark hair. It made her think of Turi.

She heard the scrape of a boot behind her.

I'm not alone.

She turned around.

There were three men there, dressed all in grey.

Calimay's serfs.

They looked hungry. They began to disrobe.

Kelly stood to face them. "Try it," she said, her voice wavering a little. "I'll break you."

She wasn't sure if she could in her current condition—and if they were to do this thing, they would probably have to kill her anyway. Nothing said that the murder had to come *after* the rape.

"Oh, no," said one of the slaves, "we weren't going to use flesh."

He held up his pick.

I should have expected this. Calimay's rape culture is as strong as Maab's, only here I have no authority.

Wounded and weaponless, a priestess without protection, she was the perfect outlet for these serfs' frustrations.

Avery limped into the room. "Well I'll be." He crossed his arms and regarded her.

The men turned in alarm, but Avery only had eyes for Kelly.

"Miss, I'll be honest with you," his lips curled into a sneer, "I've been in Hell a long time. In that time I've seen a lot of corpses. A lot of 'em. But I ain't never seen one I wanted to fuck before." He turned to the slave which had threatened her. "Give me that pick."

The slave held it closer to his chest.

Avery limped up to him. "Look at me, sonny. You see the shit I've been through? Look at my cock, you Calimay-whipped son of a bitch. You see those stitches? You see them? You know who did that to me?" Avery pointed at Kelly. "Now maybe you fuckers are used to having your pecker ripped up by little girls, but where I come from, that shit just don't happen." He looked back to Kelly for a second. "And it's time for her to pay the piper. Now give me the God damned pick."

The slave held it out. Avery took it from the slave only a moment before burying the sharp end into the slave's head.

"Run!" he shouted to Kelly.

Kelly dove into the back of one of the slaves, knocking him

over, sending his pick clattering across the stones. She grabbed it and bludgeoned the fallen slave as she moved to stand next to Avery.

She couldn't imagine how horrible they must look, standing there, her naked and Avery mostly so, each a little more than half dead.

Kelly recognized the last of them. She had sat near him, once, while they had feasted on the dyitzu Galen had brought back to Calimay's complex.

How quick we go from civilized to barbaric.

She and Avery advanced towards the man, each coming at him from a different angle. He tried to flee, heading for the water, but Kelly threw herself at his feet. He toppled over her. Then Avery was there, pick held high. He swung the flat end of the pick into the base of the man's neck. Then he repeated the strike, but with the sharp end.

Kelly looked at the three bodies. For a moment, she was worried that she might have shed enough corpsedust to make them rise—particularly the one she had tripped—but their bodies lay still.

I just bathed, and Avery didn't touch them.

She looked up to Avery. "Why? Why save me?"

His pick fell to the stones at his feet. He crossed his arms. "Frankly, you fucking whore-bitch, I would have enjoyed watching them ram those picks up your dead cunt. But Turi's fond of you. I wouldn't want him to be broken up about it."

She shook her head and stepped closer to him. "You're lying to me."

"I hate you. I have no reason to lie to you."

"I don't believe you," she said.

"Another step forward, whore. We'll find out."

She sneered. "You have to keep on lying, because if you admit for one moment that I'm a human being, then you have to admit that you're a rapist."

Avery's arms uncrossed. "I'd never rape a real woman."

Kelly swallowed. She grabbed the pick and offered it to him. "I need to tell you something. You just showed me mercy. You had me dead to rights, and you showed me mercy. You had *power* over me, but I can't say what I need to say unless you *still* have that."

Avery took the offered pick and held it over his head. He was as angry as Kelly remembered seeing any man.

"I know you don't hate me." Kelly said. "I know you're more angry at yourself, and that you're hiding it," she started.

"You fucking have no—"

"You think you're the only one?" She shouted, dropping to her knees and putting her hands behind her back so that she was helpless before him. "You raped me because you couldn't think of me as human. Big fucking deal. What, you kind of raped *one* woman? One! Do you have any idea what I'm responsible for? Where I served as priestess, I had over a hundred people who worshiped me at any given time. I had soldiers and slaves, and not a one of them had any choice when I came for them. Not one."

Avery's eyes widened. "I—"

"No! You shut up. You listen. You only did it once. You thought one person was less than human. I was taught that an entire gender was. Half of all the people who ever lived—I believed they weren't worth a damn. I was taught that no matter how hard a man tried, no matter how good his intentions were, that he was destined to want to face off against Hell, and that when he did he'd bring about the ruination of his people. But do you know what it means to believe that? Do you know what the cost of not fighting Hell is? And then there's Turi. And I met him the way *you* meet people—not as a slave, but as an equal. I met him and started to think of him the way I would have before I died. And then I saw Galen leading those serfs in Calimay's. I have ruined hundreds of men like Turi. Hundreds. So don't you stand there and tell me you hate yourself for just one. Because I'm worthy. Avery, I'm fucking worthy of Turi. I'm fucking worthy of you, and of Galen, and of the whole fucking Hell. And if you say you aren't shit for one rape, then I sure as hell am not for the hundreds."

Avery set his pick down upon the stone floor. He was crying. He got on his knees too. Kelly hated seeing men cry. He circled his mottled, half dead arms around her and she rested her head on his chest.

 — 27 —

The sword slung over Malkravyan's shoulder clacked against the wall as he leaned back against it. "You're going into the City of Blood and Stone?"

El Cid nodded.

"I've got contacts," Cris said. "A little bit of an underground movement. And Eagan over here has enough infidel fire to drop a bridge."

"And you're going to take her with you?" Malkravyan asked, pointing to Molly.

Molly felt a shiver run down her spine. Instinctively, she looked away.

"That's the idea," El Cid said.

"If you're worried that she doesn't have the training," Malkravyan went on, "I can take her back to Calimay's. Keep her there till you return."

No, I have to stay with Cris.

"Thank you, but not necessary," El Cid answered. "She won't hold us back once we're in the aqueduct."

Malkravyan let his pack and sword drop to his feet. "Be careful, there's a Minotaur out there that's pretty nasty. He's got better tracking than I've seen in one of his kind before, and he's got wights with him. I have no idea what alliance he made to pull that off. A lot of wights, and none of them are in control of other corpses."

Molly had never seen a Minotaur before, she'd only heard of

the one which had gored Michael and left him for dead on the banks of the Kingsriver. For the first time, Molly felt homesick. She had been Michael's woman, then. Everyone had liked her. She'd spent all day in the Fore. But that fight had fucked Michael up somehow. He'd wake up in the middle of the night screaming, clutching at his stomach.

He'd started to beat her after that.

El Cid was shrugging her shoulders. "From what we've heard, Lucreas Crassus is back. He's used undead before."

"It could be Nephysis, too," Jessica broke in. "We've been told that Maab is afraid he's turned traitor, or that he might be playing both sides."

Malkravyan thought about this for a moment. "It's possible he's turned, I suppose. I have a hard time seeing him accepting any authority, though. I could be wrong, but I think it's more likely he'd play both sides in hopes that he could keep a handle on his own destiny. Either way, keep an eye out for that Minotaur on your way back. He's hard to shake, so even if you think you've lost him, keep on going. Other than that, Cris knows what's going on—mostly.

"The Carrion is filled to bursting with dyitzu. Oh, and don't pass through the Deadlands. It's so full of corpses it's not even worth the protection from the dyitzu."

Cris' eyebrows raised. "Truly?"

"I'm serious, it's a mess in there. I haven't spoken to my contacts at the City recently, but be careful with how you sabotage the bridge. Maab knows that bridge is being built too—Hell, she probably knew before you found out about it, Cris—and she's not any happier about Saint Wretch coming across than we are. The best guess of my contact in her compound is that she's sending a group to take out the bridge too. Supposedly, she's got La'Ferve's best apprentice leading it."

El Cid frowned. "Cris, you sure we can't work with this Maab woman? I hate wasted motion."

"Limited objectives with her, only," Cris said, "and be careful even at that. Hell, ask Malkravyan here if you don't believe me."

"He's right, Cid," Malkravyan said. "Maab may not deal with devils, but that's about the only thing she won't do. Her societies are glorified rape dens with ritual castration, mutilation, slavery, and torture. In a lot of ways, it's better to be a slave for the City than for Maab."

"Is Calimay any different?" El Cid asked.

"Not really, but I'm working on her."

Malkravyan had more to say, but Molly could tell that he didn't want her to hear it for some reason. Of all the infidel traits, secrecy was the one that bothered her the most.

Her thoughts drifted back to Michael. To the first time he'd hit her. He'd been sorry. Really, truly and *genuinely* sorry. Molly had been able to tell that about him. She never doubted that for a minute—and it was that earnestness on his part which had made her think it wasn't going to happen again, and again, and again.

And then no one had believed her, or those that did, simply thought it didn't matter. From and infidel perspective, she could say those villagers and Citizens wanted to like Michael more than they wanted to see the truth.

But that willingness to see truth cut both ways. She had been horrific to Michael. She had hurt him psychologically, when he was at his most low. She'd given him wounds which were, in some cases, as vile and as cruel as the bruises he'd given her. The infidels would want to see that truth, too. The infidels might love her unconditionally in that they'd lay their lives down to save hers, but who the hell wanted love? They wouldn't respect her unless she became . . . she couldn't think of the word for it. A good human being? Great? Honest? All three?

Unless I become an infidel.

Cris put a hand on her shoulder. She looked around and realized that everyone was getting ready to leave. Malkravyan hugged each Infidel Friend, but passed by Molly without a thought.

Bastard.

She picked up her pack and followed El Cid and the infidels into the next chamber.

The back wall of this room was made of a shiny black, unbroken substance. It was perfectly smooth except for an inscription of a few backward and forward Cs on the side. She heard the sound of stone grinding on stone coming from behind the wall.

"Malk's got it for us," Cris said.

Eagan and Aiden walked over to the left side of the room and pressed against the stone wall. It opened like an old world sliding door. Inside, all was dark.

"What is this?" Molly asked. "This is the aqueduct?"

"Sure is." Eagan grinned. "Welcome miss, to Hell's Autobahn."

Arturus awoke.

His sleep had been fitful, small moments of rest between stretches of nightmares. He kept dreaming that his body was dead, and that it wouldn't move for that reason. Finally the morning had come, and even though he could not remember ever having a less restful night, he felt better.

My body is coming back alive. I'm probably as tired as I have ever been, it's just that I have something newly horrific to compare to exhaustion.

His friends lay nearby him. Avery's head was propped up against a stone wall. Rot still covered him almost completely, but he didn't seem to be in any pain. Kelly was already awake. She was looking at him. For some reason she was wearing the bloodied shirt of one of the rapists she'd killed. Black strands of hair were in her hands.

Her hair, it must be coming out.

"It's okay," she told him, "Galen said it was okay. The hair comes out. I'm healing. I can grow more hair. I'll be pretty for you again."

Flakes of dead skin fell down from her cheek as she spoke.

Arturus was too tired to stand, and the soles of his bare feet were hurting, so he crawled over to where she lay. "I think you are the most beautiful corpse I've ever seen."

She smiled. Her lips were beyond chapped. "You're sweet." She pointed to Aaron. "He's still in pain."

Aaron had curled up into a fetal position. He was shaking in his sleep.

The price we paid . . . are still paying.

"It's not fair," Arturus said.

"Of course it's not."

"No, I mean the whole thing. All of this. That we are born able to feel pain. That there are devils who want to hurt us.

That there are ways to make us care about things which can be taken away from us. That there is a universe out there intent on doing so. It's not fair. There needs to be some justice."

When Arturus said justice, Kelly turned her head to look at Galen. He was sitting by Calimay's priestess. There were ten soldiers with her, and about half of them were awake. To the right of the room were the twenty slaves—or there would have been. There were seventeen, now. Canvas bags of rustrock lay stacked up by the exit.

We're going to carry those all the way back.

"You want to go down?" Calimay's priestess was saying.

The woman bothered Arturus. It was the way she'd handled the news about her slave's death last night. She hadn't said a word. All she did was shrug. No hint of distress or mourning, or of any other emotion.

"Yes," Galen answered.

One of the soldiers shook his head. "Absolutely not. The mists are there. We could walk right into a dyitzu pack without noticing a thing."

"I'll be able to hear them," Galen said.

The priestess snorted. "Forgive me if that doesn't put my mind at ease."

"Look into my eyes," Galen ordered.

"I'm a priestess of Mithras, you dumb-fuck male, you don't order—"

Galen stood. "Look into my eyes."

For a second, the priestess did.

"That Minotaur followed us through these mines when we first came here. The only reason he didn't slaughter your workers while you extracted the rustrock is because he was too busy chasing us. He followed us through paths so secret, only the infidels know them. Your own soldiers have seen that he has wights at his beckoning. And he's out there," Galen pointed towards one of the ladders. "He's out there waiting for you. He thinks my group is dead, and he knows that you are going to be calling the shots. He must know the paths your people are likely to take. So do you really want to go toe to toe with a Minotaur?"

The priestess glared at him. Her lip curled up into a sneer. "You're right," she raised a hand, quivering with anger, to point at Galen. "And we *will* go the way you suggest. But when you are no longer of any use to me, you will be whipped for your insolence."

"Deal." Galen turned to the room full of soldiers and slaves. "We leave in ten minutes."

28

Julian was only bleeding a little when the morning came and the huge, ironbound woodstone door opened. This door would not swing in all the way, as its base would scrape against the hellstone floor. It was that scraping which had awakened Julian. He found himself in Edmond's arms as the firelight of woodstone torches lit up their dirty sleeping chamber.

Edmond kissed Julian in the back of his head and stood up.

I am the pick.

Julian felt blood and semen seeping out of him. It was going to leave a wet little stain in the back of his grey pants. He could pretend it was just a shit stain, if he wanted, but everyone would know better.

There was a priestess by the door. Not a little lady, but a full on priestess. She was Selena's favorite, and rumored lover, a woman called Mehlia.

"Come out," her high voice intoned, "there will be no work today. A lesson, perhaps, but no work."

He broke.

But the knowledge came as no surprise to Julian. He had known George would fall because George was a friend of the infidels. George didn't have faith. He pretended to believe in the Lord just as Julian pretended to believe in the god Ahuramazda. The torchlight danced off Mehlia's black robe, keeping her face in shadow. Julian did not know what expression was on her face, but he could imagine her wicked glee.

His friends are coming, the Infidels. If he broke, or pretended too, he could stay in their good graces and escape when the time comes.

Julian found that he couldn't really blame the man for ratting them out. The Julian that had been kidnapped by Pyle certainly would have. That Julian did break before he'd found his real faith. He had only truly found God after he had truly lost Him.

I'm sorry, Lord. I wanted to serve you. I wanted to help these people rise up against the evil here. I wanted to change this place to one that worshiped you, to one that would do your will. A place more like Harpsborough. A place that could have honey.

Julian sighed. He'd done his best. This wasn't like Earth. On Earth, he would have won. On Earth, God would have helped him. On Earth, the scales of the world tipped towards justice.

Not so in Hell.

They're going to have him point me out in front of everyone. They're going to talk about the terrible torture that they put him through, and then he's going to be brought out, a sniveling mess, and he'll point at me and any other Christian he knows. And then we'll all be tortured. The weak ones will break, the last of us will be found, and our movement will be stamped out.

On Earth, a few of the weak ones would find strength. On Earth, the Lord would make sure some of the faithful survived. On Earth, the scales of the world tipped towards justice.

Not so in Hell.

He marched with his fellow slaves out into the corridor. There were other groups of slaves there, each standing by their priestess and a requisite amount of soldiers. He looked down the hall. There must have been hundreds of people here, standing in the little pockets of firelight.

Maybe we should try to fight now, try to destroy the soldiers.

On Earth a rebellion might succeed at a moment like this. On Earth, his men might have been able to wrest the guns away from the soldiers and win their freedom. On Earth, the scales of the world tipped towards justice.

Not so in Hell.

They walked through the winding corridors of Selena's

complex. The corridors were not even, nor were they laid out in any sensical manner. This was no accident. Selena built this place as a maze because, if they were ever attacked, her soldiers would know how to navigate it and the enemy would not.

They walked up a series of stairs, and then another, and then another. There were perhaps a thousand of them now, slaves and priestesses and soldiers and Little Ladies—all moving silently through the halls. The stones echoed with their footsteps, with their breathing, with the crackling of the fire.

It seemed surreal. He almost felt as if he were outside his body, looking at himself from the crowd.

Depression began to weigh on his mind, but there was also a part of him that was looking forward to this. He almost wanted the persecution. He almost wanted to test his faith against the worst that Selena's people could give him. Let them try their hardest, let them bang stones against steel.

The largest room in Selena's complex was called the Square. It was built deliberately to mimic the ritual chamber where Maab broke the bull. It was almost as large. Two great braziers burned, bright enough to illuminate the center of the room, but dim enough to leave the outer walls in darkness. He could see those walls slightly as the firelight wavered. It appeared as if the stones were rippling.

Julian felt the crowd pulling him forward. They were coming to the stage.

Tears began forming in Julian's eyes. He felt them roll down his cheeks. He wiped them away before a Kruk could see them, but more came. He felt a sorrow in his heart that he could not explain. Maybe it was for George, for Julian knew what he had just undergone. Maybe it was for all the slaves that would never be freed. Maybe it was for the poor man Jesus who had been crucified so long ago only to have the people that he was tortured to save turn their backs on his offered salvation. Maybe, just maybe, it was for himself—because he was going to die today. Not in body, necessarily, but in soul. That young man who had daringly braved the Carrion to get food for his village would be dead. The young man who had dreaded going to church each morning would die. All that would be left was his heart's armor.

His faith.

But that's what it means to be a soldier of God.

On Earth, maybe, he would have been able to keep some of his innocence. On Earth, maybe, he would have been able to lay down his sword and return to the fields. On Earth, the scales of the world tipped towards justice.

Not here. Not in Hell. Not where Selena ruled.

The crowd was all around him. The heat of their bodies and the heat of the fire began to make him sweat. He hoped the sweat would hide his tears.

Selena appeared on the stage, or maybe she had been there the entire time and the light had just now grown bright enough to expose her. Her long shadow crept back from her robed body, fanning out across the floor before rising like the silhouette of some cruel monster across the dark stone walls behind her.

The light *was* getting brighter, he knew, because he could now see the uneven, unworked rock walls that bound them in.

"George was a slave who many knew," Mehlia's high pitched voice called out.

A near silence fell in the wake of her words. The brushing of robes and the breathing of the slaves and soldiers were gone now. There was only the crackle of the torches and the roar of the braziers.

"He worked hard. They say he never gave in to the temptations of sodomy like the rest of you sinners. They say he was a man who followed the truth of Ahuramazda. They say he was a man who would someday be baptized."

She walked in front of Selena to stand directly between the twin infernos. "But others knew the truth. Others knew he was wishing to side with Ahriman. Others knew that he had found a way to escape this complex—leaving us all vulnerable to the devils—and that he was meeting with people. People who want you all dead. And do you know what? There are those amongst us which side with him. Vale was the man who reported him. Thank you, Vale."

Julian looked about to see Vale in the masses, but not surprisingly, he could not.

They'll probably baptize him at the next ritual.

"But we are full of forgiveness!" Mehlia shouted. "And we offered to let George live if he only told us who he was conspiring with! But do you think he listened then?"

She paused and waited for an answer, none came.

"He did not."

The people around him were enraptured. Some even had grins on their faces. And why not? Perhaps this was better than working. If a man had no soul, why wouldn't he mind if his moment of rest was bought by the misery of another?

Mehlia walked all the way up to the front of the stage and stopped at the edge. There was a prop there in a burlap sack. Julian did not know what horrible implement it contained, but he knew it was going to be used on him. Mehlia looked down across the masses, and for a moment, Julian knew that she was looking at him.

My time is coming. I will not fear it. I must be strong.

"They never break soon enough, my children," she said sadly, her lilting voice echoing off the walls. "Never. So after we beat them, we threaten to take something from them. It's a shame when they don't give up early, because everyone breaks. The end result is always the same, it's just that some of you keep more of what you have. So we told him we'd take a finger, and you know that when *we* take a finger, it stays taken. Hell won't heal the wounds we give. But did he break then, children?"

Again, only silence.

"He did not. So we decided that any of his compatriots who we captured would face the same fate as he. You there, amongst the crowd, you who were his sympathizers, should know that the tortures he withstood are the exact tortures you shall receive before you die. Miserable, is it not? Miserable."

Julian was not afraid. His body was shaking, but he was not afraid.

"So then we went to take another finger. But did he break?"

Still silence.

Julian held the fingers of his right hand with his left. He did not need them. They belonged to God. He'd just been borrowing them.

"So then we went to take his hand, and did he break? Did he, my children?"

This time there was a response. "No," came the reply of a few scattered voices amongst the hundreds.

"So then we went to take his right nut. Let me ask you, my

children, did he break then, do you think?"

Oh God.

"No," the crowd replied, a few shouting.

Julian's body was shaking violently now. His heart was pumping.

Be still! Be strong.

But the flesh was weak.

"And then we went for his left. Did he break then? I ask you? Did he? Did he?"

"No!" A few more were shouting this time.

"Oh, how he screeched in pain. Tears formed in George's eyes when he became Georgette. And then we told him he would lose his pecker, and do you know what he said? He said 'take it.'" She threw wide her arms and grinned like she had just told a joke. "So we did!"

Julian felt goose bumps forming on his flesh. He was shaking so badly he was worried that he might be going into a seizure.

"I had never seen anyone so pathetic as him then. He was all tears and snot, sniveling out his whines for mercy. So then we told him he would lose his entire arm, and did he break?"

"No!" the crowd shouted.

Julian felt his teeth chattering. All of this was going to happen to him. All this pain. But he could take it. He knew he could. He had his faith. That would be enough. It would have to be enough. It just seemed so horribly unfair that he was going to have to face this. Why him? Why not someone else? Why hadn't George broken sooner?

"And then we went to take his leg, and did he break then children? Did he?"

George, you stupid bastard. Why did you hold out this long? You could have been free, and now this will happen to all of my people. Now this will happen to me."

"And then we told him we would take his eye." She paused and walked back and forth at the edge of the stage.

Julian felt his eye twitching in its socket.

Mehlia smiled and spread her arms wide. "You see, he'd thought he'd lost the worst of it. He thought with an arm and a pecker and a leg gone, there was little more we could do to him. But his face! Oh, we hadn't even touched his face. But did . . .

he . . . break?"

"No!" they cheered.

"So we dug a knife into his eye socket, only we missed and hit the eyeball a little. We had to dig around while he yelled and screamed and shouted until we could pop it out. The poor little fucker couldn't even piss himself in fear, on account of him missing a few parts—so he shit himself instead. We whipped him for that. It's a sin, you know, to shit in front of a priestess. When we were done whipping him, we had to finish with the eye. Oh, we had popped it out already, but it had just been hanging there on the end of its nerve. We severed it. Slowly."

She grinned. "And then we told him we would take his tongue and sew his mouth shut. This would be his last chance to give himself to goodness. We explained to him the righteousness of our ways. He was a blubbering mess—vomiting too. Of course, we had to whip him for that. 'Tis a sin to vomit in front of a priestess. No Kruk would fear the trembling thing that lay before us then. No person would say he could work hard. No one would baptize such a creature, this man with no arm. This man with no leg, with no dick—this man with only one eye. And he knew, oh yes at that moment, bless us Ahuramazda, he *knew*, that this was his last chance to stop the torture. He knew that if he didn't stop us then, we would just keep on going. So let me ask you children, *did he break?*"

There was silence. No one knew what to answer.

Mehlia reached down to the canvas bag at her feet.

Julian stopped shaking. His eye stopped twitching. He let his hands fall to his sides.

Oh, God, George. I'm sorry. I'm so sorry.

She emptied the bag. George's limbless and unclothed torso came rolling out. Two soldiers came upon the stage and picked it up. Two stubs writhed where legs should have been. Small bits of wrapped cloth, perhaps covering the remaining bone of his amputated arms, shook. George's face had two sunken pits of flesh where the eyes had been. His nose and the right side of his face seemed to have been torn off by the bites of a hound. There was no sign of his genitals. Scratches and whip marks scored his abdomen, and though Julian could not see his back, he was sure that had been lacerated as well. George's mouth had been sewn shut with stitches of dyitzu gut string.

George had not broken. On Earth, such torture would have killed a man.

Not so here.

"And do you know what the amazing thing is?" Mehlia asked them. "He thought that if he made it this far, we wouldn't be able to torture him anymore. He thought that if he just managed to make it past all our amputations, that he would be fine. But I've got a secret I'm going to tell you now. A secret which George might be able to hear even without his ears. Do you know what that secret is?"

No one spoke. It became so quiet that Julian could hear the crackling of the braziers.

Mehlia smiled. "The secret is that, this time, we didn't use any rustrock!"

There was a moment's pause as her voice echoed around the room. Then, as people began to understand what she meant, a great cheer erupted from the crowd.

No rustrock meant that all of George's missing limbs would grow back. It meant that they could take everything away from George again.

I was wrong. He didn't break. He had no faith, and he didn't break. He hates Jesus, but look at him, suffering on behalf of us all.

Thank you, George.

29

Arturus did not know how long they'd been walking, only that it had been longer than a day. Galen led them down into the depths of the labyrinth until they reached tunnels so choked with mist that Arturus could not see more than a few feet ahead. In those rare moments when he had enough energy to be nervous, he would fear that the mists hid the Minotaur. Usually he was too tired to care.

His muscles were sore in a way he had not remembered them being before. His sweat reeked of death and rot and had an oily consistency he wasn't used to. As they began to travel along a purple hellstone vein, he noticed that his perspiration was darker than usual, murky as if his body was trying to expunge the corpseblood from itself.

Galen led them through rivers, perhaps to get rid of the smell of their fetid sweat, or perhaps because he knew no way around them. Arturus had never felt water so cold before in his life.

The moisture was everywhere, condensing on the wall and dripping from the ceiling, and he feared for the weapons of the Carrion soldiers.

Drip drip. Drip drip.

Calimay's priestess was amenable enough, even after her verbal bout with Galen, to give them food. The devilwheat sat in his stomach and burned as if it had turned into acid. He felt at times like he needed to vomit, but that seemed like it might take too much energy.

At least the purple light on the mist was beautiful. He had to fight to appreciate the beauty since all he wanted was sleep, but he managed.

Drip drip. Drip drip.

When Galen called for a break, Arturus collapsed to the ground. The cold of the stone began seeping into his body. Avery knelt down beside him.

The hunter crossed his arms. "I need to say something to you."

Arturus nodded. He needed water. Galen would probably bring him some.

"It's important," Avery said.

With his last bit of energy, Arturus sat up. "Go on."

"I just needed to say . . . well you see—it's just that I . . . well your girlfriend . . . she's alright. You know? She's a good girl. I . . ."

Arturus waited for him to continue, but he did not. There was so much more there for Avery to say—only there was nothing he could say. He could never justify what he'd done, and it wasn't the sort of thing a person could live down—and he'd done it to *Kelly*—but for some reason, Arturus didn't hate him. He felt he should, but he didn't. Maybe it was because Avery had saved his life. Maybe it was because Avery had been wounded while raping Kelly. Maybe it was because, when compared to the evils of Maab, Avery seemed almost good by comparison.

But surely Avery knew all those things. And now that he knew he was in the wrong, he was going to suffer. But suffering wasn't the point. Arturus didn't want Avery to hurt. That wasn't justice. Justice and pain, those were different. That was what he was trying to say to Kelly earlier about things not being fair. No one, no soul, no human and no beast, could ever do enough to warrant pain. If justice was to be served on Avery, it would be in the form of an action or punishment which would prevent him from causing pain in the future. Anything that fell short of that mark wasn't justice, it was revenge.

Arturus didn't feel guilty for not hating Avery. He felt guilty for ever having hated anyone. "Avery, there's nothing you can say, but I think maybe I understand what you are trying to say."

"Is that enough?" Avery asked.

Exhaustion weighed on Arturus. He felt his eyes trying to close themselves. He shook his head and looked at Avery's half dead face. "It's got to be. It's all you've got. It's all I've got."

"I should be in jail."

"There's no time for that."

"But I—"

"Avery," Arturus said sadly, "I know you want to be punished, but it's just not possible. Isn't Hell enough?"

Suddenly Avery was angry. "Then why are you here?"

The hunter's sudden passion caught Arturus off guard. "What?"

"Why are you here? You didn't deserve this. You didn't do anything to deserve damnation. You were just born here, in Hell. You had to walk through that field of dead with me, and you hadn't done anything to deserve it. Why?"

"You don't deserve it either, Avery,"

"That's where you're wrong," he said, a little too loudly. "That's where you're wrong," he repeated, this time more softly. "I do deserve to be here. You don't know what I did back in the old world."

"No." Arturus shook his head. "No, you really don't deserve this. You're going to be here *forever*."

Avery's mouth opened like he was going to say something, but then he stopped. He stopped as if he had never thought about what forever meant. As if he had never considered what it might be like to spend an eternity dying his way down an infinite ladder of torture.

"No matter how many times you die, Avery, you'll still be in Hell. I don't care what you did before you came here. You can't deserve this."

Avery's eyes were wide, his mouth still hung open. "There's no escaping it. I can't even *die*. There's nothing I can do."

"That's where you're wrong." It seemed odd to Arturus that Avery was just now coming to this realization, but then again, Avery hadn't been raised by Galen. "There is one thing you can do, and only one. You can fight."

He watched that idea sink into Avery's soul.

"Someday, Turi, someday, maybe after I've died enough, I'm

going to find the Devil. And I'm going to hurt him. I'm going to make him understand what it means to be so hurt."

Arturus nodded, because that's what Avery needed—but what the Devil needed wasn't pain. He needed justice.

And that's if, under all these layers of Hell, there even is a Devil.

Galen stood suddenly. Arturus' hand dropped to the hilt of his gladius. But Galen was smiling.

Grey panted, black shirted soldiers came out of the mist.

They were Calimay's men.

30

They crawled down through the mist and into the secret tunnel which led into Calimay's complex. It was as narrow and as difficult to navigate as Arturus remembered. He felt bad for his father because of his size and for the slaves who had to drag the rustrock filled canvas bags behind them.

As before, they rose through a floor plate into a dark room.

The last time we had to wait here, we thought they were going to kill us.

They waited in the darkness as everyone crawled through. Slaves stayed near the entrance to help drag up the bags of rustrock. The soldiers moved into the next room, perhaps just to get into the light, or perhaps to better scout the lay of the tunnels ahead of them. Arturus remembered that the area beyond was supposed to be self contained, but that the soldiers had found dyitzu there before.

After the slaves and rust rock had been lifted out of the tunnel, Calimay's priestess led them onwards. The dark purple corridors spiraled in on themselves, leading them closer and closer to the true entrance of Calimay's complex. The soldiers were still on their guard, but they seemed far more comfortable now than in the mist filled tunnels they'd traveled through earlier. Kelly came up beside him, putting her hand in his and giving him a sense of déjà vu.

"That future," she whispered, "the one we imagined for ourselves in the Deadlands. We might get to have it."

The power of that idea lit his mind on fire. The horrible walk through the Deadlands had done something for the two of them that Arturus had not thought possible. It had taught them to trust each other.

Hell, even Avery approves of her now.

As she strode beside him, he no longer felt the need to guard his feelings—or to protect himself against her future betrayal. Oh, that might have been a real danger before, Arturus knew that much, but now . . . now things were different.

They were going to return to Harpsborough. It wouldn't be hard for her to win over the villagers, not with Avery standing up for her. The Citizens would distrust her, but they distrusted everybody. And then he and Kelly would settle in with Rick. Rick would cook them a welcome home meal. Arturus couldn't wait until Kelly got a taste of that. Then she'd be happy that she'd left her cult behind.

And Rick would love her, as dearly as Arturus did. And with Arturus' experience in the Carrion, the promise Galen had made to him so long ago about becoming a peer, that could come true. He could even help out the Harpsborough hunters. Now that he knew Aaron very well, they could even work together in times of need.

Then Kelly would want the child. Galen would train their baby, toughen it, make it the kind of person it would need to be to withstand Hell. And—Arturus felt dark thoughts creeping into his mind. He tried to shake them, to keep himself from thinking them. Those ideas were there, he knew what they were, but he couldn't let them come bubbling up from the sea of his subconscious. The Infidel would never find him. The Infidel wouldn't have the chance to give him an argument and an offer. The Carrion would never boil over. Maab would never send her people to raid Harpsborough for her war against the City of Blood and Stone. Saint Wretch would never find his way across the Erebus. And . . .

Arturus bit his lip.

How long has it been since I last bit my lip?

He stopped himself.

There will be no peace for us.

And even if there was the option, even if the Infidel truly

didn't come and all the evils of the Carrion stayed on their side of the barrier, Maab had Julian. At some point they were going to have to go and get him back.

Arturus felt his heart lighten as it let go of Alice. Hell wasn't a place to have a maiden to protect. It wasn't a place to have a girl up on a pedestal. Hell was a place where you needed someone beside you, a peer, someone who could fight—someone like Kelly.

That's what father told me, so long ago. There is little difference between a pedestal and a tower. Little difference between a knight and a dragon.

Arturus felt Kelly's hand tugging at his own. He stopped walking and realized that everyone around him had too. They stood before a wall made out of blue stone. Calimay's purple robed priestess walked up to it, two soldiers flanking her. She knocked on it twelve times. Slowly, the wall rose, and a blue undulating light shone in from the room beyond. Arturus had forgotten how beautiful the chamber was.

The ceiling of water rippled over his head as he entered, covering himself, Kelly, Galen, Avery, Aaron, the priestess, her soldiers and her rustrock burdened slaves with its soft illumination. The giant room held two long reflecting pools. Arturus remembered sitting on the edge of those pools when Galen had fed them and the slaves a feast.

Even after all that, they still tried to rape Kelly.

Marble statues rose up out of the waters, groups of men, each wearing the armor of a bygone age, carrying a body shield on one arm and a short sword with the other. On the shoulders of these men were women whose toga draped bodies wound around together into each other until their outstretched and reaching hands became one with a jar. Arturus remembered how Galen had fixed the plumbing so that the fountains could again issue forth streams of water when they were turned on.

More statues lined either side of a long, red carpet which ran between the two pools and ended with the curtain beyond which, Arturus knew, were the corridors leading into the heart of Calimay's complex—and to her throne room.

A couple of soldiers, each with grey shirts and black pants, approached, walking along the carpet.

"We have succeeded," Calimay's priestess said. "Inform

Calimay we have returned with the angel's get and the rust rock."

The soldiers nodded. "She sleeps, honored priestess, but we shall inform her when she wakes."

Avery's rotten face suddenly looked worried, and Arturus knew why. Now that Calimay had her rustrock, what reason did she have left to let them go?

Calimay's priestess turned to Galen. "You remember where your rooms are?"

"Yes," he answered.

"Good," the priestess said. "I'm sure Calimay will want to see you when she wakes. I'll have some ammo, food and clothes brought to you. Oh, and don't forget," She winked at Galen. "I owe you a whoopin'."

If they're leaving us unsupervised, it sounds like she'll keep her bargain.

And that meant that the future Kelly had brought up was a possible thing. That meant that he might actually make it back to Harpsborough. It meant that the only thing between him and all that a damned soul could dare to dream of was the river Lethe.

31

"There's another one, sir," Marcus whispered to Martin.

Together they hunkered down behind a boulder. The dyitzu Marcus had spotted was across the Kingsriver from them, nearly one hundred yards away. The Harpsborough hunters usually didn't hunt this far downriver, but Martin had brought them there today. He had done so because he figured that there might be good hunting considering how long the Carrion barrier had been down. He did so because he felt that there may have been a few wretched things which had crept in; things which his soldiers needed to kill. He did so because he needed to convince himself that he wasn't afraid.

"Jesus," Martin whispered back. "How many is that? Five?"

"Six," Marcus answered.

Martin shook his head. "That's too damn many."

"That barrier was down for a while."

But the column of corpses should have kept them out.

Marcus sat up a little, looking over his shoulder and across the river room to the dyitzu. "Could have been a small pack that came through and split up."

"Could have been," Martin said, but he didn't mean the words. "Does Tucker see it?"

Marcus peered out across the waters. "I think so, but we're closer."

"Alright, let's take the shot."

Martin lay forward across the rock, taking care to stay

silent. Marcus set up beside him.

"I'm ready, sir," Marcus said.

Martin kept the dyitzu in his sights. "I'll shoot when you do."

Marcus took in a deep breath before beginning to slowly let it out. Martin knew that when the exhale paused, the man would fire—then he saw another dyitzu.

"Wait!" he whispered harshly.

Marcus took his finger off of the trigger. "What?" His voice was almost too quiet for Martin to hear.

"Look, by the waterfall."

At the far edge of the chamber a small tributary poured out of the wall, perhaps two hundred feet high, landing in a pool where it kicked up a light mist into the air. A second dyitzu was coming out of that mist.

"Alright," Martin said. "I'll take him, you take the first one. On three—"

Then another dyitzu appeared.

God damn it.

"Does Tucker see them?" Martin asked.

"I don't know," Marcus answered. "I don't know where Tucker is."

They're probably scared. Hopefully they're smart enough to get close. We can't take three without getting some return fire.

Martin waited, peering across the Kingsriver. If Tucker was out there, he was staying the hell down.

"Should we shoot sir?" Marcus asked.

I don't know.

He needed to give Tucker more time to get in position. One of the dyitzu, the first they had spotted, bent down by the river, cupping its hands. With a surprisingly human gesture, it lifted some of the water to its lips and drank. Then it stood and started walking.

"Sir?" Marcus asked.

Tucker might need more time. Or he might not even be there.

It was getting close to one of the exits.

Marcus' rifle stayed trained on it. "Sir, if it leaves the chamber—"

"I know, Marcus."

It got closer, and closer, and—

"Now," Martin breathed.

He and Marcus fired at the same moment. Martin's shot caught his dyitzu in the leg. It dropped to its knees as the reports of the gunshots echoed over the rush of the water. Marcus had hit his in the head. The third dyitzu formed a fireball, ready to hurl it at their position, when a bullet struck it from behind. Martin chambered another round, sending his spent shell spinning through the air until it landed, ringing like a small bell—then Martin's second shot drowned the sound out.

He hit the wounded dyitzu in the chest.

It toppled over.

Tucker and James stood up from behind their cover. They'd only been fifty or so yards from their target. Tucker raised his rifle and gave out a rebel yell.

Marcus shouted back, "Got 'em. Got 'em fuckers good."

Tucker and James approached the far bank and stood there. Martin and Marcus approached theirs.

"Damn, son!" Tucker shouted. "We'll be eating well tonight, how many is that altogether?"

"Eight," Martin shouted back, "but check the fucking dead, will ya?"

"Will do sir," Tucker answered.

Martin watched as the hunter walked over to the fallen dyitzu, his rifle leveled.

"And that's not counting whatever Hux has gotten," Martin shouted.

"No, sir," James called back across the river, "We ran into him about half an hour ago. He said he ain't found shit. Must be blind."

Martin shared a worried glance with Marcus, then he quickly pulled out another round and loaded it into his 700 Remington. "But Hux was right by where the breach was?" he shouted.

James held his arms out wide.

Hux ain't going to miss a dyitzu. And there should be more by the breach . . . unless.

Martin's blood ran cold. "Tucker," he shouted, "you gut the bodies. James, get all the hunters together, as many as you can find. Mark's upstream a little, right?"

"Yes, sir," Tucker answered. "His team found three, I think."

Fuck.

Martin started looking around the room.

"Whatchya thinking, sir?" Marcus asked.

"It sounds like we've got another breach."

If that's true, Graham's going in to scout this time. I sure as hell ain't going back in the Carrion. Not me. No sir. Katie would have my hide.

But he would have to go. How could he send anyone else in his stead? What a hypocrite he would be.

But I'd be a living hypocrite.

Something else was bothering him, though. It was just too damn much to hope that two breaches in the same area could be a coincidence. If there was a breach, that meant that Nephysis wasn't done with this side of Hell.

"I feel it too, sir," Marcus said.

"What do you mean?"

"Something wicked this way comes."

James's distant form hopped over one of the dead devils on his way out of the chamber while Tucker bent down to start skinning the first dyitzu.

Martin nodded. "Marcus, you ain't just whistling Dixie."

It seemed sad to Arturus that the four bunks in the room they shared were enough to hold them. He and Kelly shared a bunk, while Galen, Aaron and Avery each got their own. There was an empty place in his heart where Johnny should have been.

Some slaves had come by with some extra grey shirts and black pants for them to wear. They'd even provided a purple robe for Kelly and some fairly serviceable dyitzu hide shoes for Arturus. Arturus was surprised at their generosity, but he wondered if perhaps he shouldn't have been. It reminded him of how Avery viewed Kelly. When he hadn't thought of her as human, he was willing to be unspeakably cruel to her. Now that Kelly was a member of his own group, Avery wouldn't treat her badly. Maybe it was the same way with Calimay's people. As strangers, they were nothing, but as people who showed them where to mine for rustrock, they were something more—something human.

Then again, it could just be that Galen's worked his magic on

Calimay.

He thought of Calista.

Hell, it might be my magic this time.

Aaron sighed from the bunk above him. "God damn, we've been through a lot."

Galen grunted his agreement.

"Fuck, it's quiet in here," Avery complained. "Who the hell let Johnny die?"

"You know," Aaron said. "I guess I shouldn't feel so bad about losing Alice's hair. Would've rotted away, anyway, in those fields."

"You're going to see her soon," Arturus said.

Aaron gave a contented laugh. "I can't wait to beat up her new boyfriend."

Arturus smiled.

"How bad is the Lethe?" Avery asked.

"I'll get Calimay's best guide," Galen said. "If we're lucky, we'll find a way through the barrier quickly. It's easier that far south—downriver as you'd call it. We didn't repair the barriers down there. Once we get out of the Carrion, assuming that the famine holds up, we should have a safe journey."

Arturus heard Aaron shifting in the stone bunk above him.

"Its dyitzu we have to worry about?" Aaron asked.

"Yes. There could be a siren, or a banshee, too, but mostly dyitzu."

"I don't want to have come all this way just to die now," Aaron said. "Even Hell can't be that cruel."

But it is that cruel.

"If it makes you feel any better," Galen said, "I'm more worried about getting through One Horn's army than I am the Lethe. If we can sneak out of here without alerting him, I think we'll all make it home."

There were some footsteps coming to the door. Arturus sat up. Kelly did too, and held his hand.

There was a surprisingly polite knock.

"Enter," Galen said.

The latch slid to one side and the door creaked open on squeaky hinges. Two of Calimay's black panted and grey shirted soldiers stood there. "Galen, you're wanted."

"See you all in the morning," Galen said. "Sleep well."

He left without another word.

Avery started snoring.

Arturus looked over to Kelly's half dead face. She seemed worried.

"What's wrong?"

"Nothing," she said with a smile. "I just thought that, well when I heard them coming, I thought they were coming for you."

Arturus squeezed her hand. "Looks like you . . ."

He heard more footsteps.

". . . were right," she finished.

There was another knock.

"Enter," Aaron said.

The door opened revealing two more soldiers. "Turi, Calista wants to see you."

Kelly sat up.

"It's okay," Arturus whispered to her. "We're so close. You've had to survive this before. I know it will be hard, but trust me. If I can avoid it, I will. But if we can make it through this, I mean, this is such a small price to pay."

Tears rolled out of Kelly's blue-black eyes. She nodded.

"I promise," Arturus said.

She mumbled something.

"What?"

"It breaks my heart," Kelly said.

Arturus felt a surge of pain. Those words, which would have been meaningless from some other girl, were powerful when they came from Kelly.

He stood up, and her hand fell out of his. He walked towards the guards. He saw Kelly for a moment as the door closed, her eyes on him, her hands clutched to her chest.

"This way," one of the soldiers said, motioning down the corridor.

So cruel.

32

"I hurt, Galen," Calimay admitted.

The bed Calimay lay on with her warrior lover was covered in blankets of cured dyitzu hide. Calimay would not be surprised if it was the most comfortable bed in hell. She'd bade her soldiers take the feathers of harpies and leave them in the Lethe to be cleaned for an entire day. After the rank smell of the harpies had been purged, she'd had them used to stuff her mattress. It had taken some time for one of her men to figure out a way to make the feathers stay even beneath her—he'd done so by making cloth compartments within the mattress. Right now she couldn't even remember which of her men had come up with the idea. Perhaps it was Dakota.

Dakota is dead.

"I was miserable," she told him. "The walls of my kingdom were falling down around my ears and my priestesses blamed me. I spent each night waiting for a knife in the back. The serfs were growing more and more bitter. They did less work each day. Then you came. You made sure my rival died in the Carrion. You made sure that Dakota, Tamara's fiercest supporter, never returned. You won back the loyalty of the serfs, and now they work harder than ever. You have brought me the rustrock I need to keep this place from falling to pieces. Please stay. You're the only man I don't . . ."

Galen's muscular back was facing her. She watched how his shoulder's flexed as he turned his head around to look at her. ". . . the only man you don't break?"

"Stay with me, Galen. I don't want to be here, in Hell. I know it sounds obvious, but it's eating at me, day by day. You're the only thing that makes me happy."

"I have to get my people home."

"I know you do."

"I have to raise my boy."

She traced one fingernail across his muscular back. "I know."

"By then Maab or the City will have found you, and crushed you. But if they haven't, I may return."

His head turned back away from her. She put her hand on his shoulder and was surprised by how hard it felt. "Why would you?"

"Before Turi, the Carrion was my home."

She propped herself up on her elbow. "And before that? How old are you, really?"

"Old."

"I could have you tortured until you tell me."

"And then I'd tell you I was so old that I'd helped change Jesus' tire."

Calimay laughed a little. "Tell me, what's going on out there? What did you find out?"

"The Furies can sense Turi. The City of Blood and Stone is digging down to where Tu-El was buried. I think they'll find him, they're digging in the right spot, at least. They've also found a way to bridge the Erebus."

Calimay sat up in her bed. "How could you fuck me without telling me this?"

Galen shrugged. "You wouldn't have been in the mood."

"No shit. How long until they bring Wretch back to life?"

Galen rolled over on his back and looked up at her. "He never died, Calimay, the Infidel tricked him across the river of darkness. That's why he can come back.

"Saint Wretch can't be hurt. Who knows how long it took him and his Archdevil to learn how to navigate Sheol? Who knows how long it took them to find a Devil city on our shores so that they might come back—a long time, perhaps—but, sooner or later, it was bound to happen. The Furies can't hurt him either. And the devils, they love him. They'll follow him. You weren't in the Hell he was creating when he toppled the ancients."

"But you were?"

"Or close enough to hear the tales."

Galen's eyes stared up through the ceiling. "We almost had it, people did. We almost had Hell whipped like we'd whipped Earth. It's just that Hell had more to throw at us, and we had no way to stop a thing like Wretch—one of our own."

Calimay frowned. "And we still don't."

Galen nodded.

"So," Calimay asked, "what do we do? Could the Infidel trick him again? Can we?"

"There are no armies large enough in these times to face the forces that he can bring to bear. Right now, in truth, he doesn't even need to be immortal."

"Then I'll surrender," Calimay said.

Galen snorted.

Calimay sneered. "You would recommend something else?"

"I've fought unwinnable battles before."

"You plan to go across to Sheol, don't you? You're going to fight a Fury and get that weapon that can hurt Saint Wretch."

Galen gave no answer, he just stared at the ceiling.

"And when you've done that," Calimay whispered, "When you've fought with every last ounce of your soul so that your son can have a Hell worth surviving in, and when I've managed to outlast Maab and Saint Wretch, you'll come back to me, and share my bed."

"There are no miracles in Hell."

"It gives me hope to think such things."

Galen stood. She marveled at his naked body. She could not have imagined a more perfect man.

He pulled on his pants, preparing to leave. "Then for hope's sake, I'll be back when all is won."

Calimay knew it was a lie. There was no beating Saint Wretch. And by Mithras, she couldn't even defeat Maab. Her bed, as comfortable as she had tried to make it, would be cold and empty from now until the day she died.

Martin's twenty men trailed closely behind him as he walked through the tunnels. "Anyone seen Huxley or his crew in the last hour?"

"Looks like James and I were the last ones to see him," Tucker said.

Well, if we end up in a fight, at least I'll have some good men beside me. I wish Hux were here, or Hidalgo. I'd give up my fucking hand again for Hidalgo.

They trotted along the far side of the Kingsriver, staying as close to the rock walls which separated them from the Carrion as they could. Martin swore that he felt the cold of the place sucking the heat away.

Now that he had seen the Carrion, Martin could tell how the architecture and rock formations had been warped by their proximity to the region. Here and there the natural caverns and red brick walls and ceilings gave way to the large dark stone blocks of the kind he'd seen on the other side of the barrier. In other places he saw archways, topped with keystones and cubbyholes which, but for their illumination, were also the same as in the Carrion.

They came to a four way fork with two purple cube markers.

Martin nodded to Tucker and James. They trotted off, one down each cube-marked corridor.

Martin sniffed the air. He thought he'd smelled blood.

Jesus Christ, it could be here. A little farther downriver than I thought but . . .

He thought he heard a whine.

Martin walked away from the fork and headed towards one of those arches. Marcus and a few of his men followed behind him.

"Stay close," Martin warned.

He raised his rifle and stepped carefully through the archway. He heard the scuffs of his men's footfalls behind him.

"Aleck," Martin whispered. "Go and warn Tucker and James to be quiet when they come back."

"Yes, sir."

The next room was a narrow one with a low red brick ceiling. Martin had to duck as they got near the end of it. There was another arch here, perhaps three feet high, and Martin could tell that its keystone was purple in color.

He crawled through it. The next room had a higher ceiling,

and its floor was littered with slain dyitzu. Near his feet was a half-dead hound. Its whine was surprisingly similar to that of an old world dog.

"Oh, shit," Martin said as he got up off of his hands and knees. "Guinness, guard the exits. Marcus, help me check these bodies out."

Tucker, James and Aleck came up behind him.

"You were right, sir, there's a bre—" Tucker's eyes widened in surprise as he saw the slaughter. "Oh, hell. What happened here?"

Martin knelt by the twitching hound. It had been hit by dyitzu fire. A lot of dyitzu fire. Its fur was a blackened mess, and its face had half burnt, half melted off. Oddly, it seemed as if its claws had all been severed at the knuckle.

Trophies maybe?

"Dyitzu look like they were mostly hit by buckshot," Marcus said, "except this one. Jesus, somebody's packing some serious ammo."

He lifted the lifeless head of the dyitzu. The entry wound was directly between the dyitzu's eyes. The back of the head had been blown to pieces. Scattered bits of skull and dyitzu brain were spread out on the wall behind the thing.

Martin whistled.

"Human over here," Guinness reported. "Looks like he wore all black."

Martin stepped over the bodies to see the man.

"We found a breach back there. It was definitely made by people," Tucker said. "Not sure how they managed to do it without getting killed, but they fucking mined through the entire barrier. It was just wide enough for a man, or a dyitzu to crawl through."

"It looks like the dyitzu were what got the hound," Marcus mused.

"Must have been an accident," Martin said absently as he knelt by the body of the dead human. "Maybe they were shooting for this guy and missed?"

The man's clothes were indeed all black. They reminded Martin a little bit of what Cris had worn when the Infidel Friend had stood on the far side of the Golden Door. Only somehow Martin doubted this man was an infidel.

"No rigor," Marcus said. "He ain't been dead too long."

Martin pulled on the sleeve of the man's shirt, rolling it up. There, on his shoulder, was a tattoo. It was of a man with raised arms, palm touching palm as if he were praying. His torso was encased in rock.

Maab's men are here.

"Should we go back and get Copperfield?" Aleck asked. "We'll have to repair this barrier right?"

Marcus was staring at the booted footprints left in the blood. "I think they went—oh shit."

Martin started, and the hound began whining and pawing the air with its mutilated claws.

"What?" Martin asked, walking over to Marcus.

"One of ours. Hit with buckshot. Took it full in the face."

"That was Steven, sir," Tucker said, "I can tell by the stain in his hoodie. He was in Hux's group, sir."

Martin unloaded a pair of rounds into the fallen hound. The whining stopped.

"Pick up the pace," he ordered. "Marcus, you're at point."

Arturus stared at the small bedside table. There was a silver backed ironglass mirror laying there next to a set of combs made out of polished hellstone.

"Are you mad at me?" Calista asked.

Of course I'm mad at you.

"No," Arturus lied.

"Are you okay?"

Arturus fought to keep his frustration down. "Just a little bruised, is all."

"I didn't mean to, I promise. I just got excited."

I slept with you so I could be with Kelly.

"I understand." Arturus tried to make his voice sound genuine. "It was an accident."

And it had been, only she shouldn't have had the chance to make that particular mistake. *I'm probably lucky she didn't leave me like Avery.*

Arturus sat up and caught a glance of his reflection in the mirror. He still looked pretty damn dead.

Calista didn't seem to care.

It was an odd realization. He had thought his ugliness

would have put her off, but it hadn't. Not at all. It was as if she really cared for him. He felt Calista's smooth fingers touch his shoulder.

Too smooth, no calluses. She never does any work.

There were footsteps in the room beyond this one coming from the other side of a woodstone door. Calimay's chambers were through there. Maybe his father was leaving, heading back to Aaron, Avery, and Kelly.

He felt a twinge of pain when he thought of how hurt Kelly had been.

I'll just lie to her, tell her I didn't enjoy it.

Calista's other hand found his shoulders. She started massaging him. It felt good. Damn good. It felt like her fingers were bringing his muscles back to life.

I shouldn't have enjoyed that. It was practically against my will. Kelly will probably be crying about it for weeks. I want to be Kelly's man, and hers only.

But he had enjoyed it. He had enjoyed it a lot—except for when she hurt him.

"It might be too early, but I swear I can feel your seed quickening inside me." Calista's voice was soft in his ear.

It will be a fatherless child she bears. A bastard.

"And that makes you happy?" Arturus asked.

"Yes," Calista said. "I'm having our baby. Good thing too, considering how easily I hurt you, you probably couldn't handle childbirth."

Arturus felt a little insulted by that, but her fingers kept massaging his back, and they felt too good for him to be mad at her.

"You love the Maab priestess, don't you? Kelly is her name?"

Arturus nodded.

"That's sad," Calista said. "I think you would have loved me if you'd had the chance. Mother says that you and your father are a different kind of man. She says you are used to choosing who you love, but I think you would have chosen to love me."

Arturus didn't answer. The warmth of her naked body was pressing up against him. Her figure was very different from Kelly's. Calista was much broader, and her breasts were much larger. Arturus had enjoyed that.

"I'd love it if you stayed," Calista said. "You could help me raise the child. If it's a boy you could raise it to be like yourself, you know? A man who chooses who they love."

Arturus felt his heart sink in his chest. He hadn't thought of that. Were he to have a son, he'd be the father of a bastard slave. Arturus looked up to the ceiling. It was covered by a red and gold Mithras tapestry.

"I can't stay."

"I know. It's not the Kelly girl either. Mother told me. It's your other father. You miss him."

Arturus' eyes hurt all of a sudden.

My tear ducts must not be all the way alive yet.

A tear ran down his cheek. She let out a gasp before touching his face, wiping the tear. She held up her finger. The tear was red.

"You cry blood," she whispered in awe. "You *are* holy!"

"From being a leper," Arturus explained, "not an angel."

"No!" she said. "You don't understand. Mithras, he's in Londinium, encased there in stone. The one who's supposed to rescue him, they say 'his eyes are idols of stone.' The person who helps Mithras come into Hell through the rock so he can fight Ahriman, that's you. You have the stone eyes which cry blood."

Arturus shook his head. "This is Hell, Calista. Prophecies don't come true here."

He felt the hard nipples of her breasts pressing into his back.

"Maybe," she said, "but I'm happy that, of all the men who've been damned, you're the one to be my child's father. Lay down with me?"

"I can't," Arturus said. "I have to go back."

Her breasts pressed harder into him. "Just pretend. You'll be with Kelly for the rest of your life. Just pretend. You were born in Hell, weren't you? Just like me. You and I are the same, you know."

It seems like every girl I meet wants to play make believe.

Arturus frowned. "I'm sorry, but—"

"You don't have to mean it," Calista said, "but lay down next to me. Let me pretend for the rest of my life that you loved me. On that day when I look into the eyes of my child, let me remember yours. Let me have this pleasant fantasy that somewhere in Hell, you're thinking of me, wishing you could return."

More blood ran down his cheeks.

Hell's gotten to me. It's gotten inside me.

He lay back down, putting one arm over her body and guiding her back into her soft sheets. Calista closed her eyes, a contented smile spreading across her face.

"I really am sorry I hurt you," she said. "It was on accident. I didn't know it would take so little." One of her eyes opened and she grinned harder.

Arturus shook his head.

He rolled over onto his back, looking up to the tapestry. Then he closed his eyes. He wondered what it would be like to finally come home. Rick's face would light up. He'd be grinning from ear to ear.

There was the distant sound of stones grinding against each other, and then the sound of rock being split in two. Arturus eyes shot open. Calista was clinging to him.

"What's going on?" she asked, her voice panicked.

Arturus heard men screaming. As calmly as he could, he got out of bed and put on his pants.

"Tell me!" Calista shouted, "What's happening?"

"This world of yours," Arturus said sadly as he picked up his shirt, "it's ending."

— 33 —

"Did you hear that?" Kelly asked.

Aaron stirred.

He looked over to Avery. The hunter was sitting on the upper bunk across the room, his hand pressed against one of the dark, fitted stones which made up their small chamber.

"There it was again," Kelly whispered, her head cocked to one side as if she were listening to something.

Aaron swung his legs over the side of his bed and lowered himself down to the ground. "I'm not hearing anything."

"Come here," Avery said. "Put your hand against the bed."

Aaron took the three steps necessary to cross over to the other bunk and put his hand against it. He waited.

"What does it—" Aaron began.

"Shh!" Kelly let out the sound harshly.

Someone else must have heard whatever it was in the chambers beyond, because Aaron could hear their worried voices. There were quick footsteps passing by their door. Then silence. Aaron could hear a slight wheeze coming from his lungs. He coughed to try and rid himself of it.

"Shh!" Avery and Kelly shushed him together this time.

Then it came. He felt it more than heard it, a vibration in the bunk. Now that he was aware of when it was coming and when it was going, he felt like he could just barely notice the distant rumble.

"A settling," Aaron breathed.

Kelly's head shook slowly.

There were a few more hushed whispers from outside, and more footsteps.

"Something's coming," Kelly said.

"Don't be ridiculous," Aaron shot back. "The stones—"

It came again, louder this time, and the vibrations lasted longer.

The hell?

"It feels like a settling doesn't it?" Avery's voice was so soft Aaron could hardly hear him. "They can be this spread out, right? A set of pillars slowly breaking or something."

Kelly shook her head again. "Get your weapons ready."

"You can't seriously think it's a devil," Aaron said.

"It is," Kelly answered. "Or Maab. But this is no settling. The blasts are too even. Someone is . . ."

The rumble came again. This time Aaron could see the bunk vibrate.

"I—" But the rest of Kelly's sentence was drowned out by the loudest sound Aaron had ever heard. Louder than a settling. Louder than the screams of the dying. Louder than the long wail of the Furies.

He was propelled into the air and his world went suddenly dark. He slammed into the back wall, hitting it so hard with his back that he lost his breath. He fell to the floor. Then, behind the rumble, there was a crack far louder than thunder, reverberating all around him and through the hollow of his chest. He found himself on his hands and knees. The chamber had once been well lit, but whatever had happened had sucked the light out of the stones. The only light he could see by was coming from around the edges of the door.

It sounded like pebbles were raining down outside of their room. Aaron noticed there was a crack now, spread throughout the stone ceiling near the doorway. It looked like it only went a little ways into the room, but as his eyes followed it, he noticed it was nearly halfway across. No, even farther.

Jesus, it's growing!

The crack's tendrils shot across their ceiling and began creeping down the back wall.

"The bunk!" Aaron shouted.

Together, the three of them took cover in Kelly's bunk.

Small stones began dropping from the ceiling, raining down onto the top bunk. Then there was another thunderous boom.

When the sound of that explosion died away, all Aaron could hear was the ringing in his own ears. He shook his head to try and clear it. Avery was saying something, but the ringing overpowered his distant sounding voice.

Aaron stood up out of the bunk and stumbled, either because the explosion had robbed him of his balance, or because there was another blast—he could not tell which. Aaron staggered through the darkness, tripping in places over the rubble, heading towards the door. His hand touched the woodstone and he tried to listen.

The ringing started to lessen, and he began hearing shouts outside.

"South quarter! Get to the south quarter!" A soldier was yelling.

Aaron slid the door's latch over and pushed. The door opened a little, letting light spill in from the hallway beyond, but it got jammed.

"What's going on!" Aaron yelled out into the corridor.

Someone was answering, but Aaron couldn't hear him at all. He shook his head again, looking back to his friends to see if they'd heard what the voice had been saying. He could barely see them in the sliver of light that the open door-crack provided. Kelly was kneeling on the ground. Avery stood protectively over her. Small pebbles and streams of dust were coming down from the ceiling.

"What?" Aaron shouted back through the door.

The light in the hallway was flickering. He saw one of Calimay's grey shirted soldiers coming up to the door. He was walking over nearly half a foot of rubble.

"Stones have got your door closed!" the soldier was shouting. Aaron missed the next part of what the man said because of the atrocious ringing. ". . . at the south quarter. Dyitzu mostly. Looks like some corpses. We'll have to break you out and move deeper into the complex."

"Not Maab?" Aaron asked.

"No," the soldier answered. "It's okay, we've got a plan for this. Help me break this door down and we'll keep you safe. Are you armed?"

There was another blast. It seemed farther away, but more streams of dust came down from the ceiling.

"Yes," Kelly shouted back, "but almost no bullets."

"Avery, help me with this."

"What?"

His hearing must be as fucked as mine.

"Help me with the door!" Aaron shouted.

Several more soldiers and a troop of slaves were passing through the hallway, heading from left to right—heading deeper into the complex.

"Why are the lights flickering?" Avery yelled.

"Light flows through skystone veins in the rock," the soldier answered loudly through the woodstone. "When the stone separates, the veins can get disconnected."

Avery put his shoulder against the door.

"One, two," Aaron counted, "three!"

He and Avery pushed while the soldier pulled. Kelly added her own weight to the effort, pushing against Avery. The door moved an inch or so, but the rubble wouldn't give.

"Again!" Aaron shouted.

Their sudden effort bought them another inch, perhaps, but nothing more.

"Again!" This time there was no progress.

"We're going to have to dig you out," the soldier said.

Dyitzu fire lit up the corridor.

"Mithras!" A shout came from down the hall. "They're here!"

The soldier dropped to one knee and raised his shotgun. A fireball whizzed over his head. Another impacted close enough to the door that Aaron had to jump back to avoid the splash of the fire. Avery got a little on his shoulder, but Kelly smothered it with her lavender robe.

"We got 'em!" one man shouted.

"It'll be just a minute," the soldier promised, and Aaron could hear him digging at the gravel by their door.

A couple more soldiers came to his aid.

"Corpses!" One of them reported.

There was another tremendous boom, and more rubble fell down from the hall's ceiling. A large stone, large enough to kill, dropped into their room. Dust filled the air. Aaron found himself on the ground again.

When the shock had passed, the light in the hallway was almost completely gone. It was flickering on and off like an old world fluorescent bulb.

Aaron coughed up dust and dragged himself to his feet.

"Quickly!" the soldier was ordering.

Aaron peered through the crack in the door, placing his head against the woodstone so that he could see down the hallway. It was nearly pitch black, but it lit up for brief moments like a strobe light. There were silhouettes moving through the dust.

"Corpses are still coming!" a soldier warned.

"You two, shoot them down," the soldier shouted. "Everyone else work on this door."

The room was filled with the sound of their shotgun blasts. Aaron could hear the reports as brief bursts through the background ringing. He felt pressure on his ears, as if they needed to pop.

The shadows of the corpses moved slowly down the hallway, stumbling through the rubble. In the brief moments after one of Calimay's soldiers fired, Aaron could see their faces in the muzzle flash. Their skin was horribly pale. They *seemed* like corpses. Maybe it was just the dust and the distance, but they didn't seem to be covered in rot.

"Can't aim for shit through the dust," one soldier shouted.

But Aaron could hear the buckshot tinkling amidst the fallen debris. The next muzzle flash showed clearly the black eyes of one of the corpses.

Not corpses. Wights.

"Bullet's ain't working!" one man shouted.

"Stone wights!" another yelled.

And they were getting closer, and closer.

The soldier left the door and leapt forward to engage one, blocking Aaron's vision of the hallway. The man's body was slammed back against the door. Dyitzu fire was sizzling through the air. Suddenly the weight of the soldier was enough to overpower Aaron, and the door was slammed shut.

"Push it open!" Avery shouted.

Again, Aaron and Avery pushed against the door.

When they had it ajar again, they did not see either the corpses or the soldiers.

What?

He heard the sound of rock crunching under a hoof.

Through the crack in the door Aaron saw the giant bull head of the Minotaur. In that sliver of vision, Aaron could see one of its eyes. That eye was looking back at him.

It stepped back, putting one hoofed foot up on a pile of rubble. Dust from the ceiling poured down around it, bouncing off its horn and pouring off its shoulders.

"He's found us," Kelly said.

One Horn roared.

"Close the door!" Aaron yelled. "Close it."

Together he and Avery gripped the handle, pulling it back. The door slammed shut and Kelly slid the latch over. Then the door was ripped back, the latch and lock splintering out of the woodstone. There was a thud from the door slamming into the rubble. Aaron could see the Minotaur's eyes. The thing was looking straight at him.

"Fuck!" Avery screamed.

"Grab the door!" Kelly shouted over his still ringing ears.

Aaron watched helplessly as One Horn closed the door and jerked it back again, getting it a little farther open.

"Grab it!" Kelly screeched.

The Minotaur pushed the door closed again, and this time Aaron grasped it with both hands before One Horn could jerk it back. All his strength did nothing. He felt like his arms were almost pulled out of their sockets as the Minotaur jerked the door open. Aaron slammed into the woodstone and dropped to the debris covered floor. Avery dragged him back to his feet and together they clutched desperately at the handle.

One Horn pulled again, overpowering Aaron and Avery as if they were children, crushing the gravel and forcing the door open another inch. This time Aaron shoved Avery away and hopped up, holding the handle with his hands between his knees and placing his feet on the wall on either side of the door. He pulled back with all his might, pushing with his legs. Avery grabbed onto his torso and tugged as well.

Again the Minotaur pulled. Aaron felt as if the muscles in his thighs tore as the handle was ripped out of his grasp. He and Avery fell to the ground.

"We need to tie it!" Avery shouted.

Kelly took off her robe and tied one sleeve around the handle.

She ran back with the robe, ready to fasten it to the bunk.

The door jerked open, and the Minotaur tried to reach in, grasping for the robe. Aaron added his strength to Kelly's and the door slammed into the Minotaur's wrist. Its thick fingers grabbed a hold of the robe. Avery picked up Kelly's shotgun and put it against One Horn's forearm. He let loose a pair of shells.

The Minotaur roared again, jerking its hand back. The door slammed shut. Kelly tied off her robe to the bunk and pulled hard on the knot. The Minotaur tried to open it again. The robe was stretched taut, but the fabric held.

"Yes!" Avery shouted.

The Minotaur tried again, and again. Cracks started to spread out from where the bunk was attached to the wall.

Oh God no!

The sound of gunfire reached Aaron's ears. Then there were more shouts. Then Aaron could hear the crunching of hooves on stone. Soldiers issued cries of pain and agony. The flashes of light coming in from the cracks around the door frame and the hole in the latch gave Avery and Kelly's faces a surreal look.

A line of blood was dripping down Kelly's face from a cut on her forehead. "One Horn will be back, but . . ."

"But what?" Avery asked.

"Turi's out there."

34

Arturus stood still.

The explosions had stopped. Loose stones and gravel were pouring down around him from the hole in the ceiling, filling the air with dust.

He had thought he was going to make it home, that he was going to love Kelly and have a child.

What a fool he was.

Hadn't his father warned him about hope?

A man screamed from the other side of the door, "The bullets aren't working!"

Calista, still nude, crossed the room to where her robe lay. "They're already here." Her voice was the voice of a hopeless girl. "The escape plan, it won't work if they're already here."

Arturus moved to the door.

"Don't leave me!" Calista was pulling on her robe. "Protect me!"

I can't protect you! I have to get to Kelly. I can't even . . . oh shit. You're carrying my child.

He remembered how he had fought in the Deadlands. He remembered the running firefights he'd had all over the Carrion. He remembered driving the silver leg spiders towards Pyle and his men.

He remembered slitting the dyitzu's throats.

Calista's purple robe hung open around her breasts. Her eyes were wide, and why wouldn't they be? She had never worked. She had never fought. She had never been forced to see Hell. This must be her first experience with pure terror.

"My father told me that facing death is the truest test," Arturus told her. "You asked me to pretend to love you, and I did. Now I need you to pretend to be brave. Will you be the woman I can die fighting for?"

She nodded.

"Then come with me."

Arturus walked over and tried the door. It opened only a little before the rubble stopped it. He put his shoulder into the woodstone a few times, but he couldn't make much progress.

He removed his razor from his pants and whipped out the blade. With the door cracked open, there was a gap large enough for him to slip the razor through. He used it to pry the pins out of the hinges on the far side of the woodstone door. The door fell outwards into the room beyond, landing with a crunch in the rubble. The light was uneven in the hallways and chambers beyond. Pockets of light—illuminating the blankets of dust that hung in the air and the life and death struggle of combating silhouettes—were separated by swaths of pitch black darkness.

He slid the razor back into his pocket.

I am a murderer. A killer. The darkness is not my enemy, it is theirs.

In the nearest pocket of light Arturus saw a man's twitching body. On top of him a corpse—no, a wight—was eating his neck. The man's throat had already been partially consumed.

The wight looked up at him, its black eyes flashing in the purple illumination.

"Your mother?" Arturus asked Calista, "Do you know where she'd go?"

"Yes, the other purple level, two floors down, near the red level stairs."

The wight stood and began walking towards him slowly—deliberately—traversing the rubble without so much as a stagger.

"In the room where we first made love?" Arturus asked.

"Yes."

He called up the mental map he had made of the place during his last stay here. He knew the way.

"Stay close," Arturus ordered.

"Yes."

He walked forward to meet his enemy.

This is my time.

Wights were faster than undead, as fast as humans, but this one was not fast enough. Arturus advanced his left leg towards the creature with a quick step. He slung his right arm around in an overhand strike, twisting his hips to add power to the blow. His blow hit the wight across the face, causing it to stumble. Even while the wight staggered, Arturus pivoted off of his lead leg and spun his body around the wight. It recovered, facing in the wrong direction, swinging at where Arturus had been. It turned towards him, but as it did so, Arturus stepped forward, throwing his arm up and around again.

This time it was not a blow Arturus was landing, not this close to his enemy, but a hold. His left hand gripped the wight's wrist as his right circled over the thing's shoulder. Arturus grabbed his own wrist, using the same hold he'd executed on the sword wielding corpse in the Deadlands. When the arm could bend no more, the corpse was forced to move around him. This time Arturus kept it spinning, pushing it downwards. He dropped his weight, ramming the wight's face into the floor with enough force to send gravel shooting through the air. Arturus let go of the thing, knelt on its back, and picked up a large rock. He slammed it down with both hands into the back of the wight's head. When that was not enough to kill it, Arturus hit it again, and again.

He stood, peering into the darkened halls, and felt Calista coming up behind him. He advanced forward into the bubble of light where the wight's victim lay. There were dyitzu moving in the shadows of the corridor ahead.

Arturus picked up the shotgun of the fallen soldier.

It is my time. Calista has my child, and I have all the weapons I need to protect it. Galen raised me, Galen trained me, Galen made me the killer I need to be to defend what I love.

But more than that, Arturus was angry. Angry at Hell. Angry at the devils in it. Angry at the gods and demons who had fashioned this place—and he wanted to hurt something. He wanted to hurt something so badly that he could feel his anger in the back of his throat. He felt it burning in his stomach and tickling his nostrils.

Someone had to suffer for endangering his unborn child. Someone had to pay for the pain Rick must be feeling even now, thinking his loved ones were lost. Someone had to give up a pound of flesh for the misery of all the people who'd ever lost anyone.

Someone has to die for taking Johnny.

And the next one to suffer was the dyitzu creeping towards him. It formed a fireball and hurled it. Arturus guided Calista back against a wall. He advanced as the fireball tore through the air by his head. He ducked low and juked to the left, the dyitzu tried to follow him but Arturus came right back up, his shotgun raised to his shoulder. He only fired when the barrel of his weapon was six inches away from his target. The buckshot pulverized the dyitzu's head and sent its brain, blood, and pieces of its skull up into the air as a heavy mist. He cocked his weapon and advanced. There were two more dyitzu that he could see, so he dropped them in quick succession—spent shells falling onto the loose stones at his feet. His next enemy was another wight, so he tossed the shotgun back to Calista.

I am a murderer.

His blood caught fire, pumping through his veins to the crescendo rhythm of his heart, boiling away the last of the corpse sludge in his body. It was an anger inside him, overwhelming him, pulsing in his ears and at his fingertips, boiling over, filling his mind with its madness and spilling out of him as tears. The blood stung his eyes, but the pain was nothing.

Kelly, I'm coming.

He flicked a jab at the wight's face, but then ducked low and closed the distance with another darting step. He got up under it, clutching both of its legs to his chest, and with a tremendous heave he lifted the thing into the air. Then he brought it down, as hard and as fast as he could, a scream issuing from between his lips. As the thing fell, its head impacted with the wall. There was a crack, but the wight still struggled. It reached up with its right arm. Arturus overhooked it, kneeling on its chest, and set his forearm under its elbow. Finding his balance and his leverage, Arturus leaned back. He felt the tendons popping. He heard the bones grinding. The sounds became hellsong in his ears, a complimentary melody to the singing of his burning blood. Then, the arm *snapped*. Oh, how the wight writhed beneath him! Oh how it suffered, reaching up helplessly with its left arm to try and push him away. This one had not suffered enough.

Arturus overhooked the remaining limb, and, with a quick jerk, broke that one too. Still it struggled. Arturus pushed its head back with his forearm, his bloody tears falling like black raindrops in the dark purple light as he bent over the wight. It struggled madly.

You are no monster. You have no idea what a monster is.

How long had it been since he'd last had the corpsedust coursing through his veins? How long since the harsh reality of Hell had been blurred by its delusions? His blood called for the stuff. The half dead nature of his body demanded it. The hatred in the back of his throat filled his mouth and his nostrils, preparing his pallet for dead flesh.

He bit the thing's neck, biting out a chunk of undead skin and muscle.

A lesser man would have choked from the bitter, copper taste, but Arturus had consumed the dead before, and a wight was not nearly as unpalatable as a corpse. He spat out the flesh and black blood of the dead and went back down for more. He tore out its larynx with his teeth.

He saw another dyitzu out of the corner of his eye, so he stood, his hand raised back to Calista, who tossed him his shotgun. He aimed and fired, but there were no more shells. Arturus did not care. He advanced quickly over the rubble, dodging left and right around the thing's fireballs and then swung the shotgun with all his might, the butt impacting with the dyitzu's head.

It fell back to the ground. Arturus put his foot on its head and jammed the barrel of his empty shotgun into its hissing mouth. He pushed the gun down so hard that he heard the rubble crunching beneath its cheek. With its head still firmly beneath his foot, he pulled the shotgun to one side, using it as a lever to pry open the dyitzu's jaw. He did not stop when the jaw locked. Cartilage crackled as the jaw dislocated, sending gleeful vibrations up through the shotgun. The dyitzu's screams intermixed with the hellsong symphony playing in Arturus' mind. He beat the thing's unhinged jaw with the shotgun's butt, and then hit it again in the temple. It stopped moving. He found another dead soldier and picked up the man's pistol. He checked the clip, seeing that it had five bullets left.

Arturus looked to the stairs ahead of him through the pockets of light and sheets of dust. He turned back to Calista and offered his hand, guiding her half naked form over the rubble. He had never received adoration before. He had seen that look in women's eyes, in Alice when she looked at Aaron, in Kara when she looked at Massan—but never had any woman looked at him that way.

"You are . . ." she started, but she didn't know how to finish the sentence.

Arturus did though. "I am my father's child."

Martin knew that, had he attempted this run a few days ago, he would have given up already. Maybe he was in better shape, or maybe he just knew now how close to its limits his body could go. Either way, this wasn't the time to stop.

The dead hungerleaf grove stood silently beyond the empty river bed.

Whenever I come here, it's bad.

He lowered himself into the empty river and then dropped to the bottom. He climbed the far side as quickly as he could. To his left and right, his hunters were coming up around him.

"They ran through here!" Marcus reported, pointing at the riverbed. "Fresh blood. Fighting's got to be hot."

"After me," Martin ordered, and he led his men forward into the grove. "I know where that riverbed goes."

Then he heard the sounds of gunfire.

"A round in every chamber," Martin ordered, "safeties off. We're coming in hot."

Oh Jesus fucking Christ, Hux, I hope you're winning.

Despite how tired he was, Martin had to stop himself from breaking into a sprint. They would be there soon enough, and he didn't want his men exhausted for the upcoming battle. The sweat of his palms made his rifle feel slippery in his hands. He rocked it back and forth like a baby as he ran.

Unlike the path through the riverbed, these halls had not been burnt into his memory from battle. Even so, he led them correctly to the temple chamber where the corpsemen had lived. He stopped at the entrance. There the battle raged. Hux had six of his men hunkered down behind the temple. Two lay on the ground, their rifles pointed towards their enemy.

The hell is he fighting here for?

Muzzle flashes lit up several of the entrances to the chamber on the far side. That's where Maab's men were. It would be possible to hit them from this distance, but damn hard.

"Hux must be low on ammo, sir," Marcus said. "They ain't firing often."

Marcus was right. Hux's men weren't firing very often at all. They only seemed to when one of the darkly dressed men emerged from the corridor.

"He's smart though, that Hux." Tucker was bent over, his hands on his knees, breathing hard.

"How's that?" Martin asked.

"They've got shotguns. In this chamber the rifle's range is going to beat 'em. In the halls back there, the shotguns are going to be better."

Damn, Hux, good move.

"Give me some ammo," Martin ordered.

He held out his hand and started pocketing the rounds they handed him into his hoodie.

"Marcus, you're with me," Martin said after he'd collected what he figured was around a hundred bullets. "Tucker, I want you to run back and lead the rest of our guys to those tunnels there." He pointed across the chamber to a group of entrances to the temple room about halfway towards where Maab's men were. "That should still give us range advantage and you'll get a better shot. As soon as you start firing, Marcus and I are going to make the run to Hux and give 'em the ammo. Then we'll have them beat. They'll have to try and pull back into the halls."

"And then?" Tucker asked.

"We head back to Harpsborough via the Kingsriver. All those chambers are large. Now go!"

Tucker stood up, taking his hands off of his knees and wiping the sweat from his brow. "Alright, gents, you heard him."

Tucker led his men back into the wilds.

Martin was breathing hard. He felt his hamstrings starting

to tense, so he began pacing back and forth.

It's just me and Marcus now.

Marcus was bouncing up and down on his toes, probably to keep his own muscles loose. "What if Tucker's fire don't distract 'em?"

"Then hopefully the range will keep us safe."

"They got pistols, too," Marcus said, peering out across the chamber.

Shit. But you can't let Marcus think you're afraid.

Martin felt his balls pulling up tightly to his body. "Well if they hit us, then at least we won't have to run so far."

Marcus leaned over, putting one hand in front of him and leaning forward like a sprinter.

One of Hux's men stood and fired. He dropped suddenly.

"You okay?" Martin could hear Hux call from across the chamber.

"I think so. Bleeding."

Got some shot in him. Oh, hell.

Then more rifles could be heard, firing all together. Across the way, Martin saw muzzle flashes lighting up a fresh set of tunnel entrances.

"Now!" Martin shouted over the gunfire.

He and Marcus ran.

"Here. The plan is that she was supposed to come to this level," Calista whispered as they hid in the stairwell.

"Thank you," Arturus whispered back.

They crept through the dark halls. This part of the complex had purple ironglass overhead, but the light was noticeably dimmer than when he had explored it before. There was a firefight going on to his right. Slaves and soldiers alike stood together, shooting down dyitzu.

At least they were bright enough to give the slaves guns.

Down one long hallway, wights were packed in shoulder to shoulder. Calimay's men fought them as best they could. They were using stones since old world stuff could not hurt these wights.

In places the ceiling had cracked. Droplets of water were pouring down, some landing on the bodies of claw-torn humans and others on bullet ridden dyitzu. To his right an entire section of the ceiling had collapsed. The water had poured out over the stones there, and he could see up into the empty ceiling.

The water must be separated into tanks.

Gunfire started up behind them. Then there was the sound of dyitzu fireballs.

Too many.

"Hide!" Arturus ordered.

Calista ran towards the collapsed ceiling. She stumbled, and Arturus pulled her back to her feet. She moved around a chest high pile of rubble and broken glass. He was about to follow her but he heard claws clicking on stone. Looking back, he saw the shadows of dyitzu coming into their corridor.

He collapsed into one corner, lying amidst the rubble.

A moment later, dyitzu, perhaps thirteen or fourteen, started running through the corridor. Arturus lay as still as he could. He kept his eyes locked in a blank stare hoping it would help him blend in with the other dead bodies.

The dyitzu were crossing over him, their clawed feet landing only inches away from his face. One stepped on Arturus' leg. The dyitzu's weight was partially distributed on the stones around it, but the pressure was enough to hurt. Arturus couldn't see it, but it had stopped for some reason.

Does it know I'm alive?

For the first time, he was happy that his body was half rotten.

The dyitzu pack had stopped moving. There was another distant cry, and then a flurry of distant gunshots

If Calimay had two hundred men, probably half of them are dead already. More dying every moment. This will be over soon, unless . . .

There were two more footsteps, as if one of the dyitzu was repositioning itself.

Have they sensed Calista?

Hot breath touched his cheek.

Oh, God.

One dyitzu must be bending down to smell him. His heart started to beat faster.

Stop! Please stop.

He felt the warmth of the creature only inches away from his own body. Surely it could hear the rhythm of his heart.

Surely it could sense the blood that was rushing through his veins. Its hand set itself down in the gravel next to his eyes. The claw on its thumb was longer than the rest, and wickedly curved. The claw on its pinky had broken off, perhaps in the body of one of Calimay's men. It crawled by him, its muscular, oddly human-looking torso, passed over his head. This dyitzu was redder than most that he'd seen. He watched its nippleless pectorals flex as it shifted its weight from one arm to the next. It started smelling the next dead body.

Behind him, Arturus heard rubble shift under the clicking steps of the dyitzu's clawed feet. The dyitzu that had just crawled over him cocked its head to one side, stood, and then stepped over him. The sounds of the devils slowly became more and more distant.

Arturus realized he'd been holding his breath. He gasped for air.

Calista was at his side in a second. She hugged him fiercely as he sat up.

Close. That was close.

He stood.

Maybe we should make a run for an exit. If I got Calista to the others, we could take her with us into the wilds.

But Calista would never survive the Carrion.

"Come on," Arturus whispered.

Calista pushed herself up to her feet. Her eyes were wide, frightened.

Together they crept as quietly as they could through the halls.

"There," she said, pointing to a corridor where men and wights were fighting. "Mother should be on the other side of that."

Well how are we supposed to get to there?

"Is there a way around?" Arturus asked.

Calista shook her head.

Arturus looked to the ceiling. The glass had been shattered here, and the water had emptied out. He led Calista up to one of the walls. He scaled it, and was about to enter into the ceiling when he noticed how sharp the ironglass was. He dropped back down and took off his shirt. He climbed up again and used the shirt to cover the edge of the glass.

It took him some effort to get any traction on the slippery substance, but he managed to drag himself up.

The tank that had held the water was only about four feet tall, but it was about a hundred yards long and maybe half that in width. The next tank over on his right was still fully illuminated, and it covered the right side of his body with its purple light. Arturus watched his shadow, a long black stain in the surreal glow, as he turned around and offered Calista a hand. She took it, but her weight started pulling Arturus back down.

She let go. "I got it."

Arturus nodded and moved away from the hole. Calista scrambled over. She tossed him his shirt. Arturus struggled into it from where he sat, and they started crawling along through the ceiling tank. The floor of the tank was full of cracks, and Arturus was worried that it might not support their weight for long.

"This looks big enough," Calista said. "It should take us there."

I hope to Hell they're following the plan that Calista thinks they are.

The water on the smooth floor soaked through Arturus pants, and loose bits of glass cut his hands. He saw some dyitzu passing through the halls beneath him. They were being chased by a group of Calimay's slaves.

"Wait!" Calista warned.

Arturus froze. Cracks were spreading out from under his knees.

"Don't move," she said. "I'll pull back, lessen the weight."

Arturus saw a few dead bodies through the cracked glass in the rubble below. Two humans, three dyitzu, and what could have been either a human or a wight. In the darkness, Arturus couldn't tell. Arturus heard some distant shouting, then the cry of a man in agony.

Calista's slow movement backwards seemed to have helped. The cracks were no longer spreading.

The sound of hooves reverberated up from the hallway beneath him.

Arturus felt his heart quicken.

Below him he saw One Horn. The Minotaur walked through

the corridor, his hooves crushing bodies and rubble alike. Just behind him were a pair dyitzu and, following them, a pack of wights.

Arturus wanted to scramble away, but he feared that would call attention to himself. He looked over to Calista. She was on her knees, holding both of her hands over her mouth.

The cracks under him spread a little more.

The Minotaur stopped as a wight walked up to him from the other direction. Arturus could not hear what the wight was saying, but the Minotaur's voice came through clearly.

MORE IN THE RED PLACE. THEY ARE WINNING THERE.

Well that's good news, at least.

The cracks spread farther.

One Horn was covered in blood and dust, but as far as Arturus could tell, he had not yet been wounded.

Has no one even managed to shoot him?

But there, there was a wound. The bullman's left forearm was bleeding a little. That blood was brighter than the rest, still showing as red even in the dark purple light.

The wight had said something else.

THEIR LEADER IS UNIMPORTANT. FIND THE WARRIOR.

One Horn walked forward—and stopped. Arturus feared that if the glass gave way, he would be impaled by the thing's single remaining horn.

Just . . .

The Minotaur looked back behind it and waved the dyitzu forward.

. . . don't . . .

The dyitzu passed around One Horn, jogging ahead into the tunnels.

. . . look . . .

The wights came next, their smooth, deliberate gait bringing them through the rubble.

. . . up . . .

The bull's head turned back and forth, scanning the hallway he was in—then, ever so slowly, it tilted back.

Their eyes met through the glass.

No.

But there was no moment of recognition. One Horn's eyes kept roving as if he was still trying to make out what he was looking at.

It's brighter up here. It can't see me. It can only see . . .

One horn turned and looked back along the ceiling.

. . . my shadow.

He heard Calista as she started to creep around.

Stop!

But he could do nothing. If he waved her back, surely One Horn would notice. And if he tried to whisper, surely One Horn would hear him. Slowly, she came into his view. She froze, suddenly, seeing his expression.

Without turning his head, Arturus moved his eyes to look down at One Horn. The Minotaur must have recognized his shape.

A small crack, as thin as a hair, crept away from where his hand was resting. It wandered, moving in lightning quick darts from one point to another, pausing for half seconds between each leap. Blood was pooling onto the glass from his cut hand. It started to run along that crack.

Arturus couldn't see the end of his shadow now because it was to his left, and his head was tilted slightly to his right. He could, however, remember the area.

One Horn can't see the end of my shadow! He'll be looking right into a wall. Maybe he didn't see my shape. Maybe he only saw movement. Maybe he'll think the cracks are what he noticed.

One Horn was still looking at the ceiling intently. It was then that Arturus realized Calista's shadow might also be in the Minotaur's field of view.

Please stay still.

One Horn looked away from the ceiling, took a few steps forward, then a few more, then he walked away.

Arturus shook his head, breathing heavily. Calista collapsed with relief, sending more cracks through the ceiling. She got back up to her hands and knees and they crawled along in silence.

When they were on more solid ground, Arturus started heading towards the far edge of the tank. Before he got there, though, Calista stopped him.

"There!" she said, her voice echoing in the tank. "There's Mother!"

The ironglass was so cracked and cloudy here, Arturus

could see only the blurred figures of the people beneath him.

"You sure?" he asked.

"Of course I'm sure," Calista said, crawling onwards.

Arturus followed.

"Dyitzu! Coming from the ceiling!" Calimay's voice came up from below.

Calista knocked on the glass twelve even times.

"No!" said a soldier. "They're ours."

"Break through the glass!" Calista yelled.

But Arturus had nothing to do that with except his pistol. He looked for a weak point in the glass. He crawled over it and started hitting it with his gun. Soldiers came over from below and starting beating at it with the butts of their guns.

The ceiling gave way.

Shit.

Arturus fell through the air, Calista at his side, amidst a shower of broken glass.

35

It had not been an easy fall.

Arturus rose, cut in dozens of places. Blood dripped down from his eyebrow, splattering across his cheek. Calista was regaining consciousness. She looked blankly, eyes wide and blinking, at the wall.

The distant sound of singing reached his ears.

"Rose, Rose, Rose, Rose, will I ever see thee wed?"

Arturus smiled.

The slaves sing as they fight.

Blood ran down his left arm, falling from his middle finger to land amidst the scattered pieces of purple-lit glass. He offered that hand to Calista. With his help, she struggled to her feet.

Calimay, as if she was recovering from shock at the same moment as her daughter, rushed over to Calista, embracing her. The Queen breathed in deeply and buried her face into Calista's brown curly hair. In the distance a man was yelling in rage. Calimay rocked her child back and forth.

The group of soldiers, along with the other priestess in the room, stepped backwards away from the pair.

"I have brought her back to you," Arturus said.

"Thank you," Calimay let go of her daughter and brushed pieces of glass off the young woman's robe. "Thank you, Turi."

The ironglass bounced along the stones. The dim light around them flickered on and off.

A soldier came rushing in, his grey shirt torn open at the chest. He was bearded, and sported a huge gash on the left side of his face. His skin, and the hair attached to it, hung loosely, peeling away from his chin.

He paused before Calimay.

"Jessie's trying to hold them off in the tunnel. We haven't heard from Alexandra at all, but a soldier joined us who said Carlotta is gathering people on the red level."

Calimay nodded. "We've got to break free and go down. There are secret ways out I know of in the depths."

"My Queen," the soldier said, putting a hand up to cover his wound. "I do not think that we can make it. Safer to go up."

Calimay shook her head. "It's five levels up before we reach an exit."

"Five levels or fifty," said the other lavender robed priestess, "it doesn't make a difference if we can't break free."

The soldier's brow furrowed. "The wights aren't hurt by our shells. We have to fight them with rocks and our fists, and they fill up some of those corridors. A Minotaur is roaming the halls. If he sees too much resistance here, he may come to destroy us."

"Come back when you've broken free," Calimay ordered.

There was a moment of hesitation. Arturus wondered if the soldier was considering rebellion. He must have decided against it because he turned around and began jogging back to the fray.

Arturus took Calista's hand. "Live, if you can. Tell our child about me."

Calista nodded.

Arturus walked towards where Calimay's men were in melee.

"Where are you going?" Calimay asked suddenly, reaching out and grabbing his wrist.

Arturus turned back. The Queen's face was drawn—pale as death in the flickering purple light. She was afraid.

"I must find my father and my friends," Arturus said.

Her fingers let go of his arm, and he started to walk away again.

"Wait," Calimay said.

Arturus looked back over his shoulder at her.

"That song, the Rose song the slaves sing, did Galen ever

teach it to you?" There was a catch in Calimay's voice.

Arturus nodded.

"He never sang anything but the first verse," Calimay said. "Do you know the rest?"

There was a shout of a man, perhaps issued with his dying breath, along with the sound of dyitzu fire.

Arturus shifted his weight, hearing the stones and ironglass grind under his feet. "It is very sad. I know why he did not sing it to you."

"Tell me!" Calimay insisted. "Tell me the words. I must know them."

Arturus could hear the tune of the slaves singing in the background. He sang the words of the third verse even as they sang the first.

"Ding, ding, ding, dong. Are these bells of November morn? Where is Rose? She's dead and gone, sire. Dead and gone, sire. Dead and gone."

Calimay's lower lip began to tremble. She looked as if she was going to cry.

Father sang that song to her. She must have thought she was Rose. Maybe she is.

"Calimay!" a priestess was shouting as she ran, robe flaring behind her, down the hallway. "We have to pull back, the Minotaur is coming."

Arturus nodded to Calimay, brushed by the priestess, and headed towards the sound of battle.

Martin's hamstrings burned more painfully than he had thought possible. Tucker's men were letting their bullets fly, the reports of their gunshots echoing across the chamber amidst the scattered booms of the Carrion men's shotguns. At any time previously in his life, Martin doubted that he could have kept running. He'd never had the will to face or overcome pain. This was something new to him—something he'd never been able to do before.

Bullets fell away from his hoodie's pocket, scattering along the stones behind him. Martin clutched one hand to his stomach, stemming the flow of ammunition.

He heard buckshot ripping through the air around him.

They've seen us.

He had not thought it possible, but he ran faster. He passed Marcus.

Thirty feet.

A wave of shot slammed into him. It must have ricocheted off something, the floor or the ceiling, because he could still run.

Am I okay?

Twenty.

There wasn't any pain.

So close.

He had heard about people who'd been shot without noticing it—perhaps he was just one of those people.

Ten.

More buckshot flew through the air. Martin dove behind the temple, rolling haplessly over the loose cobblestones.

Safe!

Marcus landed beside him, panting.

"He's been hit!" Huxley shouted. "Martin's hit!"

Martin looked at his shoulder. It looked pretty bad.

You've got to be strong, Martin.

He waved Huxley off, standing up. "We've got bullets," Martin said. "Come and get 'em."

He reached into his hoodie.

Jesus, I wish I knew if I was okay.

The hunters surrounded him. He passed out the ammunition in handfuls. His men were grinning.

Marcus walked over, peering at his shoulder. "Take off your hoodie."

"Hold your fire," Martin ordered. "Let them think we're out. They'll come into the open to try and fight Tucker."

"Take off your hoodie," Marcus repeated.

Martin pulled it off awkwardly, trying to keep his right arm as still as possible. His shoulder stung a little as he moved it, but it wasn't bad.

Marcus wiped at his wound with his fingers, peering closely. "You're good sir. They just barely pierced the skin."

Martin nodded and pulled his hoodie back over his head. "I told you I was fine."

Thank fucking God.

Martin walked up to the edge of the temple and peered

around it.

"They're getting more daring," Hux noted, coming up from behind him.

Some of the Carrion men were half out of the entryway tunnels. They would be easy targets.

"I've got a shot," one hunter reported.

"Hold your fire," Martin said. "They'll get bolder."

And they did. One man darted out into the chamber, fired a shell, and darted back in.

"Keep holding," Martin ordered.

"I could have killed him," a hunter named Alex said.

Martin walked up to hunter and put a hand on his shoulder. "You gotta trust me, you saw me fight that God damned Kyle-thing hand to hand. You know I ain't afraid of shit. You have to trust me."

His men obeyed, holding their fire.

Another Carrion man ran out, let loose a pair of shots and returned. Then came another.

"Keep holding," Martin repeated.

A group of five headed towards Tucker's tunnels, laying down a barrage covering fire. Two more of the darkly dressed Carrion men followed soon after.

"Now!" Martin shouted, shouldering his rifle.

The hunters let loose a volley. The group of five Carrion men were the first to fall under their hail of bullets.

"Again!" Martin cried.

The next two fell, and those in the tunnels scurried farther back.

Martin's men let up a cheer, and there was an answering cheer from Tucker's side.

The cheer died down, and Martin noticed two of the five Carrion men were trying to regain their feet.

"Corpses?" Martin asked.

"Fuckers must be wearing some armor or some shit," Hux said. "Takes more to put 'em down for some reason."

Martin shrugged—then he put a bullet in one's head. Huxley dropped the other.

"How many are left?" Martin asked.

"Maybe fifteen," Huxley answered. "Tops."

We're going to win. We're going to fucking win! What would I do if I were them?

Martin thought about this. He'd hightail it back to the Carrion, is what he'd fucking do. Maybe leave one or two people behind to shoot back and . . .

Someone was chanting something. Martin could hear it from across the chamber as the call echoed off the cobblestones.

Martin turned to Hux. "The hell? What's that bastard saying?"

Hux shrugged, so Martin turned to Marcus.

"Don't know, sir."

More of the Carrion men's voices were picking up the chant.

"It sounds like . . ." Marcus said. "It sounds like 'lah-irve.'"

More of them were chanting, many more than fifteen, and they were singing it louder. Now Martin could hear it clearly.

"La . . . Ferve. La . . . Ferve."

Martin saw a man, covered from head to toe with a grey skin tight suit, coming down the tunnel towards them. Martin shouldered his rifled and fired. For a moment, he was sure he'd hit the figure, but he kept on coming.

"La . . . Ferve. La . . . Ferve."

Even from this distance, Martin could tell the man had an imposing physique. His shoulders were broad, narrowing down to a lean set of hips. Some of Tucker's men fired, but they missed too. Martin let loose another shot.

"La . . . Ferve. La . . . Ferve."

"Can't y'all hit nuthin'?" Alex shouted, firing.

"We're not missing," Marcus said.

"The hell?" Huxley breathed.

Martin set his gun down by his side.

"La . . . Ferve. La . . . Ferve."

The figure pulled out a Ruger pistol and took careful aim at where Tucker's men were.

"La . . . Ferve. La . . . Ferve."

In the dim light, Aaron could barely make out Kelly's face as she peered through the small hole in the door. "He's gone," she whispered. "I'm sure of it."

Aaron heard her, he believed her, but he kept his shotgun raised. "Anything else out there?"

She moved her head around the hole. "I don't see anything. There's one wight, but it's pretty damn far down there. I think maybe . . ."

Avery had let his shotgun point down a little, but at her pause, it shot back up to chest level.

Aaron heard footsteps coming down the hall.

They said the wights were immune to bullets. My shotgun may be useless.

Kelly put her back to the wall by the door.

Aaron pointed to his own eye, and then to the lock, trying to get her to look through it to report.

She shook her head no and held a finger up to her lips.

She was probably right, if they just stayed silent, their enemy would pass them by. Then maybe they could escape from Calimay's complex into—his heart sank—into the wilds of the Carrion.

The footsteps got louder.

They've got to be right next to our door.

The footsteps stopped.

Avery's eyes went wide. Kelly held her shotgun up in front of her, ready to turn and fire.

"It's Galen," the warrior's voice announced. "Are you in there?"

Aaron nearly collapsed with relief. Kelly laughed softly, letting her head fall back against the wall. Avery's face broke into a momentary smile.

"We're fine," Aaron whispered. "What's going on?"

"One Horn," Galen answered. "Is Turi with you?"

Kelly sat up straight. "No! I thought he was with you?"

Galen cursed in some foreign language. "Open the door," he said.

"We can't," Aaron answered, "it opens outward. Too much rubble."

"I'll get the hinges," Galen said. "Then we'll have to find Turi."

Hinges? Why didn't I think of that?

"I don't know if Galen would go looking for any of us," Avery muttered.

Kelly snorted. "Maybe not you."

Aaron expected him to look angry, but Avery laughed.

He heard metal scraping as Galen worked at a hinge. Aaron heard the pin fall into the gravel outside the door. It was quickly followed by a second one.

"How did One Horn fucking find us?" Avery asked through the door. "Can he track that well?"

"I doubt it," Galen said. "More likely we were betrayed."

Galen popped the third hinge. He guided the door into the hallway and then dropped it on the ground. "Grab Turi's bag and sword."

Kelly did so, and then they poured out into the hallway, stepping on the fallen door. Down the dimly lit corridor, only visible in the flashes of light, was the wight Kelly had spotted earlier. It was busy eating something, probably a person.

"This way," Galen said.

He led them down through the rubble filled corridors. A few of the walls had collapsed inwards, and they had to climb over the piles of broken stone bricks.

"Mostly wights left now. They aren't hurt by bullets," Galen said. "As before, you have to hurt them hand to hand or with something made from hellstuff. Anything made in the old world won't work."

"We know," Avery said.

"Turi," Turi's voice echoed in from around a corner.

"Turi!" Kelly said, a little too loudly.

The young man came around the bend. He was cut in a few places, and parts of his skin were still rotten, but otherwise he looked fine.

Kelly ran into his arms. The young man hugged her back, but his eyes were on his father.

"What now?" Avery asked.

Galen's face was as stoic and expressionless as it had ever been. "Follow me."

36

Arturus felt more comfortable at his father's side. They walked through the halls Arturus had just come through, but rather than leading them into the heart of the complex, Galen was taking them back into the statue room.

When they got there, Arturus was horrified.

The blue light which had once filled the chamber was so dim that those few statues which still stood looked like ominous enemies rather than masterful works of art. Most had fallen to the ground. A stone arm lay at Arturus' feet, two of its fingers displaced. Cracks had spread through the ironglass ceiling and water was coming down through them.

"It's like rain," Kelly whispered.

The tapestry which had covered one of the far exits lay torn amidst the ruins. The golden threads which had previously depicted Mithras and the bull were drenched with blood and water. Dyitzu fire had claimed a portion of the fabric. One of the wading pools had been broken open, and the far side of the chamber was covered in an inch-deep puddle. Dead bodies of humans, dyitzu and wights littered the chamber.

Galen led them, step by cautious step, into the chamber. His MP5 was slung across his back, which made sense to Arturus since there were far more wights than there were dyitzu.

Arturus saw something move to his right, and there was a splash in the water. He turned to face it, tucking his pistol inside the beltline of the back of his pants. One of the fountains was crumbling. The stone woman who had stood, jug raised, was falling apart. Her jug had split in two, and Arturus could see where the piping, previously hidden, ran through it. She crumbled as he watched, coming down in pieces around the warriors which had supported her—her remains splashing into the water.

Arturus had looked back to his father. Somehow Galen had known to ignore the statue. He was looking straight ahead, towards something else—towards a human figure, dressed all in black, emerging from the darkness.

Malkravyan.

The lone Infidel Friend came slowly forward. Arturus remembered the hatred Malkravyan had for his father. He remembered fearing that the Infidel Friend would kidnap him and take him to see his master. He remembered that the Infidel wanted to use him as bait to draw Saint Wretch across the Erebus.

"You," Avery said, "it was you who led the devils here."

Malkravyan shook his head. "Not I."

For some reason, Arturus believed him.

The Infidel Friend continued to advance as if there were no obstructions, moving under the pattering fall of the water and over the scattered bits of stone, flesh and statuary. Arturus watched his progress, hypnotized. Galen waited silently for his arrival.

Arturus felt his hands shaking. Aaron took a step back. His gun was still pointed down, but he was ready to use it. Arturus could hear Avery's heavy breathing. Kelly was at his side.

Can Father fight one of these men?

Malkravyan stopped only a few paces before Galen.

They stared at each other, two implacable, expressionless soldiers.

How long have you hated each other? And why?

Malkravyan unslung the sword which had hung across his back. In the dim blue light, Arturus could barely make out the golden crests of the hound and the vulture which adorned the hilt of the blade. Kelly caught her breath.

Malkravyan knelt before Galen, bowing his head. The water fell down all around them as the Infidel Friend offered forth the hilt of his blade.

Kelly gripped Arturus' arm fiercely.

"My lord," Malkravyan said, "it would be my honor to fight as your vassal today."

Galen reached down and drew the sword. It was an infidel forged weapon, made of clearsteel and infused with human blood so as to be able to damage those things that were immune to other substances. It was the blood, frozen still as it swirled through the blade, which seemed to give off its own glow. The sword's light was dim, but noticeable beneath the dying, wavy blue illumination of the water that remained above, casting Arturus' father in its blood colored hue. Arturus had never seen a weapon that Galen couldn't handle—but this, this was different. Arturus knew his father—he knew that this was the weapon for which Galen was made. This was the thing that Galen had been born to use. This blade was his father's purpose.

"Give him the gladius, Turi," Galen ordered.

"No need." Malkravyan drew his own short sword, another Infidel forged blade, but this one was colored blue and had the symbol of an eagle stamped into its crosspiece. "I am ready."

Arturus drew his gladius.

Galen let his MP5 fall off of his shoulder. He tossed it to Aaron. Sword drawn, held comfortably, almost negligently, in his right hand, Galen turned towards the heart of Calimay's complex.

37

"La . . . Ferve. La . . . Ferve"

The grey figure which Martin assumed was named La'Ferve walked slowly across the chamber, his Ruger pistol, like the ones the Germans used in World War II movies, held before him. He fired round after round into the halls where Tucker's men were taking cover. Martin wasn't getting the impression that he was missing. Bullets flew back, but it was as if the man was one of those Kyle-things.

He's not, it's that suit.

Martin had seen that shade of grey before. It was Icanitzu skin. Somehow the skin kept the Icanitzu's immunity to bullets even after its death.

I can still kill him. I just can't do it with a gun.

Martin looked to the cobblestones he'd used to kill the Kyle-thing.

You poor bastard, La'Ferve. If you had come just a few days earlier, I wouldn't know how to defeat you.

"Retreat," Martin ordered his men. "Run back to the corridors. Keep the temple between you and him."

"He'll gun us down!" Marcus said. "He'll move around the temple and kill us."

Martin shook his head. "No he won't. I'm going to stay here and hold him off. I'm too damn tired to run anyway."

"La . . . Ferve. La . . . Ferve"

Martin peeked around the edge of the temple. La'Ferve was

loading another magazine into his pistol, and he was walking away from Tucker's men now—towards the temple.

"Now!" Martin ordered. "Run!"

His men bolted, leaving the temple as fast as they could. Martin lay down amidst the bodies, facing his wounded shoulder towards where he imagined La'Ferve would come.

He saw La'Ferve now, jogging after his men. The man let loose a bullet, and Martin heard one of his men cry out.

His aim is inhuman.

"To the right!" Marcus's voice called out over the chants of the Carrion men. "Keep the temple between us."

Martin wasn't sure how long he could wait, lying like this next to one of his dead hunters. Each second he delayed meant there was less distance between himself and La'Ferve, but it also meant that another one of his men might die.

But if I get shot down, they'll have no chance at all.

It was as good a reason to be a coward as any other, he supposed. La'Ferve was trotting forward, seemingly unconcerned about speed.

And why would he be? He's invincible.

Invincible to bullets perhaps, but Martin was going to deck him in the head with a cobblestone. Let the Carrion men shoot him down—Martin didn't care. What mattered was that his enemy died first.

La'Ferve fired another shot, and there was another shout. Martin hardened his heart.

La'Ferve was almost upon him—then the man's grey form passed by, only a few feet away.

Martin leapt to his feet, rock raised high. He rushed forward and swung it at La'Ferve's head.

The man's reflexes were unbelievable. Even while running, La'Ferve turned his huge frame around, his feet dancing over the cobblestones, gun arm raised to block the blow. Martin's rock impacted with the man's Ruger, sending the weapon spinning across the cobblestones, its clip coming loose.

Hell!

Martin found himself only a few feet away from the hulking figure. The grey hood had two black bulbous protrusions in place of eyeholes. The Icanitzu hide was form fitting, and Martin could see La'Ferve's rippling physique through it. The man's balance and speed had been impeccable.

Martin wasn't ready for this fight—he needed to run—but then he heard his soldiers calling.

"Mar . . . tin. Mar . . . tin."

Martin raised his fists.

Arturus had never seen such slaughter. Galen's sword whipped back and forth, his body moving in subtle ways to add its weight to the lightening quick strikes. Black blood erupted from the wounds, forced through the air from the tremendous momentum of the blows. Struck body parts would snap back as if they'd been hit by bullets. Some were severed. Skulls, seemingly made of sinfruit, gave way before the Infidel blade. The wights did show signs of fear, but they were never able to flee. Galen's darting steps kept them in range. There was no escaping him.

And where Galen went, Malkravyan followed. The infidel's technique was impeccable. It was spare where Galen flourished. Tight where Galen was expansive. Textbook where Galen was artistic. Arturus felt chills tingling up his spine because with every step the Infidel Friend took, with each display of skill, Arturus became more and more sure that he'd had the same kind of training.

Had his father not said that the Infidel owed him a favor? Had Galen learned from the Infidel Friend, or they from him? Or maybe there was one technique that was regarded as being right by all?

No, Arturus knew those couldn't be the answers. This was the way the ancients fought. The Infidel had been an ancient. Galen had said the Infidel was even their emperor. Galen was very old—it was not inconceivable to think that he had been an ancient, or if not that, then perhaps he had trained with one.

"Help back here!" Kelly shouted.

Arturus turned around and saw a pair of wights advancing. "Got it."

Neither Galen nor Malkravyan contradicted him. Arturus passed Aaron, Avery and Kelly, approaching the wights. He kept his left side forward, his sword in his rear hand to try and lure them in. The wights clawed at him, and Arturus stepped back with his left foot, switching his lead leg while striking upward with an underhand blow. His hips and footwork mimicked an uppercut, and the momentum of his body flowed into the strike. The tip of the gladius split the wight's jaw.

Leaving his weapon high, Arturus rotated his shoulder and struck again at the same wight, slashing sideways. Even as he did so, he pivoted on the ball of his right foot so that his weight would be added to the blow. The gladius tore through the cheekbone and nose of the creature, sending it sprawling to the ground.

Arturus lowered his left shoulder so that his pivot brought him slamming into the second wight. It tried to grab him, but Arturus changed levels, dropping low. His left hand caught the thing's ankle before he sprang back up. He threw the leg away as he spun, shifting his hold on his gladius into a backhanded grip and spinning so that the blade buried itself into the corpse's neck. Arturus threw a back kick to separate his sword from the wight, dropping it to the ground.

Kelly was staring at him.

"I love you," she said. "God damn, boy, I love you."

Arturus could see the blue and red glow of the destruction his father and Malkravyan were wreaking upon the enemy. Arturus hung back, trailing behind his friends, protecting them from the wights which came from behind. He hadn't been properly trained for the sword, he knew that now, but he felt inspired by his father's movements. The old lessons and footwork came back to him, bit by bit—and where his experience was lacking, he filled in his weaknesses with his hand to hand knowledge.

This thing I've become, it's nearly as good as they.

It had never occurred to him that human beings could have such power. He knew that a single Icanitzu could kill a dozen men. Those devils were immune to bullets, and excelled at types of combat for which most human beings were simply not prepared. He found that these wights were similarly vulnerable to his blade.

This is what Galen has taught me. He has made me a devil slayer. This is what we must teach every person who will lift a finger to fight the Devil.

They descended down through the complex, lower than where Calimay had been when Arturus had left her, and into a red level. The light was more stable here, flickering only slightly at irregular intervals. They passed by the statue room where Arturus and Malkravyan had spoken before. All around them the wights died. Then Arturus heard hooves clacking against stone.

One Horn.

He heard Calista's frightened orders and the shouts of her soldiers. Galen sped up to a jog, and Arturus was happy for it. Behind a flurry of strikes, Galen led them into a large complex of grey chambers out from under the red ironglass roof which had covered the rest of the level. One of the far walls had collapsed. On top of the rubble stood Calimay, Calista, and three other lavender robed priestesses. In a line before them were soldiers and slaves, each doing their best to hold off the mass of wights. With the Minotaur upon them, there was no hope. He was tearing through their line, his ham-fisted blows sending men sliding across the stones with broken noses, necks and collarbones. His quick head butts left slaves gored through the middle. He turned and kicked backwards, his leg striking with enough power to crack the skull of the man he'd targeted. He kicked again, crushing a soldier's midsection between a wall and his hoof.

The soldier he'd kicked dropped, bent over at an angle that was unnatural for a human body. The strength of the blow, even though it occurred across the room, had caused the entranceway to shake. Some of the stones over their heads were coming loose. Arturus hurried to the right, dragging Kelly with him. Aaron and Avery followed, but Galen and Malkravyan walked straight forward, their eyes on the Minotaur.

One Horn turned to regard them, standing still amidst the ruins he'd made in Calimay's line. Human blood covered its chest in streaks. In places the blood had dripped down its muscular torso before soaking into a now red tinged ring of fur at its waistline.

Arturus stopped, transfixed by the massive figure. Kelly tore her hand loose from his grasp and picked up a rock from the floor. Aaron screamed, running along the far wall and throwing himself into the back of the line of the wights. Kelly came soon after him, hammering away, swinging her rock in long arcs that ended with the head of a wight.

Avery was more cautious, but as soon as a wounded wight tried to circle around to attack Kelly from behind, he sprang to action, wrestling it to the ground.

After One Horn's devastation, Calimay's men and the wights had become mixed together. Calimay herself came charging down from the rocks, swinging a woodstone plank before her, trying to fill the hole where the Minotaur had killed her people.

Aaron chose correctly. He'll fight along the wall so he can't be surrounded completely--and he's away from the Minotaur.

Galen and Malkravyan both dropped their packs. Arturus let his own fall off of his shoulders.

One Horn didn't seem to even notice Aaron's assault. The bullman left the uneven line of men and wights, its hooves stomping an even rhythm against the stone floor. Malkravyan broke off to the left while Galen moved to the right. They began to circle the Minotaur, who himself turned around with every few steps, keeping one in his direct vision and the other in his peripheral at all times. Without communicating, Galen and Malkravyan switched directions, and the Minotaur had to step quickly to dodge Galen's sword strike.

I know this dance.

He, Rick and Galen had practiced it around a pillar.

I can do this. I should be helping. Were I a general, I would order myself to fight One Horn.

But Kelly had lost her footing. Arturus came to her aid, slashing at the wight nearest to her and sending it reeling back. Kelly was on her feet again in an instant.

One Horn's roar pulled at Arturus. He turned away from the wights.

"I'm joining," Arturus announced.

He felt Kelly's hand grip at his wrist. He turned for a second, cutting down a wight with a quick slash, and she withdrew her hand.

"Fuck him up, baby," Kelly said.

Arturus moved towards the Minotaur, gladius raised.

Almost reluctantly, it seemed, La'Ferve raised his hands.

He doesn't want to view me as a worthy opponent. Well fuck him.

"Mar . . . tin. Mar . . . tin."

All Martin knew about fighting was that he had a hard head. As a younger man, a bully had tired himself out beating him. At this point, Martin didn't mind if that was what was going to happen here. He'd found reserves of strength within himself in the last week that he had never known he had. It was time to use some of them.

Martin leapt forward, slinging a haymaker at La'Ferve. He hit nothing. La'Ferve had moved back at an angle. The man's feet were light on the ground, his huge frame seeming unnaturally mobile.

What the hell is this guy?

La'Ferve's arms lowered.

Martin swung again, he had no idea whether he hit or not, all he knew was that bright lights exploded into his vision. He stumbled backwards, finding his balance. He had not known it was possible to be hit that hard.

It was odd, but the cobblestone covered floor seemed to be vertical.

Oh, shit, I didn't find my balance. I'm on the ground.

La'Ferve was already walking away. There were shouts of alarm from his soldiers.

"La . . . Ferve. La . . . Ferve"

Martin struggled to stand, but the world wouldn't stop moving.

"La'Ferve!" he shouted.

The man looked at him, those bulbous black eyes on the hood staring into Martin's soul.

Somehow Martin found his balance.

He's trained, but I don't care. I won't go down.

Martin came forward again, his vision swimming. He threw another punch, and his vision was obscured by bright lights once more. Against his will, his body staggered to the left. He raised his hands high over his head, blocking La'Ferve's follow up strike. Even though he blocked the blow, the force was unbelievable. Martin had not thought that a human could generate that much power. The next punch hit Martin in his exposed left side, just below his floating ribs.

Despite his will, his body gave up. He toppled backwards to the ground. Martin had never felt pain like this before.

I will not fail.

Blood was pouring down from a cut he hadn't known he received, blocking out the vision of his right eye. He staggered to his feet, but his torso wouldn't straighten all the way.

God, help me. I can't win this.

Martin looked to the gun on the ground. That wouldn't help him. Even if he managed to get the Ruger, it would do no damage to La'Ferve's armored body. He looked for weaknesses. Maybe if he shot him in the eye . . . but the bulbous black covering of the eyehole in the hood was the Icanitzu's eye. That probably wouldn't work.

The hood.

Martin managed to straighten himself.

You fool, you don't need to win, you just need to get the hood off of his body, then your men can shoot him.

It wasn't fighting fair, but fighting fair wasn't what Martin was all about. He fought dirty. He would claw out the man's teeth if he had to.

He bent down and picked up a rock. He threw it at La'Ferve as a distraction and charged—not like a fighter—but like a football player. With his head lowered, Martin had no idea how his throw had done. All he knew was that when he ran into La'Ferve, it was like running into a brick wall. Suddenly the man's weight was pressing down upon him. He felt La'Ferve overhook his arm.

Then La'Ferve was beside him, a leg in front of Martin's. Martin felt himself being thrown. His head hit the temple wall and he heard a tremendous crack. When he hit the ground, he couldn't see.

My neck, is it broken?

Wasn't there something he had to do? Wasn't there a reason he had to get back up? There must have been, and it was a very important reason too, only it took too much effort to remember. Maybe it was Katie. Did she need him? Of course, he had to do something for her. But he felt so comfortable. She would understand if he did it later. She would have to understand. He was tired—so very tired. And it was nice, laying here. She wouldn't mind after he explained that to her.

Galen and Malkravyan altered their positioning as Arturus approached One Horn. Neither seemed to care that he was too young to be in this battle. What mattered, Arturus believed, was whether he moved correctly or not.

Galen was their lead man now because the Minotaur was closest to him. When Galen switched directions, Arturus copied him. When Galen juked back and forth, Arturus did too. He knew his father's movements so well that he almost sensed them before they came. He wasn't sure if he would be able to keep up with Malkravyan, but he would do his best.

The bullman charged and Galen danced out of its range, circling off to the left.

Hell, I'm up.

Arturus darted towards the Minotaur's back and slashed it. The thing's skin was unbelievably tough, and the gladius' point only pierced the skin in one place. A drop of fresh, bright red blood rose and beaded there.

The Minotaur spun, head lowered to charge at Arturus.

Now I'm the lead.

Arturus faked left, and then circled right. The Minotaur stayed with him, not fooled by his feint. Since its head was lowered, Arturus guessed that an upwards swing with his sword might be the most effective. He got ready to pivot out of the way and give the strike, but the bullman stopped suddenly and kicked backward. The kick missed the closing Malkravyan who, using some instinct that Arturus would have thought foreign to the human race, had managed to dodge the strike. One Horn turned suddenly and fired a kick back at Arturus. Arturus ducked, surprised to see how close he was to the wall. The Minotaur's foot sent cracks spreading through the stone behind him. Arturus sprinted forward as part of the wall gave way. He saw Avery and a wight go down under the rubble, but Aaron and Kelly managed to get clear.

Arturus, Malkravyan, and Galen rejoined the circle around the Minotaur.

He's smart. Those kicks are going to make it more difficult to close the distance at his back. He can be unpredictable this way.

Galen was already adapting, however, and was staying closer to the Minotaur. They needed to be closer. Their margin of error would be low, but it would be easier to strike. Such an offensive solution was pure Galen. Arturus and Malkravyan adjusted as well.

One Horn charged at Arturus again.

He thinks I'm the weakest link.

Arturus began to move back, but stopped suddenly and charged forward, sword leading.

One Horn tried to gore him, but Arturus got lower. The Minotaur grabbed at him, but Arturus guided the point of the gladius into its right bicep and pivoted towards that arm. The Minotaur adjusted, coming straight at him. Arturus grabbed on with his free arm, locking up with the beast as it came forward.

That much force was more than Arturus could ever fight directly, so he absorbed the Minotaur's momentum slowly, sliding backwards and circling. One Horn screeched in pain as it started to take damage from Malkravyan. Arturus tossed his gladius over his head towards his father.

One Horn was driving him towards the wall.

Arturus stayed locked up with the Minotaur, putting his forearm into the bullman's neck and jumping right before the upcoming impact. He had meant to use his legs to absorb One Horn's force, but the bullman kept pushing, and Arturus found himself walking backwards up the wall. Suddenly he was high over the Minotaur's head. The odd angle let him slip out of the beast's grasp. Arturus kicked as hard as he could off the corner of the ceiling and the wall. He hit the ground rolling and came to his feet. Blood was pouring out of a series of wounds on the Minotaur's back and forearms.

Malkravyan covered Arturus, stepping before the Minotaur, his blue sword flashing back and forth in a sudden onslaught. Arturus turned to his father and saw his gladius was already sailing back to him.

He caught the blade. "Ready!" Arturus shouted.

Malkravyan stepped back, fending off the Minotaur's fury. He was the lead now, and Arturus attempted to keep up with his movements. Even though Malkravyan's style was completely different than his father's, the man's motion was so intuitive, so smooth, that Arturus felt that he could simply stop thinking and move with his gut. It was as if this dance was a language all its own—a language of which the Minotaur was ignorant, but that the three of them shared. Galen leapt in, his red sword drawing darker red blood. One Horn ignored the strikes and stayed with Malkravyan. The Infidel Friend's footwork was immaculate. Though the Minotaur tried, he could not close the distance, and Galen was catching up again. This time One Horn was ready for him. The bullman stopped itself by bending over and putting its hands against the floor. So sudden was the motion that Malkravyan, who should have been striking at the bullman's exposed head and shoulders, had to catch his balance.

It kicked out towards Galen, but as always, Arturus' father was a step ahead of his enemy. And, just as before, Galen's solution was completely offensive. Arturus didn't know how much the Minotaur weighed—perhaps eight hundred pounds, perhaps half a ton—but it did not matter to Galen. Tossing his sword aside, he overhooked the leg with his right arm and powered forward into the Minotaur's body. Wrapping his left arm around the Minotaur's giant torso, and blocking the beast's untrapped leg with his calf, Galen pushed on.

The Minotaur, still bent over from its kick, tried to catch itself with its arms. They buckled and it crashed face first into the stone at Malkravyan's feet. Malkravyan drove his sword down through the Minotaur's neck at the base of its skull. One Horn screamed like a Fury, struggling upwards to its hands and knees. The bullman shucked Galen off with a powerful shove and tried to strike at Malkravyan while it stood. Even while evading the Minotaur's blow, the Infidel withdrew his sword at an angle so that it tore the wound open wider.

Were this a dyitzu, or a human, or even an Icanitzu, the blow the Infidel Friend had given it would have been fatal. The Minotaur just snorted, heedless of the stream of blood issuing from its neck. Arturus picked up his father's dropped blade and tossed it.

They reformed the circle as Galen snatched the sword out of the air.

One Horn went after Malkravyan again, this time trying to circle in from the Infidel Friend's right. Arturus rushed forward, ready to strike but wary of a sudden kick. The kick came, but not in the way that Arturus was expecting. Previously, the thing had chambered its leg before kicking backwards. This time it left its leg straight and swung it back and up. It bent its torso down as it did so, adding power to the strike. Arturus struggled to evade the awkward blow, but managed. The Minotaur, however, seemed ready for this. Its leg retracted suddenly and shot back out. Arturus saw it and tried to slip the strike. The blow caught him on the shoulder and sent him careening backwards.

He rolled carefully around his gladius and came back up to his feet to see the Minotaur charging at him. He acted dazed, but at the last minute pivoted away while delivering an upswing. The tip of the gladius tore through one of the bullman's nostrils sending blood and snot through the air. One Horn howled in agony. The howl changed its pitch, becoming a smooth, even tone which doubled and redoubled in volume. The room around them vibrated with the intensity of the call as it slowly changed from an even tenor into understandable words.

TO ME!

And for a moment, Hell seemed to center around One Horn. Arturus felt drawn to the beast. It was as if a sphere of attraction was spreading out through the room with the echo of that horrible single note song it sung, sucking in some kind of energy Arturus was only dimly aware of.

Then all was silent.

The line of wights turned, rushing away from Calimay's soldiers.

The bullman, covered in its own sweat and blood, was

hunched over, worn down from its wounds and the effort it had taken to make its call. It couldn't win on its own, and it knew it—but it didn't have to. Calimay's soldiers struck out against the wights as they turned away, but even so, that left nearly a score and a half of them coming.

Shit.

"Keep them clear," Galen ordered.

Arturus and Malkravyan broke off to face the wights. This meant that Galen would have to remain on the offensive lest One Horn get a strike in at one of their backs.

Unfortunately for One Horn, that's the way Galen fights.

What would have been reckless abandon from anyone else was cold calculation from Galen. Arturus' father rushed forward behind a series of sword swings, but those were just a distraction. Galen shot in to wrestle with the beast.

Arturus could only trust that his father knew what he was doing.

He and Malkravyan squared off against the approaching mass of wights. The gladius was a stabbing weapon first and foremost, but without a shield, he couldn't risk getting the blade caught. Arturus kept swinging at their faces, drawing black blood, then retreating. Drawing more, and then retreating. Malkravyan was having better luck. He was stepping back too, but the wights were dropping all around him.

"Forward!" Calimay screeched.

Suddenly there was a surge from behind the wights, and the soldiers and slaves were upon them, bludgeoning them from behind with stones.

Malkravyan was able to turn away first. Arturus struck and retreated, struck and retreated, struck and . . . his wights had Calimay's men to worry about.

He dashed back to One Horn. Galen had one of its legs over his shoulder and was throwing knees into its side. Malkravyan was moving around to the far side.

"We're back!" Arturus shouted.

Galen pulled away, sidestepped a kick and then raised his hand. Arturus picked up the red blade and tossed it.

They reformed the circle.

The Minotaur came cautiously forward. Arturus had seen dyitzu afraid on the Erebus, and now he saw fear in the

Minotaur's eyes. Blood poured from its dozens of wounds, dripping down its legs and pooling at its hooves.

It's time.

Without having to be told, Arturus knew that their strategy had changed.

Galen charged forward. The Minotaur had to turn and spin away to avoid the worst of the strikes, but in so doing it ran right into Malkravyan's ruthless charge. Again, out of self preservation, the Minotaur had to pull back—but Arturus was there, his bodyweight adding sting to his strikes. This time his blows cut deeper. In desperation One Horn kicked again, but Arturus was ready, and he slashed a huge gash into the fur just above the beast's hoof.

Then Galen was there again. It tried to put its foot down, but the wound Arturus had given it caused the leg to buckle. That moment was more than Galen needed. His sword struck through its eye, burying deep into its brain. When Galen removed the sword it came out with chunks of eyeball and grey matter. The Minotaur still struggled on, but Arturus and Malkravyan continued to strike.

SEEBA ALUAFI

Its brain, it can no longer speak.

It had lost coordination too. Aggressive to the core, it continued to strike out at them, but the menacing intelligence which had made the beast so dangerous was gone. Its balance was off as well, either from Galen's strike into its brain, or from the leg wound Arturus had delivered. It fought futily on, striking back at whoever had hit it last. It was too slow, and too stupid, and the wounds kept mounting. Its limbs weren't working well. They could only move in jerks, and the beast seemed to have trouble retracting its right arm. Malkravyan leveled a particularly heavy strike at its head, severing the beast's remaining horn.

AEEB FUINA KALLA

Dyitzu came pouring into the room. Arturus saw them over the shoulder of the beleaguered Minotaur. Galen and Malkravyan's backs were to them.

They were farther away. It took longer for One Horn's call to reach them.

"Behind you!" Arturus warned.

Malkravyan turned just in time to avoid a ball of fire. A dyitzu came in right behind it. Malkravyan cut it down, his blue sword humming.

The Minotaur charged at Galen's suddenly turned back. Galen, an eye over his shoulder, swung his ruddy blade at a fireball. It exploded into pitch as his sword stole its consistency, and the burning liquid splattered behind him, catching in One Horn's fur.

The bullman turned away suddenly, roaring its incomprehensible fury, falling to its knees and batting at the flames. Arturus could see the blood boiling off of its torso's fur line as the liquid fire streaked down its body. The Minotaur looked up with its remaining eye—and saw Arturus.

Oh shit.

The maddened beast came at him.

Arturus hoped his father or Malkravyan would come attack its exposed back, but they had formed their own spinning circle, this time back to back, to try and fend off the dyitzu.

Arturus backpedaled to gain some time, looking to Calimay's fighters and Aaron for support, but they were struggling with the wights.

Arturus stopped backpedaling and accepted his fate. For now, it was just him and the beast. It was limping as it approached him, stepping gingerly with its left leg. Its right eye was a mess of black blood which poured out of the gaping wound Galen had left it. The blood ran as a dark coagulated sludge down to the base of its snout.

I too cry blood.

Arturus stayed light on his feet, coming straight at the Minotaur. It swung out at him madly, its fist cutting through the air. Arturus slipped the blow and darted quickly towards its left. One Horn tried to cut him off, but the thing's weak right leg wobbled when it stepped.

Sensing his moment, Arturus darted again to its left and stabbed forward.

He had underestimated the beast.

Even with the blow to its eye and brain, One Horn's cunning was still formidable. Rather than trying to keep up with Arturus, the beast spun around completely and leapt forward off of its good hoof. Arturus' sword punctured through its abdomen, but One Horn had caught him up in its arms and was charging with him towards the wall.

Arturus pushed back, sliding his arm up to try and break the Minotaur's grip, but the beast's strength was beyond him. He reached out with one foot, trying to post it against the ground. For a second he felt the rubble, but then he was slammed into the wall.

The impact was horrific. Arturus couldn't remember ever having been hit so hard, but it was also his moment opportunity. In the instant after the collision, Arturus felt the arms of the Minotaur slacken, just slightly. He squirmed, getting both of his arms under the Minotaur's bear-hug hold. He kicked off the wall spinning away.

Arturus felt something in his mouth, and it was suddenly full of bitter tasting saliva. He spat and pieces of two crushed teeth, a small part of his tongue, and a mouthful of blood came out. Horrified, he drew the gladius out of the Minotaur's abdomen and struck. He moved backwards, his balance shaky, still spitting blood.

The Minotaur advanced, murder in its eyes, but Galen and Malkravyan were returning—coming at it from its left.

It can't see them.

Arturus stopped suddenly and rushed the Minotaur, slashing furiously before stabbing it again in the abdomen. Galen barreled into its side, sending it staggering back. Its left leg gave way and it collapsed. Galen buried his blade into the Minotaur's remaining eye. Even blind, it stood. Malkravyan stabbed it through the neck again. Arturus came in hard at its leg, severing a tendon there with three hard thrusts. It toppled again. Arturus hacked at its body. It raised its left arm to fend off the blows, but its right did nothing. Arturus could see where his father's sword thrust through the back of its shoulder had rendered that arm useless. Galen turned his attention to the beast's chest. His sword plunged into its sternum. He jerked powerfully to one side, and then the other. He shoved the sword deeper in, and, after it caught on something in the Minotaur's body, jerked left and right again. Malkravyan joined the effort, opening the rib cage to expose its beating heart. Arturus buried his gladius into the tough muscle. When it kept beating, he struck again, and again.

The heart stopped.

One Horn gasped and rolled over, organs spilling out from its open chest, and crawled blindly, thoughtlessly, towards the wall. One of its outstretched hands touch the stone and then, finally, the Minotaur lay still.

 — 39 —

Martin had no sense of his body, nor could he see—but he could smell. He smelled hellstone and blood. He could taste the blood, too, sense its tang as a nebulous cloud that was—somewhere.

And he could hear. He could hear footsteps across the cobblestones.

Am I like—my friend . . . what was his name? My best friend. The silent one. The dead one.

"You were fooled by lambs," a voice said.

"I'm sorry, La'Ferve. I was incautious. I will not underestimate these people again."

"It is understandable, they are occasionally cunning. The man, Charlie, he was that way—a cunning lamb. Maab believes now that he ran here."

"Was our contact lying?"

"No, he told the truth. The lambs slew the lepers, but there was a stonewight here, like those used by the army of the City of Blood and Stone. Its body has Nephysis' mark."

"He has turned against us."

"Or away from us. Nephysis does not like to be ruled. He may play us against the other. He may still be an ally at times."

"You're assuming your son succeeds."

"That's correct, if Callous fails, we'll all be digging rock in the pits of Cul' Nahedran."

Arturus dug like a madman through the rubble. Galen tossed Malkravyan his sword and ran to help.

"Might I have use of your soldiers, Calimay?" Malkravyan asked. "There are many wights and dyitzu remaining in your corridors, I want to clear a path to the exit for you."

"There's a secret exit below us, I'll show—"

"I know where it is," Malkravyan said.

Calimay gritted her teeth. "Follow him."

Aaron and a group of soldiers followed Malkravyan out of the room.

Arturus kept digging, tossing the stones over his shoulder. He heard Avery's agonized groan.

"Slowly, Son," Galen said. "He's alive. You don't want to let the rubble shift and change that.

Calista and Kelly were nearby, both staring at him.

Arturus could overhear Carlotta, one of Calimay's daughters and a woman he had once slept with, speaking. "It will not be easy to get the serfs to give up the weapons."

"Then don't bother asking them."

"Mother?"

"We must leave this place, and having more armed men will only help us." Calimay responded.

There was blood amidst the stones that had fallen on Avery. The urge to hurry was almost impossible to fight, but Arturus did his best. Avery's chest and arms were uncovered. Somehow the rocks had born most of their own weight and spared his life.

"Stop," Galen said. "Dig no more."

Arturus looked at his father in confusion. Then, slowly, he put his rock aside. He looked into the mound of stones, hoping to discover what it was his father feared. It didn't look like digging more would cause a collapse.

What has him worried?

And then he saw. Avery's body had been twisted completely around. He had not bled to death because the pressure of the stones was keeping his wounds closed. If they pulled him free, he would have no legs or hips. He would die.

"What's wrong?" Avery said. "What's going on?"

Arturus looked around for Aaron, but the hunter had left with Malkravyan.

"Don't move, Avery," Galen said. "The rocks that pin you are keeping you alive. If you push yourself free of them, you will die."

Kelly took Arturus' hand. "Will he live?"

Galen turned to Calimay. "You intend to flee this place?"

She nodded. "I have another place semi-prepared. With the rustrock we should be able to keep it hidden."

"Don't fucking leave me here," Avery said. "No fucking way, man. You're going to leave me here."

"We are," Galen said. "When Aaron returns with Malkravyan, we will head straight for the Lethe."

Avery shook his head. "You need a guide. You can't go without the guide."

"Malkravyan is the guide," Galen said.

"This ain't right, we've been through so much. So much."

"I'll leave you with food, a shotgun, and plenty of shells. Stay strong, Avery. Push yourself out a little, a twelfth of an inch or so, each day. If you do that long enough, you will be able to survive."

Avery's eyes were wide. "There's no way I'll last that long. This is just like what we did . . . to Kyle." He closed his eyes and took in a shaky breath. "I understand."

Soldiers came back running into the room, Malkravyan and Aaron in their wake.

"It's clear," Malkravyan reported.

Avery turned to Kelly. "I'm sorry."

"You are a thousand times forgiven."

Galen pulled out some dyitzu meat from his pack, his canteen, and some shells. He picked up a shotgun from one of the fallen soldiers and handed it to him.

"You'll need a lot of luck," Galen said, "but I may indeed see you again. Malkravyan, will you take him home if he survives?"

"If he survives, and he can find me, then I will."

Arturus knew that would never happen.

He'll have no way to find Calimay's home. And even if we could give him good directions, we couldn't do that without making him the liability that Tamara was.

"Goodbye, my friend." Arturus said.

I really am a killer now. When it was time to leave Kyle, I at least fought for him.

Calimay's troops and slaves were leaving the chamber. "You

know where to find me?" she asked the Infidel Friend.

"I do."

She stood directly before him, looking up into Malkravyan's expressionless visage. "And you will help me as before?"

"Now that you have decided to arm your serfs, my help will be in earnest."

Her broad lips formed a smile. "Good. See you shortly." She turned away towards her men. "Let's move."

They started running out.

Kelly knelt by Avery's side and whispered something into his ear. Then she stood and stepped away.

"Good hunting," Aaron told Avery.

Avery grimaced. "Good hunting."

"Quickly, we must keep up with Malkravyan," Galen said. "Follow me."

As they left, Arturus looked back to see Avery one last time. He was looking at the ceiling, his arms crossed.

"It's just me then," Aaron said as they jogged through the rock strewn corridor. "I'll be the only hunter to return. All my men are dead."

Galen shrugged as he ran. "You aren't home yet."

That's my father. A big old softy.

From Neostoicism: Philosophia

. . . as foolish children might, they killed, gluttonizing upon the herd of the sun god—so that he who was the creator of days took from them the day that was to be their homecoming.
—*Anonymous Greek*

Cavé, lest the wanderer find that horrid fear to be true: that his journey home might, in the end, be itself sweeter than his destination.
—*Kent*

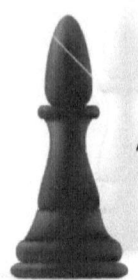

Part X
The Boy and the River

From Gehennic Law: Old Man Sisyphus

Hermes, on a day when all seemed well but all was dark, found himself supremely troubled—and in hopes that a stroll might facilitate his thinking—he took to walking. When his thoughts became too troubled, he began wandering the underworld so that the scenery would match his mood. He paused at the base of a mountain where he sat down and pondered his woes.

He heard then a great clamor as a boulder came careening down from the heights. It eventually came to rest at the base of the mountain close to where Hermes sat. Sisyphus came trotting down afterwards—for it was his eternal fate to uselessly push this boulder up the mountain as a punishment for fooling the gods.

"Hermes," Sisyphus said, "I had not thought to ever see you here, or to see you so troubled."

"I'm worried I do not exist."

Sisyphus shrugged. "Doesn't seem like a big deal to me, either way, but why would you worry so?"

"I am a god, so I understand the concept of infinity. Imagine a dartboard, and assume I throw a dart at it. There are an infinite amount of points on the dartboard where the dart can strike. I contemplate the probabilities of it hitting the dartboard at any point. It must be possible to hit the dartboard, yes? But if we assign any probability whatsoever to the dart hitting a point, and knowing those points to be infinite, then the total sum of the probabilities must end up higher than one—thus precluding that the dart could ever miss the dartboard."

Sisyphus nodded. "Sounds like you've been talking with Xeno. Look, I am a man, so I cannot claim to understand infinity, but as a man, I have a working knowledge of the infinitesimal.

The odds of hitting any one point on the dartboard are infinitesimal. There are an infinite number of infinite sets of infinitesimal numbers which, when added together, will never reach one. Also, when Max Planck dies, he'll explain to you just how many points are on the dartboard, but that's not important right now."

Hermes was grateful. "Thank you, Sisyphus. This problem had bothered me for some time. Is there any way that I can repay you for your insight? Perhaps I could have Hades free you from your torment?"

Sisyphus thought about this and said, "I don't much mind the eternal torment, but maybe you could see if that bastard has a bigger mountain."

Carlisle did not know how many epochs he'd lain there. Those fools in the old world, the ones that believed in evolution, they had talked about a thing called deep time. They were fools for two reasons. First, they denied God in their hearts. Second, the world wasn't billions of years old, it was only six thousand. Who would take a man's word over God's? A fool, that's who.

But they had been tragically right in a way, too, Carlisle found. He did not need to eat or drink. It was not possible to sleep. All that remained for him to do was lie there. He began to grasp the meaning of a decade. On Earth, it had been impossible to fathom because people and things were always distracting you. You could blink, and a decade was gone—or you could get so caught up in a moment that it seemed like a decade was an eternity. But now, lying here without moving or speaking, he began to understand time. He didn't know what portions of his stay were longer than a decade, only that they were—and that they passed. And that more passed. And that hundreds and hundreds of them had passed. And then thousands and thousands. And then millions and millions. And finally, billions and billions.

That was torture enough, but there was something worse. On Earth, a man could forget things. He would forget how to speak. He might even, given long enough, get used to the idea of nothing. Eventually, a person might become a passive thing that just watched without the need to measure the passage of time. He could be like a rock. For all intents and purposes, his soul would be in oblivion, not Hell.

Carlisle was denied this comfort. Insanity never came for him. His internal monologue never stopped because he could not forget the English language. He could never get used to nothingness because he could always remember, and somehow continue to expect, that something was supposed to be happening.

He could not imagine an agony like this one. Of all the tortures of Hell, of his infuriating pair of deaths at the hands of the Infidel, of the ruthless pain of the dyitzu, of the horrors that Mephistopheles had needed to inflict upon his mind so that he might climb the ladder of souls—none of them, not one of them even in the slightest, measured up to the horror of eternity. Nothing that he had ever imagined measured up against the

Hell that was deep time. And yet, there was something more terrifying than even that. He didn't know how much farther down he had to go to meet a horror greater than this—or even if he had come far enough down already—but one thing was certain, eventually he would find a Hell that was worse. Sooner or later, one of these people was going to ruin this eternity by speaking too loudly, and then the demons would find him.

They would claw apart this small accident, this Hell between Hells that their friend kept alive with the power granted to him by Aezcherbaelyn. That terror was in his thoughts. It had been in his thoughts through this deep time, digging a narrow trench of cowardice ever deeper towards the infinite depths of his own empty soul.

Then, one day, billions of years, perhaps, after he had fallen, that trench hit bottom.

He turned to the man next to him.

"The people," Carlisle whispered, "the ones through the cracks, they're the same."

The man nodded. "The light here is slow. That's because time is wrong."

"How long have we been here?" Carlisle asked.

The woman glared at him with her beady eyes. *Be silent,* those eyes said.

"I came here from that Hell." The man's soft voice answered. "My best guess is that people survived there for a year or so. To stay alive you have to keep yourself together. The waves of color try to tear you apart with their motion. You have to accept pain to keep yourself in one piece. You have to experience sorrow to move among the waves. You try to take on as much sorrow as you can to find a calm spot, but it destroys you, so you start taking on too much pain. You try to find a balance, and sometimes you can do alright . . . but then the storms come, and they tear you apart. I am so glad to be here."

"They only live a year? We've lain here less than a year? How much less?"

The man shrugged, and then turned away.

So Carlisle waited through the deep time. He had never thought about time before, not really. He began to understand its infinite nature. As long as he had been here, he could wait that long again. Then he could combine those two times and wait that long. And then those two, and so on and so on—forever. And ever.

So Carlisle lay down again. The epochs passed by. He could only guess at them. There was no way to really measure what millennia went where, and what million years went there.

"You speak English?" Carlisle asked.

"Yes," the man whispered back. "In Hell, souls pull at each other. We probably drew you here. The more similar, the stronger the pull."

And he waited. He waited as long as he guessed between his fall and him speaking to the man about time. Then he waited a little longer to be sure. Then he added those times together and began to wait again.

After a while, Carlisle saw a man walking up towards him. The man was wearing the same featureless grey clothes that the rest wore, except that he, like the servant of Aezcherbaelyn, had a medallion around his neck.

"Be wary of him," the man whispered. "Be wary of the Walker. Do not trust him. He has set out to explore this place. I don't understand it, but the woman over there, she says the tunnel he walks down is like some math thing called Gabriel's Horn. It goes forever, and gets forever smaller. He'll try to take you there."

"How is it different from here?" Carlisle asked.

The man sat up and gripped his arm. "How many times can you die?"

Carlisle shrugged.

"You can die forever. You will die forever. But somewhere, far far below us, there is something staring back up at us from the end of infinity. *That* is evil. It is the essence of evil. It is what people called the Devil, except our imaginations of it fell short. Just now, after all these deaths, I have *begun* to grasp the slightest inkling of the nature of the darkness that created us *and it is more horrific than any human mind has ever been able to dream.* They told you when you were growing up that the mind of God was incomprehensible, well maybe it is, but I'm telling you that this thing is incomprehensible, too, except in the other direction. Love and hatred, good and evil, they aren't even the right *words.* The concepts are too limited, too *human.* That thing out there, that thing staring at us from the other side of eternity, it's a horror that we have always tried to describe, but we have failed. Do you understand me? All our wars, all those children raped and murdered. All the deaths and torture and pain of all the animals that ever existed over all these billions of years . . . and we haven't yet, as a mass effort, begun to describe our master."

Can this be so? Could I have been so horribly wrong about existence? I must have been wrong about something. I thought I would go to Heaven.

Carlisle turned away from the old man and saw the Walker standing above him. The Walker bent down and looked into Carlisle's eyes, his silver pendant dangling down. The Walker seemed familiar, somehow. Carlisle tried to remember when he'd seen the man before. Was it the Infidel? The angel's get? Pyle? Benson? He tried to get a handle on who this man was, but he knew it might take him some time to be able to. All his memories were available to him, but because he had been lying down in this Hell for so long, for so many eternities, those memories were almost impossible to find. They were like little grains of sand amidst a beach the size of a universe.

"Carlisle?" the Walker whispered.

"Yes?"

"I have come for you."

Carlisle turned to the other man.

He was shaking his head. "Don't go."

Carlisle looked to the woman. *Don't go,* her eyes said.

"You don't deserve this, Carlisle," the Walker said. "Something has gone horribly wrong. You were brought here by . . . well, let's call it an accident. You've been mishandled. I am here to take you to the fate you've earned. Surely you know you deserve more than this."

And Carlisle thought about this. The Walker had to be right. Was the Walker Jesus? Had Carlisle somehow been tricked into Hell when he deserved something else? He couldn't remember all of his musings on his fate, at this point it would take him whole eras to collect them all, but that was a possible explanation.

"I'll go," Carlisle said.

He followed the Walker across the soft blackness. They wove their way around the cracks in the universe, past the tortured souls on the tempests of malignant color. Then they came to the funnel.

"Gabriel's Horn," Carlisle whispered. "The old man said there was something at the end of it, staring back at him. Something he feared."

The Walker nodded. His eyes were a light brown. They were so familiar.

"He told you what he knew of the truth," the Walker said.

"He told me not to trust you."

"I have no reason to hurt you, Carlisle. I simply know that you got a fate you did not deserve. I intend to correct that. I do this because I serve one greater than even Aezcherbaelyn."

Carlisle nodded. "I understand, tell me more."

"Gabrielle's horn is an infinite thing. It goes on forever. Is there a being that you know of that is infinite?"

Carlisle nodded. "God."

"That's right," the Walker said. "Not the Devil. God. That's why that man was so afraid. God is mad at him, Carlisle, but God's not mad at you."

He must be Jesus. Those light brown eyes. Soft, caring eyes.

"I understand," Carlisle said, and he felt joy rising in his heart. "I understand."

Tears were welling up from within him.

It had all been a mistake. A horrible mistake. He hadn't deserved Hell. He'd known it. He'd known it all along. Something had gone wrong, probably something that he'd done but that wasn't quite his fault. God was going to correct it. God was full of love. Carlisle had done the only thing that he'd needed to do. There were no unforgivable sins. God *was* love. The one thing he had to do was give his heart and soul to Jesus Christ, and he'd done that. And here Christ was, leading him to where he was wanted. To where he belonged. To where his family was. To that field where his blessings hung over his shoulders like a flight of angels.

He followed the Walker into the horn. It got smaller, and smaller, but Carlisle's soul fit. Souls weren't like bodies, they could get as small as they wanted—almost.

Anna McNamara's mother was *wrong*. All those doctors were *wrong*. Maab had been *wrong*. And he, he'd been right. All along, he'd known. Faith wasn't a thing that could be defeated.

He'd had his dark moments, but through it all, he'd had his faith. Even Hell couldn't shake faith. Faith was pulling him onward, sending him along with this Christ into Heaven. What a fool that Lilith had been! What an idiot! She'd tried to shake him, but she couldn't. The Devil had tried to fool him, but he'd failed.

God, I love you so much. I don't know how to thank you.

The gratitude inside him was so overwhelming he almost fell. Had he been in possession of a real body, he would have fallen. That emotion, so powerful as to dwarf all others, it was his connection with God. He felt it overwhelming him in his chest, it was a fire in his mind, it was a tingling in his fingers, it was an upswelling of a kind of indescribable hope that he had never felt so purely before. Oh, sure, he had tasted it at church in the old world, but this, this was a tsunami where the other had been a drizzle. And the feeling only got stronger as he walked down the horn.

Carlisle had been *right!* This feeling was too grand to be a delusion. Too powerful to be fake. Too real to be a lie that he told himself. It was beyond wish thinking. It was beyond *reason.*

There was a light, a brilliant light, like a train at the end of some tunnel. And then it all made sense.

He had heard of near death experiences. People on the edge between life and death would find themselves traveling through dark tunnels. Their family and friends would be there. The man far behind him, the one who had told him to be still, he had been an idiot—but he had spoken at least one truth.

Like souls draw each other together.

Of course those people who'd nearly died before coming back had seen their family! Who else could be more similar to a person than their own kin? This moment, now, this trek through the horn, it was the moment they had all been talking about. Always there had been a person, or an entity, or a force drawing them onward towards that beautiful light. He could feel the light. Its warmth was the warmth of a thousand suns. Its Love made human love, even true human love, even the love spoken of by poets and playwrights, seem like a tawdry and insincere thing.

I am in Love with God.

He stepped up to the edge. He felt the Walker behind him.

He turned around to look into the eyes of Christ the Walker.

But I never knew Christ on Earth. I never saw him, so those can't be Christ's eyes.

The Walker's face bore an expression of pure hatred. "Goodbye, Father."

The euphoria in Carlisle's soul died.

No! This is some mistake!

The light behind him was not a light of love, but of torture. It wasn't even light at all, but a darkness so putrid that it had seemed like light.

"No!" Carlisle protested. "I don't have a son! My boy died before . . . you've got the wrong . . ."

"You made me kill my mother!" The Walker screeched. "I was going to die no matter what, but you made me kill her."

The man's eyes. Anna McNamara. The Walker had his mother's eyes.

Oh.

With one hand on his medallion, the Walker pushed Carlisle backwards through the mouth of the horn. Carlisle spun as he fell, facing the darkness—facing infinity. He felt a malevolence that defied his feeble mind. It dwarfed his imagination. It was so far beyond him as to be past his scope for analogy. It was a hatred, or an apathy, he couldn't tell which, that was made all the more horrible by the fact that it wasn't even directed at him. He was just in its way somehow.

Carlisle looked into the depths of infinity and there, on the other side of endlessness, something was staring back at him.

— 40 —

It was hard for Arturus to tell as they made their way up the shores of the Kingsriver when the features of the rock and the styles of architecture went from simply seeming familiar to actually being familiar. He only knew that with each passing room they traversed he became more and more sure that he had been in them before.

Aaron had a look on his face that conveyed more joy and more sorrow than Arturus thought any man could feel at the same time. "It must be night, in Harpsborough."

"How can you tell?" Kelly asked.

"There'd be hunters in these rooms if it were day."

She nodded.

"Hidalgo lives down that way, doesn't he?" Arturus asked, pointing down a tunnel.

Galen grunted. "Indeed he does."

"We're so close." Aaron choked as he said the words.

"You'll get to see . . ." Arturus was about to say that Aaron was going to see Alice again, but Aaron had stopped walking.

Tears were streaming down his face. He turned away from them, as if that would somehow save his dignity. Kelly took a step towards him, but paused, unsure of what to do. Arturus looked to his father, but the man's face gave no hints about how he felt. Galen could have been as apathetic as the wind, or as caring as an infant's mother.

Arturus went to help Aaron, but Aaron waved him away.

Kelly's trepidation vanished, and she fell to her knees at Aaron's side, slinging her thin arms around his neck. "What's wrong?" she asked in earnest. "Tell me!"

He sobbed. Arturus looked away. Somehow it wasn't right for a man like Aaron to cry, not like this. Maybe a man like Rick, that would be one thing, but not a man like Aaron.

"Tell me!" Kelly demanded.

"Fuck!" Aaron yelled, his voice echoing off of the far walls.

Aaron was horribly angry. He leapt up to his feet, casting pebbles and earth that he'd torn up from the ground around him.

"What's wrong?" Kelly asked again.

"None of them!" Aaron shouted, towering over her. His face was red. Tears covered his cheeks and snot was dripping freely from his nose. "None of them."

Kelly turned to Arturus, but he had no answers for her. She looked then to Galen.

"His men," Galen explained, "he brought none of them back."

Aaron's tears turned to sorrowful laughter after a time, and they were able to travel again. Arturus hadn't recovered yet from the implications of what Galen had said. They'd left with a man named Mabe, who he'd never really known, who'd fallen amidst the silverlegs. So had Wistan. They'd left with a man named Fitch, who had been slain by a dyitzu. They'd left with a man named Patrick, whose face had been burnt in the tunnels. Whom Avery had slain to keep quiet. There had been Kyle, who they'd left behind. He remembered Duncan, who they'd never seen again after they fled from La'Ferve. And Johnny. And Avery.

Then they came to the rustrock road. Aaron took the lead, taking them towards Harpsborough. They followed the path for a while, and then Aaron stopped them. Arturus remembered the first time he had walked alone to Harpsborough. He had paused in this chamber also, because the Harpsborough guards were beyond it. That time seemed as if it were a lifetime ago. That Arturus had been a very different person.

"It's Aaron," Aaron announced their presence. "Don't shoot."

They entered the room with the Harpsborough guards. The

guards stared at Aaron.

"Aaron!" one shouted.

"Check his eyes!" screamed the other, and that one ran up to Aaron.

Aaron laughed as the person put his face right up next to his.

"It's you!" the guard said, jumping. "It's really fucking you."

They embraced him roughly.

There was a bit of commotion coming from the Harpsborough chamber. Arturus heard the call of some of their questioning voices. "Aaron?"

And they walked into Harpsborough. All was as he remembered it. The red bricked ceilings that soared overhead, the hovels that pockmarked the stone plain, the steeples of the church which stabbed up through the air, the chimney that rose up from Kylie's Kiln, the balconies that hung on the side of the tremendous Fore. People, pushing aside their door curtains, were coming out of their homes with sleep clouded eyes. They ran to them, hugging Aaron, Arturus, Galen and, though they didn't know her, Kelly. The shouts of joy echoed off the ceiling, such a different sound from the desperate wailing sobs that Aaron had issued earlier by the Kingsriver.

Massan was there, a broad grin on his face, though he was missing a hand, and Kara was by his side.

Arturus saw Michael appear on the balcony, his jaw hanging open.

I never did finish that chess set.

Beside the First Citizen stood the beady eyed Mancini—and even he seemed happy. And then there was a gasp which, somehow, cut through all the noise of all the shouts of the villagers and Citizens of Harpsborough. There, on one of the balconies, was Alice. She had a rag in one hand, but she tossed it aside.

"Aaron!" her voice was frantic.

She did not have the patience to run back into the Fore and descend the stairs. She climbed over the balcony rail and dropped down to the ground below. The people parted to make way for her as she ran to him.

Aaron was in tears again. Arturus had never seen anyone hug another so desperately, so intensely, as Aaron did now. He clutched her in his arms, pulling her into him as if to let go of her meant that he would lose his life.

"I'm sorry, Alice. I'm so sorry."

"You're home," she was crying too.

Arturus felt an ache in his own heart. There was a twinge of jealousy there because he had wanted her for so long, but that tiny feeling was overpowered by the sudden happiness he had for Aaron—for his friend—for the man who he had fought beside, killed beside, and damn near died beside.

"I'm sorry," Aaron repeated. "Your lock of hair, I lost it. I tried to keep it, but the river—"

Alice silenced him with a kiss. She pulled back, shaking her head violently. She chided him through her tears. "I've got more hair, Aaron."

Galen was all smiles, the politician again as he had been so long ago when they'd said goodbye to the village, shaking people's hands and telling them how he could have used their help in the Carrion.

"Damn, lad!" Massan was saying. "You've grown up pretty fast."

Arturus hugged him, looking back up towards the Citizens. There was the red headed woman, Chelsea. She was staring down at Aaron and Alice as they shared their embrace.

She looks so . . . wistful?

Suddenly there was shouting, and Father Klein burst through the crowd. He was enraged. He grabbed the lapel of Kelly's lavender robe and tore it aside, baring her breast to the Harpsborough people. He clutched her arm, and held her shoulder up to the people of Harpsborough.

"Look!" he shouted, waving his hand to them all and then pointing to her tattoo. "Look! This is one of Maab's priestesses."

Father Klein had silenced all of Harpsborough, save Aaron.

"Take your hands off of her, Klein," Aaron yelled.

Arturus grabbed Klein's hand and twisted it back, stopping just short of locking the joint.

Kelly had a malicious smile on her cruel lips. Her blue-black eyes stared at Klein like she was about to devour him.

"She's good, Father," Galen said. "She betrayed her own people. Just like you did, when you were Maab's."

Klein shook his head. "You don't understand, priestesses

don't convert."

"She's in love with my son, Klein." Galen's deep voice bellowed.

Klein's expression became confused, then angry again, and then, ever so slowly, it turned to wonder. "Is this true?" He asked of Kelly.

"It is," Kelly said, the malicious smile leaving her lips. "He has my heart."

Arturus let the Father go, and Klein clutched at her again, but this time it was her hand he took. "My apologies, Miss. Some of us, we suffered so much at the hands of Maab."

The anger that Arturus felt towards Klein fled. This priest in Hell had done something good, just then. By showing his strongly held doubts, he had addressed the fears that all the people in Harpsborough would have harbored as soon as they learned about Kelly's past. And then, by casting those doubts aside, Klein had modeled for his flock a behavior of forgiveness they could follow. It wouldn't change all the villager's minds, Hell, it might not even be enough in the end, but for now, it was the best Arturus could have hoped for.

"Come," Galen said, "We must go."

"But we just got here!" Kelly said.

Some of the villagers gave similar reactions.

"This is not our home, Kelly. And Rick, well, he doesn't even know he's waiting for us."

At the mention of Rick, just as the crowd had parted so that Alice could meet Aaron, so too did they for Galen, Arturus, and Kelly.

As they walked away, the people of Harpsborough called after them. Demanding that they not stay away for long. Begging them to come back.

"Galen!" Michael shouted even as they made it to the exit. "Tomorrow evening, we will have a feast. Come. You and all the villagers will eat from the Fore's stores."

There was a great cheer then, and Arturus thought that, at that moment, there must not be a single person in Harpsborough who was not overjoyed—except for some reason, Davel Mancini.

And perhaps also those who loved the hunters who never returned.

41

Ellen heard the sound of boots thumping across the woodstone bridge as she worked at threshing the devilwheat.

"Don't shoot, Rick," a deep voice called.

It seemed familiar somehow, like she'd heard it before.

She looked to Rick, who was cleaning a bowl where he stood behind the counter. He looked like he had been struck by something. There was the crunching of gravel.

Rick dropped the bowl, overcome suddenly by some great emotion. He looked up at the ceiling, tears welling up in his eyes. He whispered something to the stones above. Ellen couldn't be certain, but it looked like he had said "thank you."

Arturus rushed into the room and caught Rick up in a hug.

Ellen dropped her devilwheat, stunned.

Ye swore.

They had told her that there were no miracles in Hell, but they had lied. There were, and this was one of them. Galen entered the room.

A man like that, and you can have miracles.

"Galen!" she shouted, and she ran up to him.

Rick was a sobbing mess of tears. "I thought you were . . ." But even now, with Arturus in his own arms, he couldn't say the words.

Shit, I've been kissing Rick. Turi will understand. Rick knows I love his son. He'll probably have to tell him, but these people aren't like other people. It won't matter. I'll convince him that

Ellen looked at Turi, really looked at him, perhaps for the first time. His face seemed different, somehow. More adult? His facial hair was thicker, a rough dark stubble where before it had been peach fuzz. His eyes were different also, more like Galen's than before. When she had known Turi, he had carried with him an air of boyishness which—capable as he might have been—gave her the impression that he needed to be taken care of. This Turi was different.

"You're not the same," she said aloud without really meaning to.

Arturus looked at her, curious. The manner of his inquisitiveness proved her point. There was so much Galen in him now.

The Carrion is horrible, they say. The parts that weren't Galen probably burned away.

"You're not either," Arturus said. "Not by a long shot. In a good way, I mean."

That night, after Rick had fed them until Ellen feared she'd burst, after Galen had helped her move her things out of Arturus' room and into the empty one next to the forge, after she had pretended to be so happy that Kelly would be staying with Arturus in his room, she thought about what he'd said.

I'm not the same.

The Ellen Turi had known hadn't been able to fire a gun. Hadn't been able to identify a dirkenwood tree from a hungerleaf. Hadn't been able to kill a corpse on her own.

No wonder he didn't love me.

He shouldn't have judged her for these things. The old world hadn't taught her how to survive in Hell, and he couldn't have expected it to. He should have done exactly what he did do. He should have waited for her to mature, to see what kind of person this Hell would make her, before letting his heart decide. Only somehow it had gone all wrong. She couldn't think of anything that had ever gone more wrong. She cried as silently as she could.

Rick entered her room.

She looked away from him.

"I'm sorry," he said.

She didn't want to lash out, but she did anyway. "I don't want your sympathy."

"No, Ellen. I'm sorry that I was so overwhelmed by seeing my son again that I didn't think about how you must have felt. I'm sure you've dreamed about him coming home, and I know that Kelly wasn't in those dreams."

Ellen looked away from him, trying to hide her tears. "I was just so *stupid*. I was lost and helpless and damned. I was a foolish little girl who let a crush get the best of her. I'm better than that now."

Rick put his arms around her. "Ellen, you and I aren't strong like Galen. Not all people can be. But that doesn't mean that we aren't strong in our own way. You and I, we're strong because we admit our feelings and express them openly. We're strong because we're full of forgiveness and love. We're strong because we admit our sorrow and we can share it with the world."

Ellen hugged him back and choked. "It hurts," she admitted. "It hurts so bad."

He held her for a long time, but the pain didn't seem to decrease.

"Say something," she said. "Say something wise. Say something that will make the pain go away."

"I don't know that they make words like that, Ellen."

"Then pretend," she said. "Tell me a story, anything."

Rick spoke after a few moments. "There was once a Sultan that had many Magi, and the least among them was a Magi named Ferdowsi. Now this Sultan . . ."

42

Time had no meaning to Avery. In the beginning, the pain hadn't been so bad. Maybe his body had been in shock. Maybe the nerves which would have alerted him to his pain were severed. However, now, the pain was incessant. It was unbearable, except that he had nothing to do but bear it. His canteen was empty, and he didn't know how long it had been so. He'd eaten all his food, too. That had happened slightly more recently. He could feel the food in his stomach, trying to get out, but he had no way to shit.

The pain came on strong, strong enough to send tears flowing down his cheeks.

Wasted water. You need that.

He was tired of fighting. He was tired of waiting for a dyitzu or a hound to enter this place and take his life. He was tired of trying to guess when a day had passed, or how much was safe to push away from the rubble. A few days, or pushes ago, depending on how he tried to measure time, he had gone too far. The bleeding had started in earnest, and he had lapsed into unconsciousness. To his horror he had awakened again.

It's time, Avery. It's time for you to end it.

He knew how he was going to kill himself. All he had to do was push hard against the rock. His body would inch its way out of the rubble and his blood would spill and he would die.

Anything left you want to think about, Avery? This is your last chance.

But was there anything left to think about? He'd made his peace with Kelly.

There were people back in Harpsborough he missed. Jessie and Sally. He would never get a chance to kiss Jessie. He would never become a Citizen. He would never get to eat on a Fore balcony.

But those weren't his real regrets. His real regrets were the things he'd left undone in the old world. They were the loose strings that a man could leave unknotted as he traveled through life living as if he would never die. Really, he hadn't much cared about Hell. He'd never tried to make anything of his time here. He'd just been waiting to die. It seemed to be an inferior way to live.

I wish, I wish I had lived my life here like I had lived my life on Earth.

Then he would have regrets for Hell. Regrets were good. They were a sign that things had meant something. His existence here seemed so utterly meaningless that he cursed himself for having not found anything important to strive for.

Well that's a regret of a sort.

But it wasn't enough. If he was going to die like a man should die, he should have had something worth fighting for. A cause worth dying for, even. There should be a woman he loved with all his heart who he was trying to get back to—a woman who would be devastated by his death. Or better yet, a woman who didn't love him back, who he would never get the chance to tell about his unrequited love. That was the way to die. Not like this. Not as a lonely animal in an abandoned castle—alone— with no friends and only a pile of rubble for company.

I did it all wrong, somehow.

He should have a kid back in Harpsborough, or kids, who could carry on his legacy. Or maybe he shouldn't, damnation wasn't easy after all. He should have an enemy he hated.

I didn't do enough yet. Please, God, let me live.

But there was no God here—only men, and none of them cared enough for him to save him from his fate.

This isn't the death you would have chosen, but it's the one you have.

Had he really made it so far only to die like this? Had he really eaten all that corpseflesh and walked through the mobs of the dead only to be killed by hellstone? Was there any justice in that?

No, he had squandered his time here, but there was nothing to do about it now. Now it was time to die. He put his hands against the rock, breathed deeply—but where would he go next? What if the next universe he found himself in was so terrible that he would wish he were back here? But was there anything he could really imagine that he feared more than a dyitzu coming into this room while he was so helpless? Or a hound? Or a corpse?

I've got the shotgun.

He looked around for it. He had knocked it away at some point, maybe when he was eating, or perhaps when he was unconscious.

He struggled to reach it, but the distance was too far and the pain was unbearable. More tears streamed down his face.

No, it's time to die.

He readied himself again, taking in a few more deep breaths. He put his hands against the stone, but he was afraid of something more than a dyitzu. It wasn't any of the Hells he could imagine—it was death itself. Dying was so terrifying that he found he couldn't face it again.

Oh, Lord, Jesus fucking Christ. The Devil, or whatever fucked up god Calimay prayed too, anyone, anything, please help me.

He was losing blood from his efforts to reach the shotgun. The blood was fluid that he could not replace.

I can't die.

But there didn't seem to be anything else he could do. How could he have been so stupid as to have pushed too far? How could he let his impatience cause him to make that mistake? Choosing how hard to push was literally the only choice he had left to make, and he had fucked it up.

Way to go Avery. Way to fucking go.

His heart beat faster, which caused more blood to leave him, but it also caused him to be more alert.

Did I hear something?

Was it happening now? Was a devil coming to kill him? All seemed silent.

It was me fooling myself. Or maybe it was a stone falling from one of the walls.

But he couldn't make himself believe it. He looked towards the entrance to the room. That was where his friends had left him.

Oh God, is it the Minotaur?

He looked over to the dead thing. It had taken more punishment than he had thought possible. Hell, it had moved without a heart. Could such a devil heal after receiving all those wounds? Would it be rising soon from amidst the rubble? Avery's situation was hopeless enough already. He had plenty of healing to do and not enough food to fuel it . . . but things would be even worse if he was in a race against a healing Minotaur.

He heard the noise again, a footstep.

It wasn't the Minotaur.

He looked towards the shotgun. There was no way he could reach it.

I could take off my shirt and try to pull it back.

But if he moved enough to take off his shirt, he would surely die. All he could do was look to see what was coming for him.

Malkravyan entered the room.

The hell?

Suddenly his thoughts were of Aaron and Turi and Kelly and Galen. "Did they make it?"

Malkravyan nodded. "I took them down the Lethe. They were able to pass out of the Carrion. All of them were alive at that point."

Avery felt a sudden wave of relief.

"Ironic, is it not?" Malkravyan said.

"What?"

"That so many good men die, and yet you, a rapist who should have been crushed, will live."

Malkravyan walked over and sat on the rubble beside him. He dropped his pack and pulled out a canteen.

"I made my peace with the girl," Avery said.

The Infidel Friend nodded. "I am heartened to hear that. Not that I wouldn't have saved you anyway, Avery. I love all people."

"That's very Christian of you," Avery said.

"Now there's no need to be insulting," Malkravyan answered with a smile as he unscrewed the cap to this canteen. "Here, drink two swallows, no more."

Avery nodded, reaching for the canteen.

"I'm serious, Avery," Malkravyan said. "Your body has no efficient way to get rid of your waste right now. We have to time this very carefully. You have to take in enough nutrients to heal while not building enough shit up inside you to poison your system. Couldn't have happened in the old world, so you will no doubt find this difficult to intuit. Thus, I would recommend that you defer to my judgment on such matters until you have a better working understanding of your body."

Avery nodded. "I understand."

Malkravyan let him have the canteen. The metal felt cool in his hands. Drinking the water was the first pleasant sensation Avery had experienced since the collapse. He almost took a third gulp, but spat it out.

He handed the canteen back.

"You are a tough bastard," Malkravyan said. "That's good. No doubt you know that a man who wants to live heals better than one who doesn't. For you to win this race and survive, you must want life very badly."

But I don't. I feel defeated.

"I'm not sure I want to live," Avery admitted.

"I can help you with that," Malkravyan said.

Avery thought about this. "I don't see how."

"I figure I'd piss you off. It should help."

"You're an Infidel Friend," Avery said, "so I can see you being pretty damn good at that."

"Excellent. Your confidence in me is heartening." Malkravyan produced a book from his backpack.

"The hell is that? Your fucking infidel bible?"

Shit, this guy is good. I'm pissed already. He's just like that Cris fucker.

"No," Malkravyan said, "it's your Bible. I thought we'd read it together. Discuss its finer points."

Avery grinned. "I fucking hate you already."

Malkravyan's smile seemed to be in earnest. "Good. I think you just might make it, Avery."

— 43 —

"What are you doing there?" Huxley called to the man in the Hungerleaf Grove.

Galen stood and regarded them.

Marcus tugged at his arm. "You don't know what you're doing, man."

"The Hell I don't," Hux whispered back, "the Fore owns this grove, and he's stealing from it."

Galen was standing on the island where the Hungerleaf Grove grew amidst the tremendous Kingsriver chamber that housed it. He walked to the shore, standing by the stepping stones which led across the thin finger of water separating it from the land where Huxley and Marcus stood.

"I am tending to the grove," Galen responded in his deep voice. "I fear that, during my time of absence, and Rick's, your villagers have plundered it. Their work has damaged the trees, and might kill a few. I must work to save as many as I can."

"You've no claim on this grove," Huxley said.

Galen's eyebrows raised. He seemed amused.

"You do *not* want to do this," Marcus whispered to Huxley.

"My understanding," Galen began, "is that the Fore ceded me this grove after I helped them defeat the Icanitzu. Tell me, has Harpsborough declared war on my family?"

Huxley shook his head. "You can pretend this is all a war if you want, but the truth is that the Fore took this grove from Rick as a punishment for his conspiring with infidels."

If anything, Galen's amusement grew. "Took it from Rick?"

"Yes," Huxley shot back, "for conspiring with the infidels."

Galen looked to the grove for a moment before returning his attention to Huxley. "So you tell me how its right that the Fore took the grove away from me for something Rick did."

Huxley opened his mouth to respond, and then stopped. "Well, we thought you were dead, so it seemed that ownership should pass to Rick, so—"

"And you were mistaken about that?" Galen coached.

"Well, yes."

"So you'd say that your Fore gave this grove away while they were under a misconception?"

"That's true but—"

"So they were in error when they claimed the grove."

"I . . ."

"I accept your apology," Galen said.

Marcus grabbed Huxley around the arm. "Look man, Galen is . . . well, all I can say is that shit would have gone down a lot differently if he'd been there during the corpse war and the fight with Maab's people. Okay? Tell him you're sorry, that we were mistaken, and let's get the hell out of here before he decides to get pissed at us."

"But the Fore—" Huxley began, but then he stopped, thinking better of it. "Well it was nice to meet you in person, Galen."

Galen looked up from where he was tending to one of the trees. "Oh. Well nice meeting you too."

Kelly slept silently.

She was always quiet, and he liked that about her—it was the way the Carrion people were. He stood up from the floor of his own room. It was odd to be here again. It was so familiar even though he'd been absent for so long. His leather strop was exactly where he'd left it. He walked silently to the door curtain, passing through it. His steps were soft, and the gravel crunched only a little beneath them.

He could hear the gentle rush of the river and the slow, peaceful rhythm, the tranquil, harmonious beat of the woodstone waterwheel. He walked out into the river room, the cool, moist air greeting him, alighting on his cheeks and on his bare arms.

Slowly, he came up to the river his fathers affectionately called the "Mighty Thames." It was a slow and gentle stream, hardly worthy of a name, which meandered softly through the underground labyrinth of Hell without much of a fuss. Its waters were always cool and crisp, and just standing here reminded him of growing up along its banks. In this chamber the Thames was so smooth one could use it for a mirror. He often had, in the past. He used to kneel on the dark red hellstone by its bank and gauge the stubble which covered his face's reflection in the flowing water. And the chill, he'd missed the chill. It wasn't like the Carrion at all. It was . . . invigorating.

He knelt on one end of the strop, and held the other up.

Reverently, he took out the bone handled straight razor he kept in his pocket. It had been the only thing he'd taken into the Carrion that he'd returned with. His guns, his clothes, his ammunition, his food and pack—all left behind.

He began honing the razor, then, on the strop, and found after a while that he was doing so to the rhythm of the turning waterwheel. He reveled in the light whispers of vibrations that crept up from the strop, through the razor, and into his hand. To him, at this moment, this action meant that he was truly home. Somehow, even with everything he'd experienced, the truth hadn't really sunk in. But now, as he readied himself to shave, he knew in his heart that he had made it back. He held up the blade and blew off the particulates of leather. Carefully, he tested the edge on his chin and was satisfied.

Arturus washed his face, the water a blessing on his waiting cheeks. He shaved down first, on his right side, with quick, even strokes. Before he left, he had been able to cover that same area with quick upstrokes, but he could not do so now. The hair had grown in too thick, and he was bound to cut himself if he tried.

Instinctively, he placed the blade in the water a little downstream from his reflection. Above and around his own head, he saw the ceiling of this chamber. The whole of it was a soft, deep red, and it rippled around where his blade was disturbing the water—blurring where the bricks interlocked in the arched roof.

After a few more minutes, he finished and inspected his work.

Again careful not to disturb his reflection, he washed off his blade, drying the razor on his pants before folding it into its bone handle. His fingers found one of his pants pockets, and he slid the blade in it.

Then, deliberately, he looked into his reflection, meeting his own eyes as their image hovered on the surface of the oscillating water. His face was not the face he remembered. The Carrion had changed him. He could tell that he looked older. His cheekbones were a little more prominent, his face a little more angular. Maybe it was the way his reflection played off the water, but he thought he looked a little bit sadder too. It was a wistful sort of melancholy, just a touch of it. It reminded him of how Galen looked when he was thinking about times long gone.

About people he'd once known. Lovers and friends he'd lost. Maybe, during some of those times, he was thinking of Arturus' mother.

I know where this river goes.

It would meet with the Kingsriver, eventually, downstream of the Hungerleaf Grove. Its water would mix there, joining the mighty rush. But some part of it would find its way into the Carrion. Some of the water that was flowing beneath him now would pass by where those silverleg spiders lay, past where he'd killed Pyle. It would travel on to that room where he and Aaron had bathed. To the room where Galen had spoken about good and evil. Eventually it would join the river Lethe, and it might turn and fall through Giant's Tunnel. Or it might keep going, past where Maab's ritual chamber was. It might flow down into the lake where Galen said the Lethe pooled. There it could rise as mist and float through the halls where Calimay lived—to where, even now, Avery might still lay. Or it could go on past the Deadlands and the mines to where it flowed by the quarry where the workers of the City of Blood and stone labored to unearth Tu-El—to where it must finally rush over the edge of the piece of Hell they called Gehenna before falling freely into the unending depths of the Erebus. Beyond that chasm, Saint Wretch waited. He was going to come, of that Arturus was certain, and it was going to be this face, this face touched with melancholy, that Saint Wretch would be looking for.

Do you fear me, Saint Wretch, like I fear you? Do you wonder, as you wait to escape from that prison the Infidel tricked you into, if maybe, just maybe, the blood of my mother will let me hurt you? Do you have nightmares where you dream that my flesh can touch yours? That my teeth might draw your blood? That my fists might break your bones? Do you fear these things even as I fear that my strikes will be as ineffective as any other?

He left the Thames and returned to his home.

The loose rocks welcomed him as he walked back across them. He brushed through his door blanket to enter his sleeping chamber and placed his razor reverently next to where Kelly slept. She turned and looked at him. She was a light sleeper. He liked that about her, too. That was the way the Carrion people were.

He offered his hand, and she took it. He helped her to her

feet. As soon as she was standing, she reached out and brushed the back of her fingers against his cheek. His face felt smooth under her touch, as smooth as polished marble.

She smiled, not the smile of a dark priestess, but the smile of a girl—a lover. "Love me," she ordered.

Arturus smiled back. "Thus spake Minerva, and Ulysses obeyed her gladly."

"What's that from?" she asked.

"The end of a poem Galen used to sing to me."

He kissed her, and though it was painful, he loved her.

When they were finished, they napped and then stirred together. Arturus could hear Rick moving around in the battery room.

"Doesn't he know we're sleeping?" Kelly asked in mock complaint. "What business has he being awake anyway?"

"Breakfast, I hope."

Kelly frowned as if considering this very deeply. "That could be good."

Arturus grinned. "I bet you a box of shells he burns the flatbread."

This concludes the Carrion Trilogy
Hellsong continues with Hellwar: Book I (2015)

Want to be notified when sequels are released?
Register as a Citizen at hellsongseries.com

Need to look up a term?
Check out the Gehennic Encyclopedia as a free
download on Kindle or view at our website:
hellsongseries.com/encyclopedia

Submit your Fan Fiction to
contact@ehhknovel.com for possible inclusion
into an upcoming magazine.

Shaun McCoy lives in South Carolina. He is an
accomplished Pianist, Cage Fighter, Chess Player
and Writer. You can check out his fan page at
www.facebook.com/shaunomccoy